THE BRINK OF TOMORROW

Ken Gullekson

HEISENBERG PRESS
Glendale, California

THE BRINK OF TOMORROW

HEISENBERG PRESS
Post Office Box 1178
Glendale, California 91209

Cover art by Ken Gullekson, based on a design by Terry Hayes

ISBN: 0-9653136-5-4

Printed in the United States of America

Dedicated to

The Children of Proteus

Acknowledgements

My deepest appreciation to Darryl Anka and Bashar for supplying me with so much of the wisdom that graces these pages;

To Terry Hayes, whose brilliant hand-drawn design for the cover guided the electronically crafted illustration you see there now;

And to Jeanine Renne, my friend and writing partner, who gave me invaluable feedback on the manuscript.

The Platinum Principles

1: The Principle of Respect

Neither impose your will on others;
nor allow others to impose their will on you.

2: The Principle of Responsibility

Be of service to others as long as you are not of disservice to yourself;
be of service to yourself as long as you are not of disservice to others.

Chapter 1

"It's nine o'clock. You're tuned to WWKW classic radio, FM 102.4, and this is Dale Greene on The Brink of Tomorrow. I want to dedicate this first song to my parents, whom I laid to rest last week. Mom, Dad, I hope you're listening. I love you dearly, and I miss you beyond belief."

Saying these words out loud brought the lingering grief to the surface and choked up the DJ for all the world to hear. Within seconds, the melodic strains of "Teach Your Children" were making their way into the homes of thousands of deeply touched listeners and Dale Greene was shedding tears he had not expected to find.

While the station was equipped with a number of telephone lines, mainly for business purposes and the occasional request, it did not feature a talk format, so was not equipped to handle more than a few calls at a time. So most of the listeners who called the station during "Teach Your Children" heard only a busy signal. Most of those who were fortunate enough to get through only wanted to express their condolences and were satisfied to leave their messages with Dale's engineer, Bobby, who graciously thanked each caller and promised to pass the message on to the DJ. A few wanted to talk to Dale (a practice routinely avoided except under very special circumstances), and Bobby politely informed them that Dale was in the announce booth and unavailable to talk.

But one of the callers was a little girl, nine years of age, who told Bobby with tears in her voice that she had buried her parents just that morning. She sounded so sad and so sweet that Bobby didn't have the heart to tell her she couldn't talk to Dale. Hesitantly he opened his microphone to the announce booth.

"Dale, uh . . . these phones've been lighting up like a Christmas tree and I've been telling 'em you can't talk to 'em. But I got a little girl on line three who just buried her parents this morning, and she really wants to talk to you. And I just couldn't tell her you wouldn't talk to

1

her. So, do you mind talking with her for a minute?"

Dale pressed his intercom button. "Did she say how old she is?"

"Nine."

"How much time do I have?"

"A minute 'n' . . ." Bobby paused to check his timer, "forty-four seconds."

Dale considered the proposition briefly. "All right, what's her name?"

"Jeannie . . . no, Jeanine!"

"All right, I'll take it." Dale lifted the phone receiver and pressed the line button. "Jeanine? This is Dale Greene."

Recognizing the voice, little Jeanine let out a sob of relief, and for the next fifteen or twenty seconds just cried, physically unable to say a word. And Dale just let her. Finally, sensing the spell was easing, he said softly, "I understand you lost your parents recently."

Simply getting some recognition for her loss from someone who understood was a comfort to young Jeanine, but it triggered another fit of sobbing. Working dutifully to respond, she finally wrenched out a blubbery, "Yeahhhh."

Dale gave her another fifteen seconds to cry before he spoke again. "It really hurts, huh?"

"Yeahhh," Jeanine managed between sobs.

"I know. When my parents died, it hurt so much I cried for five days straight." While he spoke more simply to Jeanine than he might have to an adult, Dale was careful not to oversimplify or talk down to her.

Struggling to carry on the conversation, Jeanine stammered, "My grandparents won't let me cry."

"Really? How come?"

"I don't know." Suffering their own pain and not wanting to be reminded of it, Jeanine's grandparents, in whose care she now found herself, chided the little girl for her tears. Schooled in the old ways, they sought relief from their own grief by suppressing their emotions, avoiding the issue, and busying themselves with other things. Misguided as this was, they thought it was the best medicine for their granddaughter's grief as well.

"Well . . . I would never suggest that you disobey your grandparents,"

Dale said gently. "But I don't see anything wrong with crying, especially when you've just lost your parents."

"Me neither!" Jeanine concurred decisively. She was still whimpering, but steadily gaining control.

In the control room, Bobby pressed his mic button. "Twenty seconds, Dale."

On the opposite side of the glass wall that separated the two chambers, Dale nodded.

"Jeanine, honey, this record is about to end. So I'm going to have to say goodbye now."

"Please don't hang up!" came Jeanine's impassioned plea.

"But I have to go back on the air and start another song," Dale gently explained.

"Can we keep talking afterwards?"

She sounded so desperate for the meaningful connection her grandparents were apparently unable to give her, it just broke Dale's heart. Time was running out and he had only two seconds to decide.

"All right, sweetheart, I'll be back in a minute."

"Teach Your Children" was just ending and he was reaching for his mic switch when an afterthought struck. Despite the risk of dead air, he spoke again to his young caller. "Jeanine? Would you like to continue talking on the air?"

"On the air?"

"Yeah, on the radio. Like talk radio. Have you ever heard talk radio?"

"Yeah."

"Would you like to do that? It means lots of people will hear you, but we won't have to be interrupted every three minutes. You don't have to if you don't want to. It's up to you."

This little exchange had taken twenty seconds—which meant twenty seconds of dead air. Bobby was frantic. Signaling with his hands, he asked if Dale wanted him to spin another disc. Dale shook his head.

"Yeah, I guess so," Jeanine replied after a moment's thought.

"Are you sure?" Dale asked. "You don't have to." He was definitely not interested in talking her into anything.

"Yeah, I'm sure," she replied with enough certitude to convince

Dale he wasn't.

"All right, dear, hang on for just a second." Reaching out, he hit his mic switch and addressed the night in the velvety voice his listeners knew so well.

"This is Dale Greene. You're listening to WWKW classic radio, and that was 'Teach Your Children,' by Crosby, Stills, Nash & Young, in memory of my parents, Leonard and Dara Greene. I'm gonna do something a little different here tonight. My phones have been ringing like crazy and I've been talking to a young lady who also lost her parents this week. Her name is Jeanine, she's nine years old, and she's given me permission to put her on the air." With this, he looked across at Bobby in the control room.

Understanding from the conversation with Jeanine what Dale was up to, but not being prepared to put callers on the air with his current setup, Bobby had been working frantically to improvise the necessary connections. With the connections now made, he glanced back at Dale and nodded.

"Hi, Jeanine," Dale said when he saw Bobby's signal.

"Hi," she replied, her voice now rippling out to thousands of listeners across the city. Having regained control and moved beyond crying for the moment, her little voice was high and sweet. It melted Dale's heart.

"Would you like to tell me how your parents died?" he asked.

"They were in the plane crash."

"The one in California?" The news that week had been reporting a mid-air collision in the skies over California between an eastbound jetliner and a light plane. All souls onboard both aircraft had been killed, a total of 278 dead.

"Yeah," confirmed Jeanine in her delicate little voice.

"So they must've been on their way home," Dale ventured.

"Yeah."

"How long had they been gone?"

"A week."

Judging by his own experience, Dale suspected that a good deal of his young caller's pain lay in the multiple facts that her parents' lives had ended with no forewarning after an absence that was probably painful in itself, and that, like himself, she had been utterly unable to

4

say goodbye before they so permanently left her life.

Wanting to touch this pain to release it, he said, "So you hadn't seen them for awhile and you didn't get to say goodbye before they died."

"Yeah," she replied, choking up again.

"That part really hurts, doesn't it?" he probed, as gently as he could.

"Y-e-s," she sobbed, releasing the pent-up emotion in another flood of tears. Dale let her cry for a few seconds before speaking again.

"I'm so sorry, sweetheart. My parents died in a car crash. They were hit by a drunk driver. I didn't get to say goodbye to them either, and that's what hurt the most for me, too."

"I . . . know," Jeanine managed to interject between sobs.

"I told Jeanine earlier," Dale said, addressing his listeners, "that I didn't think there's anything wrong with crying. I believe it's an essential part of healing. So I'm just gonna let her do that for a couple of minutes here. You can tune out if you want, but I'm just going to let her cry."

As Jeanine's soft little-girl sobs infused the airwaves, Bobby worked frantically to field the deluge of calls lighting up his phone lines. Glancing up, he caught Dale's eye and gave him a desperate look. After a knowing nod, Dale signaled Bobby to get a record ready.

Jeanine cried for a good twenty-five or thirty seconds, during which not a single word was broadcast . . . and not a single listener tuned out.

When her anguish had reduced again to a whimper, Dale asked, "How are you feeling now, sweetheart?"

"I'm scared," she replied.

"What are you scared of?" Fear was something Dale hadn't personally been experiencing—at least not in the context of his parents' death—and his understanding of it, as it might have related to Jeanine, was less ready.

"That I'm gonna die," she answered.

"Oh! And why are you afraid you're going to die?"

"If my parents could die, then I could too."

"I see. And what do you find scary about dying?" He wanted to bring her fears into the open where she could see them for what they were.

"It might hurt," she replied.

"You mean it might hurt if you died violently like our parents did," he queried.

"Even if you don't," she clarified.

"Really! You mean even if you die in your sleep it might hurt?"

"Yeah."

"Hmmm. What is it you think happens when people die?"

"You get judged by God."

"Uh-huh. And how might that hurt?"

"You either go to heaven where there's music all the time and you walk on clouds, or you go to hell where you catch on fire."

"I see," Dale acknowledged, secretly amused at her childlike conception of the afterlife. "And why do you believe that's what happens when people die?"

"That's what my grandma said."

"Oh!"

That Jeanine's misconceptions about dying came from a family member was not all that surprising, but this meant some delicacy was required so as not to completely undermine grandma's well intended parenting efforts, naive though they might be. Dale considered his reply briefly, then asked, "How do you suppose your grandma knows what happens when people die?"

"She . . ." Suddenly realizing she didn't have the answer, Jeanine stopped short. Then, with some surprise, she added, "I dunno."

"Okay. Well let's see . . . you don't suppose she died and came back, do you?"

Jeanine's reply was preceded by a chortle. "No, silly! You can't do that."

"Oh! Well, then, how could she know what happens when people die?"

There was a brief silence as Jeanine considered the question. "I dunno. Someone told her?"

"Someone probably did tell her—maybe when she was little, like you. But how did *that* person find out?"

Jeanine took another moment to mull the question, then, "Someone told *them*?"

"Most likely. And someone before that probably told *that* person. And someone before *that* told *that* person. And so on all the way back to the first person. But how did the first person find out?"

Though Jeanine was only nine years old, the logic of the question penetrated her young mind and put her into a state of stunned cogitation. "I dunno," she finally replied.

"That's the problem. In order to really know what happens when people die and what heaven is like or what hell is like—or if there even *is* a hell—someone would have to go there and come back and tell us. If they haven't done that, then the only thing they can tell you is their *opinion* about what happens when you die. They can't tell you for sure what happens. So what your grandma told you was her *opinion*. Of course, she's entitled to her opinion—everyone is, including *you*. And your opinion can be the same as your grandma's, or completely different. It's up to you. Do you understand?"

"Yeah." There was another brief silence as Jeanine thought about what she had just heard. "What's your opinion?" she now asked with a fresh sense of curiosity and a budding awareness that her own opinion had value.

"My opinion," Dale began deliberately, "well, I believe a person is made up of two parts—his body, and his soul. The body you can see; it walks and talks and eats and sleeps and wears funny hats."

Jeanine gave a little chuckle. Pleased to have lifted her spirits, Dale continued.

"The soul you *can't* see. It's like invisible. It's the part of you that thinks and feels and hopes and dreams. And it comes into your body when you're born and kinda rides around in it for the duration of your life. And when that life ends, only the *body* dies. The soul leaves and goes back to where there are lots of other souls. Some people call that place heaven. Other people call it different things. I call it the spirit realm. And in the spirit realm there's no pain, only joy and happiness. This, of course, is only my *opinion*. I haven't actually been there . . . at least that I can remember. Did you understand any of this?"

"Yeah," Jeanine said thoughtfully. Then, "Did someone tell you this when you were little?"

"No, actually, I read it in some books that were written by people who died and were brought back to life."

"They were dead and came back to life?! How could they do that?"

"Most of them died in the hospital, and the doctors were able to revive them after a few minutes."

"Oh! What did they say?"

"Well, they found themselves in a long tunnel with a very bright light at the end, and they saw loved ones who had died before them. And all their pain was gone and they felt *tremendous* love and happiness. And they knew that death was nothing to be feared. Do you understand?"

"Yeah." There was a lengthy silence as Jeanine considered Dale's words. "So my parents are happy?"

"I believe they are."

"Can they see me?"

"I believe they can."

"Do they still love me?"

"I most certainly believe they do."

The sigh little nine-year-old Jeanine heaved was clearly audible, through the telephone lines, over the airwaves, and into the hearts of a whole city. "So dying's not so bad," she reasoned after some moments.

"Not for those who die. Although it's hell for the rest of us. That's *my* opinion, anyhow. Of course, you have to form your own opinion."

"I know," was her sage response.

Dale gave her a moment to let it all sink in. "How are you feeling now, sweetheart?" he finally queried. He wanted to give her the chance to recognize her uplifted spirits for herself.

"Better."

"I'm delighted to hear that! May I make a suggestion?"

"Yeah."

"Are you going to be staying with your grandparents from now on?"

"Yeah."

"Do you have a room of your own there?"

"Yeah." The lack of originality in her responses made Dale smile.

"All right," he said. "Since they don't want you crying, I suggest you don't cry when you're around them. And when you do feel like crying, go to your room where you can be alone, and cry there. And if you ever need to talk to me again, please don't hesitate to call. All right?"

"All right," she agreed in the sweetest tones Dale had ever heard.

"Okay, sweetheart . . . I'm gonna say goodbye now. I want you to know that I love you."

"I love you too."

"Thank you, dear. Bye-bye now."

"Bye."

Dale waited a couple of seconds after the connection was broken before he said softly, "This is Dale Greene and you're listening to WWKW classic radio, FM 102.4." With a glance at Bobby, who was busy fielding calls by the armload, the next song on the play list went out to the rapt audience.

Ken Gullekson

Chapter 2

Dale switched his announce mic off and hit his intercom button. "Wow, man, did you hear that?!" he exclaimed to Bobby as he relished the excitement coursing through his body. "*Jeez* that felt great! I've never felt so exhilarated in all my life! She was so sweet; she just broke my heart. I really think I helped her! I was really able to connect!"

Bobby's role in the experience had been quite different from Dale's, so he couldn't really share in the celebration. But he did recognize Dale's excitement, and nodded to that effect.

"Wow!" Dale repeated under his breath as he reviewed the experience in his mind. Having never before contemplated doing a talk format, the interaction with Jeanine suggested a novel and unexpected innovation in his radio career.

Bobby pressed his intercom button. "I'm still gettin' calls like there's no tomorrow. You wanna take any of 'em?"

Dale didn't answer immediately. He did want to take more calls, but not just then, not tonight. He felt some kind of responsibility to his listeners who were expecting to hear rock 'n' roll classics. "Uh . . . no, not tonight," he finally answered, trailing off as though he might have had more to say.

Bobby nodded his understanding and for the rest of the shift turned away all subsequent callers as graciously as he could. Dale used the time to assess his feelings, and think. A talk format would connect him with the world outside like no other format, allow him to experience life in a way he would never be able to otherwise. But he didn't want to host rantings and ravings, the venting of bilious or judgmental opinions, or mere chitchat. He wanted to help people.

But if help was what he offered, then help was what his callers would expect. And to believe he had wisdom enough to help his troubled listeners seemed to him sort of presumptuous, almost arrogant.

Still, the impulse to try was intense. He wasn't interested in coming off as superior or preachy. But ultimately, he reasoned, if he simply shared, as his opinions, what wisdom he himself lived by, and by invitation only, then, certainly, he would not come off as superior or preachy.

By the end of his shift, Dale had decided on a course of action. At 11:52 p.m., just before the final record of the shift—when he typically introduced the following show and signed off for the night—he worked up his nerve and flicked his mic switch for a special announcement.

"That was vintage ABBA from 1976, the indefatigable 'Dancing Queen.' You're tuned to WWKW and this is Dale Greene on The Brink of Tomorrow, poised to step off into the void. Before I say goodnight, however, I want to thank all of you out there who called with condolences for the loss of my parents. Your concern means a great deal to me and I very much appreciate it. To know your listeners care that much about you is an extraordinary treasure.

"If you were with us at the top of the show, you heard me talking with nine-year-old Jeanine who also lost her parents this week. To have the opportunity to talk to her and share a little of my understanding of life and death with her—and perhaps to reassure her somewhat—was a rare privilege indeed. It was so meaningful to me, in fact, that I'd like to do more of it. So I'm considering changing The Brink of Tomorrow to a talk format. But before I do that, I want your feedback. I don't claim to be a therapist or qualified to treat you in any way, but if you'd like to have someone to call when you need help over the rough spots in life, write me a letter and tell me you'd like me to go ahead with the change. If you prefer that I keep on playing the classics, write me and tell me that as well. Or if you can't decide which format you prefer, write and tell me that, too. I'll go with the majority vote. Whatever you do, stay tuned for the Midnight Express with Stan Furness, coming up at the top of the hour. In the meantime, this is Dale Greene and I'll see you again on The Brink of Tomorrow."

He flicked his mic switch and gave a final glance toward Bobby. With this, Bobby released the pause button on the final disc of the night and prepared to hand the signal off to station headquarters downtown.

"What do you think?" Dale asked as he guided his motorized wheelchair through the doorway connecting the announce booth with the control room.

"About what?" Bobby asked in return. It was not that Bobby was dense, he just needed Dale to be more specific. Plus, he was unused to having Dale ask his opinion about things, not because Dale did not value Bobby's opinions, but because Bobby, being more inclined to take life as it came rather than to study and comment on it, rarely had them.

"My idea to change the format of the show to talk," Dale clarified.

"Are you gonna get more phone lines in here?" Bobby asked before venturing the opinion.

"I guess I'd have to, along with a couple of computers to keep track of the queue."

"Then it sounds good." As might have been expected, Bobby's focus was on the technological aspects of the matter.

"I guess what I'm really interested in is what you think of the idea of my trying to help people in a talk format," Dale explained. Even after having taken the step of inviting a listener vote, questions and doubts about the proposition lingered in his mind.

"Do you wanna do it?"

"Yeah."

"Then do it."

"Yeah," Dale acknowledged limply. He had been hoping for a vote of confidence in his ability to pull it off, or perhaps a prediction about the write-in response from his listeners. Even a comment on the market feasibility of such an endeavor, given the potential loss of listeners to a rival station, which also played classic rock, would have been welcome. But Bobby was nothing if not consistent and the psychosocioeconomic nuances of such an endeavor were of no concern to him.

"By the way," Dale added, "thanks for all the extra work you did on the phones tonight. I know it was a handful."

As always, the recognition alone made all the demanding work worthwhile for Bobby and by way of thanks he simply grinned.

"See you later, amigo," Dale concluded as he swiveled and motored out the door.

"Ciao," was Bobby's stylized response.

The broadcast suite was located in the basement of the recreation pavilion and opened directly into the underground tunnel that connected the structure with the manor house. Dale motored the hundred and forty-five yards to the house, still exhilarated by his excursion into talk radio, but nursing nagging doubts about making the format change.

At birth, Dale Carey Greene had appeared to be a normal baby in every respect. Eight pounds ten ounces, bright blue eyes, glowing skin, powerful lungs, darling face—he was the chief joy of his proud parents.

Indiscriminately showing baby Dale off to family, friends, and strangers alike, Leonard and Dara Greene did not know that lurking deep within the cells of their precious offspring was an interloper which would alter their collective lives irrevocably and forever.

The Greenes had never even heard of Proteus syndrome until Dale was three years old. By the time he was four, they had learned everything there was to know about the disorder, including its common name, Elephant Man's Disease, previously thought to be neuro-fibromatosis.

The scaly patches and mottled brown spots had developed on his skin by his third birthday. Bulbous, cauliflower-like growths became evident a few months later. And by the end of the year there were marked changes in his skeletal structure.

By the time Dale was five, the flaw in his cellular makeup had turned his head and face into an unrecognizable mass of tissue and noticeably misshapen his little body. The lumpy mounds of flesh and droopy folds of scabrous skin that covered his anatomy, not to mention the unnatural formation of his young frame, disguised his features to such a degree that upon first glance, the casual observer did not immediately recognize him as human.

The one saving grace was that the disease did not affect the keen child mind or the warm child heart that had become evident at a very early age, nor did it tamper with the clarity of his precocious speech. Were it not for his disfigurement, one would have envisioned him a man of prodigious intellect and boundless compassion.

At first, young Dale was blissfully unaware of the changes taking place in his body. But before long, he began to notice the sudden gasps, the shocked expressions, the rapid withdrawal of strangers who happened to glance his way. Having previously delighted grownups with his precocious intellect and engaging personality, these new responses deeply hurt his feelings, and made his parents' hearts ache unbearably. When the community's avoidance turned to scorn, the Greenes moved to another state where they kept their beloved child carefully sheltered from the judging eyes of the outside world.

Upon learning that Proteus syndrome is a congenital disorder for which modern medicine had no cure, Leonard and Dara Greene were beside themselves with guilt. They knew they had done nothing wrong, yet they had somehow inflicted a horrible curse and immense pain upon an utter innocent. And the full extent of the young man's pain had not even begun to manifest.

The Greenes were not particularly religious, but knowing there would be no material respite from the emotional pain they were suffering, they began looking for answers in the spiritual disciplines. In the main, the organized religions they studied offered little more than the explanation that Dale's condition was God's will—or wrath— and the only solution available was simple acceptance—or penance. It was obvious to them that acceptance was requisite, but they wanted answers. And those answers were not to be found in organized religion.

So they began studying the philosophical disciplines of the East and the metaphysical movements in the West, reading volumes, attending lectures, and listening to ideas which claimed to come directly from the spiritual planes.

While the avalanche of ideas they studied represented a broad and eclectic variety of sources, the Greenes began to recognize similarities between them, and eventually discovered a consistent wisdom converging out of them, a wisdom they could embrace and apply to their lives. Moreover, these ideas and their wisdom brought a sense of relief they could find nowhere else.

Without hope for physical relief from his condition, Leonard and Dara realized that Dale could live without severe emotional pain only if he understood his condition through the philosophical principles they had discovered in their studies. So they did their best to impart the wisdom of these ideas and philosophies to their son as he grew. They taught him not to judge himself by his own appearance, even though they knew the rest of the world most certainly would. They also treated him with the highest standards of love and integrity they could possibly conceive. And their exposure to the Eastern philosophies meant very high standards indeed.

That is not to say that Leonard and Dara were perfect parents. They still had to deal with the challenges of being human. But they worked diligently to become the most loving, respectful, and responsible people they could be, so they could be the most loving, respectful, and responsible parents they could be. And their efforts were well rewarded—Dale's natural intellect and compassion flourished in that environment, and he adjusted unexpectedly well to his lot.

Fortunately, their station in life made all this somewhat easier. Born into wealth, Leonard Greene had invested wisely and built up a small commercial empire—Greene Enterprises—which made life for him and his family both comfortable and easy. Amongst his diverse collection of wholly owned enterprises were a compact-disc manufacturing plant, an offset printing company, a small book publishing firm, a city-wide fast food chain, a furniture factory and showroom, and a local radio station. And even these were mere diversions. His greatest financial resource was his investment portfolio which ranged to eight figures.

With such wealth, Leonard was able to provide his son with a life rich in interests and activities without ever having to leave the estate. The Greene property covered 147 verdant acres of varied terrain, and the compound comprised five independent structures connected by both open walkways and underground tunnels—a total of 317 rooms of every imaginable function. In addition to copious living spaces of every description, there were game rooms, two indoor swimming pools, a gymnasium, a pistol range, a library, a computer complex, a film screening room, and so on. Outdoors there were tennis courts, a driving range, an archery range, a batting cage, a fishing pond, a jogging trail, a stand of trees, and the like. While Dale was not capable of participating in most of these sports, he did experience a great deal of life as a result of being out of doors and watching others engage in these activities.

To run the huge complex and serve the various needs of the family, the Greenes kept a staff of nine—a housekeeping master, a head chef, a gardener, a valet, a chauffeur, a nurse, a financial advisor, Dale's teacher, and Leonard's attorney. The housekeeping master, the head chef, and the gardener each oversaw sizeable crews of their own which, along with the staff of nine, totaled 27 people. Even this figure grew by one as one of the housekeepers bore a child, Roberto, six years Dale's junior. This cadre, it turned out, also benefited from the Greenes' diligent work on themselves, for Leonard and Dara extended to them the same compassion and integrity they showed their son. As a result, the staff was utterly devoted to the Greene family.

For Dale's academic instruction, Leonard Greene spared no expense in hiring the finest educator and providing his son with whatever facilities were needed for his studies. For this reason, the boy received an education that rivaled the best of institutions. When all was said and done, Leonard and Dara Greene allowed Dale to learn and experience life as fully as he could—without having to interact with the cruel, judgmental world outside the estate's perimeter.

Certainly, they understood that eschewing the outside world represented some sacrifice. But this sacrifice, they rationalized, was miniscule compared to the pain their beloved son would endure had they made him face it unprotected.

Perhaps, lurking beneath the surface of their consciousness, the Greenes recognized this calculation as folly. They understood quite well that neither the Eastern philosophies nor Western metaphysics advocated hiding from one's fears. But for each insight, there is a fear to challenge it. And when it came to the Greenes' greatest fear, their wisdom was challenged indeed.

So they hid their poor disfigured child from the cruelty of the outside world and, in the process, taught him to hide from it as well.

As is common with Proteus syndrome, the misgrowth of Dale's body abated during adolescence. But the disease left him hideously disfigured. Dale's case was at least as severe as that of Joseph C. Merrick, the Nineteenth Century Englishman known as "the Elephant Man." Dale's head was distorted by an irregularly overgrown cranium which undergirded bulbous mounds of knotty flesh. And the cauliflower-like growths that began showing up at age three now covered most of his body. The disease also left him less able-bodied than Joseph Merrick. Due to asymmetric hyperostosis—uneven and irregular overgrowth of his bones—use of his left arm and legs was limited. And his feet were deformed by bone tumors and plantar hyperplasia—overgrowth of the soft tissue on the soles. At least the condition did not worsen past his seventeenth birthday. And anyone who was able to look beyond the disfigurement and into Dale's eyes saw a warmth and beauty that was rare in a human being.

One thing that became evident as young Dale matured was the effect the distortions in his skeletal structure had on his voice. Growing abnormally, his chest became relatively large, providing a particularly voluminous cavity for his voice to resonate in. The result was a deep, rich vocal quality, one which had the ability to charm the most hardened cynic.

Because it was a safe connection with the outside world, Dale spent many hours listening to the radio. Some of the time he was tuned to his father's station, WWKW, which played mostly classic rock. The rest of the time he listened to rival stations. When he was very young, he would imitate the various DJs, mimicking their individually stylized inflections, and entertaining Roberto, who had become his steadfast companion.

By the time he was fourteen, Dale had dropped the imitations—partly because he had outgrown them, partly because he had mastered them—but he did not drop his love of the radio. In fact, at the age of eighteen, he begged his father to let him be a disc jockey on the family station.

Although this seemed perfectly natural to Dale, it seemed a stroke of genius to his father. Finally, here was a way his poor misshapen son could play a role in the outside world—a real role, not a vicarious one—without having to face the judgment and prejudice that working in its midst would otherwise entail.

It started out simply enough. Dale was allowed to DJ the midnight-to-three shift one night. He did it with such accomplishment that he was thereafter permitted to work the shift one night a week. To assuage any hurt feelings, the DJ who normally covered that shift was given the night off each week with double pay.

To avoid exposing Dale to the station staff, or having to clear the station for Dale's shift, Leonard built a broadcast suite right on the Greene estate, configured to accommodate Dale's motorized wheelchair. When Dale's shift came up, the station would simply hand off control to the estate suite, and Dale would broadcast from the safety and comfort of his own home.

Dale proved so talented that two years later, when the DJ who normally covered that shift accepted a job at a station in Milwaukee, Dale was given the shift full time. By this time, Roberto, who was mechanically inclined by nature, had demonstrated a compelling interest in and ability with the technological aspects of radio. Now calling himself "Bobby," a somewhat hipper moniker, Roberto joined Dale in the control room as the DJ's engineer.

For the golden-throated, velvet-voiced Dale, the job was a cinch. Announcing record titles, reading the news, and delivering commercial messages barely challenged his articulation skills, but that was of no concern to him. Just being on the radio and talking to the outside world—from the safety of his own home—was a triumph to the young man. And he delighted in doing this for the next three years—till the age of twenty-three.

At that time, another DJ left the Greene employ, leaving a gaping hole in the popular nine-to-midnight shift. Dale and Bobby had shown such accomplishment in their previous position that they were given the more demanding shift. Dale christened his new show "The Brink of Tomorrow" and he and Bobby worked it for another three years.

Then tragedy struck.

Within a week of Dale's twenty-sixth birthday, his beloved parents were killed in an automobile accident. A drunken driver ran a red light and plowed into the Greenes' limo, killing Dale's parents and seriously injuring the chauffeur.

Needless to say, Dale was devastated. As always, he was protected from having to deal with the messy business of the outside world—the police, the hospital, the media, the funeral arrangements. The staff took care of all those details, though they too grieved the loss of their beloved employers, Leonard and Dara.

Dale's shift on the radio was temporarily assigned to another DJ, and Dale spent the next five days crying, sobbing, wailing, blubbering. Due to their exposure to the Eastern philosophies and Western metaphysics, his parents had taught him not to suppress his emotions. So he didn't. While he believed his parents' death represented a choice they had made on a higher level of consciousness—that their spirits now resided in a realm of enlightened souls and that they were supremely happy to be there—he missed them terribly. So he cried, sometimes uncontrollably, until he had completely exhausted the impulse from his being. That is not to say that he quit loving or missing them. He simply exhausted the impulse to cry about it.

Dale was, of course, the beneficiary of the entire Greene empire, so his financial future was utterly secure. After the details of the will had been settled, Leonard's attorney took Dale aside one morning and asked what to do about the staff. The question completely surprised the surviving Greene, as he had simply assumed the staff would go on about their jobs as they had for so many years. Ultimately, each and every one of them were invited to remain, and each and every one of them accepted.

Two weeks after the accident, Dale had begun to feel up to resuming his shift at WWKW. He still felt the great weight of his grief, but he knew his own life would not end just because his parents' had, and he was ready to reestablish his connection with the outside world. It was that night that he took the call from little Jeanine and asked his listeners to vote on his proposal to change the format of The Brink of Tomorrow.

Chapter 3

Knowing this was the surviving Greene's first night back on the air after his parents' fatal accident, the staffers to whom Dale was closest—the teacher, the attorney, and the financial advisor—had been listening to the show in the plushly appointed den of the manor house, and heard Dale's closing announcement.

At the end of the underground tunnel, Dale took the elevator to the ground floor where he exited into a marbled hallway. From there it was another forty feet to the double oak doors which framed the entrance to the den. The doors were open.

"Terrific show!" exclaimed Dr. Wilson Terry, Dale's teacher, as the young Greene appeared in the doorway of the den. Wilson was referring primarily to his protege's chat with Jeanine.

"Thanks, Wil," Dale acknowledged appreciatively, motoring through the doors and into the room. While he knew his beloved educator would have been impressed with anything he did, he also knew the compliment was genuine. The other two men were equally impressed, but only grinned and nodded at the young Greene, aware that Dale knew Wil spoke for them as well.

"What did you think about my announcement at the end?" Dale asked, maneuvering to a position near the deeply cushioned, velvet-upholstered chairs where his advisors sat. While Dale appreciated the praise, he ached for their comments on his proposal.

"Why ask us?" Wil asked in response.

Dale had thought his question obvious. "I want your opinions."

The question *had* been obvious, but as Dale's teacher, Wil's interest was in seeing his student trust his *own* counsel. "Seems to me the only opinions that matter are yours and those of your listeners," he replied.

"Yeah, that's what I thought, too . . . initially. But I still seem to have some doubts."

"About what?" asked Paul Norman Carr, the friend and attorney Dale had inherited from his father just two weeks earlier.

Asked to name his fear, Dale sighed. "That I can do it . . . that I really have what it takes to help my listeners. I know I made the announcement, and at the time it sounded like a good idea . . . ." He heaved another sigh before continuing. "But in the final analysis, making an announcement is vastly different from actually doing it."

"But you did do it, with the little girl," countered Shel Boerman, the financial advisor.

"Yes," Wil confirmed, "I thought you acquitted yourself quite handily with her."

"I did. But she's only one person—and a kid. There's no evidence to suggest I can do it with anyone else—particularly adults."

The three elders groaned practically in unison, alerting Dale to a flaw in his thinking.

"Come on," Wil chided. "What would your father have said about that?"

Dale looked inward. "He would've said something like . . . 'Success is a product of dreams, not evidence.'"

"Right."

"But let's face it. Who am I to think I can help anyone? Who am I to think I know more than anyone else? I haven't done any real living. I haven't faced half of what my listeners have in their lives on the outside. I've had it easy."

"You've had it different," was Wil's firm but caring reply. Sitting there, facing this bizarre-looking lump of humanity whose strength of character and emotional fortitude had exceeded all expectations, Wil found Dale's insecurities at once astonishing and endearing— astonishing because, despite his incredible disfigurement, Dale had discovered and nurtured within himself a healthy emotional center and the wisdom to go with it; endearing because Dale himself did not appreciate the enormity of that accomplishment.

"You've had it easier in some respects, *much* harder in others," Wil continued. "And in facing that hardship, you've had to come to an understanding of life far more profound than most of your listeners have ever even conceived of. You've had the benefit of your parents' teachings, you've heard enough talk-show therapists to hang out a shingle of your own, your reading of psychology, philosophy, and human behavior is extensive enough to cover any questions that might arise, and you're blessed with natural insight. But none of that really matters. What matters is how you *felt* when you were talking with the little girl."

Dale considered Wil's words for a moment.

"How *did* you feel when you were talkin' with the little girl?" asked Paul Carr, his diction accented with a hint of the South.

"I felt great! Excited! Exhilarated!"

"And what would you tell your listeners if they were that excited about a new endeavor?" Paul queried further.

The question hit home.

"'Act on your excitement,' of course," Dale replied, feeling encouraged. Then, suddenly discouraged, he shook his massive head. "Do you see what I'm doing here? I can't even follow my own advice. If I can't even follow my own advice, how can I expect to give it to others?"

"If following one's own advice were a prerequisite to giving it," Wil admonished, rubbing a brown hand over his balding brown pate, "there would be no advisors and no advice. Even givers of advice have lessons to learn."

The argument was compelling, and Dale sighed upon hearing it. "You're right. Thanks."

"Now that the question of your insecurities has been put to rest," Paul added, unfolding his slender body to its full six-foot, four-inch vertical height, "you don't have to make the format change in one fell swoop, you know. You can phase it in. Start out with one night a week and expand it if it goes well."

The suggestion made infinite sense and Dale nodded as he considered it. "I guess I'll just wait and see what my listeners say."

As expected, letters and email from listeners flooded the station. A few, indeed, expressed ambivalence about the format change. Many more expressed objections to the proposal, typically stating them in rather vehement terms. But the majority expressed everything from mild interest—repeating Paul Carr's suggestion to phase it in—to enthusiastic encouragement to make the switch swiftly and completely.

Within a week, the response had been voluminous enough to show a definite trend—in favor of a phased-in change. Dale had Bobby order a new switchboard to handle the increased call traffic, along with the computers they would need to keep track of the callers and their problems as they waited to talk to the DJ. By the end of the third week, all the equipment had been installed and Dale had announced the first night of the talk format.

Chapter 4

"It's nine o'clock. You're tuned to WWKW, FM 102.4, and this is Dale Greene on The Brink of Tomorrow. As I've been announcing for the past two weeks, we're going to be trying out a talk format one night a week here on The Brink of Tomorrow, and tonight is the inaugural event. We started getting calls a few minutes ago and we'll be taking calls till the brink of tomorrow. If you're having trouble with something in your life, give me a ring and let's see if we can sort it out together."

Dale scanned the newly installed computer monitor which displayed the list of callers waiting to talk to him. On the queue were Tim, whose mother was an alcoholic; Martina, who feared she may have AIDS; Cynthia, who had problems with her in-laws; Glenn, who was stuck in a dead-end job; Crossley, who hated his boss; Lou, who had an eating disorder; and Margaret, whose teenage daughter wanted to wear makeup. Hoping to start out with an easy one, Dale decided to talk first to Margaret.

"Our first caller is Margaret, she's thirty, and she says her teenage daughter wants to wear makeup." Dale pressed the switchboard button to put Margaret on the air.

"Hi, Margaret, this is Dale Greene and you're on The Brink of Tomorrow."

Having been waiting for several minutes, Margaret had let the phone slip down onto her shoulder, so did not plainly hear the DJ's greeting.

"Hello?" she said, fumbling to put the phone to her ear.

"Margaret?" Dale asked genially.

"Yeah, who's this?" Her call had been answered initially by Bobby, so she was unprepared to hear Dale's voice.

"This is Dale Greene and you're on The Brink of Tomorrow."

Dale's delivery was natural, conversational, devoid of the stylization he used in his DJ persona and it put Margaret at ease.

Never in a million years would she have guessed that the man at the other end of the line was a hideous freak of nature.

"Oh! I'm sorry, I didn't expect you to come on so soon," she explained.

"Oh, that's all right. This is new for me, too. But I expect it to smooth out in time. Now Bobby, my engineer, tells me your teenage daughter wants to wear makeup."

"Yeah."

"And you don't want her to and there's friction between you," Dale surmised.

"Well . . . friction?! It's more like war!"

"Uh-huh! What's your daughter's name, Margaret?"

"Katherine."

"And how old is Katherine?"

"Thirteen."

"And how do your battles come about? What does she do and what do you do?"

"She wants to wear makeup to school and I won't let her out of the house with it on."

"I see. Does she come home with it on?"

"No."

"Then you seem to be succeeding in your efforts. So, what's the problem?"

"Well, we fight over it, and that's bad enough, but I'm afraid she puts it on after she gets to school."

"And washes it off before she comes home?"

"Yeah."

"All right. Why don't you want Katherine to wear makeup?"

"She's too young!" Margaret's reply bristled with impatience, as though the answer to Dale's question should have been obvious.

"Why is that?" Dale asked, playing devil's advocate.

"Well, a thirteen-year-old shouldn't be wearing makeup!" Margaret had failed to intuit the role Dale had chosen. "Do *you* think a thirteen-year-old should be wearing makeup?!"

"Well, since you asked, I'll tell you what I think. I don't believe in 'shoulds.'"

There was a brief silence as Margaret tried to fathom Dale's meaning. "You don't believe in 'shoulds'?" she repeated.

"Right. Do you know what a 'should' is?"

"No."

"A 'should' is a disguised judgment. Now that probably doesn't mean any *more* to you, so let me explain what a judgment is, and then we'll talk about disguised judgments. Okay?"

"All right," Margaret agreed.

"Basically, a judgment is any thought or statement which declares someone or something to be right, or wrong, or good, or bad. For instance, if we think or say something is *bad*, that's a judgment. Even if we say it's *good*, that's a judgment. Of course, most people don't mind being judged as good, but saying they're good is a judgment nonetheless. Likewise, thinking or saying something is *wrong* is a judgment. So is saying something is *right*, even though most people don't mind being judged as right. Are you with me so far?"

"Yeah. But I don't see what this has to do with wearing makeup."

"All right, well, can you bear with me for a little longer?"

"Yeah . . . ."

"Good. So now, you may ask, what's the problem with judging? Well, there are a number of reasons for not judging, many of them profoundly metaphysical, which I won't get into just yet, but in this case, the problem with judging is that it's a way of shirking responsibility for our personal opinions and preferences." He spaced this last out to give it time to sink in. "When we say something is 'bad,' what we're really doing is expressing a personal opinion or preference. We're really saying we don't *like* that thing, whatever it might be. But by judging it as *bad*, we're assigning a property to it that it does not, by itself, possess. And in so doing, we're shirking responsibility for our opinion or preference. Have I completely confused you?"

Margaret giggled nervously. "Um . . . sorta!"

"All right, let me give you an example. In this region, we say the weather is *bad* when it's raining. That assigns the property of 'badness' to rainy weather. But in the deserts of Africa, rainy weather is considered *good*—because they need the moisture to survive in the desert. So you've got a situation where rain is considered good in one place and bad in another. But rain can't be *both* good and bad. And, in fact, it's not. When you strip away the judgment, you realize that rain is only water falling from the sky, a completely neutral happenstance. And because it's completely neutral, it allows people to form different *opinions* or *preferences* about it, depending upon where they live. In this region, by judging rainy weather as 'bad,' we're really just expressing our preference for dry weather, but we're not taking responsibility for that preference; instead, we're assigning the artificial property of 'badness' to the weather. Is this beginning to make sense?"

"Sorta. But what's so important about taking responsibility for our preferences?"

"Well, taking responsibility for our opinions and preferences is the first step toward taking responsibility for our actions. Now, some people may not be interested in taking responsibility for their actions, but those of us who are parents are certainly interested in getting our children to take responsibility for *their* actions, and we can best train our children to do that by taking responsibility for our *own* actions. Is it beginning to make sense, now?"

"Yeah, kinda."

"All right. I think I've spent enough time on this for the moment. Let's look at 'shoulds.' Do you understand now what I meant when I said 'shoulds' are disguised judgment?"

"Not really."

"All right. When you say *should*, you're really saying it's 'right' to do one thing and 'wrong' to do the opposite. For instance, saying 'A thirteen-year-old should not wear makeup' is the same thing as saying 'It's *wrong* for a thirteen-year-old to wear makeup and *right* for her not to wear makeup.' Obviously, those are judgments. But if you strip away the judgment, what you're really saying is, 'I don't *want* my thirteen-year-old daughter wearing makeup.' Right?"

"Right!"

"But by saying 'should'—by making it a judgment—you're not taking responsibility for your preference. You're not taking responsibility for your efforts to dictate her makeup practices. And I'd wager Katherine is perfectly aware of that, at least subconsciously, if not consciously."

"So what should I do?"

"Well, let's start by changing your question from 'What *should* I do?'—a disguised judgment—to 'What *can* I do?'"

This simple shift in wording struck a chord of enlightenment in Margaret. "Oh! All right, what *can* I do?"

"You see, by putting it that way, you're able to see that you have options and a choice in the matter."

"Okay."

Whatever misgivings Dale might have had when he first contemplated the talk format, they were quickly giving way to confidence. He felt fluent, informed. He knew just what to say at every turn. His new role felt completely natural to him.

"Well, now that we've stripped away the judgment from your original statement, let's see what you really object to. Why don't you want Katherine to wear makeup?"

For a moment, the question stymied Margaret. "Well . . . I don't think a thirteen-year-old should be wearing makeup. But you don't want me to say 'should,' so . . . I'm confused." She was becoming frustrated and it showed in her voice.

"All right, that's all right, we can clear that up. Let me phrase the question differently. What are you *afraid will happen* if Katherine wears makeup?" Dale said with deliberation.

Facing the prospect of looking directly at her fear, Margaret gasped. It took her a moment to gather her wits and courage, during which she could be heard to sigh once or twice.

Finally, "I'm afraid she's going to look like a tramp."

"Uh-huh," Dale acknowledged evenly. "And what are you afraid will happen if she looks like a tramp?"

Again, Margaret balked at facing her fears, sighing as she had before. Then, "That she'll attract boys."

"Good," Dale said supportively. "We're peeling away the layers of fear. And what are you afraid will happen if she attracts boys?"

This was the big one, but having had this little bit of experience with facing the fear, Margaret was more ready with her answer. "That she'll have sex with them."

"Right. And what are you afraid will happen if she has sex with them?"

Accustomed as Margaret was becoming to facing her fears, the one

Dale was asking her to face just now was either too complex or too awful to get a grasp of. She fumbled around for several seconds, audibly flustered. "She's too young to be having sex!" she finally blurted.

Dale noted her befuddlement. "Aren't you afraid she'll get hurt," he said with great tenderness, "because she's not yet physically and emotionally prepared for sex, because she hasn't had the experience to know how to protect herself, because the boys may take advantage of her naiveté, because she could wind up being abused or catching an STD, because her life could be inconvenienced by a pregnancy or something of that nature?"

"Yeah!" Margaret confirmed breathlessly. Facing her fears under the protection of this wise and gentle man, Margaret was beginning to envision Dale a tall, swarthy paladin.

The misshapen DJ gave his caller a few seconds to catch her breath. "Can you think of anything else you're afraid could happen as a result of her wearing makeup?"

Margaret thought briefly, then sighed again. "No."

"All right. Well, let's see ... we've stripped away the judgment, we've sorted out the fears, now the question is ... have you shared these fears with Katherine?"

"No," Margaret answered weakly.

"Why not?"

Margaret thought briefly before answering. "I guess I didn't realize I had them."

"Well, now that you do, why don't you share them with her?"

Margaret balked. "She won't listen to me."

"Why not?"

"She thinks she knows everything and I don't know anything. She's not gonna worry about my fears."

"You may be making an unwarranted assumption."

"I know her!" Margaret retorted emphatically. "I know what she'll do."

"Have you ever tried this kind of approach before?"

"No."

"Then you don't have sufficient history with it to be able to predict how she'll react."

Margaret took the point without response.

"Getting someone to do what *you* want," Dale continued, "can be very difficult—if not impossible—if *they* don't want to do it. That's true of anyone. It's even harder to get a teenager to do what you want because they're going through so many hormonal changes and spoiling for their independence. Sharing your fears is one way of guiding them toward what you want, providing you present them effectively."

"So how should I present them?"

"How *should* you present them?" Dale queried by way of reminder.

Margaret did not catch on immediately. Then, "Oh! How *can* I present them?"

"Thank you," Dale said in appreciation of her perspicacity. "Well, first of all, it's important to remember that people are far more inclined to do something when *they* want to do it and the decision to do it is theirs to make. So the most effective way of getting someone to do what you want is by getting them to want it too. And in the case of a youngster, it also helps to let them know straight up that it's ultimately their decision to make. Now, you can't force someone to want something, but you can explain *your* reasons for wanting it—your fears, your experience, your wisdom, whatever—and if your reasons are compelling enough, they'll want it too. Of course, there are no guarantees of that, but by sharing your fears with Katherine and letting her know it's her decision to make, you'll have a far better chance of her seeing the wisdom of waiting till she's older and making that choice on her own."

"See, I'm not so sure about that," Margaret countered. "I'm afraid she'd just go ahead and decide to wear the makeup and we'd be back to fighting about it."

"Well, that's certainly possible," Dale acknowledged. "But you won't be any worse off than you are now. At least there's a chance she'd decide to wait if you gave her the opportunity to make the decision on her own."

"I don't think so. If she wants to wear the makeup, that's what she'll choose."

"Well, like I said, that's certainly possible. But—"

"So that's why I have to put my foot down with her!"

"But that's what you've been doing, and you're telling me it's not working."

Margaret did not respond.

"Right?" Dale gently prompted.

"Right."

Dale sighed and paused to reconnoiter. "What makes you think she may be wearing makeup at school?"

"Well, her friends do it and she's just so dunderheaded and foolish. I don't think she has enough sense not to go along with them."

"Hmmm. If I may make an observation . . . ." Dale paused for permission.

"Go ahead," Margaret approved.

"I suspect you're confusing ignorance and inexperience, with dunderheadedness and foolishness. There's one thing we know for sure about Katherine: At the age of thirteen, she hasn't had time to gather much depth of knowledge or experience. Right?"

"Right."

"So there's a greater likelihood that what you see as dunderheadedness and foolishness is really ignorance and inexperience. Now there's a real liability in starting out assuming a young person is dunderheaded and foolish. If the kid is actually bright and sensible—which most kids are—and you mistake ignorance and inexperience for dunderheadedness and foolishness, you may fail to give them the support they need to gain knowledge and experience. And then *they* start believing they're dunderheaded and foolish, and eventually wind up doing something *really* dunderheaded and foolish. Of course, it's never too late to share fears and knowledge and wisdom, but by that time, some damage may have already been done. So I suggest you start by assuming that Katherine is bright and sensible, and will take heed of your fears and experience and wisdom."

To Margaret this seemed like an insurmountable task. "I don't know that I can do that just overnight like that."

"Well, I'm not saying you have to do it overnight. However, what you're doing right now isn't working. So if you want things to change between you and Katherine, you need to at least *start* doing something different. Right?"

Margaret did not answer immediately. Finally, she sighed, and said, "Right . . . . So what are you telling me to do?"

"Well, I'm not *telling* you to do anything," Dale gently corrected. "I'm only suggesting."

"All right, what are you suggesting?" A hint of irritation had crept into Margaret's voice.

"Basically, just what I said. Share your fears—and your experience and wisdom—with her and let her make the decision on her own."

"But I keep telling you, if I do that, she'll decide to wear the makeup!"

"As I said before, that's certainly possible," Dale said, maintaining an even tone. "But you think she's already putting it on secretly, anyway, so talking to her about it can't hurt anything." He paused to consider a different approach. "I'm getting the impression that what you'd like me to do is to suggest a more effective way of *controlling* her."

"That's right!"

"But there isn't a more effective way of controlling her. In fact, you can't really control her at all. I know that's a very scary thing to hear, but I'm afraid that's part of being a parent. The fact is, as a youngster becomes more and more mobile and develops more and more interests—becomes a teenager—you cease to have moment-to-moment control over their lives. They're often at school or at a friend's house or some activity where you have no control over them at all. So if they're intent on doing something against your wishes, they have plenty of opportunity to do it. And you're powerless to stop them short of keeping them home and chaining them to the radiator. You can punish them *after* they've done something—if you find out about it—but you can't *prevent* them from doing it. Those are just the facts of parenting. And if you put a heavy control trip on them, they'll just be resentful and may deliberately defy you just to get back at you. And they'll do it behind your back, so you won't even know they're doing it until they're in serious trouble. Putting the heavy control trip on them does more damage than it prevents. So control is not the answer."

"What *is* the answer?"

"Well, that's what I was trying to explain, but apparently it's not what you wanted to hear. The problem is that you're looking for a foolproof way to prevent your daughter from wearing makeup. And there just isn't one."

"But that's so frustrating!"

"I know. But it's a fact of life. It's like a law of nature. You don't get frustrated with the law of gravity, do you?"

Margaret sighed in exasperation. "No."

"Of course not. That's because you accept it as a law of nature. You accept it as a given that you simply have to work around. The same thing is true of working with people."

Taking a moment to consider this, Margaret did not respond.

"One of the biggest problems we have on this planet," Dale went on, "is people trying to control others instead of learning ways of interacting cooperatively. Sometimes the control works—for a while—but eventually it backfires on you and then you have a battle on your hands and it's a lot harder to establish the cooperation."

Margaret heaved a deep sigh. "This is so hard for me."

"I know. I wish I could make it easier," Dale empathized. "But that's not within my power."

"Then I don't think I can do it," Margaret lamented in return.

"I think you can," Dale assured.

"But it all just seems so hopeless."

Battling Margaret's resistance to suggestion, Dale was feeling the gnaw of frustration. Could it be that his confidence earlier was premature? Could it be that he was only able to penetrate surfaces, powerless to incise deeper? How long would he last as a radio advisor if that were true? He reached deeply into his training for a new angle. Finally, a flicker of an idea.

"Margaret . . . when I look at the pattern of this conversation in the last few minutes, I notice that I've been giving you all kinds of reasons for sharing your fears with Katherine and you keep coming up with reasons not to—which is your prerogative. But it suggests there's still something you're afraid of. What do you think that is?"

"I don't know," Margaret replied honestly, but sensing Dale was right.

"Hmmm." Dale paused briefly to think. "Let's see. You're thirty, Katherine's thirteen. You had her when you were . . . seventeen. When did *you* start wearing makeup?"

Margaret hesitated, clearly anxious about revealing something embarrassing.

"No one's judging you here, Margaret," Dale assured. "You can tell me."

"About twelve or thirteen," she finally replied

"And you attracted boys and started having sex and were pregnant by the time you were sixteen."

"Yeah." Margaret sounded at once discovered and relieved.

"What did *your* mother say when *you* started wearing makeup?" Dale asked.

Margaret again hesitated. "Well . . . she absolutely forbid it."

"But you did it behind her back?"

"Yeah. All my friends were doing it."

"Just like Katherine."

Margaret chortled with recognition. "Yeah."

"Did your mother explain to you why she didn't want you wearing makeup?"

"No, she just said I was too young."

"I see. Pretty much what you said about Katherine."

"Yeah."

"Tell me, Margaret . . . if you had it to do over again, would you do it differently?"

"Oh, yeah! I mean, don't get me wrong; I love my daughter. I just would've waited."

"Why?"

"Well . . . I know better now."

"Back then, you didn't know what could happen to you," Dale confirmed.

"Right."

"Would that be because your mother didn't share her fears and wisdom with you?"

Margaret mulled the question before answering. "Probably."

"By not sharing your fears and experience and wisdom with Katherine, aren't you condemning her to the same ignorance?"

Margaret's sigh of recognition was audible. "Yeah."

"What I'm suggesting is not an easy thing to do because the outcome is so uncertain, as we've already noted. But ultimately, I think it's more effective than trying to prevent a child from doing something she's determined to do. It may help to remember that children aren't shrubs that you can just prune to whatever shape you want. They're human beings who, as they grow into adulthood, will shape themselves according to their own needs. If their needs are to resist and defy you—because you've tried to control and confine them—then they'll shape themselves accordingly. And that's true of Katherine." Dale gave Margaret a moment to assimilate what he had said. Then, "Would you like some pointers on how to approach her with all this?"

"Sure!"

"Okay. Well, first . . . when you sit down to talk with her, tell her right off the bat that the decision to wear makeup will be hers—so she knows you're not going to try to lay the control trip on her—but you want to talk about what wearing makeup means. Then tell her about your experience and your fears. Bear in mind, your fears alone will probably not be enough to dissuade her. She's liable just to tell you 'get over it.' And she'd have a point. So you have to put them in terms of the jeopardy she could be putting herself in by wearing makeup at her age. And that jeopardy would have to be credible. If it's not, she'll see through it and reject it. Go into detail about your own experiences. Whatever you do, don't come off hysterical.

"Second . . . many teenagers are very sensitive to any suggestion that they can't take care of themselves. They're kind of funny in this way. They may secretly be very insecure about their ability to relate and perform, but they bristle at the suggestion that they can't handle themselves, especially when it's their parent who's making that suggestion. It's a real contradiction."

"So what do you do about it?" Margaret asked.

"Well, credit her with having intelligence and ability. Let her know that you believe she's capable of making sensible decisions and handling whatever challenges that might arise in her life, but that life challenges even adults, and understanding the challenges helps to meet them. Basically, talk to her as an equal.

"Third . . . keep in mind that Katherine is human, and she *will* learn the lessons she's here to learn, regardless of your efforts to protect her from them. If those lessons include learning the easy way—from your wisdom and experience—then she'll act on what you have to say. But if her lessons require that she learn the hard way—by making her own mistakes—then there's nothing you can do to prevent it. You can't protect her from the lessons, and you can't protect her from herself. Ultimately, the best thing you can do is give her your love, your wisdom, and the freedom to make her own choices, and hope she applies that wisdom to those choices. And if, after you share your wisdom with her, she chooses to make mistakes, you have to let her make them. If you don't let her make her mistakes, she won't be able to learn from them."

Margaret groaned at this prospect.

"And finally, be prepared to compromise. She might be willing to keep her makeup to a minimum to get your approval, yet still fit in with her friends. So keep that in mind."

"Okay."

"And that's about it. If you, as a parent, do your job of guiding and preparing your kids to make their decisions wisely, then, for the most part, they'll make wise decisions. But whether they make wise decisions or not, letting them make their own decisions demonstrates that you trust them. That eliminates the resentment and defiance, and usually they're so appreciative of your trust that they'll work extra hard to make decisions that please you." Dale waited for a reply from Margaret, and getting none, asked, "Does that help?"

"Yeah," Margaret replied thoughtfully. "Quite a bit."

"Good! Let me know how it turns out."

"All right, I will. Thanks for your help. You've really been terrific."

"Well, thank you, and you're very welcome. Best of luck."

"Thanks. Bye."

"Bye."

Dale pressed the disconnect button and waited a second before announcing, "You're listening to WWKW, FM 102.4, and this is Dale Greene on The Brink of Tomorrow. I'll be back with more calls after this commercial break."

Switching off his mic, he glanced over at Bobby. The engineer had started the commercial tape and was busy answering another call, so Dale simply raised a misshapen thumb. But beneath his disfigured exterior, the DJ was elated.

The call from Margaret had turned out to be much harder than Dale had originally anticipated, but he felt at once satisfied that he had met the challenge and delighted to have been able to help someone. From this he derived an elevated sense of confidence—until he realized that if what looked like an easy call turned out to be so hard, then what looks like a hard call might be impossible.

While the commercials were airing, he scanned the callers displayed on his monitor. The number had increased threefold. Amongst the newcomers, some of the interesting ones included Greg, who was addicted to sex; Cindy, who was contemplating an abortion; Yolanda, who was trying to hold a relationship together; John, who was sexually abused as a youngster; Argus, who was dating a married woman; and Cameron, who feared marrying a rich woman.

Noticing that Bobby had just finished with a call, Dale punched the intercom button.

"Boy, we've got quite a selection here," Dale observed.

"Yeah," Bobby confirmed. "From about half-way through that first call, they started soundin' real anxious to talk to you."

"I guess that's a good sign."

"I guess," Bobby replied. Then, "Thirty seconds."

For the next half minute, Dale looked over the list, then decided on his next call.

Chapter 5

"You're listening to WWKW, FM 102.4, and this is Dale Greene on The Brink of Tomorrow. In case you've just tuned in, we're talking with WWKW listeners who find themselves facing tricky challenges in their lives and we're trying to help sort them out. If you're having a tough time with something, give me a call and let's see if we can find a solution for it together."

Dale glanced at the monitor and readied his hand on the appropriate line button for his next caller. He was not sure if his motivation for this selection was just curiosity or something closer to home.

"Our next caller is Cameron, he's thirty-nine, and he says he's afraid of marrying a rich woman." He pressed the button, engaging the call. "Hi, Cameron, this is Dale Greene and you're on The Brink of Tomorrow."

"Hi, Dale. How ya doin'?" Cameron's voice was strong, steady, and masculine.

"I'm doing just fine, Cameron. How about yourself?"

"Pretty good, pretty good."

"Now, did I get this right, Cameron, you're afraid of marrying a rich woman?"

"Yep."

"I don't mean to make fun or anything, but this isn't the kind of thing you run into every day."

"I know."

"I mean, it's not like you're obligated to marry a rich woman."

"I know."

"So it seems to me the solution is to just avoid dating rich women in the first place."

"Too late for that. Already dated her and popped the question," Cameron explained.

"Oh!" Dale exclaimed, taking a second to assess his error. "Boy, I misread that one. I thought you were just talking about a general fear of marrying rich women. But you're talking about marrying a *specific* rich woman."

"Yep."

"Well, I apologize for misreading it. I guess that would be the most logical reason for being afraid of marrying a rich woman."

"It's all right. It kinda throws me once in a while, too."

"Well, now that we've got that cleared up, what about this woman makes you afraid of marrying her?"

"She's rich."

"Oh! So it's her *money* that you're afraid of?"

"Yeah."

"I take it you don't have money of your own."

"Only what I earn."

"Do you love her?"

"Crazy about her."

"Hmmm. Why are you afraid of her money?"

"Well, you know what they say, 'Money is the root of all evil.' I guess I'm afraid I might be getting myself into no good."

"Ahhhh. What kind of person is she?"

"She's terrific. Kind . . . loving . . . down to earth. Couldn't hope for better."

"So you don't think she's out to mistreat you."

"Nah!"

"Aside from the saying you just quoted, how do you feel about her money?"

"It's okay. I mean, it's nice to have money. You can have a lotta nice things."

"But it's not a big deal to you?"

"Nah."

"Okay. Well, I'm going to reveal to you, and to my entire listening audience—and I wish I could reveal it to the whole world—a grave misconception that has been propagated by all those who harbor jealousies of the well to do."

"All right."

"That saying you quoted—'Money is the root of all evil'—while it's quoted that way more times than not, it's actually taken out of context. The complete quotation is, 'The *love* of money is the root of all evil.'"

"Ohhhh!" Cameron exclaimed.

"You can see that by taking it out of context, people portray money as an evil it isn't. Even then, the quotation—'The love of money is the root of all evil'—still isn't a statement of fact, it's only speculation. In order to make it a statement of fact, someone would have had to examine every evil that ever existed and every evil that ever will exist and determine for certain that the love of money was indeed the root of *all* of it. I don't think anyone has conducted a study like that, or ever could. Now, we certainly see the love of money at the root of *some* evil in this world, but I think we can find other evils which have as their root *other* human weaknesses. So the best we can say is that the love of money is the root of *some* evil. But since you don't seem to love money, it wouldn't seem to a problem for you anyway. What do you think?"

"I think that's right!"

While he had hoped this to be the case, Dale was a little surprised to actually hear the confirmation. "So . . . does that take care of your fear?" he asked in conclusion.

"Yep! Sure does," Cameron replied.

"Terrific! Well, I wish you the best of luck with your lady. Have you set a date yet?"

"August fourteenth."

"Well, congratulations! I'm sure you'll be very happy."

"Thanks, Dale, I think I will. And I sure appreciate your help."

"It's my pleasure, Cameron. Keep in touch."

"I will."

"All right, bye."

"Bye."

Dale disconnected the call. "I love it when a plan comes together," he said, addressing his listeners at large. "I'm sure we all wish Cameron happiness in his marriage. Well, let's see . . . that was so quick, it looks like I have time for another call."

Having successfully handled two calls whose themes were, at least on the surface, somewhat lightweight, Dale felt encouraged to take on something just a little more pithy.

"Let's try Yolanda, who says she's trying to hold a relationship together." He punched the line button. "Hi, Yolanda, this is Dale Greene and you're on The Brink of Tomorrow."

"Hi," Yolanda said in a timid voice.

"You're trying to hold a relationship together? Is this a relationship between yourself and someone else or between two other people?"

"Myself and my boyfriend."

"I see," Dale acknowledged gently. "So there's something that seems to be pulling you apart?"

"Yeah."

"Why don't you tell me about it."

There was a brief silence. "My boyfriend says he wants to start seeing other girls," Yolanda finally replied, her voice becoming unsteady as she choked up.

Dale checked his monitor. "You're twenty-two, is that right, Yolanda?" he said tenderly, noting her emotional state.

"Yeah."

"All right. How old is your boyfriend?"

"Twenty-six."

"Twenty-six. And how long have you been going together?"

"About . . . six months."

"Uh-huh. Did your boyfriend . . . what's your boyfriend's name, Yolanda?"

"Rick." Yolanda was still sniffling, but otherwise recovering her composure.

"Did Rick tell you why he wants to see other girls?"

"He said he wants more variety."

"What kind of variety?" Dale asked, intrigued.

"I dunno. All kinds, I guess."

"He wasn't any more specific than that so that you could determine if *you* could supply the variety he's looking for or if he definitely had to go outside the relationship for it?"

"He said he wants to meet someone with a different look and different interests."

"I see. So what are you doing about it?"

"I bleached my hair. I started wearin' workout clothes an' goin' to the gym. I'm tryin' to get my nerve up for bungee jumping, an' I'm trying to . . . fulfill some of his sexual fantasies."

"Uh-huh. Does any of that come naturally to you?"

There was another brief silence, and a sigh. "Not really."

"What does come naturally for you?"

"Well, my hair is black, and I just wanna stay home with him. I don't wanna go out and do all these things. I just wanna cuddle with him."

"Do you think his stated need for more variety is really more about fulfilling sexual fantasies than anything else?"

"No," Yolanda said thoughtfully. "It's part of it, but not all of it."

"And is what you're doing working?" Dale asked. "Do you seem to be able to satisfy his need for variety?"

"Uh-uh," she replied forlornly.

"Hmm. Do you know if he's already started seeing other girls outside of your relationship?"

"I don't think so."

"How certain are you of that?"

"Pretty certain. He wants to break it off with me so he can start seeing other girls and I keep begging him not to. So he keeps seeing me. But I know he's not happy."

"And you want some advice on what you can do to keep him from leaving you."

"Yeah!" Yolanda replied as though it should have been obvious.

"Well, without talking to Rick, I can't say for sure what's happening. But I can guess. It sounds to me like he's being honest and above board with you, which means you may not like what I have to suggest."

"Oh?" Yolanda's response sounded worried.

"This may not be something you can fix, dear. You see, life is a process of experiencing who we are. And it may be that Rick needs a kind of variety you simply can't supply him, because that's what he needs in his process of experiencing himself. It's not a failing of yours, it's simply a fact of who he is and who you are. That's not saying anything against Rick, either, it's just recognizing that the level of compatibility between you and him is no longer high enough to sustain the relationship. I'd guess he's experienced everything in the relationship he was in it to experience, and now he has to move on to other relationships in order to experience what he couldn't experience with you."

"Well, then, what can I do to make it so he *can* experience with me?"

"I'm sorry, sweetheart, it doesn't work that way. It's not a matter of what you do—or don't do. It's a matter of who you are. And apparently, you aren't who he needs you to be."

"Then, how can I be who he needs me to be?"

"You can't. You can only be who *you* need to be, which is to say you can only be who you *are*. You can't be who someone else needs you to be unless and until you're who you are. That's because in the process of living life, we attract ourselves to people who act as our reflection. If you're not who you are, then you'll only attract people who are not who *they* are. That is, by not being who *they* are, they will reflect back to you the fact that you are not being who *you* are. And if they're not who they are, then what they want *you* to be is all screwed up. So trying to be someone you aren't for Rick will not get the job done. The only way to get it done is to be who you are. Then, it's up to the *other* person to determine if you are who they need."

"But, then, what you're saying is that I can't have Rick!" Yolanda exclaimed plaintively.

"Yeah, that's what I'm saying. But you obviously don't need him."

"Why?!" She was not so much asking why she didn't need Rick as why Dale believed she didn't.

"Well, we generally stay in a relationship only as long as we need to in order to experience what we're in it to experience. And since *he's* apparently experienced everything he was in the relationship to experience, it's most likely that *you've* experienced everything *you* were in it to experience, as well. It's just that you haven't recognized that yet."

"But I don't care about any of that!" Yolanda pleaded, dissolving again into tears. "I just wanna have Rick!"

"I know that, dear," Dale said tenderly. "But I don't get the sense that having Rick is in the cards for you. If it were, you wouldn't have to be doing things that aren't natural to you. He'd be attracted to you just as you are. Now, sometimes relationships run into difficulties which can be resolved by a variety of means—counseling, improved communication, et cetera—and in those cases I would encourage the partners to take advantage of those means. But in other cases, the two partners are simply looking for things they can't find in one another. So they simply have to look elsewhere. It's not a failing on anybody's part, it's just a fact of the makeup of the individuals involved in the relationship."

"I just don't believe that," Yolanda whined.

"What do you believe?"

"That there's gotta be something I can do to make him want me."

Dale drew a deep breath. He had said essentially the same thing three different ways and it appeared that Yolanda was simply unable to get it. He had learned from his interaction with Margaret that he did have the stuff to penetrate, so this didn't try his patience exactly. But he did feel a sense of frustration, since he knew she would suffer until she reached sufficient awareness in her life to get it. Still, he wasn't through trying.

"Well, I'm sorry to say, I don't think this is something you have a say in, sweetheart," he explained. "This is like a law of nature. It's just the way it is. There are certain personal problems that you can take care of all by yourself. But when another person is involved, as in a relationship, the only thing you can take care of is *your* side of the problem. You can't do anything about the *other* person's side; you can't make them do something they don't want to do or feel some way that they don't feel. To try to do that will only bring you heartache."

"But isn't love supposed to conquer all?!" Yolanda argued plaintively.

"It *is* reputed to. But I think that saying is only intended to mean that love will resolve all problems. I don't think it means that love will get you everything you want. Sometimes resolving a problem means letting go of something, even letting go of a lover. Do you love Rick?"

"Of course! That's why I don't want to lose him."

"All right. Do you love him enough to want for him what he wants for himself?" Dale posed the question with measured deliberation.

Yolanda sensed the trickery in the question and hesitated before answering. "Yes," she replied cautiously.

"Then, if what he wants is to stop seeing you and start seeing other women, then loving him would require that you let him do that."

"But if I let him go, I don't know what I'm gonna do," Yolanda said desperately. "I don't think I can live without him!"

"I think you can," was Dale's heartening reply. "But since you're having doubts about that, let's take a look at what you're really afraid of. Do you have any idea what that might be?"

"Yeah! Losing my boyfriend!" Yolanda replied emphatically.

For effect, Dale gave an intentional pause. "I'd guess it goes much deeper than that," he said softly. "I'd guess you're afraid you don't have sufficient value—all by yourself—to attract another relationship. Does that sound right to you?"

"What?" She had heard the words, but was so out of touch with the fear that the meaning hadn't registered with her.

"Aren't you really afraid you won't be able to attract another guy because you don't believe you have what it takes to do that?"

Dale's question did strike a resonant chord, and Yolanda could be heard to emit a shallow gasp. But the thought was just too frightening for her to really seize, and she shied.

"I dunno," was her noncommittal reply. "I guess."

"That's what I'm thinking, too," Dale continued. "But as I see it, it's simply not true. Although I'm sure you're not aware of it, I believe that you possess *exactly* what you need to attract *exactly* the right person for you. But in order for that to work for you, you need to begin to see your value, all by yourself, and cease looking for it in the eyes of others."

While this produced a flicker of recognition in Yolanda, it was still a bit beyond her at the moment, and she accepted it with little more than a sigh.

"Don't forget," Dale added, "Rick may be leaving you so he can find someone more compatible with himself, but at the same time, he's freeing *you* up to find someone more compatible with *yourself.* If you go into this separation with that in mind, I believe you *will* find someone more compatible."

"But I don't want someone more compatible! I want Rick!"

Recognizing this as a retreat from the core fear, a return to desperation, rejection of a superior future in favor of an inferior present, Dale wagged his huge, misshapen head in private amusement. "I'm sure you feel that way now," he countered gently, "but if you were with someone more compatible, you'd feel a whole lot different."

His logic being irrefutable, Yolanda had no response.

"As I said earlier," he continued, "I believe life is designed to show us who we are. And I suspect that one of the things you'll be learning from all this is that you do have value—all by yourself, without reference to Rick or anyone else—and that by virtue of that value you can and will attract a man with whom you can be yourself, who also just wants to stay home and cuddle, someone for whom you will not have to compromise yourself, and with whom you can enjoy greater compatibility than you ever did with Rick."

Yolanda heaved a sigh of futility. "I can't imagine that right now."

"I know. And I don't hope to convince you of it. It's something you'll have to learn on your own as you live your life. It may happen quickly, or it may take awhile. It may come easily, or it may be very painful, depending on how strongly you resist it. And other things may have to be learned first. But whatever the case, learn it you will."

Dale waited for a response, and getting none, continued.

"I know that what I've told you tonight isn't what you wanted to hear, and I'm sorry I haven't been able to help you more. But that's all I can do. It's up to you from this point on. I know it's tough, but I believe you *will* get through it and learn what you need to, and come out of it in better shape than you went in. And I wish you the best of luck in doing that. Call me again if you need to, dear. And if you're ever feeling unloved, just remember: *I* love you."

"Thanks," Yolanda replied, more perfunctorily than genuinely.

"You're welcome. I'll talk to you later."

"Okay. Bye."

"Goodnight."

Dale pushed the disconnect button. "This is WWKW, FM 102.4. I'm Dale Greene on The Brink of Tomorrow and I'll be back with more calls after these messages."

Dale threw his mic switch and looked over at Bobby as the commercials rolled. This time it was Bobby who, sensing that Dale had been discouraged by the last call, raised his thumb. Dale took the accolade with a nod.

Although he knew he had done everything he could for Yolanda, he wished he could have sent her away feeling better. *Were the successes of his first two calls flukes?* he wondered. *Was the failure of this last more representative of what he could expect in the future?* It was disheartening, but he did not have the luxury of bowing to discouragement. He still had two and a half more hours to go and dozens of callers waiting to talk to him.

During the break, he looked over the calls that had been added to the list. They included Bev, who was trying to dump her boyfriend; Tyrone, whose father beat his mother; Jill, who wondered if she was a Lesbian; Jimmy, who was picked on by classmates; and Angela, whose brother abused her. None of them looked easy. But then again, easy was not what he was here for. So he selected one that looked challenging.

Chapter 6

"You're tuned to WWKW, FM 102.4, and this is Dale Greene on The Brink of Tomorrow. If you're just joining us, we're talking with WWKW listeners who are having difficulty with the challenges in their lives. If you're having difficulty with a challenge in your life, give me a call and let's see if we can sort it out together.

"Our next caller is Jill. Jill's fifteen and says she wonders if she's a Lesbian." He pressed the button which connected the call. "Hi, Jill, this is Dale Greene and you're on The Brink of Tomorrow."

"Hi, Dale. How are you?" Her voice was youthful and sweet, but intelligent.

"Just fine, Jill. And you?"

"I'm fine, thanks. I've really been enjoying your show tonight. You've given everybody such good advice, and I just ... I've just really gotten a lot out of it."

"Well, thank you, Jill. That's very kind of you to say, particularly after my conversation with Yolanda, to whom I'm afraid I wasn't much help."

"But you did everything you could. I thought you were wonderful."

"Well, thanks again. Hopefully, I can be of greater help to you. Speaking of which . . . my notes say you wonder if you're a Lesbian."

"Uh-huh."

"What makes you think that?"

"Well ... I'm ... attracted to girls," Jill explained somewhat apprehensively. "I don't have any interest in boys, I never have, and I don't think I ever will."

"Have you dated boys?"

"A few times. Just little things, you know ... school dances, the movies, ice skating once."

"And how did you feel on those dates?"

"I felt okay. I felt kind of like I was out with my brother or something."

"Did you hold hands or anything like that with these boys?"

"I held hands with one."

"And how did that feel?"

"Like holding hands with my brother."

"There was no tingle to it or extra excitement associated with it?"

"No."

"Have you ever kissed a boy?"

"No, not since I've been a teenager. And I don't want to."

"Mmmm. And do you feel different when you're with girls?"

"Yes."

"Tell me what that's like."

"I feel kind of tingly inside. I feel a strong attraction to them. It's like I don't want to say goodbye at the end of the day, especially with my friend, Teri. And I can't wait to see her again the next day."

"Have you held hands with Teri, or any of the other girls? Or kissed them?"

Jill took a deep breath before answering. "I've kissed Teri," she said finally.

"And how did you feel when you did that?"

"It was exciting," she said forthrightly, but nervously.

"Uh-huh. So what is it you'd like me to help you with?"

"I want to know if I'm a Lesbian or not."

"I see. Well, you know, my dear, that's a question only you can answer. I could make a guess, based on what you've told me. But it wouldn't be worth much compared with your own assessment. So I wouldn't do it."

He waited for some response from Jill, but none was forthcoming. "I assume," Dale continued, "since you called me, that this is problem for you."

"Yeah."

"Why?"

"Because I don't know if the way I feel makes me a Lesbian or not."

"Why do you need to know? Or let me put it another way: Why do you need to label yourself one way or the other? Why not just enjoy the feelings you experience with the people you're with?"

"Well, I do, but . . . ." Her emotional state, as indicated by the tone of her voice, had escalated to anxiety.

"But what?" Dale prompted, after giving her a moment to complete her sentence.

"I . . . I don't know." She sounded very confused.

"All right," said Dale in his gentlest tone. "What about being a Lesbian scares you?"

"That it's wrong, that it's not normal."

"Ah! Is there anything else about being a Lesbian that scares you?"

Jill thought for a moment. "No."

"When you're with your girlfriends, does it *feel* wrong—or abnormal—to you?"

"No. It feels good."

"So you're afraid that it still might be wrong or abnormal, even though it feels good to you while you're doing it."

"Yeah."

"Do you feel as though you're hurting anyone by doing this?"

Jill thought about this for a few seconds. "No . . . not really. Except that I think it would hurt my parents if I turned out to be a Lesbian."

"Uh-huh. And by that you mean it might disappoint them or hurt their feelings in some way?"

"Yeah."

"All right. But otherwise, you don't think what you're doing is hurting anyone, including yourself."

"I don't think so. But I don't know if it's hurting me or not."

"You mean, even though it doesn't feel like it's hurting you, you wonder if it really is and you're just not aware of it?"

"Right."

"And how do you imagine it might be hurting you without your being aware of it?"

"If it's wrong, or not normal."

"Okay, we're back to wrong and abnormal. What makes you think it might be wrong or abnormal?"

"Because people say it is."

"Do you believe they know what they're talking about?"

She hesitated. "I don't know."

"But you think *I* know what I'm talking about, so you'd like *me* to tell you if it's wrong or abnormal."

"Yeah!"

"Okay. Well, of course, that's very much like telling you whether or not you're a Lesbian, and I won't do it. But I can help you determine that for yourself. Were you listening earlier when I was talking with Margaret?"

"Yes."

"Then you heard me say that ideas of 'right' and 'wrong' are judgments, and that they represent a failure to take responsibility for what amounts to no more than personal opinion."

"Uh-huh."

"Good. So let's look at another aspect of this. By saying 'right' or 'wrong' it makes it sound as if these judgments are absolutes, as if there's some ultimate authority which determines absolutely, once and for all, what is right and what is wrong. But if you listen carefully, you'll hear people saying 'I *think* this is right' and 'I *think* that is wrong.' 'I *think*' confirms the fact that they're only expressing their own personal opinions. And for every person you find who says something is wrong, you can find someone else who will say it's right. And even when people are absolutely convinced of their judgments, those judgments still boil down to no more than personal opinion. So if judgments are no more than personal opinions, then we're not talking about absolutes that you have to concern yourself with, we're only talking about opinions. And that means *your* opinions are just as valid as theirs. Of course, I recommend that you put your opinions in non-judgmental terms—'This is what I *like*' and 'That is what I *don't like*'—and in so doing, take responsibility for your opinions. Are you getting this?"

"Yes!"

"Good! Then, let me go a step further. One of the problems with this whole judgment thing is that people judge others on things they have no business sticking their nose into. If I like to blow bubbles with my spit in the privacy of my own home, then it's nobody's business but my own. Still, some people who object to spit-bubble blowing will try to dictate my behavior according to their own preferences, even in my own personal, private domain where it in no way affects them. And they do it by judgment—by saying it's 'wrong'—which makes it sound like some ultimate authority has passed judgment on the practice. And by doing that, they're able to make the practice sound like a transgression against God or humanity, or a violation of law or ethics, or sound worse than it really is. And by doing that they're able to influence people without their knowledge. I don't mean to sound paranoid or anything, as though there's some conspiracy out there to influence people against their will—there might be, but that's not what I'm saying. I'm only saying that out of habit and ignorance, we often influence people without their knowledge by using judgments, and we often allow ourselves to be influenced without our knowledge by accepting the judgments of others."

Dale paused a moment to assess Jill's understanding and further receptivity.

"Basically what I'm saying," he continued, sensing that she was still with him, "is that you don't need to be influenced against your will if you're aware of judgments and how they can influence you. So you don't need to concern yourself with the 'right' or 'wrong' of what you are or what you're doing, provided you're not hurting anyone, or yourself, in the process. Understand?"

"Yeah."

"Does that help?"

"It helps . . . ." She sounded only half committed.

"But . . . ?" Dale asked, reading the uncertainty in his caller's voice.

"But even if it's not wrong, that doesn't mean it's normal," Jill explained, sounding still worried.

"Oh, yeah," Dale recalled. "You were also concerned that it may not be normal. Well, this is something I can tell you for sure. Lesbianism is *not* normal."

As expected, this elicited a subtle gasp from his caller, plus most of his other Gay and Lesbian listeners.

"But that's a very misleading statement," he went on. "And the reason it's misleading is that most people don't know the real meaning of the word 'normal.' Do *you*?"

Sensing this to be a trick question, Jill thought for a moment. "I don't know."

"All right," Dale acknowledged. "Most people interpret the word 'normal' to mean 'natural,' so that anything that's *not* normal is considered *un*natural. And of course, by portraying things as unnatural, they can be portrayed as ungodly, and undesirable. But 'normal' means something quite different. 'Normal' comes from the word 'norm,' which means 'average,' or 'like most everyone else.' Since homosexuals make up only a small percentage of the population, they are definitely not like most everyone else. So homosexuality is, by definition, not normal. But that doesn't mean it isn't natural. For that matter, since lefthanders also make up only a small portion of the population, lefthanders aren't normal either. But no one would argue in this day and age that lefthanders aren't natural, because we all know they are. This is just a case where, again, people try to mislead you by the words they use. By saying homosexuality is 'not normal,' they try to give the impression that it's not natural. But it occurs naturally, so it is natural."

"I'm left-handed, too," Jill revealed.

"Well, there you go," Dale replied jauntily. "You're a perfect example of natural abnormality. Bill Clinton was also a lefty, and he was president of the United States. So being abnormal in some respect doesn't make you unnatural or wrong."

Jill laughed for the first time, giving Dale the impression that she'd resolved her problem.

"So how does that feel now, darlin'?" he queried.

"It feels better. But what if I am a Lesbian and it hurts my parents?"

Knowing this to be a very tricky subject, Dale drew a breath.

"Well, that is a good question. This is a very delicate issue, because it straddles a very fine line, a line that few people perceive, and even fewer understand. And that line is the line between your actions and the other person's feelings. Basically, it's this: Each person is responsible for his or her own *actions* and his or her own *feelings*. So if you do something which is clearly an imposition on someone else and it hurts their feelings, then you've crossed the line and you share in the responsibility for their feelings. However, if what you do is *not* an imposition on them and it hurts their feelings because they choose to judge your actions, then you haven't crossed that line and their feelings are their own responsibility. Do you understand?"

"Uh . . . I'm not sure."

"Okay, let me give you an example. Let's say you're living under your parents' roof and eating their food and wearing the clothes they buy you, and you get pregnant, and now they *also* have to pay for feeding, clothing, and housing your baby. And the extra costs are a hardship on them and they feel angry and betrayed. In this case, your actions are an imposition on them and you share in the responsibility for their feelings of anger and betrayal. If, however, you've left home and you're supporting yourself completely on your own, and you get pregnant, but you take care of all the baby's needs yourself, and your parents *still* feel betrayed—because, say, they judge the fact that you're pregnant and not married or something—then your actions are not an imposition on them and their feelings are their own responsibility. Because whether you're married or not, by that time, it's really your business and your business alone. They may *feel* it's still their business, because of the judgment or because they retain their parental protectiveness way into your adulthood, but it wouldn't be. So their feelings of anger and betrayal would be their own responsibility, not yours. Do you understand?"

"Yeah. So you're saying that being a Lesbian is my own business and if it hurts my parents' feelings, it's their responsibility?"

"Essentially, yes. However, I must alert you to some very important distinctions. *Being* a Lesbian and *practicing* Lesbianism are two different things. That is to say, feeling attracted to girls is different from actually having sex with them. I don't believe it's anyone's business but yours how you feel . . . because that's completely internal. But how you *express* those feelings—how you *act* in response to those feelings—may indeed be someone else's business if you do it in their presence or on their property or in some way that imposes your will on them. I mean, if you were having sex with your girlfriend on your parents' couch and they walked in on you, that would make it their business. So if your *actions* as a Lesbian somehow constitute an actual imposition on your parents, then I believe it becomes their business. So I suggest that if you act on your feelings, you make sure it doesn't impose on anyone else. It's a very delicate balancing act, but if you understand that fine line, then I believe you can keep your balance in tricky situations such as this."

Knowing this was a lot to assimilate, Dale gave it time to sink in. But he did have other listeners to consider, so after a short while, asked, "So is that better?"

"Kind of," was Jill's reply, her tone suggesting something still unresolved.

"What else is bothering you about this, hon?"

"Well, I'm still not sure if I'm a Lesbian or not."

Hearing the original question resurface somewhat puzzled Dale. He had covered judgment, covered the threat of hurting her parents' feelings, and she was still asking the original question. The key conundrum remained undiscovered.

"All right," he said tentatively. "What is your definition of a Lesbian?"

"A female who's attracted to other females. But I talked to another radio psychiatrist, and he said—"

Dale abruptly cut in. "Excuse me, Jill. I apologize for interrupting you, but I want to make sure you understand that I'm not a psychiatrist or therapist of any kind."

Jill was silent, as though having failed to understand what Dale was driving at. Noting this, he clarified.

"You said '*another* radio psychiatrist,' implying that *I'm* a psychiatrist, too, and I just wanted to be sure you understood that I'm not."

"Oh! No," replied Jill. "I know you're not."

"Good. Go ahead with what you were saying."

"Well, I talked to another . . . to a radio psychiatrist, and he said I wasn't sure I was a Lesbian because I'm at an age where I feel awkward with boys and more comfortable with girls, and I'm misinterpreting that as attraction to them."

"Ohhhh!" Dale exclaimed as the light dawned. "I see." This wasn't the first time he'd heard of talk-show therapists laying an opinion on a caller and leaving the caller at odds. "Does that assessment feel accurate to you?" he asked with pointed gravity.

Jill took a long time to answer. "No," she finally said.

"As I said earlier, I won't voice an opinion as to whether you're a Lesbian or not, but I will declare positively that you have the prerogative and the proficiency—if you'll excuse my alliteration—to determine that all by yourself. And I encourage you to go with your own sense of things. Sure, listen to other people's opinions. And if their opinions strike a chord in you and work for you, then feel free to adopt them. At that point of course, those opinions become your own. But if someone else's opinion feels unnatural to you or doesn't work for you, feel free to discard it and form your own. This is what the great men and women of history have done. And I encourage *you* to do it, too. So *you* decide if your attraction to girls is just awkwardness with boys or real attraction. *You* decide if you're a Lesbian, or just someone who likes girls. Your opinion is the one that matters for you."

"You don't think I'm too young to be a Lesbian?"

Dale felt like shaking a good-naturedly reproving finger at her. "Come on, now, Jill. You know what my answer to that is."

"Decide for myself?"

"Absolutely. I will repeat one thing. Pay very close attention to whether your actions are hurting you or imposing on someone else. If you feel that you may not have enough experience to know if you're hurting yourself—or imposing on someone else—then one option would be to wait until you do. Girls will always be there when you decide for sure."

"That's true." She heaved a huge sigh.

"Feel better now, dear?" Dale asked.

Jill sighed again. "Yeah. A lot."

"Excellent!" acknowledged Dale. "I'm delighted to hear it."

"Thanks so much. You've really helped me. I really love you."

"Oh, thank you, sweetheart! I really love you, too. Call again any time you want."

"I will. Bye for now."

"Bye-bye."

Dale disconnected the call, waited a second, and said in a soft voice, "This is WWKW with Dale Greene on The Brink of Tomorrow. I'll be right back."

Although, like Yolanda, a small handful of callers throughout the evening did not feel better after talking with Dale—mostly because they resisted facing the painful truths required to resolve their problems—the majority of them hung up elated by the insights they had received.

Dale was equally elated. Having helped the satisfied majority and at least shown the unsatisfied minority the truths behind their problems, he felt he had accomplished what he'd set out to do, and shown himself that he did have what it takes to really help people.

That night, as he lay in bed, reliving the evening and his successes, he thought again of his parents, as he did every night, and tears came to his eyes. Silently he thanked them for giving him the opportunity to participate in the outside world, to contribute to the well-being of his fellow humans, and to do something with his life that he loved, despite a disfigurement that would most assuredly have otherwise denied him those rewards. He concluded with a pledge to do it with the greatest integrity and compassion he knew, then promptly fell sound asleep.

Chapter 7

Over the next ten months, letters and email poured in to the main offices of WWKW from listeners praising Dale and applauding his new talk format—all physical mail addressed to Dale was picked up from station headquarters by the estate driver; email was automatically forwarded to a private email address—and the show expanded gradually from one night per week to seven.

In the course of that time, Dale heard several times from little nine-year-old Jeanine, who found living without her parents difficult, but manageable. Margaret called again to report that she had reached an amicable compromise with her daughter, who was content to wear just enough makeup to be accepted by her peers. Yolanda called in several times, pining for Rick and wanting to know how she could get him back. Jill wrote to thank Dale again for his help and to say that she had decided she *was* a Lesbian, but that she and her girlfriend were abstaining from "going all the way" until they were older. And Cameron invited Dale to his wedding. Though Dale declined the invitation, citing prior commitments on the day of the nuptials, he did send Cameron and his moneyed bride an exquisite bouquet, along with his fondest wishes for their success.

A good number of other listeners who talked with Dale during those months wrote in to reiterate their thanks and give Dale updates on their progress. Listeners who had never called the program wrote letters testifying to the benefits they had derived from Dale's chats with those who had called. All but a few raved about the new show and Dale's advice, both in general and in specific. Many of them included the words "I love you," or some variation thereof, and some requested photos of the revered radio talk-show advisor. There were even a few propositions, sight unseen.

The few who had negative comments were split between those who missed the classic rock and those whose values were based on moral judgments or religious dogma. To those who missed the classics, Dale apologized on the air for changing the format, and invited them to tune to the rival station. To the others, Dale simply thanked them for expressing their opinions. The fear of judgment and ridicule being ever present beneath the surface of his consciousness, should his appearance become known, the requests for photos were simply—but not cold-heartedly—ignored, for lack of a better idea. The propositions met a similar fate.

"What do you look like?" Dale was asked one night by seventeen-year-old Amanda toward the end of her call.

Like a dagger, this most public question about his appearance stabbed painfully at Dale's core, evoking his terror of being revealed and causing his heart to race. His impulse was to lash out in defense of his privacy, but he knew that would only betray the secret, so he counseled himself toward composure. "What do you imagine I look like?" he queried in return, ducking the question.

"Oh, I'd say tall, slim . . . kind of muscular, but not muscle bound . . . long dark hair, blue eyes . . . very handsome!"

"Well, thank you very much," Dale acknowledged artfully. "You have an *excellent* imagination."

"All right!" Amanda exclaimed, believing she had nailed the description. "Can I ask you something else?"

"Absolutely!"

"Could I have a picture of you—would you mind sending me a picture of yourself?"

Cringing at this even more direct threat of exposure, Dale took a deep breath to steady his pounding heart. "I'm sorry, sweetheart," he replied evenly. "I don't mean to disappoint you, but if I sent a picture of myself to *you*, I'd have to send one to *everyone*." Dale's heart sank with shame as he engaged this time-honored but false trick to deflect Amanda's request. But he saw no alternative. He waited for a response, and getting none, added, "I'm sure you understand."

"Yeah," Amanda accepted, not thinking to question further.

The very next caller, twenty-eight-year-old George, was not so accepting. "The way you answered her question," he said in reference to Amanda's query, "you made it sound like she guessed what you look like. But you didn't actually say so."

"Very good! I applaud you for being so attentive," Dale praised, concealing his fear that he might not get out of this one and hoping George would just drop it.

"So what do you really look like?"

"You know, George, I'd really rather just let you use your imagination on that."

"Why?!" George pressed.

Dale thought for a second, then decided to tell the truth . . . at least one truth. "What's really important in the interactions I have with my listeners is the message, not the messenger. So I prefer to minimize the emphasis on me in order to keep people focused on the message."

"Oh," George said, a mite deflated. He had expected something more exotic.

"Does that make sense?" Dale asked, by way of confirmation.

"Yeah," George returned. "I get that."

Dale breathed a sigh of relief that George had accepted this explanation and moved on.

Concomitant to all the praise being heaped on The Brink of Tomorrow, the show's listenership grew quickly and steadily as word spread of the wisdom available nightly on WWKW. As the program expanded in popularity, it became more and more difficult for callers to get through. Listeners began calling the station hours before the show started, just to get a place in line on the switchboard. Even so, since the switchboard could hold more calls than Dale could handle in a night, some callers wound up waiting on hold all evening, only to be disappointed when Dale was unable to get to them.

For this reason, Dale closed each show with an apology to all the callers to whom he had been unable to talk, and signed off each night with "I love you," a response in kind to the sentiments expressed to him so often in the letters and during calls. He meant it with all his heart, and his listeners knew it.

It was in recognition of the lucid wisdom that Dale shared with his listeners each night and the growing popularity of the all-talk Brink of Tomorrow program that the local chapter of the Archers Association voted to present Dale with their prestigious and coveted Man of the Year award.

In a formal letter directed to Mr. Dale C. Greene at the main offices of station WWKW, Roger Hampton, the president of the chapter, informed Dale of the award and invited him to accept it in person at their monthly awards dinner.

Desperately fearing his disfigurement would shock and disillusion a lot of people if he appeared in person to accept the award, Dale, with the accordance of Wilson Terry, Paul Norman Carr, and Shel Boerman, penned a letter to Mr. Hampton, thanking him for the honor and accepting the award in principle, but declining to appear in person for reasons of a conflict in scheduling. "If you would be so kind as to forward my award to the radio station," Dale wrote, "I will be happy to issue a letter of appreciation to the membership of the Archers Association to be read at your next meeting."

Of course, the conflict-in-scheduling excuse was a lie. While Dale did have decisions to make regarding the various businesses comprising Greene Enterprises, Paul and Shel pretty much ran the organization, leaving Dale adequate spare time to do whatever he pleased.

Lying to Cameron to avoid attending his wedding was bothersome. Lying to the Archers Association to avoid appearing in person to receive an award honoring *him* was agonizing. But his experience with strangers, and the terror it struck in his heart, informed him that his appearance alone would offend a great many people and possibly raise misgivings about voting him the award in the first place. So, in the ratiocination of Dale and his advisors, the lie was justified in the interests of protecting the Archers members. And with the mailing of his letter, Dale considered the matter concluded.

But the Archers were serious about their awards and their ceremonies. If Dale were unavailable to attend the monthly awards dinner, the Archers would arrange a special meeting to accommodate Dale's schedule, whatever that might be. Such was the content of a second letter from Roger Hampton, which Dale received not three days after posting his reply to Hampton's first letter. Floating between the lines of this second letter was the well known fact that the Archers Man of the Year award was the source of a good deal of the publicity the organization relied on to promote their charitable activities and bring in much needed contributions.

Mr. Hampton's persistence and pliability came as somewhat of a surprise to Dale and his people, although it probably shouldn't have. Since the Archers were willing to accommodate Dale's schedule, Dale and his advisors had to come up with some other excuse for declining to accept the award in person. As had been their habit when Dale's father was alive, the trio of advisors met informally over coffee and bagels each morning in the luxurious ambience of the den. Now, in Leonard's stead, Dale attended these meetings.

"We could say you're planning to be out of town for the next few months," Shel suggested feebly, knowing the proposal didn't stand a chance.

"If we did," Dale countered, "we'd have to explain that I'm broadcasting from a remote location."

"It would be awkward, but it could be done," Wil said. "Of course, then we'd still have the same problem when you 'got back to town.' Any other ideas?"

"Do you think they'd believe agoraphobia?" Dale asked.

The three advisors gave this proposal several seconds of thought. "It might work for someone else," Wil finally tendered, "but you come off too well adjusted for that to be convincing."

"Then how about excruciating bashfulness?" Dale cracked. The other three men chuckled at the absurdity.

"Is there any disease we could say you have?" queried Paul, "somethin' that would be contagious to your public, but wouldn't keep you from broadcastin' every night."

The four men looked at each other helplessly. As an educator, only Wil had any medical knowledge beyond the scope of Proteus syndrome, and he was at a loss. "For the most part, anything that would be contagious to your public would also be contagious to Bobby and everyone else they presume you work with at the station. It would be a tough sell . . . but I'll give it some thought."

"Well, we could tell them the truth," Shel offered, a twinkle in his eye. The other three men eyed him expectantly.

"That I'm just too ornery to be let out of the house?" Dale proffered. The others laughed.

"Anything else?" Wil queried, hoping to elicit at least one viable idea.

After a moment of thought, the other men shook their heads.

"Well, let's give ourselves a few days to think about it. Maybe one of us will have a brainstorm." The others concurred with faint nods.

When a week passed without response from Dale, Mr. Hampton called the main offices of **WWKW** to see if he could actually talk to someone, preferably Dale. The receptionist said no one was available at the moment, but promised to have someone return his call. Then, as she had been instructed in the event she received any business calls for Dale, she called a private number which connected her with the estate. Paul Carr answered and took the message.

Knowing they had delayed too long in answering Hampton's second letter and that a response of some sort was urgent—if Greene standards of courtesy and good relations were to be maintained—Paul called another meeting with his employer and his two associates to decide on a way to address Hampton's phone call.

"Why don't you ask him if we can send someone else over to pick it up?" Dale suggested. "Just tell him I very much appreciate the award, but I'm very busy and very sorry I can't accept it in person."

"This is their Man of the Year award," chimed in Shel Boerman, doubtful of Dale's proposal. "This is a really big deal to them. Do you really think they'd go along with something like that?"

"They might," Wil Terry offered, scratching his neatly cropped salt-and-pepper beard, "if given no other options."

"Don't forget," reminded Paul, "they've already offered to arrange a special meetin' to accommodate Dale's schedule. They might find a way to slip around whatever options we offer, and still make a case for Dale acceptin' the award in person."

"If they do," Dale asserted, "we can always decline the award altogether."

The protest from his trio of advisors was instantaneous and vociferous.

"I don't think *that's* a good idea, Dale," Paul cautioned. "This is the Archers Association! Even if you don't need the award, you don't need the negative publicity turning it down would generate."

Dale shook his woolly head as if to dismiss any concerns about negative publicity.

"You may not be concerned about negative publicity for yourself," Wil countered, "but your listeners might feel betrayed in some way if their hero turned down an Archers Man of the Year award."

"I'm not a hero," Dale cautioned modestly. "I'm just a guy sharing my opinions. I don't want anyone putting me up on any pedestals."

"I recognize that. But I'm afraid that's not under your control," Wil argued. "You've helped a lot of listeners and they love you. You can caution them not to apotheosize you, but you can't stop them from doing it, and you know it. On the other hand, you don't have to go to some unnecessary extreme that could be misinterpreted. I'm not suggesting you try to protect a hero status, but I am suggesting you not knowingly do something to hurt your listeners' feelings."

The argument was persuasive and Dale mulled it for a moment. "All right," he conceded, turning to Paul. "Don't turn it down. But that means we have to come up with something the Archers will accept."

"What was it you told a caller a few months ago?" Shel queried. "You want to put the focus on the message, not the messenger. How about that?

"That sounds like he's turning it down altogether," Wil observed.

"Oh, yeah," Shel replied.

Paul sighed. "Why don't I just talk to Hampton and feel him out?" he asked, secretly dreading his own suggestion, but knowing they had few other options. "Maybe he'll be more accommodatin' in a two-way parley."

That being the most sensible approach the four men had no choice but to concur.

"He's extremely appreciative to be honored in this way," Paul told Roger Hampton over the phone, "but his schedule's so full, it just makes it so hard for him to find time to accept the award in person. Couldn't we send an envoy to pick up the award and convey Mr. Greene's gratitude to your members?"

"In the seventy-four years we've been bestowing this honor, we've never had anyone decline to receive it in person, except once when our nominee died the week before the ceremony. If I didn't make it clear in my last letter, let me do so now. We can arrange the meeting to suit Mr. Greene's schedule and even send a limousine to transport him to and from the ceremony. He wouldn't need to be there longer than twenty minutes, just long enough for the presentation and to let the media get some photos and videotape." Having made his sales pitch, Hampton now softened his voice. "This is our seventy-fifth Man of the Year award, and that makes it very special for us. Would you *please* see if there isn't some way to make the time for us?"

Paul felt boxed in, unable to say *yes*, unwilling to say *no*. He considered saying something like, *Mr. Greene just doesn't make personal appearances*. But having used a busy schedule as his reason for declining, this would most certainly have come across as an excuse, and a very transparent one. He nervously ran his hand through his thinning blond hair. "All right, I'll talk to him and see if his schedule will accommodate any adjustments."

"I would appreciate that very much," Hampton acknowledged sincerely.

"I'm not promisin' anything," Paul cautioned. "But I'll see." In fact, he knew there was no hope of satisfying Hampton's request.

"Thank you. When can I expect to hear from you?"

Paul thought for a second. "Within the week, I should say." Even now, he was dreading that next call.

"Excellent. I look forward to hearing from you, then."

"They've got seventy-four years of history into this thing," Paul told Dale and his other two advisors at the next meeting, "and this bein' their seventy-fifth, he didn't want to hand the award to anyone but Dale."

"God, I feel terrible about this," Dale lamented. "No matter what I do, I'm going to disappoint or disillusion somebody."

"Ya know," Shel Boerman began, "they may not want to give the award to an envoy, but they don't know what Dale looks like. So we could send an envoy and tell them it's Dale, and they'd never know the difference."

The four men eyed one another in alert silence, hastily checking the expressions on each others' faces. This was the one possibility which would disappoint no one. But it had its own set of complications. Finally, Dale shook his head. The other three men relaxed; they had known this would be his response.

"It might work," Dale reinforced, "but it's deceptive and I don't want to be involved in anything like that."

The other men nodded their concurrence.

"Well, I told him I'd give him an answer by the end of the week," Paul said. "So we've got a few more days."

"Big deal," countered Shel. "We're back to where we were this time last week."

"Well, maybe something will occur to one of us this time," offered Wil Terry. "There's got to be some way out of this."

The other men nodded their concurrence.

Two days later, a brief story appearing on the back page of the city's largest newspaper, *The Chronicle*, reported on the award predicament.

DJ DECLINES MAN OF YEAR AWARD

Station WWKW DJ and talk radio personality, Dale C. Greene, has reportedly not accepted the Man of the Year award offered to him this year by the local chapter of the Archers Association. Sources say Greene has been unwilling to commit to a personal appearance at the presentation of the prestigious award, citing schedule conflicts. Local chapter president, Roger W. Hampton, denies suggestions that Greene will decline the award, but Archers officials close to the issue speculate that the DJ may turn down the award altogether. The local Archers chapter voted Greene the humanitarian award in recognition of the community service rendered to troubled listeners on the advice talk show.

Paul was the first to spot the article. He brought it up at the morning meeting the next day. Stepping over to Dale's wheelchair, he handed the news clipping to the young Greene, then returned to his seat on a sofa.

"I haven't *rejected* the damn thing!" Dale exclaimed after perusing the piece. "I just can't accept it in *person*. I wish I could make them understand the difference!"

"That's going to be pretty hard without revealing your reason," Wil replied. "Then, of course, if you reveal the reason, you may as well accept it in person. They're interpreting what they see the only way they can, given the only information they have."

"Well, I'm afraid that's all we're going to give them. So I guess we're all stuck with it," Dale rejoined in frustration.

"We've still got a few more days before I have to get back to Hampton," reminded Paul. "Something's bound to come up."

"Yeah, all right," Dale agreed. But he was not hopeful.

Chapter 8

"It's nine p.m., you're tuned to WWKW, FM 102.4, and this is Dale Greene on The Brink of Tomorrow. As always, my thanks to all of you who've written letters. For those of you who were wondering about Regina"—a previous caller who had been torn between two men—"she writes and says she decided on the mechanic, and they were married last week. Congratulations and good luck to both of you."

Regardless of what else was happening in his life, Dale could always count on his interactions with his callers to be invigorating and therapeutic.

"Well, we've got a switchboard full of calls, and I'm eager to see what challenges are facing my listeners tonight. So let me not waste any more time flapping my lips and let's get right to it. Our first caller is Rosie, she's thirty-one, and she says she's unhappy with her life." He connected the call. "Hi, Rosie, this is Dale Greene and you're on The Brink of Tomorrow."

"Hi, Dale." Rosie had a pleasant, rather girlish voice.

"My notes say you're unhappy with your life. Is this right? You don't sound unhappy."

"I don't?"

"No. Are you?"

"I think so."

"Hmmm, that's an interesting response. And you're thirty-one?"

"Uh-huh."

"You sound much younger than that."

"Oh, I know. I hear that a lot."

"I bet you do. How could someone who sounds so young and pleasant be unhappy with her life?"

"I dunno."

"Well, then, why don't you tell me what's going on that's making you unhappy."

Rosie started with a big sigh, then spoke apprehensively. "Well . . . I have a terrific job, I'm about to be married to a terrific guy, and I'm utterly miserable."

"Really! And why is that?"

"I don't know. That's why I called you."

"Could this be a case of premarital jitters?"

"I dunno. Maybe."

"When's the date of your wedding?"

"In about eight weeks."

"Eight weeks . . . . Well, that's a ways off to be feeling jittery. Do you love the guy?"

"He's a terrific guy! I'd be stupid not to."

Noticing Rosie had not really answered his question, Dale opened his mouth to quiz her further on the matter, then decided to wait. "What kind of work do you do?"

"I'm a pharmacology technician."

"Oh, that sounds interesting! What does that actually entail?"

"I work with a pharmacologist in preparing and testing pharmaceuticals. It sounds real glamorous to most people, but when you get right down to it, it's a job like any other. But it's a great job! The pay is great, the benefits are great . . . the people are great."

"Well, that sounds really great," Dale acknowledged, intentionally using Rosie's word of approbation. "What kind of education do you need for a job like that?"

"I have a B.A. in liberal arts. But I minored in biology. That's how I got the job."

"I see. Well, you're obviously very bright. And you've got a great guy, and a great job. So why on earth are you unhappy?"

"I don't know! I can't figure it out. Everything in my life is perfect. I'm thinking there must be something wrong with me."

"Like what?"

"Like I don't know. Like maybe a brain tumor or some kind of psychological problem."

"Well, if it's either one of those, then I can't help you. Have you been experiencing headaches or dizziness or blackouts?"

"No. Nothing like that at all."

"Any other physical complaints?"

"Uh-uh."

"Okay. Well, if you had had some physical complaints, I would've just advised you to go to a doctor and have some tests run and left it at that. You might still want to see a doctor, but as long as you're feeling all right we can talk about this some more. So, tell me about your fiancé. What does he do?"

"He's a lawyer."

"Ah! What's he like?"

"He's very attractive, very attentive, he's got money. What would you like to know?"

"Do you love him?"

"Of course!"

Dale furrowed his lumpy brow. "You say 'Of course' as though it would be *dumb* not to love him."

"Well, it *would* be dumb not to love him."

"But love isn't a matter of smart or dumb. Love is a matter of the heart, not the head. And the heart has no smart or dumb to it. I haven't actually heard you say that you love him, only that you'd be stupid not to. So let me ask you again—and I want you to give me a direct answer—do you love him?"

It took Rosie a moment or two to muster the answer, and when it came, she didn't seem too sure of it. "Yeah."

"I hate to say this, darlin'" Dale confessed, "but that didn't sound all that convincing. Is it possible that maybe you don't really love him?"

"No, I do. It's just that—" She stopped mid-sentence and heaved a huge sigh.

"It's just that what?" Dale asked after giving her time to complete her thought.

"I'd be stupid not to love him."

"It's just that what?" Dale repeated, completely ignoring her non-responsive utterance.

Rosie made several abortive attempts to voice her answer, then finally offered with resignation, "He just doesn't turn me on."

"Ohhh!" Dale exclaimed, a piece of the puzzle having just fallen into place. "Do you mean he doesn't turn you on sexually?"

"Sexually, yeah . . . in *all* ways. But see? That's stupid! He's a wonderful guy. There's no reason in the world he shouldn't."

"Ah, we're back to reasoning where the heart is concerned." He paused to shift gears. "All right, let me ask you something else. Do you like your job?"

"Of course. It's a great job."

"It may be a great job, but do you *like* it?"

"Well—" She interrupted herself again and sighed with exasperation at the question. Dale just let her struggle with it. "Not really," she finally admitted, "but that's *me* again. It's a great job! There's no reason I shouldn't like it."

"Even liking a job is a matter of the heart, not the head. Do you understand what I mean when I talk about the heart and the head? By heart I mean emotions, by head I mean intellect. Do you know the difference between the two?"

"Yeah, I think so."

"You think so," Dale repeated. He took a breath and let it out as he prepared to explain himself. "See, the problem here is that a matter of the heart can't be understood with the head. It can only be understood with the heart. And knowing the *difference* between the head and the heart involves both intellect *and* emotions. So if you only *think* you understand the difference, then you don't. You also have to be able to *feel* the difference. And you don't give the impression that you do." He paused for a moment to reconnoiter. "Would it be fair to say that you're unhappy with your life because you're not doing something you really enjoy, and you're engaged to marry a man you don't really love?"

Rosie heaved a troubled sigh, then said, with some trepidation, "I dunno."

"All right. That's close enough for now. If I'd been off the mark, I believe your answer would have been much different. So what would you prefer to be doing with your life that you're not doing now?"

Rosie blew through her lips as she thought about it. "I don't know. I just . . . . He's a terrific guy; it's a great job. I really don't know what I'd prefer to be doing."

"Hmmm . . ." Dale breathed, momentarily stumped. Then, "All right, let's try it using *your* terms. What would be the *dumbest* choice you could possibly make in your life?"

Rosie snorted and answered, without hesitation, "Touring with a rock band."

Dale laughed appreciatively. "Now that's an interesting answer! I guess I meant something you might actually consider."

"I've actually considered it!"

"Really?"

"Yeah."

"Whoa!" Dale exclaimed. "Now that's what I call a one-eighty! What do you see yourself doing on tour with a rock band?"

"Keyboards and vocals."

The specificity in Rosie's response was telling and Dale knew exactly what it meant. "Oh, you're a musician?" was his surprised reply.

"Yeah. I majored in music."

"No kidding?!" This turn of events fascinated the DJ. "Do you have a specific band in mind or are you just dreaming in general?"

"I have a specific band. Have you ever heard of Man's Inhumanity?"

"Oh, sure!" Dale replied. "They were local up-and-comers a few years back."

"Yeah. Well, they're touring now. I dated the lead guitarist in college, and he asked me to join the band. Also asked me to marry him."

"Really! How did you feel about this guy?"

"I was crazy about him. I would have followed him to the ends of the earth."

"Why didn't you?"

"My dad had just died and my mother was sick and I had to stay home to take care of her."

"How's your mother now?" Dale asked with genuine concern.

"She's fine."

"I'm glad to hear it. So do you ever hear from the lead guitarist?"

"Oh yeah. We write, and talk on the phone every few months."

"Oh, that's great! So, is his invitation still open?"

"To join the band or marry him?" Rosie queried.

"Both," Dale answered.

"I guess. He keeps asking me."

"To join the band or marry him?" Dale asked.

"Both," Rosie replied.

"So why don't you?!"

Rosie heaved a troubled sigh. "It would be completely irresponsible."

Dale cocked his head. "Irresponsible to whom?"

"Everyone!"

"Name one person."

"My mother."

"Ohhh!" Another piece of the puzzle had just fallen into place. "All right, anyone else it would be irresponsible to?"

Rosie struggled with the question for a moment, then finally said, "I guess not."

"So, unless I miss my guess," Dale ventured, "after you nursed your mother back to health, you felt responsible for her ever after."

Rosie hadn't thought of it in exactly those terms. "I guess," she answered tentatively.

"I have news for you, my dear. You're an adult. Unless you have children—and apparently you don't—you're not responsible for anyone but yourself. You're responsible *to* everyone for conducting yourself with integrity, but you're not responsible *for* anyone but *you*."

"But I'm the only family she has. I can't just leave her and go on the road for months at a time!"

To Dale's ears, there seemed to be too much tension in Rosie's voice and he ventured a guess. "Is that what she tells you?"

Wondering how Dale knew, Rosie hesitated. "Yeahhhh," she drawled dubiously.

"Uh-huh. I'd lay odds she also tells you—probably more often than you're aware—that your job is a great job and you'd be stupid to quit, and your fiancé is a terrific guy and you'd be stupid not to marry him. Am I right?"

"Yeah. How'd you know?"

"I'm just repeating what *you* told *me*. I think we've hit on the source of your problem here, darlin'. Your mother tells you something, you believe it, and you adopt it as truth that rules—and apparently ruins—your life. You can't expect to be happy with someone else ruling your life, you know. That's like a law of nature."

"But I can hardly just up and leave."

"Do you live with her?

"No, I live a few blocks away."

"So what does she need you for?"

"I'm the only family she has."

"And you'll continue to be the only family she has. Are you her only source of income or transportation or companionship or any of those kinds of things?"

"No, none of those things. It's just that I'm the only family she has left."

"Well, you know, it sounds to me like you *could* just up and leave."

"No, I can't! You don't understand!" Rosie's tone had become somewhat petulant.

Dale remained calm. "Okay, well, let's see. If I understand you correctly, she's healthy, she can get around, she has friends—am I right?"

"Yeah."

"Okay. If you left, it wouldn't be like you died, you know—you'd write and call and visit when you could. Don't forget, it's the way of nature for the young to leave the nest. It's sometimes traumatic for *human* parents when that happens—it's called separation anxiety—but that doesn't negate the nature of it. Your mother would just have to get used to it. And she would. She's been afraid to let go and she's used manipulation to keep you in the nest. But she'll get over that, too."

"But what if she's right?"

"What if she's right about what?"

"That I'd be stupid to quit my job and not marry Todd."

"Again, you're back to reasoning where the heart is concerned. Sweetheart, there *is* no 'right' or 'wrong' to this. So there's no 'what if' about it. There's only the adventure of life, and learning what it has to show you about yourself. And that's not a matter of 'right' or 'wrong,' it's a matter of choice—*your* choice, strictly and solely—of what *you* want to do, what *you feel* like doing. That's all there is to it. There's nothing more—period. So go do it!"

To Rosie, this seemed a tall order. "I don't think I can," she sighed.

"Why not?"

"I just . . . ." She trailed off in exasperation, then fired back, "She's my mother!"

"You're right, she *is* your mother. But so what?" Dale was not being disrespectful, only playing devil's advocate.

"So what?! What do you mean, so what? She's my mother!"

"I'll bet she uses *that* phrase on you, too. Right?"

"Yeah, so?!"

"So you're reading a whole lot more into those words than is really there. Let's take a very close look at exactly what those words say. 'She's my mother'—all those words really do is state a familial relationship. But when *you* say them, you're saying a whole lot more than just that. You're also saying that your mother is someone for whom you're responsible and to whom you must listen and to whom you must be obedient, even subservient. And this is exactly what *she* means when she says them. By loading them with all those hidden meanings, she's convinced you that her parental status entitles her to rule your life. But that simply isn't true. The phrase, 'She's my mother,' simply doesn't contain all those hidden meanings. The truth is that you're an individual with your own individual needs, and you're entitled to your own life."

"But that's so selfish."

"Does she say *that* to you, too?"

Rosie considered this briefly. Then, "Yeah."

"Just listening to you and the things you say to justify working a job you don't like and marrying a man you don't love—at the expense of the life you'd prefer to be living—it's abundantly clear to me that your mother uses the whole vocabulary of manipulation to keep you in the nest. Don't get me wrong, I have nothing against parents. I loved my parents, very deeply, and I was shattered when they were killed. But I didn't love them because they were my flesh and blood, I loved them because they were wonderful, caring people who treated me with the utmost respect and love. What I'm trying to get you to see is the distinction between loving your parents and allowing them to impose their will upon you because they are your flesh and blood. So I don't mean any disrespect toward your mother when I say she's being manipulative. I'm sure she doesn't do it maliciously; I'm sure she really believes it herself. She's just scared to death. Her husband left her—"

"He died," Rosie interjected.

"Okay. But the result is the same—and that was very painful. And no doubt she's afraid she'll experience the same pain when *you* leave her. But that fear is unjustified. That fear is something for her to face and work on and overcome, not for you to reinforce by subjugating your will to hers."

"So you're saying this is all my mother's fault?" Rosie countered, more than little offended by the suggestion.

"No, no, not at all. I'm not laying blame or finding fault in any way, shape, or form. I'm only trying to help you identify the dynamics of your misery. Sometimes—*most* of the time—we discover that someone, usually ourselves, but frequently also others, are acting out of fear. And by identifying those fears and the dynamics of the resultant actions, we can understand what's making us unhappy. In your case, your mother and you are in a dysfunctional, co-dependent relationship in which she fears your leaving the nest and you fear making her unhappy. And in doing so you enable her to just go right on being afraid."

"*I* enable her?" Rosie said with some surprise.

"Absolutely! Actually, I have to amend something I said earlier. She hasn't exactly been manipulating you. The fact of the matter is that she's been *trying* to manipulate you and *you've* been *permitting* her to. She's been feeding you the lines and you've been swallowing them hook, line, and sinker. You've been just as responsible for the manipulation as she has."

"But it just seems so selfish to go off and do what *I* want to do when she's so unhappy with her life."

"Ah, so you're not the only one unhappy with her life," Dale surmised.

"No."

"So let me ask you this: Has your willingness to stick around and work a job *you* don't like and marry a man *you* don't love made *her* happy?"

"What?" Rosie had not expected this question and it took her somewhat by surprise.

"Has your willingness to stick around and work a job you don't like and marry a man you don't love made her happy?"

"Well . . . no."

"And it never will . . . because it isn't within your power to do that, no matter how you conform to her wishes. *She's* the only one who can make her happy. Just as you're the only one who can make *you* happy. And doing what makes you happy is not selfishness. A lot of people have a huge misconception about selfishness. They tend to think that anything you do for yourself constitutes selfishness. But that's not true. Only those things you do for yourself at the *expense* of another is selfishness. All the other things you do for yourself are 'self-fulfillment.' And there's nothing selfish about self-fulfillment. But because people often fail to distinguish between the two, self-fulfillment winds up being mistaken for selfishness and you get accused of being selfish when you're really just taking care of yourself. Do you understand?"

It was a little too much theory for Rosie to absorb and she answered tentatively, "Sort of."

"All right, let me put it this way: Treating yourself to an ice cream cone, for example, isn't selfish unless you get that ice cream cone by depriving someone else of it. Likewise, treating yourself to your own life isn't selfish unless you're depriving your mother of her life."

"But if I left, that's what I'd be doing," Rosie insisted.

"No you wouldn't. That's what she wants you to believe; that's how the manipulation works. But the fact is, your mother has the prerogative and the ability—and the responsibility—to create her own life. Actually, by trying to keep you from living your life as you wish, *she's* the one who's being selfish. She's treating herself to *her* life—such as it is—by depriving you of yours."

This point made an impression on Rosie and she gave it a moment of thought. "But what if the life she wants to create for herself includes me?"

"That's a very good question, and it brings to light a very fine line that few people distinguish, and even fewer manage to understand. I use what one of my references calls the 'Platinum Principles' to sort out things like this. Have you ever heard of the Platinum Principles?"

"No."

"Well, they're a couple of guidelines for living respectfully and responsibly. They can help distinguish selfishness from self-fulfillment, and service from servitude. The first Platinum Principle, which is the principle of respect, says: 'Neither impose your will on others, *nor allow others to impose their will on you.*'" To emphasize its pertinence, Dale enunciated the second half of the principle with greater deliberation. "The second Platinum Principle, which is the principle of responsibility, says: 'Be of service to others as long as you are not of disservice to yourself, and be of service to yourself as long as you are not of disservice to others.' As applied to *your* question, if there's any imposition of will by one party on the other party, that's selfishness. Or, if there's any disservice by one party to the other, that's selfishness. So it seems to me that any effort your mother makes to manipulate you into marrying a man you don't love and working a job you don't like—or in any way keep you from doing what you want to do with your life—qualifies as both an imposition and a disservice."

"But wouldn't leaving her be a disservice?"

"No."

"Why not?"

"Well, this is where it gets tricky, because the line becomes very fine. The only reason the prospect of leaving your mother feels like a disservice is because you're overlooking the fact that she's *already* imposed her will on you by manipulating you into staying in the nest and not following your dreams. The fact is, by leaving and following your dreams, all you'll be doing is *stopping* her from imposing her will on you, which is what the second half of the first principle guides us to do. The problem with dealing with parents is that we often overlook their imposition on us when we're examining our own choices for the disservices we think we may be doing them."

"What?!" Rosie blurted, not understanding the complicated language.

"I'm sorry. This is kind of a complex subject and I didn't explain myself very clearly. What I was trying to say was that, in the process of emancipating ourselves from the will of others, we often *think* that we're imposing our will on them. But in fact, we're only doing what we need to do to *stop* them from imposing *their* will on *us*. But we're so used to subordinating ourselves to their will that we're blind to it, and all we see is our own imposition of will on them as we put our foot down against their impositions on us. And that horrifies us. The solution is to get a clear perspective on how they've been imposing their will on us." Dale paused to sense Rosie's response. "Does that clarify it for you?"

"Yeah, sorta."

"Good. So, leaving your mother would not be a disservice to her. Of course, if you really *want* to stick around the nest, that's another matter. But then, you'd be doing what you want with your life and you wouldn't be miserable, as you are now. Is this beginning to make sense to you now?"

Rosie heaved a tentative sigh before answering. "Yeah . . . ." In the tone of her response, Dale could hear that she had, for the first time, let go of some of her resistance. "But it's hard," she added after a moment.

"I know it is," Dale consoled softly. "And it may be painful, at least at first. You obviously love your mother very much, and I'm sure it's hard to imagine her getting along without you, even harder to break the habit of subjugating your needs and desires to hers. But I believe that, at some level of her consciousness, she needs you to break away and follow your dreams and experience growth in your life so that she can break free of her dependence on *you* and experience the kind of growth in her life that she's here to experience. My references tell me that we're sometimes here for the purpose of setting an example for someone else. Yours may be to show your mother how to follow her dreams. She may discover dreams she's long forgotten. And even if she doesn't have dreams or choose to grow further, you won't be being unloving or disrespectful or selfish if you leave and follow your dreams."

"I guess."

"I think you'll find that your mother's attempts to manipulate you into staying close to home are largely based on her fear that she can't have a life without your being nearby, and the belief that someone else can make her happy. Of course, both the fear and the belief are misconceptions. And if you were to do with your life what you really want to do with it, she'd discover that she *can* create a life of her own, and be happy, without you. It would be a shame for you to pass up your dreams, only to fail to make her happy, and discover, after she's passed away, that your sacrifice was in vain."

"*That's* for sure." With this, Rosie heaved a tremendous sigh. "So how can I break it to her that I'm quitting my job and breaking off my engagement and joining a rock band." She had become increasingly anxious while saying this.

"Just tell her you love her and that you appreciate her opinion, but that you have to follow your own dreams. And when she says all the things she usually says, just repeat yourself. 'I love you, Mom. I appreciate your opinion'—be sure to include that—'but I have to follow my own dreams.' That's all. It may take awhile, and she may be offended at first and get upset with you and throw a fit. But when she sees how happy it makes you to be following your own dreams, she'll come around."

Rosie blew another tremendous sigh. "Well, I guess I've got my work cut out for me, don't I?"

"So you're going to do it?"

"Yeah. It scares me to death, but I don't wanna be miserable for the rest of my life."

"Excellent! Terrific! I predict great things for you, my dear."

"Thanks! And thanks for your help tonight, Dale. You've been so sweet and patient."

"Well, you're certainly welcome. Let me hear from you from time to time. Let me know how your tour's going."

"Oh! Okay. Sure!"

"Best of luck, sweetie. And—"

"Oh! Oh! Dale?"

"Yes?"

"I wanted to ask you . . . I read in the paper this morning that you had turned down the Archers Man of the Year award. Is that true?!" She sounded almost distressed by this news.

The question took Dale completely by surprise and rocked his composure for a couple of seconds. "No, no, I haven't turned it down," he replied at last, feeling very much on the spot and putting on a facade of innocence. "I just haven't been able to schedule it yet. That report was premature."

"Oh, I'm glad!" Rosie said, obviously relieved. "I'd hate to see you turn it down. You've done *so* much for me and people I know. You just really deserve it."

"Well, thank you, sweetheart! I really appreciate that. Be sure to let me know how the tour goes, now."

"I will, I promise. I love you."

"I love you, too. Goodnight."

"Goodnight."

Dale pressed the button to disconnect the call. "This is WWKW, FM 102.4, and I'm Dale Greene on The Brink of Tomorrow. Back with more calls after these messages."

Now *Dale* heaved a sigh. He had not anticipated his listeners getting wind of the award controversy and putting this kind of pressure on him. Even Bobby had been unaware of the award and the discussion it had prompted between Dale and his advisors.

Dale's very next caller had also seen the report and mentioned it—it was practically the first thing out of his mouth. Over the course of the evening, six out of the sixteen callers he talked with mentioned the award. What had started out a minor problem was becoming a major predicament. And he was beginning to feel nauseous at the thought of dealing with it.

Chapter 9

The day had started out bright and sunny. Dale was being wheeled along a cheery grass-lined walkway. Suddenly, a large matronly body stepped in front of the sun, darkening the sky. The smiling face of the intruder was focused on something above and behind Dale, and he tilted his head up and back to look at the object of the intruder's gaze. The object he found himself looking at was a face, upside down, but familiar and pleasant.

Then, the intruder shifted her gaze downward, and looked for the first time at Dale. A stunned look crossed her face and a gasp escaped her lips. "Oh, my God!" she uttered as the look on her face turned to one of horror.

Suddenly, other people were there, looming close, peering directly into Dale's face and grimacing uncontrollably, shrieking and holding their hands over their mouths, becoming nauseous and turning to run as if from a carrion mess.

Dale felt a sudden pain stab deeply at his heart. The muscles in his face tightened and threatened to cramp. Tears blurred his vision and moistened his cheeks. In the blink of an eye, the strangers had fled, leaving him wounded and crying like a child.

He looked up and back for the familiar and pleasant face he knew was behind him. But the face was gone! He had been abandoned—left utterly alone in a world devoid of friendly faces. The hurt was beyond his wildest imaginings and he cried out, "Nooooooo!!!"

With a start, Dale woke to find himself in bed, drenched in sweat, the victim of a familiar nightmare. After his show the previous night, he had gone straight to bed, exhausted by the tension of being quizzed about the Archers award.

Unfortunately, the light of morning wasn't much comfort. The pressure was on to arrive at a solution and he knew it would be the first thing on the agenda at the morning meeting.

"I just feel so bad about it," Dale lamented to his trusted trio. "If it were just a matter of disappointing the Archers Association, I'd just turn the damn thing down. But now the whole city's in on it." He sighed and looked inward for a moment. "How complicated would it be to send an envoy posing as me?"

The trio collectively drew a breath and eyed one another. This was the solution Dale had rejected just three days earlier. Slowly, reluctantly, the three men began laying out the complications.

"We'd have to swear him to secrecy," offered Wil Terry.

"Of course, he wouldn't need to see Dale," Paul Norman Carr clarified. "The only thing he'd need to know is that he's impersonating him. So the secret wouldn't be all that damning if it were to come out."

"He'd have to sound enough like Dale to fool the Archers," Wil included.

"He'd have to sound enough like me to fool my listeners," Dale added. "The local news media will be all over the presentation."

"Oh, yeah, that's right," Wil acknowledged "Well, we could solicit voice samples."

"That'd be the place to start," Paul agreed. "But he couldn't be a local boy."

"No. We'd have to bring in an outsider," Wil asserted. "We could approach voice agencies in New York or Los Angeles. They're teeming with talent and wouldn't give a damn about the seamy goings on in Springfield."

"We could have the agencies send the tapes to my brother-in-law in New York," Shel Boerman offered. "That would give us an extra bit of insulation."

"Might also be a good idea to specify we're lookin' for unknowns," Paul interjected. "Get someone who's hungry. Less likely to ask questions."

"Right," Wil acknowledged. "We could narrow the field to a handful of candidates, fly in and conduct interviews at their agencies, and fly the winner out on a charter. He wouldn't even need to know where he's headed or the real circumstances of the job, just that he's playing the part of a DJ accepting an award."

"That would certainly simplify things as far as swearing him to secrecy goes," Dale said. Wil nodded.

"What else? Anything else we need to consider?" asked Paul Carr.

"Yeah," offered Shel. "What are the consequences of the plan falling apart?"

"You mean, what if we can't find a guy to do it?" Wil queried.

"No. What if we're found out?"

Everyone in the room drew a breath, and held it.

Paul finally broke the silence. "We apologize and give back the award," he drawled quietly. "In the controversy, Dale might have to give up broadcastin' for a while. But it shouldn't be any worse than it'll be if we don't come up with somethin' to satisfy the Archers. There's nothin' illegal in what we're proposin'."

"And it *is* for a good cause," Wil added, somewhat languidly. As no dissenting opinions were expressed, the room was quiet for a moment.

"So, can we do this?" Dale asked, just to get a consensus.

The three other men thought briefly, consulted one another with their eyes, then nodded their heads.

Seeing the agreement, Dale heaved a sigh of relief. Then furrowing his brow, he lamented, "I just wish it didn't have to be this way."

"You didn't ask for your disfigurement," Wil counseled supportively. "It just happens to be a complication of your life that invites special ingenuity. You were given both the disfigurement and the award; obviously, you were meant to deal with them in the least objectionable way possible. And this appears to be it."

"Yeah," Dale acknowledged blandly, mulling the proposition. "And it *will* make everyone happy." He was thinking of the Archers and his listeners. He was failing to consider himself.

That afternoon, Wil Terry obtained a list of agencies that represented voice talents in Los Angeles and New York City. Selecting ten agencies in each city, he placed orders with each firm for voice samples of young, attractive unknowns with deep, resonant voices—giving them the address of Shel Boerman's brother-in-law. Paul Carr had the telephone company set up a toll-free line to enable the agencies to call the estate without giving away its location. And Shel made arrangements with his brother-in-law to accept and forward the tapes to the estate.

Within a few days they had a pile of audio cassettes and CDs featuring the voices of over a hundred film, television, and radio aspirants. Most were accompanied by professionally photographed headshots. Each sample ran only a few minutes in length, so the four men were able, within a day, to listen to the entire batch and cull the half dozen or so which best met their needs. By the end of the next day, they had made arrangements with the pertinent agencies to meet for interviews with the top candidates in the various agency's offices.

By this time, a full week had elapsed since Paul Carr's last conversation with Roger Hampton. As promised, and with less anxiety than he had anticipated, Paul phoned the Archers president.

"Well, I have good news and bad news," he told Mr. Hampton. "The good news is that I've talked to Mr. Greene, and he's happy to make an accommodation in his schedule."

"Oh, good!" Hampton interjected.

"The bad news is that we haven't been able to open up a specific a date yet. But we're workin' on it. Perhaps if you could send me a list of dates that would be most convenient for you, we'd have some framework to work within."

"Of course," replied Mr. Hampton. "I'll have one made up and faxed to you this afternoon."

"Excellent!" Paul acknowledged with more enthusiasm than he actually felt. "I appreciate your cooperation."

"Oh, don't mention it. We're delighted just to know Mr. Greene will be able to accept the award."

"No more delighted than we are, Mr. Hampton. It is a very great honor the Archers Association has bestowed on my client, and we appreciate it very deeply. *And* we're sorry for the delay in making these arrangements."

"Well, these things happen, Mr. Carr. After all, it's for the very reason that our Men of the Year are active, productive, and very busy members of the community that we offer this award. As long as we're able to make our presentation, we're happy."

"As are we. I should have word for you on a specific date within a week of receiving your list, if you'll be so patient."

"Absolutely," acknowledged Hampton. "I look forward to

receiving your call."

"Thank you, sir. And good day."

"Good day."

Hanging up the phone, Paul heaved a sigh of relief. Unfortunately, the exhalation didn't completely quell the anxiety he felt over this operation. Even though their plan had been hatched and was under way, there were no guarantees that they could accomplish it without being discovered.

Four candidates for the role had been selected from three agencies in Los Angeles; three had been chosen from as many agencies in New York City. The interviews with the candidates in New York City were scheduled two days hence; those in Los Angeles for two days after that.

Flying to New York armed with contracts and a sample acceptance speech specially worded to keep the nature of the job ambiguous, Wil and Paul sat down individually with the three candidates from the Big Apple. The Greene duo needed to see how they looked, sounded, and carried themselves in person and under extemporaneous circumstances.

As it turned out, the conversational voice of the first of the three men was considerably higher than his "announce voice" and during casual intercourse he tended to lapse into it. The next interviewee looked quite a bit older and more haggard than his photo—certainly not what someone would imagine Dale to look like. The final candidate had a very pleasant look and sounded so much like Dale as to be nearly indistinguishable. But he wasn't quite as open and personable as Wil and Paul had hoped. Still, they marked him down as a contender in the event that the nominees in Los Angeles failed to meet their standards.

If the two Greene representatives had too few viable candidates to choose from in New York, they had too many in Los Angeles. Although one candidate was a single father who was unable to leave the area, even for three days, because of his young son, the other three seemed ideal for the part. They were all attractive, personable, and sounded as much like Dale in person during extended conversation as Wil and Paul could possibly have hoped. Reading the sample speech and answering sample questions, they were utterly believable as Dale Carey Greene—almost spookily so when Wil and Paul closed their eyes and listened to them in personal darkness.

Upon further examination, however, it was discovered that one of the candidates was a local DJ who enjoyed a small but loyal following in the area—a little too well known for safety. Of the remaining two men, one was the playboy heir to a small fortune, the other an unemployed locksmith, both unknowns aspiring to success in the field of acting.

Either of these candidates could have filled the role perfectly, but Wil and Paul had their doubts about the playboy. While the pay they were offering for the one-night gig—$7,500—was phenomenal for an unknown, it would have been insignificant to the rich boy, and therefore represented little incentive to keep his participation in the project secret. The locksmith, however, struggling to get acting parts and out of work after his father's lock shop was bought out by a developer, seemed hungry enough to do whatever was necessary to get the job, even if it meant signing a contract which enjoined him from revealing the location or nature of the work he was to perform.

After informing the locksmith, Elliot Draupau, that he was their leading candidate and ordering a comprehensive background check on him, just for safe measure, Wil and Paul called Dale with the news of the find, then celebrated by taking in the sights of Los Angeles. When the background check came back two days later, it showed no arrests, no warrants, no known vices, no subversive activity—no trouble of any kind, for that matter—and only minimal credit difficulties. Apparently, Elliot was as nice a guy as he seemed, and the two men phoned to let him know he got the part and to arrange a contract-signing meeting.

Keeping the details of the job somewhat ambiguous, Wil and Paul told Elliot that he was simply playing the part of a DJ accepting an Archers Association Man of the Year award in a publicity event. That was enough to satisfy the excited actor and he signed the contract, including the strict non-disclosure clause, without further question.

Calling Roger Hampton that afternoon from his luxury suite at the Bonaventure Hotel, Paul settled on a date for the award ceremony—fourteen days hence—and made final scheduling arrangements with

Elliot.

In the days before the event, Dale worked with Wil, Paul, and Shel to write his acceptance speech and develop some plausible background material for Elliot, something to help the locksmith get a feel for the character he would be playing, in case the media insisted on comments from the new Archers Man of the Year. They didn't really expect Elliot to have to field questions, but they felt more secure erring on the side of safety. During the same period, the Archers Association issued press releases and generally played up the event in the media. And Dale informed his listeners that he had finally been able to make arrangements to accept his Man of the Year award. They were understandably delighted.

As preparations for the event neared completion and Dale and his advisors found time to relax, the questions, the misgivings, the second thoughts about the rectitude of what they were doing had time and opportunity to resurface in their minds. And resurface they did, with even greater urgency than before.

What they were contemplating wasn't illegal, but it was dishonest. What they were undertaking wasn't evil, but it was unethical.

Still, the honest, ethical approach was sure to upset everyone involved. The history of people's response to Dale and others similarly disfigured demonstrated *that* beyond doubt. Dale's reputation, the Archers Association's award plans, the feelings of Dale's devoted listeners, and, worst of all, the beneficial work Dale did for the community with his show—the very thing he was being honored for—would be torn apart by the judgment and prejudice endemic to our society. The media scrutiny following any revelation of the truth would see to that.

No, despite the apparent dishonesty and unethical nature of it, what they were doing was the least objectionable, least painful solution to the problem, for all involved. That was the conclusion each of the four men reached in the privacy of his own thoughts, without reference to or conference with the others. And particularly for Dale, it meant not having to face his fear of appearing before his public. So the plan moved forward with unrelenting momentum, unimpeded by concerns of higher principle.

Two days before the event, a limousine arrived at Elliot's North Hollywood address and transported him to a small airfield in Burbank. There he was escorted to a specially chartered jet bound for he knew not where. In Springfield, he was met by Wil and Paul, who had timed his arrival to provide him ample opportunity to study his speech and background material before the ceremony. To keep Elliot as far away from Dale as possible, he was lodged in a premium hotel suite for the three-day duration of his stay.

The first order of business after settling in was a fitting for a custom tailored tuxedo. For the out-of-work locksmith, the regal treatment he was being accorded was a personal validation and he studied his part with conscientious diligence.

Taking adjoining suites just down the hall from Elliot, Wil and Paul made themselves constantly available for comments, consultation, companionship at meals and light recreation so as to make their charge feel welcome and comfortable in what was to Elliot a city full of strangers.

The ceremony had been scheduled early enough to allow "the DJ" to be back at the radio station in plenty of time for his nine o'clock show. Of course, Dale already knew the speech Elliot was to give, as well as the background material he had prepared. But just in case any of his callers happened to watch the media coverage on the evening news and ask him about it, Elliot was fitted with a hidden wireless microphone that would transmit the proceedings, plus any interactions he might have with the media, to a compact receiver/recorder in Wil's pocket. Immediately upon conclusion of the affair, the tape was to be rushed to the estate where Dale would listen to it so that he could respond specifically to any of his callers' questions about the event.

As the hour of the ceremony approached, the two advisors were pleased to see that Elliot was relaxed and had a firm grasp of the material he had studied. In keeping with the aristocratic treatment he was being given, Elliot was transported to the ceremony in a white limousine, along with Wil and Paul, with whom he had by this time become quite friendly and upon whom he had come to rely for direction and guidance.

While the Archers Association Man of the Year awards were nothing even close to the gala events of Hollywood, the local media were out in force, and the sidewalk outside the hall hosting the event was mobbed with Brink of Tomorrow fans who wanted to get a glimpse of their favorite, but heretofore unseen, radio talk-show personality.

The white limo pulled up in front of the hall to wild cheers from the crowd and Elliot was escorted inside by two tuxedoed Archers. As instructed, he grinned and waved to the crowd, just as Dale might have. Watching from just a few steps behind, Wil and Paul exchanged obviously pleased looks. So far, so good.

Ken Gullekson

Chapter 10

"Ten months ago, he lost his parents, Leonard and Dara, in a tragic automobile accident. A drunk driver ran a red light and slammed into the limousine they were riding in. He was off the air for two weeks, and when he returned, the grief he felt at their loss was still very much evident in the quaver in his voice. But he did not let that tragedy daunt him; did not let his sorrow stop him. Instead, he turned that tragedy into triumph.

"That night, he took his first on-air call, a little nine-year-old girl named Jeanine, who had also lost her parents that week. Imparting a kind of wisdom with which we are all by now quite familiar, he comforted little Jeanine, and helped her to better understand the nature of this sometimes inexplicable phenomenon we call life.

"Since then, he has shared this wisdom nightly with the citizens of Springfield, helping so many to face their fears with courage and character, to solve their problems with intelligence and integrity. For this service to the community, the Springfield Archers Association has voted him its highest honor. On behalf of all of the Archers of Springfield, I am extremely proud to present this plaque recognizing Mr. Dale Carey Greene, our Man of the Year."

Stepping back from the lectern, Roger Hampton turned toward Elliot Draupau and clapped his hands in enthusiastic applause, along with the entire gathering of 187 Archers. From his seat of honor at a row of tables flanking the lectern, Elliot stood—his grin wide, just a hint of embarrassment on his face—and approached the speaker. As he did, the entire assemblage rose in a standing ovation. Extending his hand, the Archers president shook Elliot's hand in congratulation and handed over the beautiful, gold-trimmed plaque.

As he had been instructed by Wil and Paul, Elliot accepted the plaque, looked at it for a moment in extreme appreciation, then turned toward his admiring audience with a mixture of extreme gratification and painful modesty etched on his face. Mr. Hampton directed him to the lectern with a hand gesture and took his seat at the row of tables, and Elliot stepped up to make his acceptance speech. He had it written on a piece of paper stuffed inside his jacket pocket and had been coached to take it out and read from it. But as he stepped to the lectern and adjusted the microphone, Elliot seemed to dispense with that altogether.

The applause took a good while to die down, and by the time it did, Elliot had said either "Thank you" or "Thank you very much" six times.

"Thank you very much, ladies and gentlemen," he said again as the applause finally faded out. For all practical purposes, he sounded indistinguishable from Dale, but Wil and Paul were somewhat alarmed that he had not taken out his prepared text. Everything had gone exactly as planned up till now. Was Elliot going to blow it after all?

"I am deeply, deeply honored to be named the Springfield Archers Man of the Year," Elliot began, remaining perfectly faithful to the text of the prepared speech. "I didn't set out to win any awards when I changed the format of The Brink of Tomorrow from rock 'n' roll to the discussion program it is today. I set out only to surrender to my passion to share what I held to be true in my life with others who wished to hear it. In so doing, I hoped they would find benefit in what I had to share.

"In the beginning, I had many doubts that what I had to say would be of interest, or benefit, to anyone but myself. But the thousands of calls and letters I've received over the months from my listeners, along with this award, informs me that I have succeeded, in ways beyond my wildest dreams. It's not the success for myself which I find so gratifying, however, but the success of my callers—and all my other listeners—who have made some sense out of the myriad of challenges we call life, and improved their lives. Therefore, I accept his award, with great pride, on behalf of them. Thank you. I love you all very much."

The room erupted with applause as Elliot stepped back from the lectern and displayed the plaque prominently just off his left shoulder, a courtesy to the press who wanted photos of the triumphant moment. Roger Hampton stood and again shook Elliot's hand, a further courtesy to the media. Applauding wildly, Wil and Paul were celebrating not only Dale's award, but Elliot's letter-perfect impersonation of their beloved friend and employer. Not only had he delivered the speech exactly as written, he had made it sound entirely extemporaneous.

Roger Hampton made some closing remarks—thanking the Man of the Year, thanking the community, thanking the assemblage for their attendance—and officially ended the proceedings. Afterwards, people milled about talking, many of them seeking an opportunity to shake Elliot's hand and congratulate him. With Wil and Paul at his side, he handled the mob with pleasant aplomb and soundly confirmed, in the minds of all, the wisdom of naming Dale Carey Greene the Archers Man of the Year.

The media eventually had their opportunity with Elliot, most of the time shouting too many questions to permit any one of them to be intelligible. Of course, since the media's questions could not be known in advance, the answers could not be rehearsed verbatim. During coaching sessions, Wil and Paul had floated sample questions, and Elliot had had to compile his answers from the background material he had been given. But handling real questions from real reporters intent upon getting a scoop was much more challenging. And Wil and Paul were more than a little anxious at the prospect of someone asking something unforeseen that Elliot couldn't answer convincingly.

"What are your plans now?" one reporter shouted.

"To go back to the station and do my show," Elliot replied with a grin, understanding the real intent of the question but opting for humor. It got the laugh and the reporter did not pursue the question further.

"Where are you going to put your plaque when you get it home?" came another question.

"On the mantle, right next to my Peabody," Elliot answered.

"Oh, you have a Peabody?" the journalist queried further.

"Not yet," Elliot quipped. More laughter.

"Do you have any advice for the television viewers out there?" asked a TV reporter.

"Yeah. Listen to the radio—FM 102.4." Again, laughter. He had been instructed, in the event someone asked for advice, to advise them to call the show, so as to preserve anonymity.

All in all, Elliot exceeded his coaching, answering those questions which managed to rise above the din with grace and humor.

As the hour was approaching half past eight, Wil and Paul urged their charge to say goodnight and make his exit. The limo was waiting outside and Elliot and Paul were whisked away. Wil took possession of the plaque and the audio tape he had made and proceeded alone to the Greene estate.

In the limousine, Paul showered Elliot with heartfelt praise, remarking that he had performed his part beyond expectation. Understandably, Elliot beamed at the accolade.

Dale, too, was impressed with Elliot's performance as he listened to the proceedings on tape in the den of the manor house.

"You guys did a terrific job with Elliot," Dale told Wil when the tape ended. "I couldn't have done better myself."

"Are you referring to the coaching we gave him?"

"No, his performance. He's even funnier than *me*."

"Jealous?" Wil asked gently, detecting a hint of sensitivity in his young friend.

"A little," Dale replied honestly. "But not so much the quality of his performance as the opportunity to meet the public face to face—to actually touch my listeners." He heaved a sigh. "Oh, well. It isn't the first time and it won't be the last."

"You're a wise man, Dale C. Greene," Wil said sincerely. "And that's why I love you."

Dale smiled softly in acknowledgement, then asked, "So what happens now?"

Wil looked at his watch. "It's almost time for the show."

"No, I mean with Draupau. Does he just fade back into the background?"

"Hopefully. Then things can get back to normal around here."

"Yeah," Dale agreed. Despite the award, and the success of the operation, he felt uneasy about the deception, and was eager to put the whole affair behind him.

Wil stood to go, then turned back, gingerly touched Dale's award, and said with utmost sincerity, "By the way . . . congratulations."

"Thank you, my friend," Dale acknowledged, the soft smile

returning to his lips. Wil left and Dale looked a last time at his Man of the Year plaque before motoring off to do his show.

Chapter 11

"It's ten thirty-three, you're tuned to WWKW, and this is Dale Greene on The Brink of Tomorrow." Dale had just returned from the mid-show commercial break. "My next caller is Ross. Ross is twenty-nine and says he doesn't understand women." He pressed the button which connected the call. "Hi, Ross, this is Dale Greene and you're on The Brink of Tomorrow."

"Hey, Dale, how's it going?"

"Just fine, Ross. And you?"

"Just fine! Hey, I saw you on the news getting your Man of the Year award just a minute ago. Congratulations!"

"Oh, thank you very much."

"You're welcome, man. Hey, what does it say on your plaque?"

Since this particular question had not been foreseen when Dale and his advisors had discussed their plans for the Archers affair, no specific arrangement had been made with regard to the plaque. So it occurred to Dale as fortunate that Wil had brought it back with him—as opposed to leaving it with Paul—and that he had taken the time to actually read the inscription.

"It says," Dale replied, looking at the picture of the plaque in his mind, "'In recognition of exemplary service to the community, we name Dale Carey Greene, Man of the Year.'"

"Well, I think it's really cool that you got it! Hey, you know when you were sitting at the tables up at the front there, that guy sitting on your left looked familiar. Who was he?"

Dale's heart skipped a beat. Of course, he had no idea who had been sitting to Elliot's left and could not answer the question. He hated being put on the spot and cursed silently for getting himself into a position like this. But he could not afford, at this juncture, to betray the scheme through carelessness. He would have to sidestep the question. His mind raced for an answer.

After what seemed like a very long time, Dale replied, "Actually,

Ross, since that person didn't specifically give me permission to broadcast his identity, I don't feel comfortable giving out his name. Sorry. But that doesn't mean we can't talk about *you*. Shall we?"

"Oh, sure," was Ross's quick reply.

"Good," Dale acknowledged. "Now, you say you don't understand women?"

"Yeah!"

"Is there a particular woman you don't understand?"

"It's all of 'em—my wife, my mother, my daughter, my boss. I don't understand any of them."

"And what do they do that you don't understand?"

"Everything! They just . . . I don't understand anything they do."

"Nah, nah, nah, you have to be specific. Otherwise you get into generalizing and stereotyping and judging. So what specifically don't you understand?"

Ross heaved a ponderous sigh. "Well . . . my wife can't seem to make up her mind about anything. She asks my opinion about *everything*, and even after I give it to her, it still takes her forever to actually make a decision. And then half the time she doesn't do what I tell her anyway. So what's the sense of asking my opinion in the first place?" Ross's delivery was somewhat akin to a jackhammer. "And when my wife and my mother get together, there's no decisions on anything, ever. My dad complains about the same thing. Then, my boss yells at me for making decisions she says *she's* supposed to make. She wants me to come to her all the time instead of making 'em myself—like I can't make a decision on my own. I tell you, Dale, I don't know if I'm comin' or goin'."

"And what don't you understand about your daughter?"

"She does *everything* I say. I guess if it wasn't for that, the other women wouldn't be so hard to understand." He paused a second, then corrected, "Yes, they would."

Dale chortled to himself. "How old is your daughter?"

"Six. And the sweetest little thing you ever saw."

"I don't doubt it. Well, it sounds to me like you're confusing a few things and I think I can give you a couple of pointers to sort them out."

"Please! Anything!"

"Bear in mind, I can only give you *my* understanding of it, which is all anyone can do. Some experts may disagree with me—there's not a lot of scientific fact on the subject—but I'll give you what I can."

"I'll take anything you can give me."

"All right. I must warn you, though, I might have to get metaphysical on you. Are you ready for that?"

"Lay it on me."

"All right. First of all, you can't understand women if you think of them as completely and utterly different from men. Sure, women are anatomically different from men in many respects—and that would seem to suggest that they're different in *every* respect. But that anatomical difference is misleading, and, by itself, is insufficient reason to consider them—or treat them—as totally and completely different from men. Likewise, women often try to understand men as totally and completely different from women, and in so doing, fail to get a clear understanding of men. In fact, aside from their anatomical differences, men and women are actually very much alike. So forget about thinking of women as totally alien beings. And you women out there, forget about thinking of men as totally alien beings. What I'm going to tell Ross about women also applies to your understanding of men.

"All right . . . the metaphysical perspective on this is that humans are basically spiritual beings with gender-differentiated bodies. Obviously, the concept of physical gender is meaningless when applied to a non-physical spirit. So, how can genderless spirits exhibit so many different and seemingly contradictory traits in bodies of the same gender? I'm referring to either gender, here. Well, it turns out that spirits are *both* genders, in an energetic sense. That is, each spirit is made up of two kinds of energy—one that could be called 'masculine energy' and one that could be called 'feminine energy.' Masculine energy is essentially—" Dale momentarily deepened and hardened his voice "—assertive, protective, consuming, intellectual. Would you agree that that describes the typical male, Ross?"

"Oh yeah."

Now Dale softened his voice. "Feminine energy is essentially receptive . . . creative . . . nurturing . . . emotional. As you can see, the masculine and feminine energies complement each other quite nicely."

"Hmm . . . you mean like interlocking puzzle pieces?"

"Yeah! Now, each of us possesses *both* of these energies. But we possess them in different amounts—we each have our own unique mix. In general, the gender of a person's body will predispose him or her to a predominance of energy in that gender—which is to say, a male will usually exhibit more masculine energy than feminine energy, and a female will usually exhibit more feminine energy than masculine energy—but both genders have *both* kinds of energies. You with me so far, Ross?"

"Yeah, pretty much."

"Okay. Now, it actually works out best if there's a pretty close balance between the two types of energies. But that's not always the case. In fact, it's *frequently* not the case. Some people exhibit *way* more of one kind of energy than the other—which means that some women will exhibit way more feminine energy than masculine energy, and others will exhibit more masculine energy than feminine energy. Those who exhibit way more feminine energy may seem overly emotional, overly reserved, overly vulnerable. Such women tend not to make decisions easily or quickly, tend not to display their strength, tend not to determine their actions through thought processes." He paused to catch his breath. "Does that generally describe your wife?"

"That's right on the money," Ross acknowledged.

"All right. On the other hand, women who exhibit a predominance of masculine energy will be more assertive, more protective, more intellectual—which means they'll make decisions more easily, be protective of their turf, and generally *think* their way through life instead of feeling their way through it. Does that sound like your boss?"

"Oh yeah!"

"Well, there you go. That's why different women can have very different dispositions."

The light was beginning to dawn on Ross. "Wow! That's pretty wild."

"Yeah. Of course, you see the very same phenomenon in men. Men with a predominance of feminine energy will be more sensitive, more creative, more emotional, that kind of thing."

"Wimps," Ross interjected. He was not being derisive so much as simply making an observation.

Dale chortled at the remark. "Well, some people do label such men as 'wimps.' But of course, that's an inaccurate and meaningless judgment. In fact, these men often turn out to be our artists—writers, painters, composers, actors, and so forth—men whose sensitivity often shapes our society and who we tend to admire and respect. On the other side of the coin, of course, are men whose masculine energy far outweighs their feminine energy—what we call 'macho men.'"

"Isn't that how it's supposed to be?" Ross challenged. "I mean, isn't that what a real man is?"

"Not in *my* opinion," countered Dale. "What you're referring to are men who, while they may display great strength and courage, may also be quite brutal and insensitive, even anti-social. For all we know, it may have been those very men who started the myth of the 'real man.' They told us *they* were real men, and as a society we believed them, mainly because they were more assertive than the rest of us. But if we set that blind belief aside for a moment and examine what we really admire in people, we discover that the people we admire the most are those whose masculine and feminine energies are just about balanced."

"How do you figure that?" Ross puzzled.

"Well, if you take a close look our *heroes*, I think you'll find them to be men whose strength and intelligence are balanced out by sensitivity and compassion—you know, the guy who risks his life to rescue a group of God's creatures from mortal danger, then grieves when some of them don't make it. Isn't that what we generally consider to be a 'real man?'"

"Yeah, I s'pose it is," Ross agreed, genuinely getting the picture.

"Same for women. A 'real woman' is a woman whose vulnerability and emotions are balanced out by strength and intelligence. And I don't mean *cancelled* out, I mean *balanced* out. Both are there, and they both surface when it's appropriate. So when you're trying to understand either men or women, look past the physical gender and see if you can figure out the ratio of their masculine and feminine energies. Then it'll all begin to make sense."

"I see. So how does my daughter fit into this? Does this mean she has more feminine energy than masculine energy?"

"Well, it may be a little early to tell with her at this stage. But I suspect you may be confusing her gender energies with something else, and that's the fact that little girls just generally tend to love their daddies, and will do anything for them. If you want her to grow into an emotionally healthy woman, I suggest you not abuse her love for you by overtaxing her willingness to serve you. You could wind up really confusing her and unbalancing her energies."

"Really?!" By the tone of Ross's voice it was clear that the prospect of emotionally harming his daughter was of genuine concern to him. "So how do I balance them?"

"Well, *you* can't actually balance them in *her*, but you can help *her* balance them."

"How?"

"The only way I know is to set an example, so she has the opportunity to see, in a role model, what it's like to be balanced. You can start by recognizing that *you* contain both kinds of energies, and by allowing both of them to manifest in yourself in approximately equal amounts."

"How do I do *that*?"

"Okay, well, let's see. First of all, how do you feel about crying?"

"You mean myself, or others?"

"Both."

"Well, I think it's a sign of weakness, so I never cry. I guess the women can't help it, but it bugs me when they do it."

"All right. Well, you might want to reconsider that point of view, because from a metaphysical perspective, crying isn't weak."

"It isn't?" Ross asked with some surprise.

"No. Crying is a natural expression of an emotion that's an essential part of being human. If you don't allow yourself to cry when you feel sad—or whenever you feel like crying—you can never be an emotionally whole and healthy person. If you look at this objectively you'll find that crying is a completely natural act, even for men. It's only that our society teaches us this myth that it's not manly to cry. So if you resist crying when you feel like it, you can inhibit your feminine energy and upset the balance. And if you frown on the women in your life crying, they may try to inhibit that expression in themselves, and become unbalanced as a result."

"Oh, I see." Genuinely trying to grasp these concepts, Ross mulled Dale's words briefly. "So I hafta cry to balance my energies?" he asked at length, none too thrilled at the prospect.

Dale smiled at Ross's narrow interpretation of his explanation. "Well, it takes a little more than that, but yeah, that's part of it. As I said, the first step is to recognize that your vulnerability and emotions—all those things you've considered to be weak—are just as vital a part of you, as a man, as your strength and intelligence. So let those emotions express themselves; don't hide or inhibit them in yourself, or others." Knowing this idea challenged some of Ross's basic beliefs, Dale gave him a moment to absorb it.

"Boy, that goes against everything I've ever believed," Ross said at length.

"I know. Unfortunately, what society has taught you to believe has left you without the knowledge to understand women."

"Well, that's true."

"As for helping your daughter balance her gender energies: While you're balancing your own energies, you can also recognize that *she* contains both energies, and allow them to manifest in her naturally. This is done by allowing and encouraging her to both think for herself *and* feel deep emotions. If she feels like crying, for instance, hold her and encourage her to cry as much as she needs to in order to completely release the emotion. Also, encourage her to be both strong *and* vulnerable, as appropriate to the occasion; and support her both when she stands up for what she believes *and* when she yields to someone else. Are you seeing how this works?"

"I think so," Ross replied thoughtfully. "But now you've got me wondering why someone's energies would be out of whack in the first place?"

Dale chuckled softly at Ross' choice of words. "Well, I think 'out of whack' is a little strong when you're talking about gender energies," Dale gently counseled. "That makes it sound as though there's something 'wrong' with an imbalance, and I don't mean to give that impression at all. The word 'imbalance' simply means 'unequal in weight or measure,' and there's no implication that there's anything 'wrong' with an imbalance. There are certain personal advantages to being pretty much balanced, but there's nothing 'wrong' with an imbalance. In fact, I tend to doubt that a perfect balance is even achievable. Everyone's gender energies are going to be unequal to some degree—if for no other reason than the fact that our gender-differentiated bodies tend to predispose us to some measure of dominance by one energy or the other. So it would simply be inappropriate to judge someone by their energy imbalance. So please, all of you out there who are listening to this, don't approach this with judgment. Agreed?"

"Sure."

"As for your question about what causes the imbalance in the first place, it's pretty complicated. Are you sure you want me to go into it?"

"Go for it."

"All right. Well, obviously, the gender differentiation of our bodies contributes to it. But more than that, it's a consequence of our fears. And these can come from a variety of sources—imitation and adoption of the fears of our parents and whatever other role models we might have; childhood and adulthood traumatic experiences; local cultural influences; and whatever we bring with us from past lives."

"Wait a minute. Can you run that past me again?"

"All right, let me put it this way: Depending on the dynamics of our parents' relationship, we'll either adopt or reject their gender energies in the formulation of our own. For instance, if we're a male and our father has a weak masculine energy, but he manages to avoid fights with mom by surrendering easily, we may adopt a weak masculine energy for ourself as a way to survive in a hostile world. This, of course, is all done subconsciously. On the other hand, if dad's weak masculine energy means mom walks all over him, we may *reject* a weak masculine energy for ourself as being too vulnerable. We'll do essentially the same with our mother's energies."

"Even if we're a male?"

"Well, obviously, a male makes some adjustments in the modeling of his energies after his mother's, but her energies do play a significant role in the formulation of his own. It really begins to get complicated if our parents' relationship is co-dependent, or if one of our parents leaves the picture through death or divorce and we don't find a suitable role model to replace them. We can become quite unbalanced. This is somewhat of an oversimplification, but it gives you some idea of the dynamics which shape us."

Ross thought briefly. "So my daughter's energies will be kind of a composite of mine and my wife's?" Ross confirmed.

"In a sense, yeah," Dale replied.

Ross sighed. "Then she's in deep trouble!"

Finding Ross' use of exaggeration rather charming, Dale smiled to himself. "No more than anyone else, actually. I believe we all come here knowing pretty much what we're getting ourselves into. We don't remember that once we're here, of course—that would take all the surprise out of life—but as spiritual beings, we know what we want to experience and we pick our life circumstances for the express purpose of experiencing it. Of course, part of our experience involves the experience of others, so if you find yourself interested in balancing your own gender energies, then your daughter may have come here to be a part of that."

"Oh, I see." With this, Ross heaved an audible sigh and Dale gave him a few moments to assimilate it. When he had, Ross continued, "Now, you said a minute ago that I was confusing a few things. What did you mean by that?"

"Okay, well, this brings us back to your wife. What I was referring to was the fact that when she asks your opinion about something, she's probably not asking you to make a decision about it—which is apparently what you thought she was doing—she's more likely just conducting a survey of other people's opinions, including yours. That would be true even if you're the only one she's surveying. This is an example, by the way, of her feminine *receptivity* in action: She receives the opinions of others, allows them to mingle with her own opinions and emotions, and then acts on the resultant feelings. It's a perfectly valid approach to decision-making, just as valid as your more intellectual approach. Of course, our society tends to judge her approach, because it has this unfounded belief that intellect is better than emotion, but that doesn't make her approach any less valid or viable. I suggest you not judge it either."

"Okay," Ross acknowledged, not entirely sure he could comply with Dale's suggestion. "Now what about my boss?"

"All right, now, refresh my memory. She didn't like your making decisions for her; is that right?"

"That's right."

"Okay, well, I suspect that if your boss were male, you wouldn't even be thinking about making decisions that were his to make. You'd let him make them and be happy about it. And if you did make decisions in his place, he'd be all over you, just like she is. Am I right?"

Ross thought about this for a moment. "Probably."

"All right. Well, first of all, it would seem that your boss's masculine energy is well developed and she uses it to good advantage in her work. But I'd guess the problem you have with her has less to do with her gender energies than it has to do with the fact that people in command generally don't like their subordinates exceeding their authority and making decisions they're not charged with making. I also have a feeling you might have a somewhat sexist attitude when it comes to women in authority, and maybe you've failed to recognize her position just because she *is* a woman. Am I right about this?"

Ross wasn't all that eager to admit the truth and hedged a bit. "Mmmm, yeah, probably."

"All right. Well, I encourage you to find a way to make a shift in your attitude and give her the respect you'd give a man in the same position. I think you'll do a lot better with her if you do. By the way, you'll be surprised at the response you'll get from the women in your life when you're open with your emotions."

"Really?!"

"Oh yeah. Of course, there are no guarantees, but if you can make that emotional connection with them, I believe you'll be more effective in your interactions with them. You may feel very vulnerable in doing this, but I believe the results will be well worth the effort."

"Hmmm . . . . Well, this does give me something to think about," Ross said thoughtfully. "Thanks."

"You're welcome, Ross. Thanks for calling, and best of luck."

"Thanks, Dale. Talk to you later, buddy."

"Goodnight." Dale disconnected the call, glanced at Bobby, and, getting a signal to go to commercial, added, "This is Dale Greene on The Brink of Tomorrow. I'll be back with more calls after this."

With a moment to relax Dale heaved a deep sigh. Having to field Ross's initial questions about the award ceremony had been stressful and he felt unusually fatigued. Neither he nor his triumvirate had anticipated the amount of stress this undertaking—this *deception*, innocuous though it might be—would produce.

A few days earlier, Dale had briefed Bobby and the crew that kept up the Greene estate about the fact that an envoy posing as Dale would be accepting the award for him. As expected, all had voiced understanding and support of the plan. But for Dale, asking such a large number of people to keep this secret induced in him a vague discomfort, an ineffable pressure.

In anticipation of this briefing, Dale and his advisors had considered, and dismissed, the potential problems. After all, the secret of Dale's disfigurement had been successfully kept by the entire group for over two decades. But this new secret contained a deception which the old one did not. There was no doubt in anyone's mind that the secret was safe. But still, for Dale, the pressure was palpable.

He savored the three minutes and twenty seconds of rest the commercial break provided. Following the break, he took five more calls before the end of the show. Two of the callers referred to the media reports on the award ceremony, but fortunately, neither of them asked questions he found difficult to answer, and the rest of the evening went off without event. But for Dale, it was still a little too close for comfort.

Fatigued as he was, the show couldn't have ended soon enough and he breathed a sigh of relief the instant he signed off. At last, the Archers ordeal was over and he could go back to being heard but not seen. The relief brought with it a new appreciation for the anonymity of his job.

Ken Gullekson

Chapter 12

The next morning, Wil and Paul escorted Elliot to the chartered jet which would fly him back to Burbank.

"Thank you, Elliot," Wil said as he handed the young actor an envelope containing a cashier's check for his fee. "You did an extraordinary job. We couldn't have wished for more."

Having never held a paycheck that big, Elliot wanted to look in the envelope, but was unsure it would be the mannerly thing to do.

Paul noticed. "Go ahead," he urged with a soft smile.

With a subtle grin of his own, Elliot lifted the flap on the envelope and pulled out the check. As promised, the amount was $7,500, a small fortune to the former locksmith. A quiet sigh escaped his lips. "Thank you," he said softly, earnestly.

Wil extended his hand and Elliot reciprocated. "Safe flight home," Wil wished him.

"Thank you," Elliot said again.

The gesture was repeated by Paul. Then Elliot turned and boarded the jet. In Burbank, another limousine would take him back to his tiny North Hollywood apartment.

With the praise of a job well done ringing in his ears and the cashier's check nestling in his pocket, Elliot was a happy man. Never mind the fact that his contract enjoined him from listing his role as Dale Greene on his resume or even talking about the experience. He now had the wherewithal to get his car fixed, catch up on his overdue bills, and buy some new clothes. The financial pressures were off for at least four months, and he would be able to pursue his acting and voice work full time without concern.

In Springfield, however, the pressure was just beginning to build. That afternoon, the business phone at the radio station began to ring with urgent, sometimes insistent requests for Dale to give media interviews, local TV talk-show appearances, product endorsements, and speaking engagements. Over the next few days the phone receptionist at the station dutifully took a total of twenty-seven messages, subsequently calling the private number at the estate and relaying the numerous requests to Paul.

Requests of this kind were nothing new. They had been coming in at an average rate of about one per week since Dale had changed the format of The Brink of Tomorrow to all talk. But the manifold increase in the frequency, urgency, and insistency was new.

In deference to Dale's fear of appearing in public—justified by the rationale that his disfigurement would seriously disturb his listeners and undo all the good he's done—all the previous requests for personal appearances had been summarily, though graciously, declined. Vaguely citing "privacy" and "principle" as Dale's reasons for declining these earlier requests, Paul was easily able to turn away all previous callers. But the current callers had a form of leverage the previous callers did not possess: Whereas before they were just interested in the DJ who conducted the most popular radio talk show in the city, now they were asking for the Archers Man of the Year, a personage of undeniable distinction in the community. Moreover, the fact that "Dale Greene" had already made a public appearance significantly weakened his claims on privacy.

Fortunately, the claim of "principle" was still available, at least partially. Accepting a Man of the Year award was one thing; chitchatting with a reporter or TV talk show host was another. And endorsing products was in a different category altogether. While Dale owed his fortune to his father's commercial ventures, exploiting a position of honor for the commercial motives of television producers and marketing executives who wished to make a buck for their organization seemed crass. Therefore, all such requests could be turned down for reasons of, again, principle.

But the requests to speak were different. Among them were invitations from both public and private schools asking Dale to address student assemblies, and from charitable organizations asking him to speak at fundraising events. Since these requests were not motivated by profit, but by the desire to help others—the same desire that drove Dale in doing his show each night—they were much harder to turn down on the pretext of principle.

Again, he found himself in consultation with his advisors, and he was not happy.

"We don't have much choice but to turn them down," advised Paul, taking a seat on the sofa opposite Wil.

Nervously twitching his joystick from side to side, Dale nudged his wheelchair about the den in an oscillating pattern. "The interviews and talk shows and product endorsements, yes. But what about the speaking requests? I mean, these are schools and charities!"

"We don't have much choice but to turn them down, too," Wil replied.

"How's that going to look?" Dale queried irritably, jerking his chair to around to face Wil. "I'll accept a Man of the Year award but I won't speak to school kids or help a charity raise money."

"We both know very well," Wil countered, "that appearances don't matter. It's the character of your actions that matters."

"Yeah, well, in this case, the appearances reflect the character, and they both stink."

"I think you're being a little hard on yourself," Wil counseled. "You have a compelling reason not to accept these invitations."

"Yeah, but they don't know that, and I can't tell them—for the very same reason I can't accept the invitations!"

"What would you like me to do?" Paul asked, hoping to move the discussion toward resolution.

"I don't know. I don't know if there's anything we *can* do," Dale replied dejectedly. "It's like we're right back where we were a month ago. How did we fail to foresee this?"

"We can't expect to anticipate *every* problem," Paul offered.

Dale sighed. "I'm beginning to wish I'd never even gone to the talk format."

"I don't believe *that*," Wil said, knowing Dale was just suffering under the pressure. "You've helped a lot of people and it's all been worth it. And you know it."

Dale sighed again, even deeper. "I know. It's just that this is so damned frustrating."

"So, I guess that means we turn them down," Paul surmised.

"Yeah, turn them down," Dale replied. "There's not much else we can do."

"I'm open to suggestion as to what to tell them," Paul said. "We can tell most of them you're just not interested. But I don't think you want to say that to the schools and charities."

Dale put his large, lumpy head in his gnarled hands and groaned. Having no suggestions of their own, the other men just waited for Dale's response.

"Tell them I'd like to do it, but that I'm too busy right now . . . and that we'll let them know when I have a break in my schedule. That would've worked with the Archers if they hadn't wanted to give me a damned award, for Christ's sake."

"All right," Paul acknowledged.

One by one, Dale's advisors stood to go about their duties.

"This is just one of those things you can't change or control," Wil added in an effort to console his former pupil. "Your only option is to accept it."

Surrendering, Dale heaved a final sigh. "Yeah. You're right. C'est la vie."

Paul spent the next few days returning calls and declining requests. Although everyone he talked to sounded disappointed, he noticed subtle differences in the tone of voice from one contact to the next. The media, TV, and product endorsement contacts, while clearly disappointed not to have been able to land a commercially potent subject for their enterprises, sounded personally aloof from the rejection. In contrast, those who represented the schools and charities had an obvious emotional investment in the invitation and their disappointment sounded personal. Having to turn them down left Paul feeling heavyhearted.

It took about a day and a half for the students of Bret Harte High School to learn that their beloved radio advisor had turned down their school's invitation to address the student body.

The invitation from Bret Harte High had been conceived four weeks earlier when the student council had voted to nominate Dale as its choice for speaker at the SBEA—the Student Body Elective Assembly. This was the one assembly each semester for which the students were permitted to invite the speaker of their choice. Of course, the ultimate decision was never entirely theirs, since the selection had to be approved by the principal, Mr. Smalley. Having never tuned in to The Brink of Tomorrow, Mr. Smalley was reluctant to cast his vote for a radio DJ. But upon learning this DJ had won the Archers Man of the Year award, he had at last relented, breaking the standoff and approving the nomination of Dale Greene as the SBEA speaker.

Immediately upon receiving the call from Paul declining the invitation, Mr. Smalley's student aide notified David Moon, the chairman of the student council, and by the end of the school day the entire school knew of the rejection. Disappointment was the majority reaction, anger the minority response. The disappointed majority had the cooler heads and, typically, prevailed over the angry minority in an emergency meeting of the student council as it discussed the matter and tried to understand why their beloved DJ would turn them down. Ultimately, it was decided that someone should call the show that night and make a personal plea.

"My next caller is David. David is seventeen, and says he's been snubbed by someone he loves." It was the third call of the evening. "Hi, David, this is Dale Greene and you're on The Brink of Tomorrow."

"Hi, Dale. How's it goin'?"

"Fine, David. How's it going with you?"

"Oh, all right, I guess."

"Well, that's better than a poke in the eye with a sharp stick."

David laughed.

"Now, you say you've been snubbed by someone you love?" Dale continued.

"Yeah," confirmed David.

"What's going on?"

"Well, I'm a student at Bret Harte High, and my school invited a local celebrity to speak at an assembly and he turned us down. And me and the other students are having a hard time understanding why he would do that."

Though David's statement was somewhat cryptic, Dale now knew exactly what—and who!—his caller was referring to. Dale's heart skipped a beat. Was this call destined to reveal Dale's refusals to his entire listening audience? "I see," he replied calmly, despite the fist of anxiety that had suddenly seized his gut. "Has this turned out to be a problem for you or the school?"

"Well, not a problem exactly. But the student council voted to invite him to speak and everyone was real excited about it because we really thought he'd do it, and it's just real disappointing."

"I see," Dale acknowledged with feigned composure. "And why is that?"

"Because everybody really loves him and we thought he'd want to speak to us."

"Are you taking his turndown personally? That is to say, do you think he turned you down because he doesn't love you or your school?"

David thought this over briefly. "Well, I'm not sure." David and the students of Bret Harte High had no way of knowing that theirs had been one of twenty-seven invitations.

"What reason did he give you for turning down your invitation?" Dale asked, still remaining outwardly unruffled, but churning anxiously inside.

"He said he was too busy."

"Uh-huh. Have you considered that maybe he declined your invitation not because he doesn't love you, but because his schedule does not, in fact, permit it at this time?"

David sighed. "Yeah. But that doesn't really do it for me."

"By that you mean it doesn't leave you feeling satisfied."

"Yeah."

"Well, sometimes the choices other people make in the context of their lives are disappointing and confounding to us when we want those lives to somehow interface with our own. But we have to respect their choices."

"So you're saying this isn't a scheduling problem, but a choice? That means he didn't want to speak to us after all."

For a youngster, Dale thought, David was unexpectedly sharp. "Well, that's not exactly what I meant," he replied. "But I can see how you might have misinterpreted it." Externally, Dale was managing to maintain a facade of seamless serenity. Internally, he was cursing himself, cursing his choices, cursing his disfigurement, cursing the situation. Whatever excuse he gave for turning down a speaking invitation, Dale knew that everyone whose invitation he had declined would also hear the excuse . . . and possibly see through it. "Actually, I was referring to the fact that how someone schedules his life is a choice," he concluded, hoping to keep the focus on scheduling and deflect further questioning.

"Hmmm," David replied, thoughtfully. "Well, I thought I'd try to make a personal plea to him. Do you think that would help?"

Dale's heart sank. He had hoped his previous response would dig him out of the hole he was in. But David's latest question just dug him in deeper. To discourage David from making such a "personal plea" would deny the philosophy Dale had espoused so many times on the show—the value and efficacy of direct interaction and communication. But to encourage David to make the feared plea would possibly invite that very interaction and communication right there on the air for all to hear! What was Dale to be—high-minded or hypocritical? He took a deep breath.

"I've always been a proponent of direct interaction and communication. Otherwise, how would anyone know what you want?" Having encouraged the personal plea, he braced against the painful consequence of having to answer a direct query from David.

David thought briefly about Dale's reply. "Yeah. That sounds about right." Despite the obvious opening, David felt it unnecessary to be more explicit and ask the DJ directly to speak before the students of Bret Harte High. For some reason, he felt Dale had received the message as loudly and clearly as he had intended it. "Well, thanks, Dale. I really appreciate your help."

Dale was stunned that his caller was already thanking him, obviously ready to say goodbye. That meant that Dale was, at least in the most immediate respect, off the hook. However, in his heart, he knew he was more securely hooked than ever—not because of any pressure David had brought to bear, but because of the pressure his own sense of integrity and compassion was bringing to bear. He had indeed received the message. "You're welcome, David," Dale replied. "I trust everything will work out for you."

"Thanks. I hope so. I'll talk to you later."

"Bye-bye." Dale disconnected the call. "This is Dale Greene on

The Brink of Tomorrow. I'll be back after this commercial break."

The call with David had been relatively short, so Bobby was expecting Dale to take another call and was unprepared to go to commercial. It took him only a second to make the adjustment and he got the spot on the air without delay, but he knew the call had upset his disfigured friend. He engaged his intercom.

"You okay in there, buddy?"

Dale sighed and pressed his intercom switch. "Yeah, I guess."

In fact, he was not okay. It was happening again. The invitation to public exposure, the decision to turn it down, the pressure from his listeners, the gut-wrenching agony. The old Yogi Berra pleonasm, *deja vu all over again*, rang in Dale's ear.

During the break Dale scrutinized his queue for caller descriptions which might betoken anyone disgruntled over a declined invitation. He didn't want another confrontation like the one he had had with David, mild though it had turned out to be. Not everyone, Dale knew, would be so pleasant or discreet as David had been.

At the moment, the queue included Eileen, who thought her boyfriend had given her gonorrhea; Julie, who was frigid and losing her husband; Gary, whose little brother was becoming malicious; Sheila, who was afraid she was dying; Dana, who was molested by her stepfather; and Fern, whose boyfriend didn't want her to have an abortion.

They all looked safe, and he breathed a sigh of relief. Had he been this vigilant—this suspicious—a few minutes earlier, he might have avoided being blindsided by David. Of course, the downside of suspicion, he discovered, was the unaccustomed gnaw of guilt. That's what dominated his awareness for the duration of the commercial break.

Chapter 13

"We're back," Dale announced when the commercial break ended. "You're tuned to WWKW, FM 102.4, and this is The Brink of Tomorrow with Dale Greene." Still troubled by his conversation with David, he made a point of modulating his delivery to conceal his anxiety. "My next caller is Dana. She's thirty-three and says she was molested by her stepfather." He connected the call. "Hi, Dana, this is Dale Greene and you're on The Brink of Tomorrow."

"Hi, Dale." Dana's voice had a weary, though not unpleasant, quality to it.

"Did I get that right, Dana, you're thirty-three?"

"Yeah."

"So I'm guessing that this probably happened a number of years ago?"

"Yeah. It started when I was fourteen."

"Hmm . . . nineteen years ago. And you're still troubled by it?"

"Uh-huh. It haunts me daily."

"I understand. Would you care to tell me about it?"

Dana took a deep breath and released it with a sigh. "When I was eleven, my mom remarried. He was very charming and very good-looking and we got along really well. Of course, at eleven, I was still just a kid, so there wasn't anything going on at that time. But as I started to mature and fill out, he started noticing. And the more he noticed, the more attention he paid to me. And . . . I loved it. My real father never had much time for me, so getting all this attention from the new father figure in my life was really wonderful. And he started telling me how beautiful I was and how sexy I was and I . . . I ate it up. And one night my mom was out with her bridge club or something and my stepfather and I were watching a movie on TV and we were sitting right next to each other and he had his arm around me—like any loving father would—and . . . I don't know what happened, but suddenly we were kissing. And it felt really good. I wasn't creeped out or anything because he was really good-looking and a really good kisser and I was a really horny fourteen-year-old girl. So, one thing led to another and . . . we had sex." She stopped to give Dale a chance to react.

"I see," Dale acknowledged evenly, his concerns about the conversation with David fading as this new challenge drew him in. "Did he force himself on you?"

"No. I let him do it. In fact, I think I kind of encouraged him a little. I didn't really know what I was doing—sexually—but I was a willing participant. I knew it was wrong, I knew he was my mother's husband and I shouldn't be doing it, but he made me feel so sexy and desirable. I realize now that, at that age, it was just my hormones running rampant." She heaved a deep and troubled sigh.

"So, do I understand you to say that this happened more than once?"

"Yeah. We did it every week—when my mom was at her bridge club—till I was fifteen. But she came home early one night and found us together and that was it. She kicked him out—threatened to call the police on him—and divorced him. And we moved to another state."

"Ah. Was she angry with you about it?"

"No. She thought he had raped me and I was too scared to tell her the truth. He tried to tell her that I'd gone along with it, but she didn't believe him. I mean, who would? Isn't that what any guy would say to get himself off the hook?"

"Very possibly," Dale conceded. "So she thought you were an innocent victim in all this."

"Yeah."

"Did you ever tell her the truth?"

Again, Dana heaved a heavy, troubled sigh. "No. She died before I had a chance—cancer. But I don't know that I ever would have. It might have killed her sooner."

"I see. Have you heard from him or has he been in your life in any way since then?"

"No. I never saw him again after that."

"Okay." Dale gave Dana's lament a moment of thought. "Tell me, Dana, are you married? Do you have kids?"

"I'm married with two girls."

"How's your relationship with your husband?"

"It's good."

"Does he know about this?"

"No."

"Do you think it affects your relationship with your husband? Or your girls?"

"I dunno. I mean, worrying about it every day probably doesn't help, but it doesn't stop me from having sex with him or anything."

"Okay, fair enough," Dale said. "Well, let's see if we can't narrow this down some. What specifically about this event troubles you?"

"Well . . . everything! I let this grown man have sex with me when I was underage—even encouraged it! I betrayed my mother by having sex with her *husband*. How sick is that?! It *all* troubles me."

Seeing that Dana was becoming overwrought and wanting to soothe her, Dale responded especially gently. "I see. Have you tried conventional therapy to deal with this?"

"Oh yeah. I've been to half a dozen shrinks. But it hasn't done any good. I still think about it every day and kick myself for being so stupid. I mean, not only did I do it, I broke up my mother's marriage to him by not telling her the truth. I feel like a real shit."

"I appreciate how you feel about this, Dana, but I have to ask you to remember that this is family radio and not to use four-letter words."

"Oh, God, I'm sorry! Oh, I'm . . . I'm really sorry. See, that's what kind of person I am. I really . . . ." She sighed again. "I'm really sorry."

"It's okay, dear," Dale said softly, the troublesome call from David by now completely forgotten. "I forgive you."

"But I really am sorry," Dana persisted.

"I know you are, I truly do. And it's important to me that you realize that I've forgiven you, and that you forgive *yourself*, and allow yourself to recognize this as a lesson *learned* and move past it. Okay? Will you do that?"

Dale heard Dana inhale sharply. "Okay," she pledged, then exhaled.

"Good. Now I have to ask you some questions about how you are today. Okay?"

"Okay."

"Did he hurt you in any way that left any physical scars or

disabilities?"

"No. Not at all."

"Good. And you say you've never heard from him since your mother divorced him and you moved away?"

"Right."

"So there are presently absolutely no physical signs of him in your life."

"That's right."

"And you've been able to do everything in your life that you wanted to do: Marry the man you wanted to marry, have your kids, do the kind of work you wanted to do. Is that correct?"

"Yeah."

"All right, good. Now it's very important that you recognize the following facts: Right now, in present time, there is absolutely nothing in your life that physically connects you with him or forces you to deal with him. He's not calling you or otherwise talking to you; you have no physical scars or dysfunction to remind you of him; he doesn't have you locked up in some basement; he's not forcing himself on you; he's not physically abusing you. He's really physically completely out of your life. Right?"

"Right."

"All right. Now, in what I'm about to say, I want you to understand that I'm in *no* way minimizing the trauma that this experience represents for you, but it's important for you to understand this point."

"Okay."

"The *only* connection you have to him is . . . *in your mind.*" Dale said these last three words very gently, so as to not to appear accusatory or judgmental. He paused to allow them to sink in. "By 'mind,'" he continued, "I don't mean to limit the concept to 'intellectuality.' I really mean all things non-physical: your emotions, your thinking, your memory. So everything about that time in your life that's presently affecting you is entirely in your mind and nowhere else. Do you see that?"

"Hmm . . . yeah," Dana replied thoughtfully.

"Good. So then the solution to this problem is actually quite simple. All you have to do is . . . *change your mind.*"

At first, there was only silence on the other end of the line as Dana worked to see how this overly simplistic solution could possibly resolve what she considered to be a massively tangled problem. "Change my mind?" she finally squawked.

"Yep."

Dana heaved a sigh as she gave the proposition several more seconds of thought. "Okaaaaaay," she drawled at last. "But that seems too simple. I mean, all the shrinks I've gone to seemed to think it would take a lot of work."

"Well, it *could* take a lot of work, if you aren't ready and willing to change your mind. But it doesn't have to. I liken emotional problems to a big barrel of rotten, stinking fish. In general, in order to rid the barrel of the stink, shrinks get their patients to sort through and examine each fish. But the fish don't tell you anything. The most elegant solution is to just chuck the whole barrel. Do you follow?"

"I understand what you're saying, but . . . it still sounds too simple."

"I know it sounds that way. But what else is there? There's nothing *physical* to change. So the only thing *left* to change is your mind. In fact, that's all the shrinks and therapists are trying to get you to do, except that most of them don't see the simple truth of this, so most don't tell you that.

"But how can I change my mind? It *happened*. The memory is there!"

"You can change your mind about how you *feel* about it. The way you feel about it is based on how you look at it—your judgment of it—and *that* you can change."

"Hmmm." Again, Dana drew a deep breath and let it out. "Okay, so how do I do that?"

"Well, the first thing we need to do is address your willingness to change your mind about this. You know, some people really like their problems and don't really want to get rid of them. Or maybe they don't *like* them, exactly, but they wouldn't know what they would do without them. Going to therapy and talking to a shrink or a group gives them something to do—a feeling of purpose. So they don't really want to get rid of the problem and through all their therapy they never really change their mind about it. So my first question to you is: Are you willing to not have this problem anymore?"

Not wanting to give a glib answer to something this critical, Dana pondered the question for several seconds. "I think I am," she replied at length, still mulling the matter. "Yes, of course I am!" she confirmed after several more seconds. "I hate it! I want to be free of it! Definitely, I'm willing to not have it anymore!"

"Excellent!" Dale commended. "So let's start by exploring the practical rationale for changing your mind about this, then we'll get into the metaphysical rationale."

"Okay," Dana agreed.

"Now, we've already established that your intimacy with your stepfather didn't leave any physical effects on you. Did it have any other lasting effects on you, or anyone else?"

"It broke up my mother's marriage. *That* was a lasting effect."

"Okay, let's analyze this. Why do you think your mother divorced your stepfather?"

"Because she thought he had raped me."

"Do you think she would have stayed with him if she knew he was merely *cheating* on her—with her own daughter?"

This stumped Dana. "Hmmm. Probably not. But I still caused him to cheat on her, so I'm still responsible for breaking up the marriage!"

"Okay, well let's look at that. You said he was a willing participant in it, right?"

"Yeah."

"Then his cheating on her was *his* doing, too."

"But he couldn't have done it without me."

"That's not exactly true. He could have done it with someone else. Wouldn't that have just as effectively broken them up?"

"I s'pose."

"Think of it this way. He chose to cheat on your mother. That, all by itself, is a divorcible offense, irrespective of who he cheated with. Right?"

"Right," Dana said, the light beginning to dawn.

"And with you, couldn't he have prevented it all by himself, simply by controlling his urges? Don't forget, he was the adult. He was the one with the experience and—supposedly—the maturity to understand the consequences of what he was doing, and to prevent it from happening. All he had to do was not kiss you back. It would have been very easy for him to do that. But he didn't. Right?"

"Right."

"So you're not responsible for breaking up your mother's marriage."

"But I was *partly* responsible. Wasn't I?"

"Well, it's important to make the distinction between what you *did* and the consequences that ensued. You're responsible for having sex with him and he's responsible for having sex with you. But *your* participation in that was not responsible for breaking up your mother's marriage. *His* participation was responsible for that, because it was *his* marriage and he could have prevented it, all by himself."

"Oh, I see." The intake of breath and the sigh that followed told Dale that she had released some of her trauma. "But I'm to blame for having sex with him."

"Well, 'blame' is judgmental and we're not doing that here. You're *responsible* for having sex with him because you chose to do it, but you're not to *blame* for it. This is a metaphysical distinction, so we might as well get into the metaphysical rationale. Do you have any idea why you might not have changed your mind about this already?"

Dana gave this a few moments of thought. "No."

"Okay, this is quite simple, too. It boils down to one thing: judgment. In your description of the event—and your expression about what type of person you are—you made several judgments. By holding onto those judgments, you're preventing yourself from releasing the trauma. You need to release those judgments to put this problem behind you."

"What judgments are you talking about?"

"Well, you indicated that you believe there was something 'wrong' with what you did with your stepfather. And two decades after it happened, you're still kicking yourself for being—to use *your* words—'so stupid.' Those are judgments."

"Oh!"

"But what if there *wasn't* anything 'wrong' with what you did? What if it *wasn't* stupid?"

"Wait a minute, wait a minute! Go back. Are you saying it isn't—or shouldn't be—against the law for adults to have sex with kids?!"

"No, no! I'm not saying that at all. First of all, I'm not commenting on *his* act of having sex with you. I'm commenting on *your* act of having sex with him and I'm saying it wasn't 'wrong' for *you* to have done that. *Unwise* maybe, in retrospect, but not 'wrong.' I'm emphasizing that *you* didn't do anything 'wrong' by having sex with him. Second, in our society, we *have* to have laws against adults having sex with minors because there are plenty of people who act without restraint on the darkest sides of their nature, and I'm in no way suggesting we repeal those laws or anything like that. But our society isn't structured on metaphysical principles, and in order to understand the metaphysical rationale, you have to put the legal considerations aside for a moment. I'm just saying the legal considerations aren't part of the *spiritual* underpinnings of our lives."

"Oh, okay."

"So, what if your intimacy with your stepfather *wasn't* stupid? What if it was exactly what was *supposed* to happen? That is, what if your soul had created that scenario for you for some purpose of spiritual growth? And your only 'mistake' was listening to someone—maybe your own ego—which led you to believe it was 'wrong' or 'bad' and wasn't supposed to happen; or was supposed to happen differently?

"My ego?" Dana queried, suddenly lost.

"All right, I guess I need to explain that a little. To begin with, disregard whatever you might have read about Freud's concept of ego. That's not the ego I'm talking about. The ego I'm talking about is a mental construct that's recognized in metaphysics. The job of the ego is to keep you focused in physical reality, so you can live your physical life. Without your ego, you—your soul—would pop right out of your body and zip back to the spirit realm. So you need your ego. Unfortunately, the ego in most people has gotten too big for its britches and often runs—and *ruins*—our lives. It's responsible for all the negative things in our lives—judgment, negative emotions, unwarranted fears, unkindness, bigotry, self-doubt, et cetera. Okay?"

"Okay."

"Your soul, of course, is the spiritual part of you and it's chosen to incarnate this lifetime in order to experience and learn certain things. Some people call this your karmic path."

"Karmic path . . . all right."

"So what if your intimacy with your stepfather was *supposed* to happen? What if it was part of your karmic path? What if you've been kicking yourself all these years for doing something that you *needed* to do in order to fulfill your karmic path—to experience something or learn some lesson your soul wanted to experience or learn? Would that put a different spin on it?"

Dana took a moment to consider this. "So . . . you're saying having sex with my stepfather was like . . . *fate* or something?"

"Well, I wouldn't use the word 'fate' to describe it. 'Fate' connotes something outside yourself predetermining the course of your life, and I believe we determine the course of our lives ourselves, at a higher level of consciousness. This event would be something that would have been chosen by *you*—your soul—not anything outside of you. So it doesn't qualify as 'fate.' But, yes, I'm suggesting it was something you chose to do, at a level of consciousness you aren't normally aware of."

Presented with this novel idea, Dana released another sigh. "I see," she answered thoughtfully. "So I need to stop judging what I did?"

"That would be *my* recommendation. The fact of the matter is, the soul actually relishes all those experiences the ego judges. It's important to realize that the objective of the soul in incarnating into physical reality is to explore all aspects of itself, and that includes the negative end of the spectrum—its dark side—as well as the positive end of it. The negative energies don't manifest in the non-physical realms, so the examination of the negative energies can't be done in those realms, it can only be done in physical reality. So we incarnate into physical reality, in part, to examine the negative energies. And we typically incarnate hundreds of times in order to examine—in great detail—the full spectrum of both positive and negative energies. That means that, in past lives, most of us have all done it all—stolen, raped, killed, manipulated, betrayed . . . been raped, been killed, been manipulated, been betrayed. You name it, we've done it all, had it all done to us, and watched others do it. Since we're here to experience all these things, it just makes no sense to then judge and punish ourselves for doing what we're here to do. As I said, part of what we're here to do is to learn certain lessons. Sometimes those lessons teach us what we don't like, what kinds of experiences we don't enjoy and don't wish to repeat. Obviously, it doesn't make sense to judge and punish ourselves for having done things that have taught us those lessons. So judging our negative acts doesn't serve us. Does that make sense?"

"Yeah."

"Good. Also, we may choose or allow a negative event to happen to us in order to balance karmic energy. Balance is one thing the universe seeks and karma is the urge to balance the energies. That is, if you do something negative to someone, then spiritually you have an urge to reverse the roles and balance the energies. For example, after we have chosen to impose our will on someone in one lifetime, we may then seek to balance that act in another lifetime in which the roles are reversed. In this way, as a soul examining all things, if you had previously been an older man who had illicit sex with a young girl, you might want to know what it feels like to be that young girl, to be in her shoes, to feel what she felt. So you would put yourself in her role in this lifetime. I'm not saying this is what you did, but this is the kind of thing the soul does to learn and experience and balance the energies. And again, it just makes no sense to judge yourself for doing what you're here to do.

"Finally, sometimes we do things just to be of service to another. You don't know what would have happened between your mother and your stepfather. For all you know, he was destined to flip out and hurt her, or even kill her—or vice versa. Your soul has access to all kinds of information that you don't have access to, and maybe it knew something tragic like that could happen and guided you to have sex with him to prevent it. You just don't know. So you really need to just trust that what you did was *exactly* what you needed to do to be of service to yourself and everyone else. See what I mean?"

"Yeah!" The tone of Dana's voice was now brighter, more spirited.

"Good. So let me ask you this: Have you learned all the lessons from this experience that were in it to learn?"

"Oh, yes!"

"Good. And if you had it to do over, would you do the same thing?"

"No way!"

"Excellent. Then you've gotten everything out of it that was there to be gotten. Continuing to judge and punish yourself for it is just a waste of time and energy, and you can stop doing it. Okay?"

Dale heard Dana heave a long healing sigh. "Yeah," she said breathily, "I think I do. She drew another breath and released it. "Wow. This is really incredible. When I called, I was at the end of my rope. I . . . I didn't think anyone could help me, since none of the shrinks had been able to help. But I think this is finally going to do the trick. In fact, I know it is." She released another healing breath. "Thank you *so* much. This is really incredible. I guess I already said that, but it really is! Thank you!"

Dale chuckled lightly to himself. "You're quite welcome, my dear. I'm delighted to be of service. Please feel free to keep in touch and let me know how you're doing."

"I will, I promise. Oh, I don't want to say goodbye! This has been so incredible! But I know you have other callers. I really appreciate you spending so much time with me."

"That's what I'm here for, dear."

Again Dana released a cleansing breath with a sigh. "Thanks again, Dale. I love you so much."

"Thank you, Dana. I love you, too. Good night," he concluded softly.

"Bye."

Dale disconnected the call and announced a commercial break.

With the success of his conversation with Dana, Dale's concerns about being confronted about speaking invitations had completely evaporated. After the commercial break ended, he took calls for the next two hours and thirteen minutes without incident.

By 11:51, with time for just one more quick call, Dale was beginning to feel a bit cocky. Thinking he had dodged a bullet and forgetting that cockiness bred carelessness—and sometimes disaster— he looked over the callers remaining on his list. There were Ann, who needed eyeglasses for her three-year-old; Dennis, who was stuck in a dead-end job; Terence, whose father was an alcoholic; Carl, whose teenage son was a drug addict; Vicky, who felt manipulated by her mother-in-law; and Nancy, who was feeling depressed.

Hoping for a topic he could dispatch quickly and easily, Dale selected Nancy. "My next caller is Nancy; she's twenty-seven, and she says she's feeling depressed." He pressed the button which put the call on the air. "Hi, Nancy, this is Dale Greene and you're on The Brink of Tomorrow."

"Hi, Dale."

"I won't ask you how you are because it says you're feeling depressed. What are you depressed about?"

"I'm depressed because you turned down our invitation to speak at our fundraising banquet." There was the subtlest hint of resentment in Nancy's voice.

Oh, no! Here we go again, Dale thought, his core fear seizing him again. He took several deep breaths while trying to think of a response. "I see," he replied at length, again calm on the outside, turbulent on the inside. "Well, I'm very sorry to have disappointed you. That certainly wasn't my intention. Did you hear what I told—" he had to think for a moment to recall the name "—*David*, at the top of the show?"

"I guess you turned *him* down, too!" Nancy speculated. She didn't mean it to sound accusatory, it just came out that way. Likewise, Dale hadn't meant to reveal that David's "local celebrity" had been himself, but it suddenly struck him that he had, and he winced in anticipation of the self-inflicted pain to come.

"What I was referring to," Dale corrected, trying his best to repair the damage, "was the fact that these things are sometimes very difficult to schedule. So you shouldn't take it personally."

"Okay, you're right," Nancy allowed. "But it seems to me like this kind of thing is important enough to find a way to schedule it."

"Who do you represent, Nancy?"

"The Springfield Community Mental Health Center. We're a non-profit organization; we service hundreds of mentally ill, and we depend on the community for financial support." Having uttered these words many times in the course of her work, she had become very polished, very articulate in her delivery of them. "I know you're not obligated to help us, but I know how passionate you are about helping people—I listen to you all the time—and as the Archers Man of the Year, I know you'd make a big impression on potential contributors." She paused briefly, as though awaiting an acknowledgement. Getting none, she continued, "It's not like we're asking you to endorse a product or anything, we're only asking you to help raise funds for a charitable organization." She paused again, then added, "I just felt like you turned us down without even talking to us."

Dale drew a deep breath and let it out slowly. He knew reacting defensively to Nancy's query would only paint him in a hypocritical light, and though a *mea culpa* would reveal more than he really wanted to reveal, he knew it was the only way to avoid the semblance of hypocrisy. "Well . . . as embarrassing as it is for me to admit, I did turn you down without even talking to you. The fact is that I received a great many invitations to appear on talk shows and endorse products, as well as to speak at various—" not wanting to give away the fact that he had turned down both schools and charitable organizations, he searched for a more generic term "—venues. I wasn't at all interested in the talk shows or product endorsements and told my staff just to turn them down. I guess the other venues also got turned down without due consideration. I apologize for that. It would have been more considerate of me to at least talk to you."

"Does this mean you'll speak at our fundraiser?" Nancy queried with animated enthusiasm.

"I can't make any promises at this time, except to say that I'll review your invitation. I agree that your work is important—the work of your organization, that is—well, *your* work, too, but I was referring to the Center—"

"I know what you meant."

"—Thank you. Whatever I do, I have to take into account my other obligations."

"I know, and I know it might take a while to schedule it. But I hope you'll consider it." By this time, Nancy was sounding quite hopeful, her tone having changed from subtly indignant to subtly supplicant.

"I'll definitely consider it. That I *can* promise."

"Oh, thank you so much. On behalf of the Springfield Community Mental Health Center, thank you."

"You're welcome, Nancy." Nancy's effusive gratitude made it sound as though Dale had agreed to speak, and he contemplated reiterating the limitations of his promise, just so there would be no misunderstanding. But that, he thought, might sound as though he were less than enthusiastic about helping their fundraising efforts when he was not—when he was only less than enthusiastic about appearing in public. "Thanks for calling," he concluded.

"Thank *you*. Bye-bye."

"Goodnight." Dale disconnected the call and began his wrap-up. "Well, that's all we have time for tonight. You're tuned to WWKW, FM 102.4; it's The Brink of Tomorrow and I'm Dale Greene, poised to step off into the void. As always, thank you all for letting *me* share with *you* my understanding of this odd thing we call life. If you're having trouble with some aspect of *your* life and you'd like some help with it, call me on The Brink of Tomorrow. In the meantime, stay tuned for the Midnight Express with Stan Furness coming up in just a few minutes. This is Dale Greene; I love you all, and I'll see you again on The Brink of Tomorrow."

He closed his announce mic as Bobby rolled the top-of-the-hour commercials and prepared to hand the signal off to station headquarters. Getting a look from Bobby, Dale opened his intercom. "Well, the fat's in the fire again."

Understanding fully, Bobby raised his eyebrows and twisted his mouth.

Chapter 14

Having heard the show, Wil, Paul and Shel were waiting for Dale when he wheeled into the den from the broadcast suite. Their young friend and employer looked as frustrated as they had ever seen him and Wil wondered why it was that someone who carried such a burden to begin with, who harbored ill will for no one, and who did so much good for his fellows would be faced with such additional challenges.

"I hate it, I hate it, I hate it!" Dale bellowed, his resonant voice giving the complaint a thunderous power. Pitching the joystick of his wheelchair forward, he lurched across the room and jerked to a stop at the picture window where he stared out across the estate. Having seen him in the throes of frustration over his disfigurement as a youngster, the trio knew his current frustration was not with his admirers' demands for his services, but with his inability to provide those services, to make the personal appearances. More than anything, it was Dale's nature to want to be of service. They knew also that no amount of consoling would comfort him, that in time he would reach out and ask for their help, and that only then would there be any relief for him. So they sat quietly, said nothing, and let their dear friend stew.

Sure enough, after several moments, Dale slowly swiveled his chair and spoke. "So how much more trouble could we be in if we got Elliot Draupau back here to do these appearances?"

It was an unexpected question and the three advisors, as if on cue, raised their eyebrows in unison. Thinking over the ramifications of such a venture, they took some moments to formulate their answers. Paul was the first to speak.

"Legally, none," he said at last, somewhat cautiously. "Tactically, plenty. The challenges of the last time would be multiplied by . . . who knows how much."

"Right now," added Wil, "Elliot's pretty much in the dark about what happened last week. We were careful to keep him occupied during your show, so he's not a hundred percent sure whether Dale Greene is a real person or a fictional character. But—"

"—That would change if he were to do these personal appearances," Dale surmised, finishing Wil's thought.

Wil nodded. "I don't see how we could avoid it."

"So, let's say we do bring him back," Dale hypothesized. "What do we tell him about Dale Greene? Do we tell him he's disfigured?" He looked at the others for some response. Getting none, he added, "Or do we just say he's shy?" Although it might have been a viable explanation, the three other men knew Dale was being facetious and smiled appreciatively. In Wil, it also triggered a thought process that began to work in the back of his mind.

"I don't think he even needs to know that much," asserted Paul after a moment. "In fact, I'm not so sure he needs to know much of anything."

All eyes turned toward Paul.

"I think he's hungry enough," he continued, "even after that chunk o' change we dropped on him last week, that for the right price he'd do what he's told and make no bones about it."

"He'd have to be here for several months in order to fulfill all the speaking requests, and whatever else we wind up having him do," Wil challenged mildly. "How would we keep him from hearing the show and getting suspicious?"

Realizing his proposal was unsound after all, Paul replied, "We could put him up here at the estate, give him a luxury apartment, pay him a bundle, see to his every need, and—I don't know—bust his radio."

The four men laughed.

"What bitter irony," Dale observed with a smirk. "The guy who's playing the radio talk-show advisor can't even listen to his own show."

"Obviously, that's unrealistic," opined Wil, with a dry edge in his voice. "With the bundle we'd be paying him, he could buy another radio."

While it didn't match Paul's quip, this from Wil drew appreciative chortles.

"Whether he hears the show or not," Shel observed, now entertaining a serious thought, "he'd have to stay out of sight while it was on. If people get to know his face and he's out on the town during the show, they're going to know something's fishy."

"Good point," Wil acknowledged. "And it brings up a crucial question: How secluded can we keep him?"

"Maybe a better question is: How secluded do we *need* to keep him?" Paul corrected. "And how secluded is he willin' to be kept?"

"Oh, boy," Dale moaned, putting his mountainous head in his gnarled hands, anticipating trouble.

"The answer to the first question," Wil offered, "is that he would definitely have to be lodged on the estate, as Paul suggested, and he would definitely have to be in each night for the duration of the show. He could go out at other times, but he'd have to be escorted any time he's off the grounds. And we should minimize his exposure to the public—at most, take him out shopping for clothes, occasional meals, maybe a little sightseeing . . . .   What else would he have to go out for?"

The other three men thought, but had no answer.

"The answer to the second question," Wil went on, "is that we have all the activities he could possibly want right here on the estate. And if he wants something we don't have, we could more than likely import it. So, hopefully, his willingness to be kept secluded would be high, given sufficient financial compensation."

"If he's going to have access to the recreation pavilion," Dale added, "we'd also have to restrict his access to the subway so he couldn't stumble onto me during a show." Dale was referring to the underground tunnel to the broadcast suite, which occupied the basement of the recreation pavilion.

"We can put locks on all the doors that lead to that section of the subway," Paul suggested.

"We'd have to put some kind of a lock on the elevator in that building, too," warned Shel, remembering that the elevator provided access to the tunnel from the upper floors.

Shel didn't say much outside of his field of finance, Dale observed silently, but once in a while he came through with a crucial observation.

"I'm sure we can get a special key lock to replace the basement button on the elevator," Wil posited.

"What about mail and phone calls?" Dale asked. "Certainly, we can't isolate him from the other people in his life."

"No, that would be unconscionable," Wil replied. "But it would be preferable if his people didn't know exactly where he was."

"He can give them my brother-in-law's address in New York," Shel offered. "My brother-in-law can overnight any mail he receives for Elliot. It'll only arrive a day late."

"And for Elliot's phone we can use the eight hundred number we set up for the agencies to obscure the area code," added Paul.

Dale gestured with his hand to signal his agreement with the plan.

"What else do we need to consider?" Wil asked.

"Oh!" Dale exclaimed, thinking of something. "We probably ought to make the manor house off limits, too—except, say, by special invitation—so he can't come waltzing in here and discover me in my pajamas."

The other men chuckled. "Good point," Wil acknowledged. "Anything else?"

"What about women?" Shel wondered. "How's his appetite in that arena?"

"Unknown," was Wil's response. "But he told us he didn't have a girlfriend, and since it wouldn't do to have Dale Greene consorting with women of ill repute, he'd have to be willing to forgo the fairer sex while he's here."

"It'll only be for a few months," Paul observed. "Surely, we can pay him enough to make a little celibacy worth his while."

"Well, that would simplify things a bit," Dale commented with some relief.

"There's something that concerns me, though," Wil said thoughtfully. Everyone's attention focused on Wil. "What would keep him from revealing the secret after he leaves, say a year or two down the road?"

"Well, the contract will enjoin him from revealing the nature of the job, just like the last one," Paul explained.

"Yes, well, something bothered me about the last one," Wil confessed. "It may have enjoined him, but it didn't prevent him. I know there are no guarantees in this sort of thing—shy of physically locking him up—but that last one didn't even stipulate a penalty were he to reveal the secret."

"It's understood we'd sue him," Paul replied.

"For what? He doesn't have anything to lose," Wil challenged.

"True. We assume the hassle alone's enough to scare him into honorin' the terms of the contract."

"I know that's what you're counting on, but it doesn't take into account the vagaries of human nature; it doesn't have any muscle behind it; it's too theoretical and tenuous."

"But there wasn't that much at stake on that one," Paul reminded. "The worst he could do is reveal that he stood in for a DJ named Dale Greene. He didn't know any more than that and didn't have any motive to reveal what he knew."

"Well, this time is different," Wil countered. "This time Elliot will know more about everything. There's more to know and more to keep secret."

"What are you driving at?" asked Dale.

Wil hesitated before answering. "We might want to consider letting him know you're disfigured."

Dale was stunned. "You can't be serious," he challenged, the fear of judgment and ridicule that motivated his seclusion suddenly gripping his chest.

"Well, I think it's something to talk about," Wil gently urged, the thought that had been brewing in the back of his mind now coming to the front. "In fact, there's even a case to be made for introducing him to you."

Dale stiffened, more than a little alarmed, his heart racing. "You're suggesting I meet with him?!"

"Strangely enough, that could work to our advantage."

"How?!" The tone of Dale's voice was biting.

"Well, I'm not necessarily advocating this, mind you," Wil replied, taking note of Dale's tone, "but I think it bears examination. If you meet with him, then he understands why he's been hired; he feels included as a partner, in a sense, in an endeavor to provide a service to the community; and he cooperates on the basis of compassion, loyalty, and community service. If he doesn't meet you, particularly if he doesn't even know you're disfigured, then there's a mystery, a sense of exclusion, and less incentive to be loyal."

"Wouldn't just telling him I'm disfigured have the same effect as meeting me?"

"I think anything less than a face-to-face meeting would breed the same sort of mystery as saying nothing at all."

Dale knew Wil's position had some merit, but it was just too frightening and he looked for a compelling argument against it. "Okay, if he meets me, the mystery is gone, but the secret we're asking him to keep is huge and its revelation is disastrous!"

"But if he doesn't reveal the secret," Wil countered, "irrespective of what that secret is and how much he knows of it, then it doesn't matter and we've accomplished our mission. My only interest is in finding the most compelling incentive possible for Elliot to keep the secret, and if meeting you constitutes that most compelling incentive, then I think it's worth considering."

"All right, well, you're proposing that he meet me face to face. What if it freaks him out and he's unwilling to do the job no matter what we pay him? Then we're right back where we started from, only *then* we don't have *anyone* to take my place, because we will have already wasted the *one* person in the world that the community recognizes as *me*."

The point was compelling and it left everyone nonplussed.

"We don't know that he'd react that way," Wil countered after a moment.

"No, and we don't know that he wouldn't," Dale pressed.

Again, his argument was persuasive and the other three men were silenced by it.

"Was there any evidence of prejudice or intolerance in his background check?" Shel asked.

"Nothin' that's been documented," Paul replied.

"That only means that we don't know one way or the other," Dale pointed out. "Even Elliot may not know how he'd react to coming face to face with the likes of me."

The point was valid and the trio of advisors all nodded their consensus.

"All right, so, let's weigh the options we've discussed," Dale went on, his heartbeat beginning to return to normal. "We can most probably get his cooperation if I don't meet with him, but that cooperation may be compromised in the long run by the mystery factor. Or I can meet with him, eliminate the mystery factor, and risk not getting his cooperation at all."

"The unknown is Elliot," Paul observed.

"Well, I don't want this to sound paranoid or anything," Dale said, "but given the unknowns, I'd feel safer not meeting with him."

Despite the counter-arguments that had come before, the trio were forced to agree and nodded as much.

After a brief silence, Wil sighed. "Well, that decided, how can we put more muscle into the contract?"

"Trust fund," suggested Shel, looking to Paul for support.

Paul nodded thoughtfully. "In addition to his regular pay, we could open a hefty trust fund that would transfer to Elliot's control in, say, twenty years, if he keeps the secret, and revert if he reveals it." He looked around at the other men to find them listening intently. "And to keep him honest in the short term we could deposit his regular pay in an escrow account that releases to him when he finishes the work, as long as he hasn't revealed the secret. We'll be takin' care of all his livin' expenses while he's here, so he won't need his pay till he's done."

"That sounds feasible," Wil acknowledged. "Of course, we haven't actually decided on exactly what the secret is going to be."

"Why don't we tell him the truth?" Dale said, with a mischievous gleam in his eye. It confused everyone.

"I thought you were just arguing against that," Wil challenged, speaking for the other two advisors as well.

"Not exactly," Dale replied, enjoying the suspense he had just created. "The truth I'm suggesting we tell him is that my reason for not telling him the secret is the same as my reason for not telling my listeners the secret, which is the reason for hiring him in the first place. If he didn't have to keep the secret, we wouldn't have to hire him, and he wouldn't be getting the job."

It was a truth that seemed to solve a number of problems and Dale's advisors endorsed it with pleasant and somewhat animated surprise.

"That's pretty slick," Wil observed. "It makes the secret responsible for putting him to work. Keeping the secret equates to keeping the job."

The next day, Paul placed a call to Elliot. Leaving a message on his answering machine, he asked Elliot to call the toll-free number that had been established a month earlier for communication with talent agencies.

Picking up the message a few minutes after five and knowing it would be some two or three hours later in Springfield, Elliot decided to wait until the following day to return Paul's call. In fact, he was not all that eager to talk to the Greene Enterprises advisor.

Since returning home from Springfield, Elliot had had the extraordinary fortune to audition for a newly created recurring role on the daytime drama "Days of Our Lives." The call notifying him of the audition—which was scheduled for the day after his return from Springfield—had been waiting for him on his answering machine and he had nearly missed the opportunity for being late in responding. But luck had smiled on him and he made the audition just under the wire. By the time Paul left his message, Elliot had already been invited back three times—to audition for progressively higher levels of production executives—and was in competition with only two other actors for the part.

His reluctance to return Paul's call stemmed from a sense of confidence that his acting talents exceeded those of his two competitors, and a feeling that he was going to get the part.

It had been a heady week for Elliot. In the previous six months he had had only nine auditions and just two callbacks—one for a bit part in a TV Movie-of-the-Week which he did not get, and another for an even smaller part in an industrial film which he got, but which was ultimately cut from the finished film. This had naturally left him discouraged. But the soap audition, following upon the Dale Greene gig, had elevated his spirits into the clouds.

It was late morning on the West Coast, early afternoon in Springfield, when Elliot dialed the toll-free number which connected him with the Greene estate.

"Hi, Paul, it's Elliot," he said brightly when the attorney came on the line.

"Hey, Elliot! How's it goin'?" Paul asked cheerfully in his genteel

Southern drawl.

"Just fine, Paul," Elliot responded, himself slipping into a subtle Southern inflection. By some impulse of nature, he had done it in Springfield all the while he was in Paul's company. Paul had never noticed. "How's it goin' with you?"

"Fine, as well, Elliot, thank you."

"What can I do ya for?" Elliot asked.

"Well, I called to see if you're interested in doin' some more work for us out here."

"Same kind as last time?"

"Uh-huh, only a lot more of it."

"Hmmm," Elliot replied cautiously. He sincerely appreciated the invitation and did not want to offend Paul by turning it down too abruptly. "Well ... that sounds real good, except I'm up for a recurring role on 'Days of Our Lives'—a choice part for an unknown like myself—and I couldn't give you an answer till they decide. Can you wait a few days?"

Elliot's answer took Paul completely by surprise. That Elliot might not be available to stand in for Dale had never occurred to him—or any of them—and his heart sank. This could ruin everything. "How many days do you think it'll be?" Paul asked as though unaffected by Elliot's news.

"Well, it's hard to say for sure—it's out of my hands, you know—but they said probably two or three."

Remembering how desperate for work Elliot had been when they first met, Paul considered saying he could not wait that long—telling him, *this is a sure thing, but you have to act now to get it.* But he knew it was he, and Dale, who were desperate right now. And should the actor not get the soap role, he could hardly reverse himself two days later and hire Elliot after all, after issuing such an ultimatum. No, this required a more delicate touch.

"Oh, okay!" he said cheerfully. "I can wait that long." He knew waiting would be uncomfortable, what with the pressure Dale's listeners were bringing to bear, but he and his employer had little other choice. "But if you wouldn't mind callin' me at this number when you find out—one way or the other—I'd appreciate it."

"Oh, sure, no problem!" Elliot replied. That, he figured, he could agree to.

"Well, I appreciate that. Good luck with your . . . the part you're up for," Paul said, sounding utterly sincere. In fact, he wasn't at all sincere—he was scared—and he hated the pretense.

"Why, thank you, Paul. I appreciate that. I guess I'll talk to you in a few days."

"I'm lookin' forward to it. Bye, now."

"Bye-bye."

The two men hung up simultaneously, Elliot elated that he had an option were his soap part to fall through, Paul devastated that he was without options were Elliot's part to come through.

Paul was not eager to tell Dale the results of his conversation with Elliot; not because he feared his employer's wrath—even under such trying circumstances, Dale would not be imperious with his employees—but simply out of compassion and a desire not to disappoint. But tell him he did. Needless to say, Dale was both anxious and unhappy; not with Paul's failure to win Elliot's cooperation, but with the lousy luck of his draw.

For two days, maybe three—maybe more—Dale would have no choice but to wait it out. His fate rested in the hands of others—people he didn't even know, conducting their lives and businesses more than half a continent away with absolutely no knowledge of or regard for his problems. And he was utterly powerless to do anything short of felonious about it.

If Elliot didn't come through, Dale would be faced with turning down his speaking engagements for good and always, and disappointing many worthy fans, or showing his hideous face in public and ending all that was good about his life. Nothing had prepared him for this kind of challenge and a feeling of quiet terror took hold, churned his insides, and would not let go.

Chapter 15

"My next caller is John, he's thirty-three, and he says he's losing his friends."

Three days had passed since Paul had talked to Elliot and not a word had been heard from the Thespian. Now, well into the fourth show since then, the verdict was overdue.

Doing the show each night had turned out to be a mixed blessing. On one hand, advising his callers on their problems had helped Dale take his mind off of his own. On the other hand, the program was a naked reminder of his own vulnerability.

Before the Archers award, before all this mess, when he was happy, when doing the show each night was a sheer delight, Dale had had no concept of what it was like for other personal advisors to give advice while struggling with their own problems. Now, he had a very clear understanding of it and he did not like it. Like them, however, he had no choice but to conduct himself as though he had not a care in the world.

Fortunately, none of his callers had pressed him on the issue of personal appearances—or even mentioned them—but his anxiety and uncertainty about the immediate future remained ever close to the surface.

"Hi, John," he said, with much more enthusiasm than he felt, "this is Dale Greene and you're on The Brink of Tomorrow."

"Hi, Dale," John replied, sounding very forlorn, his voice ripe with resignation.

"Oh! You don't sound at all happy," Dale observed. "What's going on?"

"I seem to be losing all my friends."

"So I understand. What did you do to bring this about?"

"Well, it's kind of a long story, but the short version is that I'm an enabler, I'm in therapy and I listen to your show, and I've finally been taking some command of my life; I've been applying the Platinum

Principles and setting some boundaries so people don't walk all over me—which means I've been telling my friends 'no' a lot—and now they're not calling me." He heaved a big sigh. "In certain respects that's good, because most of them I don't want hanging around anymore anyway. But still, I see all these people that used to be my friends just kind of disappearing from my life and it's scaring me; I'm afraid I'm going to wind up with no friends at all. You know what I mean?"

"Absolutely," Dale replied, remembering the disappearance of his parents' friends as they watched his little four-year-old body transform from beautiful to hideous. "Are you married or do you have a significant other or anything like that?"

"Not anymore. My girlfriend was one of the people who disappeared from my life."

"I see. How do you feel about that?"

"Well, not too bad. She was a big part of the problem."

"Well, that's good . . . good that you don't feel too badly about it, not that she was part of the problem."

"I knew what you meant," John assured.

"I assume you knew that as soon as you started establishing your boundaries," Dale confirmed, "some of the people who had been your friends, if not all of them, would no longer find you useful and abandon you."

"Yeah."

"So what you're seeing you had kind of expected, right?"

"Yeahhhh," John said cautiously, bracing for a *So-what-are-you-complaining-about?* type of comment from Dale.

"Well, it's a difficult and very brave thing you're doing, John, and I respect you very much for doing it." In months past, Dale would have felt much more ardor and conviction in praising his callers. Now, in light of his own problems, those emotions were subdued. He knew intellectually what he needed to say, and he said it with the same enthusiastic inflection as before—in fact, he did it so well that no one could really tell the difference—but it didn't feel the same.

John drew a short breath and let it out. "Thanks."

"It sounds to me like you're on track, here, John; you just have to keep going on it. I don't know what else I can tell you."

"Well the problem is, it doesn't feel like I'm on track. It feels awful."

"Ah," Dale acknowledged, "and you'd like another perspective that will give you more confidence that you are on track."

"Right!"

"All right . . . ." Dale took a moment of thought. "Tell me, which would be worse—having no friends at all, or friends who use you?"

John sighed and thought about his answer. Finally, "I guess I'd rather have no friends at all. I'm really tired of people using me and I'm trying to get beyond that period in my life. And when you put it that way, even though it feels bad not to have friends, it feels worse to be used. So I guess I'd rather have no friends at all."

"Good! Does that feel better?"

While it felt better, it didn't give John the satisfaction he was looking for and he moaned, "Uhhhhh, sort of."

"But not totally," Dale confirmed.

"No."

"All right, tell me this—which is worse, the feeling of loneliness of being without friends, or the fear that you'll never have friends again?"

John again thought about his answer, taking several nervous breaths as he did. "The fear of never having friends again," he replied.

"That's what I thought. Are you doing anything to make friends?"

"Oh, sure! I'm going to mixers, striking up conversations in the supermarket, answering personals ads, things like that."

"You're working pretty hard at it," Dale confirmed.

"Oh, yeah! Doing everything I can think of."

"All right, are you ready for a suggestion?"

"Sure!"

"Stop."

There was a brief silence before John, puzzled by Dale's suggestion, repeated, "Stop?"

"Stop looking for friends."

"Stop looking for friends?"

"Yep. It's my guess that you're working *too* hard at it."

"But . . . I feel like if I don't look for new friends, I'll wind up with no one."

"I know," Dale acknowledged. "But that's just your fear, not an accurate prediction of the future. And I really don't think that'll happen. For one thing, you sound like a sensitive guy who would make a good friend to someone. So you ultimately won't have any trouble attracting friends. For another thing, it sounds to me like you're in the middle of a healing crisis. Do you know what a healing crisis is?"

"Yeah, it's where you're healing from something, but before you notice things getting better, they seem to be getting worse."

"Very clearly put! In physiological healing, such a crisis usually arises because, during the healing process, disease toxins are released by the tissues into the bloodstream to be cleansed from the body, and you feel lousy until they're all filtered out and eliminated. Although there's no *scientific* basis for it, it would appear that we go through similar healing crises when recovering from emotional traumas, too. You've just made a major change in yourself, you're recovering from chronic emotional trauma, and you have a lot of healing to do."

"That's true."

"If you fail to recognize your healing crisis for what it is, you're liable to misinterpret it as an indication that your remedy isn't working, when in fact it is. Then you stop applying the remedy, undermine the healing process, and wind up right back where you started."

"I don't wanna do *that*."

"No, of course not." Dale paused briefly, giving the lesson a moment to sink in. "In addition to that, this healing crisis will give you an opportunity to learn something about yourself that you wouldn't be able to learn if you started replacing your friends right away."

"Oh? What's that?" John was genuinely intrigued.

"That you don't need anyone else to complete you—that no one else *can* complete you—and that you're a whole being all by yourself. That's not to say it's not enriching to have friends and other forms of companionship. Surely, what we learn in life, both about others and about ourselves, comes from our relationships. But as a human being, you're utterly complete in and of yourself and you don't need others to be whole. All you need, really, is to realize that. So if you *are* without friends for a while, you'll have the opportunity to see that you're already complete. Does that make sense to you?"

"Yeah, it does, it makes a lot of sense." John sighed again as another question came to mind. "So let's say I take your suggestion and stop looking for new friends. How will I know when to start again?"

"You won't need to know. You'll start attracting friends automatically—unless you start worrying about it."

"Unless I start worrying about it?"

"Yeah. It seems to me you're in the process of evolving in some very significant ways: You're becoming aware of the existence of higher levels of integrity, you're aspiring to a higher level of integrity for yourself, and you want people in your life who are of like mind and heart. Now, we attract people into our lives to reflect back to us our own internal reality. So if you allow yourself to slip back into your previous mode of worrying about things, which is really a lower level of integrity, then you'll only attract the kind of people you used to attract."

"Oh!" John exclaimed, understanding clearly. He thought briefly before continuing. "So maybe I am on track, all right . . . ." But something still bothered him. "But if I can be on track and still feel bad, how am I gonna know when I'm on track and when I'm not?"

This was always a tough call, given the inscrutable nature of humanity's charter, and Dale blew through his teeth. "Well," he began, pausing to think before going on, "feeling bad is sometimes part of being on track. Ultimately, as I understand it anyway, you can never really be off track—metaphysically speaking—so you don't have to worry about it."

John groaned.

"I know," Dale responded, "that's not very satisfying."

"No, it doesn't tell me anything at all!" The frustration was evident in John's voice.

"Well, actually it does," Dale reassured. "It just seems like it doesn't because we like to break down and analyze every little detail of our lives, and this asks us to accept the whole of life as perfect."

"Yeah, and that doesn't sound very realistic. There must be some way of knowing whether you're on track or not."

"Sometimes there is and sometimes there isn't. Sometimes you just have to surrender to the process and let it take its course."

"Surrender? You mean, like, *give up?*" The idea of giving up was clearly loathsome to Dale's caller.

"Well, no, not exactly. 'Giving up' means 'ceasing to desire.' 'Surrendering' means continuing to desire, but allowing the process of achieving that desire to unfold by itself, possibly in wonderful ways you couldn't possibly imagine if you were completely in charge of it yourself. What you're surrendering is your fear—your fear that it won't turn out the way you want it to—and your impulse to control or manipulate things into going your way. You continue to desire and dream, but you release your worries that your dreams won't come true. I mean, let's face it: If you were to try to conceive and control all the processes of your life all by yourself, you could wind up inhibiting or limiting them for lack of imagination or perspective."

"Are you suggesting I'm not in control of the processes of my own life?"

"I'm suggesting there are other aspects of yourself which are also active in the creation of your life. For this to be meaningful, you pretty much have to accept the premise that we're basically spiritual beings with roots in a spiritual realm that we draw upon for strength, emotional nourishment, guidance, support, that sort of thing."

"I accept that."

"Good. Surrendering, then, means letting go of the fear and the impulse to control, and allowing the *details* of whatever it is you desire to be taken care of by those parts of yourself that are in the spiritual realm. You do that by knowing what you desire, not worrying about how you're going to get it, and acting on what excites you—provided you always act with integrity."

"According to the Platinum Principles, for instance," John confirmed.

"Right! Very good! Your excitement, by the way, is your indicator from the spiritual realm that you're on track."

"Oh!"

"And actually, there's another indicator that you're on track, and that's your fear."

"The *fear* is?" The tone of John's voice suggested incredulity.

"Yeah. I know this sounds strange, but fear turns out to be the same vibration as excitement. It's basically excitement that's been turned 'inside out' either by a traumatic experience in the past in which you misjudged something you were excited about and experienced an unpleasant surprise, or by simply failing to act on your excitement in some area of your life the first time it came up. When you surrender your fear, you're actually releasing your judgment, which allows the fear to convert back into excitement. So the guiding principle is: Do what you're excited to do and do what you're afraid to do—as long as you always act with integrity. In your case, what you're afraid to do is to cease to look for friends. So this principle would suggest you relax on that, and just let the process unfold by itself. If you do that and don't worry about the details of the process and don't let your doubts discourage you, then I believe it will automatically happen just as it needs to for you to experience life and evolve at exactly the right pace for you."

"Experience life and evolve. That doesn't necessarily mean you get what you want."

"No, it doesn't. But of course, life doesn't come with a guarantee."

"I know." John sounded a little disconsolate.

"On the other hand," Dale continued, "as you experience life and evolve, your ability to create your reality as you desire it also evolves."

"Oh! Yeah." At last, the tone of satisfaction that Dale liked to hear in his callers' voices was evident in John's.

"Ultimately, John," Dale concluded, "you might find yourself without friends for awhile. But if you do, and you've done everything we've talked about here, you can rest assured that that's exactly what you need for your own personal growth at this time, and you'll come out of it with the knowledge and experience you came here for. On the other hand, you might get excited by something, act on that excitement, and find yourself meeting all kinds of new people. It all boils down to doing what you're excited to do or what you're afraid to do, with integrity. And if you fight the process—worry about the details, give more credence to your doubts than your desires, and not surrender to it—you could wind up prolonging it, and the discomfort. I suggest you just get out of your own way and let it happen."

John took a few moments to allow Dale's words to settle in, breathing deeply all the while. "I can see there are no easy answers, but this helps quite a bit," he said at last, heaving a final, releasing sigh.

Dale, too, sighed. "Well, I'm glad," he acknowledged. "You're on a challenging but exciting journey, my friend. Keep in touch, and let me know how it turns out."

"Oh, sure! And thanks a lot. I really love you. Your shows have really helped me over the last year, and I really appreciate it."

"Well, thank you, John. I love you as well. Have a great evening."

"Thanks, I will. Goodnight."

"Goodnight." John hung up and Dale pushed the button which took the line off the air. On the far side of the glass wall, Bobby was signaling for a commercial. "You're tuned to WWKW, FM 102.4," Dale announced. "This is Dale Greene on The Brink of Tomorrow, back with more calls after these commercial messages."

That night, as he lay in bed, Dale recalled his advice to John and did his best to surrender the fear that had been vexing him so much in the last few days. He did achieve a measure of relaxation, and surrender on an intellectual level. But the thought that Elliot might not be available to stand in for him, that he might have to disappoint thousands of listeners, that the secret of his disfigurement might be found out, and that he might be ignominiously rejected by the entire community in one fell swoop was just too terrifying at this time. So he was unable to surrender on the *emotional* level, the only level where it would be effective.

Chapter 16

The next day, late in the afternoon, Elliot called. With disappointment clearly evident in his voice, he reported that he had been turned down for the soap role. Apparently, one of the production coordinators had commented that Elliot looked "an awful lot like John," referring to John Cochran, one of the leading men—something everyone else had overlooked—and Elliot had been nixed on the spot. But he was pleased to say he was free to talk about working for Paul and Wil.

Paul asked Elliot if his schedule would allow him to spend two or three months in Springfield, at a rate of a thousand dollars a day, whether he worked or not, and an extra fifteen hundred on the days he did work. That suited Elliot's schedule just fine and they made arrangements for Wil and Paul to meet with Elliot at the Bonaventure the following day to discuss the particulars of the job and sign the contract.

The next morning, Wil and Paul boarded a charter and jetted west to Los Angeles.

After describing the nature of the job, Wil and Paul laid out the terms of the contract between Greene Enterprises and Elliot Draupau: Again, the need for secrecy; a trust fund in the amount of $350,000 as reward for keeping the secret; an escrow account to hold Elliot's daily earnings until the work was complete; the virtual restriction to the estate, offset by the luxury accommodations and the availability of the numerous activities; admittance to the manor house by invitation only; the temporary celibacy; et cetera.

Elliot wanted to keep his apartment in North Hollywood and asked the two Greene representatives to pay his monthly rent and utilities so he would not have to pay them out of his earnings. For three months, the total expenditure for this would be less than five thousand dollars and Wil and Paul readily agreed.

Given the amount of money he would be earning in the three

months—close to $100,000, with all his living expenses taken care of—Elliot was delighted with the terms of the contract, despite the restrictions. Still, he asked if he could show it to his attorney before signing, to which Wil and Paul had no objection.

The next day, Elliot's attorney, Darryl Britlaw, a close personal friend, scrutinized the document. For the most part, the instrument seemed sound, and with Darryl's blessing, Elliot met again with Wil and Paul, signed contract in hand. Hearing from Paul later that afternoon and learning that Elliot had signed on, Dale, finally able to relax after weeks of anxiety over this whole affair, breathed a blustery sigh of relief. In a few months, his public would have had their fill of personal appearances, and he could return to the relative safety of just being a voice in the dark. In the meantime, his biggest challenge was deciding what he could say to school kids that would hold their interest, yet educate and enlighten them.

Elliot was given a week to put his affairs in order, during which time Wil and Paul returned to Springfield and began scheduling speaking appearances—one every week or two for the next three months—with the schools and charities which had made requests. In addition, Dale began drafting the first address Elliot would be delivering. Locks were put on the doors to the underground tunnel leading to the broadcast suite, the "basement" button in the recreation pavilion elevator was replaced by a key lock, and a seven-room apartment was prepared for Elliot in the luxury complex on the estate where Wil and Paul made their homes with their families.

At the appointed time, just as before, a limousine picked Elliot up at his North Hollywood apartment and delivered him to the Burbank airfield. There, he boarded a charter destined for somewhere halfway across the continent. Even more than before, Elliot considered this to be a great adventure and enjoyed the exhilaration of its launch. Again, he was met in Springfield by Wil and Paul, but this time he was taken to the extraordinary Greene estate.

After being shown his apartment, whose appointments were even more elegant than he had dreamed, Elliot was given the ambassador's tour of the estate—the ten-room apartments occupied by Wil and Paul and their families, the estate crews' apartment complex, the recreation pavilion, and the garage which housed the classic cars Dale's father had been so fond of. He was even invited to tour the manor house, though reminded of the terms of his contract regarding this structure. Dale sequestered himself in his bedroom all the while Elliot was in the house.

Elliot realized he had lucked his way into the lap of luxury, and whereas the size of his fee had been his initial incentive for accepting the restrictions stipulated in his contract, now his very surroundings were incentive enough. And the tennis, racquetball, swimming, batting—Elliot was eager to partake of them all.

For the first few days, while Dale finished drafting his text for the first address—to the students of Bret Harte High—Elliot had little to do but play and explore the more remote regions of the estate. In his exploration of the underground tunnels, the former locksmith noticed that subway access to the recreation pavilion was blocked by doors secured with shiny, freshly installed locks. Since none of the other doors in the tunnels even had locks, Elliot found this rather intriguing.

He also noticed, while sampling the indoor sports, a shiny new key lock in the recreation pavilion elevator where none of the other elevators on the estate had key locks. While it meant nothing to him at the time—nor even concerned him, for that matter—he did conclude that behind those doors was something Greene Enterprises did not want him to see.

A week before the first speaking engagement, Wil gave the completed address to Elliot to study. Elliot wasn't expected to memorize the speech, just be familiar enough with it to make a creditable presentation from the text.

Along with the address, Wil also gave Elliot an expanded version of the background material he had studied for the Archers event, in case he was asked to field questions about "himself." Wil further suggested the actor start listening to Dale's show each night. Although Elliot was instructed, as before, not to respond to any requests for advice when amongst the public, Dale and his advisors thought their emissary should get a taste of Dale's conversations with his callers, as well as the depth of the love and admiration his listeners held for him, so Elliot could flavor his performance accordingly.

"My first caller is Marilyn," Dale was heard to say that evening. "She's thirty-one, and she says she can't get her kids to behave without screaming at them." As the call went on the air, Elliot was glued to his radio, eager to get his first sampling of the mystery man he was portraying. "Hi, Marilyn, this is Dale Greene and you're on The Brink of Tomorrow."

"Hi, Dale, how are you?"

"As well as can be expected, Marilyn. And you?"

"I'm really sick of yelling and screaming at my kids."

"No doubt your kids are sick of it too." If there was one thing Dale was passionate about it was parenting. He had had some of the best, but he knew how much some children suffered at the hands of ignorant or abusive parents and found it quite disturbing. "How old are they?" he asked.

"Five, seven, and eight."

"Their genders?"

"Oh!" Marilyn said this as though she should have thought to mention it on her own. "The two older ones are boys and the youngest is a girl."

"Does the kids' father live with you?"

"No, we're divorced. But he has them every other weekend."

"How long have you been divorced?"

"A year . . . well, almost a year—about ten months."

"How were the kids before the divorce?"

Marilyn drew a breath, then grunted and mulled the question for a moment. "About the same, really. Maybe a little better."

"So would it be fair to say that you've always had a discipline problem with them?"

"Yeah, I guess. But their father was the disciplinarian. He did most of the yelling and I didn't have to do so much. But since it's been just me and them, I get so tired of screaming and yelling at them all the time. They don't seem to pay any attention."

"Well, all that screaming would tend to desensitize them to your authority. How did *your* parents get *you* to behave?"

This question also made her draw a breath, deeper this time, and more startled. After a couple of grunts and several seconds, she finally said, "Well, I guess they yelled at me a lot. I never thought about it much, but that seems right."

"Sounds like you tuned them out just like your kids tune you out."

There was an instant of silence. Then, "Yeah!" She said it as though it were a revelation. Dale found it somewhat odd that, with all the enlightened talk about parenting these days, including on The Brink of Tomorrow, Marilyn had not examined the parallels between the parenting she had received and that which she was giving.

"One of the frailties of our society," Dale offered, "is the way we pass our parenting practices on to our children. The problem is, most of us do it by inadvertent example, instead of by deliberate example and instruction. That is, we learn how to parent from the way our parents parented *us*. So if our parents' parenting skills were poor, *ours* will be too. And for anyone who tunes their parents out like you did and your kids are doing, the lessons become implanted subconsciously—which makes them extremely resistive to remediation."

"Phew!" Marilyn exclaimed. "What can you do about that?"

"The only way to break the cycle is to start paying attention to how we parent our children and make an effort to unlearn what we learned from *our* parents and learn new skills. Apparently, you're repeating the same—" Dale wanted to be delicate in his choice of words "—*patterns* your parents used on you. And if you don't make a conscious effort to break the cycle, your children will learn your style of parenting and do the same to their children—your grandchildren."

Marilyn groaned at the unpleasantness of the thought.

"Luckily, you've already started the relearning process by making this call," Dale added.

"Thank God."

"I can give you a few pointers to get you started, but if you're serious about this, and I sincerely hope you are, you'll have to supplement my suggestions with some reading or parenting classes. There are a lot of books and courses available on the subject and I urge you to look into some. All right?"

"All right. But I would like something to get me started."

"All right. Well, first of all, the objective of parenting isn't to get children to behave, it's to give them a foundation for emotional health and to show them how to be responsible adults. If you do that, then acceptable behavior is automatic. If your only interest is in getting them to behave, you only wind up controlling them, which means they only learn how to control *others*. That's what bullies do. So they grow up neither emotionally healthy, nor responsible. Does that make sense?"

"Yeah. But I can't very well just let them go around screaming and yelling and tearing up the house!"

"Well, now, don't forget, they've learned the screaming and yelling from you and your husband, since that's how you speak to them."

"Oh!" This was the first time Marilyn had seen this connection.

"So you can't very well blame them for that."

"Mmmm."

"So the first thing you have to do is stop screaming and yelling at them. It may take a while for them to notice the difference and pick up on the new example—and I mean it may take months—but they'll eventually get it."

Dale heard Marilyn heave a sigh of exasperation.

"I know," he responded. "Now you're imagining that without screaming and yelling at them, they'll be running completely wild."

"Well, yeah!"

"Well, there's something you can do that's a lot more effective than screaming and yelling."

"What?!"

"Do your kids know the rules of the house?"

Having never even conceived her household to have rules, exactly, Dale's question took Marilyn quite by surprise and she was unable to respond.

"Do *you* know the rules of the house?" he asked, picking up on the meaning of her silence.

"Well, I know when they do something wrong."

"Uh-huh . . . . Would you do me a favor?"

"What?"

"Quit thinking in terms of right and wrong."

"That's what you always say. And I know what you mean for adults, but I don't see how it applies to children."

"Well, it's not really any different."

"Then I don't understand. You can't just chuck right and wrong;

you have to draw the line somewhere, otherwise they'll tear the place apart."

"That's absolutely correct. But I'm suggesting that right and wrong are not that line."

Marilyn heaved another exasperated sigh. "Okay then, what's the alternative? What should I use instead?"

Dale considered cautioning her against "shoulds," but he didn't want to stray too far from the subject.

"Try thinking in terms of respect and responsibility. Respect for other people and their property, and responsibility in one's actions and relationships."

"Oh!" She had not expected such a practical answer.

"If you do that, you can focus on what's really meaningful and avoid a lot of arbitrary restrictions that are just meant to control. Can you do that?"

Realizing it was a challenging proposition, Marilyn hesitated before finally answering, "I think so."

"Good. Now, if neither you nor your kids know the rules of the house and you're just reacting every time they do something you don't like, they don't get any sense of consistency in your discipline, so they have no way of knowing what behavior will be acceptable and what won't. On top of that, they're always stressed out by the fear of getting yelled at. And you know what fear does to people."

"What?"

"Makes them run around and scream and yell. You see what you're up against?"

"Hmmm!"

"So, after quitting thinking in terms of right and wrong, the next thing to do is to come up with rules of the house. Take some time with this. Think them over and write them down. And be sure to get your kids to help you. This gives *them* a say in their formulation, and you'll be surprised at how well they'll take to the task and how much more willing they'll be to follow the rules after they've had a hand in writing them. Now, when you write these rules, make sure they apply to everyone equally. In other words, don't come up with rules that apply to *them* but not *you*."

"How can I do that?! They're too young to do all the things I do—

like using knives and the stove and dangerous stuff."

"Well, for things they're too young or inexperienced or uncoordinated to do, you can put an age limit in the rule. For instance, if you don't want them using the stove, you can make the rule something like: 'No one under the age of ten is permitted to use the stove.' They'll perceive it as applying to everyone in the household, but with age a determining factor. This gives *you* permission and *them* something to look forward to as they grow up. It also gives you the opportunity, when you include them in the rule-writing process, to explain some of the hazards of the household. They'll understand these things much better than you think they will."

"Ya think?"

"I do. Now, to make these rules work, there have to be penalties for their violation. But be careful not to confuse penalties with punishment."

"Penalties and punishment . . . what's the difference?"

"Well, punishment is a form of retribution that causes pain or discomfort—scoldings, spankings, having to stand in the corner, going to bed without supper, that sort of thing. A penalty would be a form of *amends* like fines or loss of privileges—no TV, early bedtime, grounding, et cetera.

"That doesn't seem like much of a difference."

"Well, the distinction may *seem* fine, but it's actually quite significant. Penalties don't inflict physical and emotional pain like punishments do, they only remove the benefits that a kid earns by behaving respectfully and responsibly. In other words, if the kid wants the privilege of watching TV or going out on a date or earning an allowance or whatever, they have to behave respectfully and responsibly. If they don't, they don't get the privilege."

"Oh, I see."

"Now, to be most effective, penalties must be specified right along *with* the rule, so when someone breaks a rule, they already know what the consequence is going to be. When *I* broke a rule, my parents would very calmly say to me, 'What's the penalty for breaking that rule?' and I'd tell them, because I already knew it. I'd already agreed to it. So I *had* to accept the penalty, and usually did so somewhat sheepishly. As you can see, this takes the anger and revenge out of the equation, and when that goes, it puts an end to most of the yelling right there."

"Wow!" Marilyn exclaimed, having suddenly seen the wisdom of it all.

"Wow is right!" Dale acknowledged. "Is this enough to get you started, or do you want another hint?"

"I'll take another hint."

"Excellent. I suggest that at the same time you write the rules, come up with chores for each of the kids to do, for which they'll earn a specified amount of money. You pay them at the end of the week for every chore they do. If they do all their chores every day that week, you can reward them by paying them double. They soon find out that the more chores they do, the more they earn. *Then*, one of the penalties for rule violations can be fines against their earnings. It takes a little trial and error to get the balance just right so you don't fine away all their earnings and destroy their incentive to do their chores, but a nice balance can be obtained with a little diligence."

"I dunno," Marilyn groaned. "This sounds like a lot of work."

"Whoever said parenting would be easy?"

"Well . . . ." She really didn't have an answer and wound up saying nothing more

"Right. I admit, it is a lot of work. But trust me, it's a whole lot *less* work than yelling at your kids all the time and still not getting anywhere."

"Oh," Marilyn said, getting the point.

"By the way, this system of rules, chores, rewards, and penalties is modeled after our society and does a pretty good job of preparing kids for life in the real world."

"Oh!"

"Keep in mind, though, there's a lot more to effective parenting than just this. You need to hug your kids daily, spend quality time with them on a regular basis, *really listen* to them when they talk to you, and answer their questions clearly and meaningfully. In other words, give them the same respect you'd give an adult. If you write up the rules of the house and do the things we've talked about here, I believe you'll be way ahead of where you are now."

"You really think this will work?"

"Most definitely. I'm living proof of it."

"Oh!" Marilyn acknowledged, impressed. "Okay, I'll try it."

"Atta girl! Call me in a couple of months and let me know how it's going. Will you do that?"

"Sure!"

"Great! Thanks so much for calling."

"Thank you!"

"You're welcome. Bye-bye."

"Bye."

Marilyn hung up and Dale disconnected the call, announcing softly, "This is WWKW, FM 102.4, and I'm Dale Greene. I'll be back with more calls on The Brink of Tomorrow after this."

Elliot turned the volume down on his radio. During the commercial break, he assessed his feelings for the man he had just heard. He definitely liked him. There was something familiar, something relaxing, something comforting about the fellow. In many ways, he felt a special kinship with Dale and the ideas he embraced.

After the commercial break, Dale took a somewhat unusual call. The caller didn't have a particular problem to discuss, but just wanted clarification of a metaphysical principle Dale had mentioned many times in talking with listeners. Elliot turned his volume up again to listening level.

"Welcome back. I'm Dale Greene and you're listening to The Brink of Tomorrow on FM 102.4. My next caller is Aaron. He's twenty-seven, and he wants some clarification on *judgment*." He connected the call. "Hi Aaron, this is Dale Greene and you're on The Brink of Tomorrow."

"Hi, Dale. How's it goin'?"

"Very well, thank you, Aaron. How are you?"

"I'm good, I'm good." Aaron's manner was somewhat free and easy, with a slight backwoods flavor to his speech.

"I'm glad to hear it," acknowledged Dale. "So what would you like to know about judgment?"

"Well, I keep hearin' you say we shouldn't judge, but I'm still not sure why. This may be a dumb question, but what's wrong with judgin'? Why shouldn't I judge?"

"Well, first of all, Aaron, there are no dumb questions. Every question you have is valid. So don't ever be afraid to ask a question. Second, I'm not saying there's anything *'wrong'* with judging. That, in itself, is a judgment. Nor am I saying you *'shouldn't'* judge. As I've said many times before on this program, 'should' and 'shouldn't' are disguised judgments."

"Oh, right, I do remember you sayin' that."

"Right. So I'm not saying you *shouldn't* judge. I'm saying that judging doesn't *serve* you, and may in fact disserve you. And *not* judging *does* serve you."

"Okay. So how does not judgin' serve me—or judgin' not serve me?"

"Are you prepared for a heavily metaphysical answer?" Dale queried, not sure Aaron was aware of the depth of his question.

"Sure, why not," was Aaron's relaxed response.

"Okay. Well, for one thing, if you choose not to judge, you can achieve a peace of mind that cannot be achieved when you are in the habit of judging. When you choose not to judge, a whole army of uncomfortable emotions just kind of fades into the background. They don't *vanish* from your energy makeup, but they don't impose themselves on your awareness with the intensity that they do when you judge. And when those emotions are not upsetting you, your life is magically more peaceful. It's something you can't really imagine or appreciate until you've actually done it."

"Okaaaaay," Aaron drawled dubiously. "Go on."

"For another thing, your life can begin to go more to your liking."

"Just by not judgin'? How's that supposed to work?"

"Well, when you judge, you cut yourself off from a great portion of your power as a spiritual being. You know, ultimately, we are all one thing: the consciousness of God, or Creation, or All That Is—however you prefer to think of it. Only we have been particularized, both spiritually and materially."

"Huh? Partic—?" Aaron wasn't sure enough of the word to even repeat it.

"Sorry, Aaron. I'm just saying that the single consciousness of God or All That Is has chosen to partition itself and express itself as individual souls and individual particles of matter, and by doing so has created the experience of living in a physical reality. And the fact is, the power that we can exercise or express in our life is the power of that consciousness. And the more connected we are with that consciousness, the more power is available to us to create our lives the way we want them. Is this making sense so far?"

"Yeah, I guess."

"Okay. Now, when you judge someone or something, you create an artificial separation between you and that person or thing. And by doing so, you cut yourself off from a portion of the power that's available to you. And that reduces the amount of power you have to create your life as you wish it."

"Whoa, whoa, wait a minute. I don't see how judgin' cuts you off from your power."

"Well, it happens on a subconscious level, to be sure, but it can be thought of like this: No one wants to be part of something that's 'bad,' or that's 'wrong.' So the instant you judge something as 'bad' or 'wrong,' at that subconscious level of awareness, you separate yourself from the people or things you're judging. And this separation cuts off access to the power of God or All That Is that is embodied in those people or things. It's quite automatic and completely subconscious, but it happens nonetheless. And when you practice judgment, like most people on this planet do, the amount of power you cut yourself off from is astonishing—because you're usually not judging just one person or just one thing at a time, you're judging whole categories of people and things, and this separates you from vast portions of God/Creation/All That Is. But in addition to that, when you judge others, you're subconsciously judging *yourself*, and that really disconnects you from your power."

"How do you figure *that*?" Aaron puzzled, echoing the question that had formed in Elliot's mind as he listened to the conversation.

"Well, as I've said before, we attract people and circumstances into our lives to provide a reflection of ourselves, to allow us to see ourselves in a sort of mirror that they hold up to us. In fact, they're there specifically to reflect back to us our beliefs, our judgments, et cetera. And when we attract into our lives people or things that we're uncomfortable with—that we *judge*—they reflect those aspects that we judge in *ourselves*. It's really quite automatic. And this subconscious self-judgment is *really* where judgmental people cut themselves off from their power. So just by ceasing to judge, you make a huge leap in your spiritual growth."

"So does that mean I have to like and accept everyone and everything?" Aaron seemed somewhat overwhelmed by the prospect of having to interact with people he disliked. "I mean, *jeez*, what if you got yourself mixed up with the Mafia or somethin' 'cause you accepted them into your life? Couldn't that be kinda disastrous?!"

This question was a natural consequence of the logic Dale had just expressed and Elliot was champing at the bit to hear the answer, too. But Dale was prepared for it.

"To answer your question literally: Yes, it means you have to accept everyone for who they are and everything for what it is. But it doesn't mean you have to *like* everyone and everything, or *interact* with them. Here's how it works: You *accept* them by recognizing that they have a *divine right to exist* and to be on this planet, and to express themselves in any way they choose, as all the various ways God or Creation or All That Is has of expressing itself. In other words, it's not 'wrong' for them to be here and to be who and what they are, and to do what they choose to do. This is what you accept. You don't, however, have to *like* what they do, or involve yourself in *their* expression of themselves, or express *yourself* in the same way. So you may choose to keep your distance from them because what they do doesn't resonate with who and what you are. But you accept them as valid expressions of All That Is within existence on this planet."

"But isn't liking or disliking just judgment in a different form?"

"No. What I'm talking about here is *preference*. Judgment is the act of discerning between different people and things by assigning values to them—this is good, that's bad, this is right, that's wrong. But those values aren't properties those people or things naturally possess. They're really just your *opinions* about those people or things, opinions you're not taking responsibility for. That's in large part what creates the separation. *Preference*, on the other hand, is the act of discerning between different people and things by determining your personal feelings toward them—I *like* this, I *don't like* that, I *prefer* this, I *don't prefer* that. By doing that, you take full responsibility for the distinctions you make between different people and different things, and don't create the separation. And when you take responsibility for those distinctions, suddenly you're empowered, at least in part because you don't have to rely on other people's opinions about what is good and bad or right and wrong.

"So while you accept the validity of the Mafia—and everyone else—to be here and express themselves as they choose, you also recognize that you prefer not to express yourself as they do, and you put enough distance between you and them that their expressions don't affect you. Putting distance between yourself and something you don't like or prefer is a perfectly nonjudgmental way of arranging your life so that you're not negatively affected by their expressions. This is *preference*, and it's how enlightened beings discern the various people and things in their reality without judgment. Is this beginning to make sense?"

"Yeah, somewhat," Aaron answered gamely. "I may have to think about it a little while for it to sink in completely, but I think I'm beginnin' to see the difference. It's an interesting way of lookin' at it."

"Yes it is. And when you get really good at perceiving your reality through preference rather than judgment, your level of responsibility and peace of mind comes *way* up." Dale gave this thought a moment to sink in, then asked, "Does this give you the clarification you were seeking?"

"Uh, yeah, yeah, I think it does," Aaron said.

"Excellent. And for what it's worth, Aaron, I'm sure your question has helped a lot of listeners who were afraid to ask it for fear of looking dumb."

"Ya think?!"

"I'm quite sure of it."

"Wow, that's cool, that's cool."

"Is there anything else I can help you with tonight, Aaron?"

"Nah, that does it. Thanks!"

"You're quite welcome. Thanks for calling."

"See ya!"

With that, Dale disconnected the call. "This is Dale Greene on WWKW, FM 102.4," Elliot heard Dale say in conclusion. "Back again after these commercials."

His radio muted for the commercial break, Elliot laced his fingers behind his head and contemplated the wisdom Dale had shared with Aaron. Although he had never given thought to this specific idea before, now that he had heard it, it certainly rang true to him. When he tuned in at nine o'clock, he didn't know how interested he would be in sticking it out to midnight. But after just two calls, he knew he wanted to hear everything Dale had to say. Settling back for the remainder of the program, he imagined playing this man to his public. Yes, without a doubt, there was something about this role that really felt right.

Ken Gullekson

Chapter 17

The day of the address to the students of Bret Harte High came quickly. After a week of intensive listening to The Brink of Tomorrow, Elliot felt secure in his understanding of the man he would be portraying for the next three months. In addition, his study of the expanded background material on the DJ gave him confidence that he could handle any questions he might be asked in the course of the morning.

Dale, by contrast, was nervous. As had been the case during the Archers ceremony, he had no control over the moment-to-moment events of the address. Such events had the potential, slight though it might be, of going devastatingly awry. Elliot could suffer stage fright and stumble through the speech, or he could be shot and killed in the middle of the talk by a crazed gunman, ostensibly ending the life and career of radio advisor Dale Greene. Or "he" could bore the kids to tears and lose a whole segment of his radio audience in one fell swoop. Sure, his advisors had assured him it was a good speech, but they weren't hormone-ravaged high school students. Only now, sitting alone in the manor house while his advisors and secret emissary got underway, did Dale realize just how risky it was having a virtual unknown deliver an untried address under potentially unpredictable circumstances for which contingency plans could only be sketchily discussed.

Ignorance of the details of the event, such as had tripped him up on his show the night of the Archers ceremony, was to be avoided this time by hiring a professional cameraman to videotape the proceedings. Theoretically, the videotape would provide Dale with a visual reference for any questions his callers might ask on the show—and experience showed that ask they would—after the event.

Instead of a limousine, Elliot was driven to the high school in a Plymouth Voyager, a comfortable and attractive, but much less ostentatious, vehicle. Wil and Paul accompanied Elliot at every stage of the process—finding the school's administration offices; checking in with Mr. Smalley and David Moon; and getting settled backstage in the auditorium in which the students were to assemble.

Elliot's anticipation of the address, as was typical for him, manifested as excitement rather than nervousness, and he chatted amicably with Mr. Smalley and David Moon in the wings during the final minutes before the program. At last, the auditorium was filled with clamoring students and Mr. Smalley stepped to the lectern to quiet them down. As he was not well liked by much of the student body, it took him several moments to secure the desired peace. When he did, he made a few miscellaneous announcements, then introduced David Moon, who took the lectern with a big smile.

"Okay, you guys," he began informally, "here's what we've all been waiting for. It took some doing to get him, but he's finally here. You all know who he is and what he does, and some of you have even talked to him on the air, so I won't bore you with a lengthy introduction. Please join me in welcoming the SBEA speaker for this semester, the Archers Man of the Year, WWKW radio advisor, Dale Greene!"

With this, David stepped back from the lectern, and Elliot strode onstage to thunderous applause. While he had committed the entire address to memory, just as he had the Archers acceptance speech, he laid out the prepared text on the lectern to use as a place-keeping tool, just to be on the safe side. In the next 42 minutes, everyone would learn whether Dale's words, as delivered by a pretender, could hold the attention of 474 restless high school kids.

Watching the videotape of the Bret Harte High address that afternoon, Dale was pleased with the raucous applause Elliot drew at the end of the speech as he thanked his audience for their attention and stepped away from the microphone.

Elliot's performance had been flawless, but the recording had revealed several passages in the address to be less than captivating and Dale noted to himself that they would need adjustment for the addresses yet ahead on the schedule. Still, the speech had been generally well received and the deception had come off without a hitch.

Fast forwarding through the lengthy applause and the curtain call it evoked, Dale slowed the tape to normal speed as Wil, Paul, and Elliot exited the backstage entrance to the auditorium. There, a throng of students was gathered at the Plymouth Voyager to see and touch their beloved radio advisor. Some of them thrust scraps of paper toward Elliot for autographs.

Oddly enough, this obvious eventuality had not been anticipated— no one had asked for autographs at the Archers ceremony—and Dale watched intently as Elliot looked to Wil and Paul for some quick advice. The two advisors eyed each other, and with a shrug decided to give the kids their way. With a nod from Wil, Elliot started scribbling "Dale Greene" on the scraps of paper.

Dale pressed the pause button to freeze the image on the TV screen. "What are the ramifications of that?" he asked, directing his question mainly to Paul. He and his three advisors were gathered in the plush den in the manor house.

"I dunno," Paul replied. "We're pretty much breaking new ground. But it's not like these are legal documents or anything."

"It can't be any more complicated than anything else we're doing," ventured Wil. "But it's probably better than refusing them and disappointing a bunch of innocent kids. After all, that's why we're doing this whole thing in the first place."

Dale nodded and unpaused the frozen video image. There was only a minute or so more of autograph signing before the kids rushed off to their next class, leaving the Greene team alone. A few seconds later, the video picture turned to snow.

As it turned out, the precaution of the videotape hadn't been entirely necessary, except for purposes of review. Though a couple of callers mentioned the Bret Harte address that evening on The Brink of Tomorrow, neither asked embarrassing questions. In fact, they were extremely complimentary, and Dale acted appropriately appreciative. While he *was* appreciative—after all, it was his words they were praising—he couldn't fully suppress his misgivings about the deception. Fortunately, no one seemed to notice.

Elliot listened to the show that night, too, just to see what kind of response he would get from Dale's listeners. He had hoped for more callers who had seen his performance, but he contented himself with the praise the two students heaped on "him."

For his part, even without such praise, he knew he had done well. His success here reminded him of earlier successes, particularly in high school plays, where the acting bug had first bitten him. He knew then that he had the passion, the personality, and the prowess to really move an audience. He hadn't realized at the time that success in the acting business—or even getting a measly walk-on—would hinge less on talent than on having the desired look, making his own opportunities, and being in the right place at the right time. After so many years of study—and a handful of minor roles—he was finally getting the chance to prove himself. Too bad no one who could help his career would ever know it.

Before Jefferson—the heavily attended private school next on Elliot's address schedule—Dale made the requisite adjustments to his text, taking a hint from several skillful *ad libs* and on-the-fly adjustments Elliot had made during the Bret Harte address. In fact, using Wil as a go-between, he even solicited Elliot's comments on the revised text before the address. Elliot was flattered, reviewed the videotape of the Bret Harte presentation for ideas, and made a couple of minor suggestions.

With the adjustments to the text, the Jefferson address was even more successful than the Bret Harte appearance. Following that, addresses at four other schools—interspersed with appearances at three locally televised charity fundraisers—came off with increasing polish.

In contrast to the addresses at the schools, the charity appearances involved more glad-handing than speechmaking. At one event, Elliot happened to meet the mayor of Springfield, and at another—an environmental awareness rally—sang songs with Joan Baez. Of course, he pulled these off with his usual affable aplomb.

All in all, the appearances by Elliot in Dale's behalf seemed not to be causing any problems. But Dale found it somewhat disconcerting that he was now getting calls on The Brink of Tomorrow from the mayor. Being a "personal friend" of the popular radio advisor, mayor Braunmuller sometimes phoned the show on the pretext of discussing city problems. Dale was, as always, gracious. But he knew that in reality, the mayor was, in this election year, only plugging his political agenda.

During the three months that elapsed over the course of the nine events, the weather turned cold and the leaves began to fall from the trees. As the days wore on, Dale became accustomed to the routine and pushed the onus of the deception to the back of his mind. Somewhere along the way, he celebrated the one year anniversary of the all-talk Brink of Tomorrow.

Also during that time, he heard from some of his former callers. Rosie wrote from Boca Raton, Florida where she was happily singing and playing keyboards on tour with Man's Inhumanity. Ross called with more women problems—he was handling them better, now, but still needed help. And John wrote to share the good news that he had happened onto a group of animal rights activists and was "making great friends like crazy."

From time to time over the course of the three months, Elliot went on shopping trips into the city, always accompanied by Wil and/or Paul, and was asked on several occasions to sign autographs. Although he enjoyed the attention, he was acutely aware that the name he was signing—the name he was being identified with—was someone else. It didn't keep him awake at night, but it did gall him some, and he looked forward to the day he would be signing his own name on scraps of paper thrust his way by admiring fans.

With each appearance, as the adjustments to Dale's texts became fewer and fewer, Elliot had to spend less and less time preparing, so was able to spend more and more time at leisure activities: watching movies in the estate screening room, working out, swimming, and playing tennis and racquetball. He found in Bobby a worthy opponent in these sports and they began spending much of their free time together. He phoned his answering machine back home in North Hollywood to pick up messages daily, and returned the few calls that mattered. Two or three times a month, he placed a call to Darryl, his attorney friend, just to be sure his rent and utilities were being paid on time and everything was okay back home. True to its word, Greene Enterprises was taking care of all his home maintenance expenses in exemplary fashion.

As the end of the three months neared, Elliot started looking forward to returning home, redeeming the escrow account in which his earnings were being held, and hitting the audition trail again, this time without the financial pressures. During the months he had been in the Greene employ, the frequency of his audition calls had more than doubled and he had been forced to pass up eleven auditions—one for a juicy part in a super-budget action thriller starring Vin Diesel. Anxious about losing the face recognition that came from personal contact with industry operators that was so important to an acting career in its early stages, Elliot was eager to take advantage of his increased popularity with the Hollywood casting agencies and actually go on some auditions.

He was also eager to see his father—his mother had passed away six years before—and start dating again. A thousand dollars a day was an adequate substitute for female companionship for a while, but it didn't hold up in the long run. Despite its many rewards, the Greene gig was pretty confining.

But Elliot wasn't the only one who felt confined. Whenever Elliot was on the estate—which was most of the time—Dale had to stay in the manor house or the broadcast suite, the only two places on the entire 147 acres he was sure not to be seen. And neither place was much fun for long.

Then, to add insult to injury, he got to see a whole lot less of his best friend, Bobby, whom he could hardly ask to share the long hours with him cooped up in the manor house. He wasn't exactly jealous of the time Bobby spent with Elliot—he wasn't that petty—but he was envious.

As the months wore on, Dale instructed Wil and Paul to take Elliot into the city with increasing regularity so Dale could have some time out of doors. His only real relief from the confinement and monotony came from the belief that it would all be over soon.

But the residents of Springfield had other ideas.

Over the months, word had spread that Dale was doing appearances and calls started coming in again. As before, most were for TV talk shows, product endorsements, and the like. And as before, they were summarily declined. But there were four more charities and two more schools—one of which was a middle school—in the mix. And this time, a handful of hospitals and community service organizations were also bidding for Dale's time.

What little discussion that took place between Dale and his advisors concluded as before—they could hardly turn down schools and charities, or hospitals and community service organizations—and Elliot would have to be retained for another two or three months to make the requested appearances. Dale's heart sank at the prospect of another two or three months of isolation.

Elliot wasn't particularly sanguine about the idea either, given his eagerness to escape his confines and go home. But Wil and Paul offered him a raise of $500 per day, plus $3000 per event, to sweeten the offer. When Elliot's response was a thoughtful twist of his mouth, they knew they hadn't offered him enough and Wil quickly upped the raise to $1000, bringing Elliot's daily fee to $2000.

At that rate, Elliot calculated, in another three months his escrow account would be hovering near $300,000, and he would have an investment sum on which the bank interest alone would be enough to pay his modest living expenses. And after all, the first three months hadn't been all that bad. For another two hundred grand he could stand to stick it out for the additional three months. And with the hospitals and community service organizations on the agenda, there would be a little more variety in the presentations. Sure, he'd be willing to do another three months—on one condition . . .

Wil and Paul eyed each other with shared dread.

. . . That Greene Enterprises pay the insurance premium—due next month—on his car, which was sitting unused at home. Wil and Paul sighed with relief and the deal was struck.

Ken Gullekson

Chapter 18

"My next caller is Cathy. She's twenty-three and says she's considering having an abortion."

Ten weeks had passed since Elliot had renewed his contract with Greene Enterprises and he was dutifully doing appearances in Dale's stead. They were going well, and for Dale, things were seemingly back to normal. He had even resigned himself again to the restrictions on his freedom forced by having Elliot on the estate.

"Hi, Cathy, this is Dale Greene and you're on The Brink of Tomorrow."

"Hi, Dale," she replied. "Thanks for taking my call." Her voice was strong and steady, suggesting intelligence and confidence.

"You're welcome, Cathy. How might I be of service to you?"

"Well, I'm ten weeks pregnant, and recently I had an amniocentesis done, and, um . . . it turns out my baby's gonna have Tay-Sachs disease."

Taking the rare opportunity to show off his medical knowledge, gleaned while studying his own affliction, Dale explained, for the benefit of his listeners, "Tay-Sachs disease is a genetic disorder which causes rapid mental and neurological deterioration and is always fatal in early childhood."

"That's right. My husband and I lost a previous child to Tay-Sachs, and it was just so painful, we don't want to go through it again. And we also don't want to put another baby through all that pain and suffering."

"And one solution is to terminate the pregnancy," Dale confirmed.

"Right. My question is: If I decide to have an abortion, how does that affect the spirit that's incarnated in my baby's body? I mean, are we imposing our will on it by having the abortion? Is it really murder, like the right-to-lifers say?"

"Wow! What a refreshing question. I was expecting you to ask me whether or not you should have the abortion—which, of course, I wouldn't have commented on one way or the other."

"We've been listening to you long enough to know not to ask something like that," Cathy explained.

"Oh, thank you, Cathy. I very much appreciate your attentiveness, and your wisdom. To answer your question: As I understand it—and all I can tell you is what my references tell me—the spirit which has dibs on your baby's body won't actually incarnate until just before birth or just after birth. So, while there's usually a consciousness which has associated itself with the fetus, even at this early stage of the pregnancy, aborting a fetus isn't the same as killing a fully developed, postnatal human being."

"Okay. But still, isn't it imposing our will on that consciousness somehow? I assume the Platinum Principles would apply to unincarnated spirits as well as incarnated ones."

"Yes, they do apply to noncarnate consciousnesses as well as carnate ones. But the reverse is also true."

In the silence that was his caller's response, Dale could almost hear Cathy grunt with confusion.

"A noncarnate spirit following the Platinum Principles—I don't know if they call them Platinum Principles in the spirit realm, that's just what we call them here—a noncarnate spirit following the spiritual equivalent of the Platinum Principles also wouldn't impose its will on you, meaning that it wouldn't expect you to bear a child whose ill health would cause you pain you're not willing to experience."

"Then why are babies born with birth defects? I mean, both the baby and the parents suffer."

"The first thing to understand is that everyone, every consciousness on the planet, comes into physical reality to *experience* itself, including its darker energies, which is something it can't do anywhere else. Of course, most of us don't remember that that's our purpose in coming here—we don't even remember *deciding* to come here, for that matter—but that's our purpose anyway, as I understand it. For example, in its native spiritual state, in the spirit realm, a spirit can't experience such coarse feelings as pain and suffering—it can only experience those kinds of feelings in the coarser physical reality. So it incarnates here for a lifetime. When it returns to its native spiritual state after the lifetime is over, it returns with experience and insights it can't get anywhere else but the physical plane.

"Now this may be hard to understand, but some spirits come here to experience some very extreme and intense feelings in their physical lives. And one way to experience such feelings is to incarnate in a defective body. Of course, compared to the infinite life of a spirit, the lifetime of a physical body is extremely brief, so these extreme and intense feelings only last for what amounts to the blink of an eye to the immortal spirit. But the result is that the spirit comes away with a *very* profound understanding of those feelings. A very great deal is learned from a very difficult lifetime." Dale sighed with an unaccustomed self-consciousness at secretly describing his own life. "Likewise, parents who choose to bear defective children do so to experience some very special things in the process. Does this make any sense to you?" Dale queried.

"Yes, but . . . so are you saying I came here to experience what it's like to have a defective child?"

"Well, yes and no. The things we come here to experience have more to do with the *feelings* associated with our experiences than with the *events* of those experiences. But to answer what I think you meant by your question: You've already had a defective child, which means absolutely that you came here to experience the feelings associated with that kind of thing. But the fact that *this* baby has the Tay-Sachs defect doesn't necessarily mean you came here to *repeat* the experience. The fact that you chose to have the amniocentesis done and that you're considering an abortion suggests to me that you're finished with that and you're taking steps *not* to repeat it. Of course, there'll undoubtedly be something else to experience in whatever course you wind up taking."

"Why?"

"There always is. I mean, a lot of the challenges and experiences we create for ourselves are designed to reconnect us with feelings and emotions we've denied in the past, and there are a great many of them."

"Oh." Cathy thought briefly. "So maybe having the abortion would be okay . . . . But that still doesn't tell me whether or not I'd be imposing my will on the spirit that's gonna incarnate in my baby."

"Well, no, it doesn't. The answer to that is that all interactions are co-created. That is to say, every interaction that takes place in the physical world is agreed to, at least at the spiritual level, if not the physical level, by the souls involved in that interaction. So interactions such as bearing a defective child, so-called traffic accidents, and even murder, are all agreed to by the souls involved in them."

"Murder?! Really?"

"Sure. On the spiritual plane, one party looking for the experience of extreme victimhood finds another party looking for the experience of extreme victimizer—or vice versa. Their karmic paths in the physical plane bring them together under circumstances conducive to murder, and boom, they both come away from the interaction with the experience they were looking for."

"But one guy ends up dead and the other guy ends up in jail!" Cathy was obviously bothered that anyone would seek such a result.

"The first guy ends up back in his native spiritual state with insights about the feelings associated with allowing others to impose their will on him. The second guy doesn't get back to his native spiritual state quite as fast, but when he does, he has insights, not only about the feelings associated with imposing his will on others, but also about others imposing their will on him, which he gets from his experience in jail."

"Oh! I see. Painful experiences!"

"They *are* painful experiences. But although painful experiences are dreaded on the physical plane, they're treasured on the spiritual plane. You can't get them anywhere else." Dale paused to let Cathy come to grips with this, then added, "In any event, these things are all co-created, so you don't have to worry about imposing your will on the consciousness that's associated itself with your baby."

"Okay," she said, sighing with finality. Dale was just about to conclude the call when Cathy spoke up again. "But wait a minute! Now I'm confused. Are you saying that even if we impose our will on someone, we're not really imposing our will on them, because on the spiritual plane we all agree to the things we do to each other?"

"Mmm, that's not exactly what I'm saying. On the spiritual plane, it's true, there is no real imposition of will. But on the physical plane there *is*. Even though we're agreeing to these interactions on the *spiritual* plane, within the context of the *physical* plane, we *aren't* agreeing to them, so we have to consider them real impositions on the physical plane. I know, it's kind of a paradox, but that's how it has to be for us to experience the things we're here to experience. So, you can't use this as an excuse for intentionally imposing your will on someone on the physical plane—it doesn't negate the Platinum Principles."

"I get that," Cathy acknowledged. There was a lengthy silence as she mulled Dale's words. "But . . . now I'm even less clear about the abortion now that I know about the paradox. I understand that I've made an agreement with the spirit that's associated itself with my baby, but I don't want to use that as an excuse to impose my will on—" She stopped abruptly and sighed with frustration.

"All right," Dale said, sensitive to the meaning behind her sigh, "let me see if I can't simplify it a bit. There are just two things to remember. Number one: In addition to guiding you not to impose your will on others or to be of disservice to others, the Platinum Principles also guide you not to allow others to impose their will on *you* or be of disservice to *yourself*. And that's very important. You have to remember *that* when making your decision about the abortion. And number two: As long as you're mindful of the Platinum Principles, and act with genuine love—which translates into integrity—you can trust that whatever you decide to do will be a co-creation that satisfies the needs of all the parties involved, including the consciousness that's associated itself with your baby's body. Does that clear it up a little?"

Cathy sighed. "Yeah . . . quite a bit. But why would any being want to have its body—the body it's going to incarnate in—aborted?"

"That's a very interesting question," Dale replied, smiling to himself. "The answer is that physical reality is very demanding and, as I understand it, not all noncarnate beings are ready to commit themselves to a complete lifetime in it. Some just want a taste before they order the whole enchilada. And they have several options for acquiring that taste. One is to connect up with a couple whose spiritual consciousnesses want to experience the feelings associated with losing a child in a spontaneous miscarriage. Another is to connect up with parents whose spiritual consciousnesses want to experience the feelings associated with choosing to abort a fetus. In both cases the pregnancy doesn't go to term, and the brief connection the spirit has with the fetus during the first few months of gestation gives it all the taste of physical reality it's looking for.

"And for beings who have a little more sense of adventure but still don't want to commit to a lengthy lifetime, death in early childhood may be the answer. They simply connect up with parents whose spiritual consciousnesses want to experience the feelings associated with losing a child to a childhood illness, or sudden infant death syndrome, or a birth defect such as you've already experienced."

"I didn't want to experience the feelings associated with losing a child to a birth defect!" Cathy interjected emphatically.

Sensing some unresolved trauma, and maybe a touch of guilt, Dale responded with deliberate tenderness. "Not consciously, no; of course not. You make most of these choices at a spiritual level of consciousness which you may not be aware of on the physical plane. If you made them on the physical plane, you wouldn't interpret such things as the death of a child as a *loss*. Which means you also wouldn't experience the *feelings* associated with that loss. But it's likely that you denied these feelings in a previous life and chose this experience to reconnect to them. As you can see, you have to trick yourself into believing you're not making these choices in order to experience the feelings associated with them. You do that by intentionally forgetting the paradox when you incarnate."

"Oh!" Cathy gave a moment of thought to this idea. "But if we intentionally forget the paradox when we incarnate, how are you and I able to know about it now?"

"Well, according to all my spiritual sources, we're living in a very special time, a time that the collective consciousness on the planet has chosen for a sort of transformation, during which many of us will be evolving to higher states of awareness. In these higher states of awareness, we'll be simultaneously aware of our physical selves *and* our spiritual selves. And in this new state, we'll be aware of how we create our reality with our thoughts, and begin to consciously create the reality we most desire, both individually and collectively. Thus, we'll be able to see the paradox at work while facing the challenges of our lives."

"Hmm, that's pretty wild. But, now . . . won't knowing about this paradox kind of defeat the purpose and ruin our experiences?"

"Ruin them? No. Change them? Yes. If you can keep this paradox in mind when you're in the middle of a very challenging experience and see the experience from both perspectives at the same time—the perspective of your physical self, and the perspective of your soul—then you'll truly have evolved and accomplished one of the objectives of incarnating in physical reality in the first place."

"Which is what?"

"To understand yourself—experientially—as a spiritual being."

"Oh! Yeah, you said something like that earlier. Hmmm."

"Anyway, the consciousness who incarnated in your first baby knew what he was doing. And it was his choice both to choose you as his parents, and to die young. The choice to leave a physical incarnation is always made by the consciousness incarnated in it. The consciousness who's associated itself with your new baby likewise knows what he's doing. And you can trust that whatever decision *you* make will be exactly what he's after."

Cathy mulled this for a moment, then heaved a tremendous sigh. Dale could tell by the sound of it that not only had she resolved the issue of the abortion, she had released trauma that she had been holding onto from the loss of her first child.

"Does that help?" he asked, more to confirm it for her than for himself.

"Yeah . . . a lot!" With this, she began to cry. She tried to hold it back, but the release was not to be denied, and she blubbered. "Thank you so much," she managed to say between sobs. It was a couple of moments before she could speak again, and when she did, she could only repeat, "Thank you."

Sensing no imminent letup in the flood and wanting to let her cry in private, Dale said simply, softly, "The privilege is mine, Cathy. My love to you and your husband. Good night."

Disconnecting the call and dispensing with the station I.D., Dale waited a respectful moment, then signaled Bobby to roll the commercial tape.

As Bobby took each new call, the name of the caller would pop onto the bottom of Dale's computer screen, along with the description of the caller's subject, for Dale to review. As the commercial break drew to a close, a curious subject appeared on the list and Dale decided to take it.

"It's eleven fifteen, you're tuned to WWKW, and this is Dale Greene on The Brink of Tomorrow. My next caller is Steven. Steven is thirty-four and he says he disagrees with my advice on a previous call." He connected the call. "Hi, Steven, this is Dale Greene and you're on The Brink of Tomorrow."

"Hello." Although not hostile, the tone of Steven's voice was certainly not friendly. Warned that Steven had a disagreement, Dale was prepared for a less-than-warm reception and did not let the chill in his caller's voice dampen his typically amicable manner.

"Which call did you disagree with, Steven?"

"The last one, from the girl who asked you about getting an abortion."

"Oh, okay. What did you disagree with?"

"Abortion is murder!" Steven pronounced fervently, "and you shouldn't be encouraging anyone to do it!" The emotional content of Steven's assertion seemed a little extreme to Dale, as though coming not from rationale, but dogma.

"Ah!" Dale exclaimed evenly. Certain of his position, he did not let the fervor in his caller's voice throw him off balance. "Are you saying that from a religious point of view or a legal point of view?"

Unprepared for this sort of question, Steven had to think briefly about his answer, but quickly replied, "Religious."

"Okay. Did you listen to the whole call from beginning to end?"

"Yeah."

"Then, did you not recognize that I wasn't encouraging Cathy to do anything one way or the other?"

"Yeah, but what you told her made it sound like it was okay to have an abortion."

"Would you have preferred that I tell her *not* to have an abortion?"

"Yes!"

"So you think I should be telling my listeners what to do?"

"Yes!"

"So I should tell *you* what to do?"

Again, Steven was unready for Dale's question. "Well, no!" he finally asserted.

"So I should tell *Cathy* what to do but I shouldn't tell *you* what to do?"

"Uh, yeah."

"Well that doesn't sound fair," Dale countered.

Unable to answer Dale's head on, Steven snorted, then reverted to his original complaint. "But we're talking about murdering children!"

"Well, actually, we were talking about saving an unborn child from a very brief life of pain and suffering."

"But that's God's decision, not yours."

"Okay. Is it God's decision to put that baby through the pain of the disease?"

Suddenly forced to advocate an unsavory view, Steven was temporarily silent. But he ultimately held his position. "Yes."

"Why would He do that?"

Again stumped, Steven had to think about this one. "I don't know," he finally replied. Then, thinking he had the perfect rebuttal, added, "But we don't have to know. All we have to do is follow the Bible."

"All right. How well do you know the Bible?"

"Very well," Steven asserted proudly.

"Good," Dale said sincerely. He, too, knew the Bible. "Does it ever specifically denounce abortion, or even say when life begins?"

As these questions were not directly addressed in any English version of the Bible, Steven was again confounded. "But killing is wrong!" he impressed again.

"Well, now you're making a judgment, which I've demonstrated in the past is no more than personal opinion. But let's consult the Bible on this. Doesn't the Bible call for the taking of one life as punishment for the taking of another?"

As this question put him at a distinct disadvantage, Steven again delayed answering. "Yes, an eye for an eye," he finally said, reluctantly.

"Then the message is that killing isn't always 'wrong.' Sometimes it's 'wrong,' but sometimes it's right. Isn't that correct?"

"But the Bible is specific on when it's right to take a life and when it's not," Steven added firmly.

"Okay. If we're following Scripture literally, then we need to look for an express sanction either for or against abortion. A lot of people think they see dicta on this matter in the Bible, but they have to interpret the text extremely liberally to find it. But when you take the Bible literally, as *you're* doing, it gives nothing about aborting a fetus either way, especially when the baby is definitely doomed to a brief life of pain and suffering."

"But I still think it's wrong!"

"Okay, you're back to judging. How do you justify judging when Scripture says 'Judge not, lest ye be judged'?"

Steven opened his mouth and took a breath to respond, but stopped short with nothing to say.

"Would you prefer to doom the child to a brief life of pain and suffering?" Dale continued.

"No," Steven said, clearly distressed by that prospect.

"Look, Steven, I'm not advocating abortion. But I also can't advocate putting a little baby through the trauma of disease just because the Bible can be loosely interpreted to forbid it. The foundation of the principles I embrace and advocate on this program is respect for and responsibility toward others. That means not imposing your will on others, and wanton killing certainly is an imposition of will. But allowing others to impose their will on you is no better, so sometimes it's necessary to kill in defense of one's own life. As I said a minute ago, even the Bible calls for the death of those who kill. That complicates the issue of killing. The same has to be said for abortion. The only thing I'm trying to do is make sense of a very complicated issue."

In the background, Steven could be heard to sigh.

Dale continued, "Cathy would have much preferred her child not have a genetic disease that would put it through a lot of pain and suffering and end its life very early. Her questions about abortion were not because she wanted to get rid of the child, but to compassionately rescue it from a brief life of pain. She wouldn't have even considered abortion if the baby were going to be healthy. But God didn't give her that option. If you believe the Bible is the Word of God, then you have to recognize that God sometimes leaves difficult decisions up to people, and that compassion is sometimes the deciding factor. The insights I shared with Cathy were completely consistent with that."

"I still think it's wrong and don't think you should have encouraged her."

With this, Dale recognized there was no hope that his caller would see his point of view. He wasn't hoping to change Steven's mind, only to agree to disagree. "Certainly, Steven, I respect your right to have a differing opinion. I only ask that you do the same for me. Like I said before, I wasn't encouraging Cathy to get an abortion, I was merely sharing with her my understanding of the operation of spirit as seen from the metaphysical perspective. And I did that at her request, so I was not imposing my perspective on her. Can you say the same?"

"I'm doing God's work!" Steven asserted.

"So am I," Dale replied.

"Bullshit!" Steven interjected.

"This is family radio, Steven, and I need you to keep it clean."

The next sound that went out over the airwaves was the click of Steven's phone hanging up.

"Everyone is entitled to his opinion," Dale said in conclusion. "I just urge you all not to impose your opinions on those who don't wish to hear them. This is Dale Greene on FM 102.4. Back after these messages."

Ken Gullekson

Chapter 19

If Dale and his advisors had imagined that the community would lose interest in seeing their beloved "DJ" in person and that the requests for personal appearances would abate, they were sorely mistaken. The interest only grew and the station continued to receive calls from organizations worthy of Dale's attention. Having trapped themselves in a pattern of accommodation, Dale and his advisors found themselves unable to turn down these organizations' requests and continued to schedule appearances, even as the end of Elliot's second three-month term came and went. Unfortunately, the Greene team couldn't find the nerve to broach the subject with Elliot. Embarrassed by their errors and oversights, they just kept dispersing his daily fee to his account and sending him out, hoping he wouldn't notice as the three-month mark slipped by. This happened not by plan—there had been no discussion or scheming—they just didn't make any effort to stop it. Each man knew, in his heart of hearts, that they were being less than forthright, less than scrupulous. But they had created a problem for which there was no other solution, and their fear of losing the one solution they had kept them from acting.

Elliot, for his part, was very much aware of the passage of time—and of a sudden reticence in Wil and Paul—and found it odd, if not disconcerting, that he was still being scheduled for appearances without so much as a word from his employers. Of course, not knowing the awful secret that was responsible for his employment, he had no concept of the magnitude of the problem they faced. But he did find it uncomfortable to be working without a contract or any discussion of when the job would end.

He also found it very taxing. In the last three months, his feelings of confinement, weariness with the role of Dale Greene, isolation from Hollywood and the world at large, discontent with the injunction against claiming credit for the work, frustration at the inability to pursue other roles, and plain old wall-climbing horniness had grown exponentially. And seeing appearances being scheduled into the indefinite future made him even more anxious.

But it wasn't Elliot's way to march up to Wil or Paul and demand to know what was going on. He was more inclined to accept it as a mystery; then ponder it, puzzle over it, and try to figure it out on his own. Not that he approached it systematically or found any fascination in the intrigue, he just wanted to avoid a confrontation.

One of Elliot's first clues to this mystery came in the form of his tennis and racquetball buddy. Despite the friendship that he had forged with Bobby over the preceding months, Bobby remained somewhat of an enigma to Elliot. He knew Bobby to be athletically coordinated and technically inclined, the son of an estate housekeeper who had died a few years earlier, but beyond that he knew little of the man, and nothing of his relationship with Dale Greene. And to the best of Elliot's knowledge, Bobby performed no useful function on the estate. These details of his life, of course, Bobby was careful to keep to himself.

But Elliot had noticed that Bobby always seemed to disappear shortly before nine each night. Even if they were in the middle of a tennis match or racquetball game, Bobby would forfeit the contest and excuse himself ten or fifteen minutes before the hour. On those occasions, as the hour approached, Bobby would start checking his watch and rushing his shots, as though hurrying to finish the game before some unstated deadline. Elliot often took the opportunity to return to his apartment and tune in The Brink of Tomorrow, and speculated that Bobby might be doing the same—although he never quite understood Bobby's readiness to accept a loss just to catch the beginning of the show.

But as Elliot began to ponder this mystery—and that of his continuing uncontracted employment—he began to take notice of details which had seemed unimportant before. After excusing himself from a racquetball game one night, Bobby hurried into the recreation pavilion elevator which shuttled between the ground floor and the observation mezzanine. Curious to see what his friend was up to on the mezzanine, Elliot bolted up the stairs and watched from the landing for Bobby to emerge from the lift. But he did not, nor was he anywhere in sight on the mezzanine. After waiting a few moments,

Elliot walked over to the elevator and pressed the call button. When the elevator arrived, it was empty. This elevator was not so speedy, Elliot calculated, that it could have beaten him up the stairs by a sufficient margin to give Bobby time to emerge, walk the length of the mezzanine, and disappear unseen down the back stairway.

The only other explanation for Bobby's instant disappearance lay in the shiny new key lock Elliot had noticed the first time he had ridden the elevator, over six months ago. Situated immediately below the "Ground Floor" button, it obviously dispatched the elevator to a lower level—the underground tunnel—specifically, the portion of the subway secured by the new locks on some of the tunnel doors. This must have been where Bobby had gone.

Prior to that night, Elliot had given little thought to the location of the radio station. Having never seen WWKW's facilities, he assumed that The Brink of Tomorrow, like all of its other programs, originated from its headquarters, which he figured were located somewhere in town. He had had no reason at all to associate Bobby with the broadcast, so Bobby's disappearance each night in no way alerted him to the presence of the suite from which Dale broadcast the show. But spurred by the mysteries he had begun contemplating, he decided to find out where Bobby had gone. That night, he resolved to discover what that shiny new key lock was concealing.

Mariangela, the housekeeper who cleaned Elliot's apartment each day, typically hung her passkeys on her supply cart, and the next morning, as she busied herself in his bathroom, Elliot took a clandestine peek at her key ring. The elevator lock was of a make with which Elliot was intimately familiar and the key that fit it was easy to spot, amongst its tarnished companions, by its still shiny finish. Thanks to his years as a locksmith, Elliot knew key blanks and notch heights by sight and he readily memorized the configuration of the shiny key on Mariangela's key ring.

That afternoon, Elliot phoned his attorney friend, Darryl Britlaw, and asked if his contract with Greene Enterprises stipulated any penalty for entering the secured portion of the underground tunnel beneath the recreation pavilion.

"You planning a heist?" was Darryl's snap retort.

"Ha, ha," Elliot replied sarcastically. "No, there's just a mystery here I want to get to the bottom of."

"What kind of mystery?"

"Uh . . . I don't want to say just now; it may be nothing. It's best just to leave it at that for now."

Darryl grunted dubiously.

"So what about that penalty?"

Darryl was silent for a few moments on his end of the phone as he looked over the document. "There's no mention of any underground tunnel here," he replied finally, "much less a penalty—except for unauthorized visitation to the manor house."

"That much I knew," Elliot acknowledged. He briefly mulled the course of action he was contemplating. Then, "Are you absolutely sure about this?"

"What am I, an idiot?"

"Come on, Darryl, this is important."

"Yes," Darryl replied, feigning annoyance. "I'm absolutely sure."

Elliot released a quick sigh, then thought a moment longer. "All right, thanks, Darryl. I'll let you know if there's anything to this."

"All right," said Darryl, dropping the feigned annoyance. "Talk to you later."

Moments later, Elliot phoned his father and asked him to make up a key of the required configuration—Mr. Draupau had retained all his locksmith equipment after the developer bought him out. To allay any suspicions the outline of a key in an envelope addressed to Elliot might raise, Elliot asked his father to mail the key taped inside a stiff greeting card. It would arrive in a few days, and in the meantime, Elliot decided simply to relax, take in The Brink of Tomorrow, and review his text for a luncheon chat with the local Rotary Club scheduled for three days hence.

Having decided on a risky course of action, Elliot found the passing of the next few days interminable. He filled them with activities—tennis, racquetball, batting practice, swimming, even a shopping trip into the city—but doubts and apprehensions about what he was contemplating weighed heavily on him.

What if the secret he was about to uncover in the underground tunnel altered his perception of his employers and the way he portrayed Dale? Could he continue to be effective in his performances? Would it be noticed by his audiences? Would that somehow betray the secret? Would he then forfeit the earnings accumulating in the escrow account and sacrifice the nest egg waiting for him in the trust fund?

What if the secret he was about to uncover represented some illicit activity that he was thereafter bound legally, morally, and ethically to reveal, but by covenant to preserve? Certainly, revealing such illicit activity would represent the noblest course, despite the sacrifice of covenant. But it would also deprive him of the fruits of his labors. Would he be able to part with that money when it came time to actually bare the secret? This would surely be a test of character, character which had heretofore never been so rigorously challenged.

Of course, even after the key arrived, Elliot could still opt out of the plan. His decision would hinge upon how he felt when he actually held the key in his hand, actually slipped the key in the lock, actually breached the security of those subterranean galleries. Would he go through with it then?

Preoccupied as he was with these questions, Elliot failed to win a single contest with Bobby at tennis or racquetball. Knowing he and Elliot were fairly evenly matched, and used to winning only about half the time, Bobby found his opponent's losing streak strange and asked if anything was amiss. Of course, Elliot was forced to lie and pass off his losses as nothing more than a biorhythmic dip or some unexplained lapse of concentration or dexterity. Being an accomplished actor, though, he pulled off the prevarication with perfect aplomb.

As it happened, mayor Braunmuller was a member of the Rotary Club and made a point of attending the luncheon where his "old friend Dale Greene" was addressing the gathering. Elliot had caught most of the shows during which the mayor had called in and talked to Dale, so was sufficiently familiar with the subjects they had discussed to seamlessly continue the relationship.

In a way, Elliot delighted in the deception he and his employers were perpetrating on the mayor. As Elliot had come to expect of politicians, the mayor's plan for the city had turned out to be mostly smoke and mirrors, and Elliot felt it was appropriate that the official got a taste of his own medicine, even though he didn't know he was getting it. After the luncheon, the two men stood around talking politics while Wil and Paul sat silently nearby.

Arriving back at the estate that afternoon, Elliot found waiting for him the greeting card containing the key he had requested from his father. Excitedly opening the envelope, he carefully inspected its cargo. As expected, it was just what he had ordered. The card was equally appropriate, a humorous "You Hold the Key to My Heart" message.

Eager as he was to find out what was behind those locked doors, the recreation pavilion and subways tended to be fairly active during the day, so he dared not start his investigation right then when he was most at risk of being caught. Better to wait until after nine that night when Bobby was not around and the place became really quiet.

"My first caller is Antoine," Dale said as he opened the show that evening, utterly oblivious to the fact that his alter ego was only moments from breaching his precious, horrible secret. "Antoine is fifty-six and says his wife is divorcing him after thirty-one years of marriage. Hi, Antoine, this is Dale Greene and you're on The Brink of Tomorrow."

Elliot had his radio on but wasn't really listening. He was too busy dressing for his excursion into the nether world of the Greene estate.

Despite his apprehensions upon first conceiving this plan, Elliot had not accurately guessed how anxious he would be upon actually executing it. Slipping the illicit key into his pocket, stepping into the chill night air, and zipping his jacket to the collar, he found himself literally weak-kneed and tremulous. He paused at his doorstep, trying to calm down. It took several moments. The only thing that seemed to work was to imagine himself playing a role—a cop or spy or private eye. Even then, the stark reality of his undertaking prevented him from completely steadying his nerves.

Furtively watching for onlookers, he briskly walked the two hundred yards to the recreation pavilion, avoiding the little pools of light thrown by the lamps which lined the walkway.

Being inherently secure there on the estate, the pavilion was never locked, and Elliot easily slipped in and made his way to the elevator.

Once inside the lift, he reached into his pocket and grasped the key. There he hesitated. His mind was abuzz with questions, doubts, and fears, none of them distinct or intelligible. Now was the moment of decision.

But the buzz in his mind was too cluttered and formless to mount a compelling argument against continuing, and he slowly pulled the key from his pocket and aimed it at the shiny new lock that would dispatch the lift to its lower depths.

Just inches away, his hand moving closer, he found that he had crossed into a bizarre frame of mind. He was no longer in control. He was on autopilot, executing a program conceived at another time, another place, out of touch with the reality of this moment. Had he been in touch, he might have faltered. But he didn't. And he was thankful for the programming as his hand drove the key slowly toward the lock.

With a delicate click, the key made contact, then slid cleanly into the keyway. In a last-gasp effort to be heard, his mind made a final stab at logic. Even now he could abort the mission. Even now he could retreat and return to his apartment with no questions asked, no harm done.

But that would leave him with even more questions and none of the answers he sought. And delaying would only prolong the anxiety. It was now or never.

He let the programming prevail and rotated his wrist.

The key turned in the lock.

Without warning, the vehicle's motor clunked to life and the car lurched downward. Compared to the quiet of the moment before, the noise of the elevator motor seemed loud—*very* loud—loud enough to attract unwanted attention. His heart skipped a beat, then began pounding.

The elevator would continue down to the tunnel below and there was no way of stopping it en route. He could not push a button or turn the key back or wave a magic wand and reverse its direction in mid-descent. It would stop when it hit bottom, and no sooner. What if they were waiting for him when he arrived? What if they nabbed him as the doors opened, the illicit key still in his hand?

In anticipation, his heart hammered his ribs even harder.

The ride seemed interminable. Finally, the car slowed and stopped and it was quiet again. He was safe.

Then, suddenly, the doors opened. They were onto him!

No, that's just how elevators work! he scolded himself. He put his hand to his brow and silently laughed at himself. *What an idiot!* Had this been a movie and he a player in it, this scene would have provided the comic relief. He stepped out of the compartment into the subterranean corridor.

The tunnels were relatively well lit. He had hoped they would be dark and shadowy to provide him some semblance of cover, should he encounter anyone down here. But they were lit just like the tunnels outside the secured area. Why should they be any different? Again, *What an idiot!*

From his vantage point directly in front of the elevator, Elliot could see nothing of interest. In both directions—right and left—the ten-foot wide tunnel curved around out of view. This gave him two apparently equal options for exploration and, flipping a mental coin, he chose to go right.

For some reason, he felt more comfortable right next to the bare white wall and hugged it as he made his way around the gentle curve. The floor of the corridor was linoleum and his deck shoes made a faint chirping sound as he walked. He tried walking slower, faster, even tiptoe—but to no avail. The sound was inescapable and it made him even more nervous than he had been before.

Only after walking another twenty yards did it occur to him to take off his shoes and make the trek in his stocking feet. *Some spy I would have made!* For a moment, he wondered how he would explain his shoes in his hands instead of on his feet if he were caught, but that quickly gave way to the realization that he would have much more serious explaining to do than his footwear.

After eighty-five or ninety yards, he came to a door which was secured by a shiny new lock. As best he could figure, this was the door under the garage. He had already been on the other side of this door, wondering what was on the side he was on now.

"Humph," he murmured in disappointment.

He turned for the trip back and exploration of the other end of the tunnel.

Arriving back at the elevator without incident, he moved confidently into the remaining portion of the corridor. As far as he could see, this part of the tunnel looked just like the other end as it curved away in the distance. His gaze was focused into that distance when the wall on the inside of the curve, the wall he was hugging, suddenly disappeared into a recess.

Stunned, he stepped back and froze against the wall. His heartbeat was suddenly up and he took a moment to calm himself.

Screwing up his nerve, Elliot slowly peered around the corner into the recess. It was about eight feet deep, and dark, compared to the rest of the tunnel. At its far end was a heavy door. A small window at eye level provided visual access to the room on the other side, but it was also relatively dark and Elliot was unable to identify any of what he saw through the window.

But there was movement, the flickering of lights, and a low drone. This must be what he came to see.

He moved slowly, carefully, into the recess. As he approached the door, the drone became distinguishable—a man's voice effectively muffled by the weight of the door. And the view through the window became broader, though still unrecognizable.

Now, close enough to touch the door, but being careful not to, Elliot peered obliquely through the window. On the other side, he could make out another door leading to yet another room, and what appeared to be a thick glass partition between the two chambers. On the wall of the far room were what appeared to be racks of some sort. An indistinct reflection on the glass partition made it difficult to see what, exactly, was on or in the racks.

Seeing no one from his current perspective, Elliot moved cautiously to a more advantageous angle. Presently, there was a movement, and the form of his friend, Bobby, rose into view in the far chamber. Startled, Elliot stepped back into the shadows.

Turning away, Bobby did something at the racks on the wall, then returned to his seat. Elliot slowly moved forward again until he could see Bobby's face. Bobby was looking through the glass partition at something in the near chamber. Fortunately, he gave no indication of having seen Elliot, owing, Elliot figured, to the darkness in which he was standing. But what was Bobby looking at?

Moving across the plane of the window, Elliot began to make out, in the near chamber, a swing-arm lamp, a computer monitor, and what appeared to be a control panel with lights all lined up in rows. In the glass partition was the reflection of something strange, something unrecognizable. It had a nodular, organic sort of shape, but was oddly amorphous.

Suddenly it moved, and Elliot jumped back. What was it?! It was roughly the size and shape of a bear's head. But that made little sense. He peered again at the odd reflection. Presently, it settled into its former position.

In the reflection, Elliot could see the faint glimmer of eyes. They darted and blinked with an intelligence well beyond that of an animal, but whatever they belonged to, it certainly wasn't human. What was it? What could it be? Was he standing outside some subterranean chamber of horrors, witnessing some bizarre scientific—or *un*scientific!—experiment? Could his unassuming racquetball opponent possibly be part of such a foul enterprise? Wouldn't their role in keeping this secret, by necessity, implicate his friends, Wil and Paul?

Wait a minute! he cautioned himself. *You've seen too many movies. This isn't what's happening.*

Presently, Bobby gave some sort of a hand signal to whatever it was he was looking at. Without delay . . .

"We're back," came the deep resonant voice of Dale Greene through the door. It was muffled, but unmistakable. "You're tuned to WWKW, FM 102.4, and this is The Brink of Tomorrow with Dale Greene. My next caller is Stacey . . . ."

Elliot was stunned. From his vantage point he couldn't see the DJ's face. All he could see was the strange faint reflection in the glass partition, and he studied it intensely. For sure, there were the eyes— their expression matched the intent of Dale's words. And below the eyes, there was a mouth, its movement matching phoneme for phoneme what Dale was saying.

Moving to peer through the window at a very oblique angle, Elliot could now make out the back of the creature's head. It was bulbous and tumescent, with long, coarse hairs jutting sparsely from its mottled surface, its movement matching bob for bob the movements of the reflection speaking. Could this be?

Elliot looked again, studied the spectacle sharply, watched it for several minutes. It was unmistakable.

Dale was this ... *thing*! And this was the booth from which he broadcast his show each night!

Elliot drew back from the window and leaned against the wall, his breathing shallow and fitful, his emotions a strange mix of compassion and revulsion. No wonder Dale couldn't meet his public himself. Who would want to know their beloved radio advisor was a ... monster?

It was so bizarre that Elliot was still having trouble believing it. He wanted a better look at his employer, but his perspective through the window limited him to what he had already seen.

He thought about waiting for the show to conclude and watching from some refuge as Dale exited the booth for the night. But the tunnels offered no such refuge.

He considered waiting and confronting Dale directly, but it really wasn't his intention to make the DJ uncomfortable—nor himself, for that matter—and that certainly would be the result of such confrontation.

He entertained the notion of staying and watching more of the proceedings through the window, but that would make him vulnerable to discovery.

Thinking better of it, he decided his best course of action was to simply return to his apartment and decide what to do from there. He turned to leave, but found it strangely difficult. What he had seen through that window had changed something in him, fused him in some way to what was behind that door.

He felt odd, not himself. He had the sudden urge to burst in and make himself known. *That,* he knew, would be disastrous.

Startled back to reality by this irrational impulse, he abruptly turned, made his way out of the catacombs, and returned with no further delay to his apartment.

Ken Gullekson

Chapter 20

"My next caller is Quentin, who's thirty-five and says he's losing his job. Hi, Quentin, this is Dale Greene and you're on The Brink of Tomorrow."

A week had passed since Elliot's excursion into the Greene estate catacombs. Having seen what he saw down there, Elliot had become fascinated with The Brink of Tomorrow and not missed a minute of it since. Knowing Dale's monstrosity and listening to him dispense his very wise, very insightful advice in that liquid-gold voice presented a haunting study in contrasts. There was no way Elliot could discern the DJ's disfigurement from how he sounded or what he said. Yet, he knew the awful truth.

Knowing this truth, Elliot now viewed everyone and everything in the Greene domain differently. He saw Bobby as a principled soul, a talented engineer, and a dedicated friend. Wil and Paul and Shel were obviously loyal, loving guardians of Dale and his interests. And the estate was Dale's own private Camelot.

And he saw himself differently as well. He was no longer just playing a role under very odd and confining circumstances. He was now a contributor to a cause, a representative of a principle, a trustee of a sacred promise. Whereas before he felt like an outsider, now he felt like a member of a team. Whereas before he was doing the job for money, now he was doing it for Dale. Whereas before he wanted to quit and go home, now he wanted to stay and help.

Not that this was to be his life's work. But for now, knowing the circumstances and his role in them, he was willing to stick it out for a while longer. After all, if he left while Dale's public was still clamoring for appearances, Dale couldn't simply hire someone else to take his place. Now that half the city accepted *him* as Dale Greene, he knew that no one else could do the job. If he were to leave, he would leave Dale without options. And that didn't seem fair.

He had already called Darryl and told him he would be staying on.

An appearance at a convalescent hospital was scheduled for a few days hence and Elliot, in his new frame of mind, was approaching it with fresh purpose and enthusiasm.

"What line of work are you in, Quentin?" Dale was asking his caller as Elliot's thoughts drifted back to the show.

"I work for a defense contractor," Quentin replied blandly. "I can't get any more specific than that for security reasons."

"I see. Are you being fired or laid off?"

"Laid off, along with a few hundred other guys—and gals. It's part of the defense cutbacks we're being hit with."

"Uh-huh. Aside from being temporarily out of work, what exactly is the problem?"

"Well, given the nature of my work, there just won't be any jobs for me in this area after this one's gone."

"Are you getting any kind of severance package to keep you afloat while you decide what to do?"

"Oh, yeah, I'm getting a very generous severance package. But it won't last forever and I have a family to support."

"Can you find another job elsewhere and relocate?"

"Well, aside from the fact that I really don't want to move—I have all kinds of family here—I'm afraid there won't be much call for the kind of work that I do anywhere else. Because of technological advancements, my expertise is all but obsolete. So I'm kind of stuck."

Dale drew a breath and blew it out again as he mulled his next question. "You know, Quentin, I don't mean to sound unsympathetic when I say this, but humans are a very adaptable life form, and, given sufficient resources—a generous severance package, for instance—they can adapt to all kinds of new circumstances. So I have difficulty sympathizing with complaints that one's job is becoming obsolete. My answer is: Adapt and do something else. Does this ring true to you?"

Quentin sighed loudly. "I guess so."

"Good. So with that understood, what are you excited to do?"

Quentin thought briefly before answering. "Well, I could put the severance package in the bank and work for my father-in-law. I wouldn't make much, but at least I'd have a job for the rest of my life. But I really don't have any interest in livestock feed and he and I really don't get along that well."

"You don't sound at all excited about that."

"Well, no, I'm not."

"Then what *does* excite you?"

"Well . . . I'd like something that pays as much as my last job . . . with some stability . . . ." Quentin's voice trailed off as though he had run out of answer.

"I don't mean this as a reprimand, Quentin," Dale said softly, after giving his caller a moment to say more, "but your response doesn't answer my question. I point that out because it's quite illuminating to see how one's mind responds to this question. What I want to know— and, more importantly, what you have to answer for yourself—is: What *excites* you? What really gets your engine cranking?"

"You mean, like, what kind of jobs excite me?"

"What kind of *anything* excites you? What revs you up when you think of it? Don't restrict yourself to *jobs*." Dale pronounced the word in exaggerated announcer tones even deeper than his normal voice. "What are your wildest dreams?"

"My wildest dreams?! To spend all my time skydiving!"

"Skydiving! Now that *is* exciting. Is that what you do in your spare time?"

"Uh-huh."

"Hmmm. Have you ever considered opening a skydiving school here in Springfield? That would certainly give you plenty of opportunity to skydive all day long."

"I'd *love* to do that. But starting a business is pretty costly you know."

"Can be. Is there any chance your severance package is big enough to cover the start-up costs of opening such a school?"

"Yeah, but it'll take every penny of it, and going into business these days is so risky. It scares me to death."

With Quentin's admission of fear, Dale finally knew how to help his caller.

"All right. Well, I think we've hit on the crux of the matter and I have some ideas to share with you. First of all, I must preface this by saying that I don't give business advice. All I do is share my philosophy of life as it might apply to the problems my callers present me with. It's up to you to extract from that philosophy the guidance you seek—or not. It's entirely up to you. And with that in mind, I have a couple of things to say about your dilemma."

"Okay."

"First of all, the practical side: At the age of forty-eight, my great grandfather got tired of working his fingers to the bone for other people and started a business of his own, with his life savings. It took every penny he had, and he had some pretty lean years as the business grew. But when he died, he was worth over fifteen million dollars. That may not sound like much now, but back then it was a fortune. I never met my great grandfather, but my parents told me that if he was adamant about anything, it was the wisdom of following your dream. It can pay off—and big. And it doesn't take a stroke of genius or some wonder product. All it takes is faith in yourself and a lot of hard work. You may be familiar with the business my great grandfather started: Harvest Moon?"

"The supermarket chain?!"

"That's right. He finally sold his interest in it, but not before he had amassed his fortune. So it can happen."

"I *guess*!"

"Now for the philosophical side: As you know, if you listen to this program at all regularly, we're all here to experience ourselves as the spiritual beings we are. And everything we do, we do in the service of that. Now, it seems that we're closest to our native spiritual state when we're doing either what we're *excited* to do or what we're *afraid* to do. Fear and excitement go together here because they're basically the same energy; the only difference is that fear is excitement that you've judged or failed to act on in the past. Anyway, doing what we're excited or afraid to do leads us to the various experiences we're here to have. Of course, these experiences may contain varying degrees of joy and pain, depending on what we're here for, but irrespective of what we encounter in our lives, we're closest to our native spiritual state— closest to our soul, if you will—when we're doing what we're excited to do or what we're afraid to do. Of course, there's nothing difficult about doing what we're *excited* to do, it's doing what we're *afraid* to do that presents the real challenge. And it can be quite a challenge! Many of us allow our fears to immobilize us and we accept a life of mediocrity and boredom and stagnation."

"Well, fear's not really a problem for me. I jump out of airplanes, after all."

"Were you scared the first time you jumped out of an airplane?"

"Well . . . ."

"Be honest. There's no shame in feeling fear."

"Yeah, I was afraid, sure. But after a few times the fear went away and it became just a huge rush."

"You mean the fear turned into excitement."

Quentin hesitated for a moment as he assessed the transformation of his feelings back then. "Yeah, that's about right."

"That's because, as I said, fear is just excitement you've judged or failed to act on in the past. And when you do what you're afraid to do, the judgment comes off and the fear converts to excitement. That's what happened after you did what you were afraid to do and jumped out of that airplane the first time."

"I get it."

"So if you'd love to open a skydiving school but the idea of investing every penny of your severance package scares you, do you see the potential of the fear converting to excitement, once you've done what you're afraid to do?"

Quentin heaved a huge sigh. "Yeah, but we're talking about risking everything I have to do that."

"Aren't you risking your *life* every time you jump out of an airplane?"

This one caught Quentin short and he was at a loss for an answer. Finally, he murmured, "But that's different."

"You're right, it *is* different. But what's different isn't the nature of the risk, it's the way you're responding to it. With skydiving, you responded to the fear with your *soul*, and you jumped anyway. With the idea of starting a business, you're responding to the fear with your *ego*, and you're backing away."

"How's that?" Quentin queried, unsure how the ego fit into the equation.

"All right, I've talked a little about ego before, but I guess I need to go into another aspect of it. Without going into detail about how the ego works or why it is the way it is, suffice it to say that the ego is most attuned to fear, while your soul is most attuned to excitement. So when you contemplate undertaking a challenging experience, your ego will respond with fear, while your soul will respond with excitement. If you're in touch with your *soul*, then you'll feel *excitement* at the prospect of undertaking the challenge. If you're more in touch with your *ego*, you'll feel *fear* at the prospect of the challenge. Now, your soul wants you to be all that you can be, while your ego wants to protect you."

"From what?"

"From anything it imagines is a threat, whether it's really a threat or not. That includes your own aspirations."

"I see."

"So, in response to the fear, your ego steps in and does what it can to rescue you from it. It does that, basically, by feeding you thoughts which talk you out of your fear, or show you how to avoid the fear. It might feed you thoughts like, 'This severance package is my security blanket and I can't afford to invest it all in a business.' Or, 'If I put that money in the bank and work for my father-in-law, at least I'll have some security.' Does this sound at all familiar?"

Quentin drew a deep breath and exhaled noisily. "Of course."

"Right. And if you decide not to undertake the challenge, then your fear is assuaged and your ego has succeeded in rescuing you from it. But you're also less than you can be, and you don't get to experience the excitement that that fear will turn into."

"I get it."

"As you can see, the process of converting the fear into excitement is really the process of getting in touch with your soul. So, you can either do what scares you—which, in this case, also excites you—or allow your ego to rescue you from your fear and limit yourself. The choice is yours. What do you think?"

Quentin sighed again. "It's ... it's *really* scary. But if I'd never jumped out of that airplane, I never would've known the thrill of it." He paused to mull the issue further, and Dale just let him, despite the silence it produced—he knew his listeners, who fought these very battles every day, were glued to their radios.

As for Elliot, hearing Dale's explanation of the phenomenon of ego reminded him of Dale's own predicament and the fear that had prompted the disfigured DJ to hire an actor to meet his public for him. Had Dale's own ego rescued him from his fear of meeting his public? Was Dale at all aware of this himself?

"All right," Quentin concluded at last. "You make a good point. I'm gonna do it."

"Don't let me talk you into anything," Dale cautioned emphatically.

"No, no! This is my decision," Quentin affirmed. "It's scary as hell, but it's also exciting. So I'm gonna do it. Thanks!"

"You're welcome," Dale replied with a chuckle. "Keep in touch and let me know how it turns out."

"I will! In fact, if you ever want to skydive, your lessons will be on the house!"

"Why, thank you, Quentin! I certainly appreciate that. Good night, now."

"Good night."

Dale disconnected the call and announced, "This is Dale Greene on The Brink of Tomorrow. Back in a moment with more calls on FM 102.4."

Hey, Elliot thought to himself, *maybe I can get free skydiving lessons out of this!*

"It's nine forty-seven," Elliot heard Dale announce upon returning from the commercial break, "and you're listening to The Brink of Tomorrow on FM 102.4. My next caller is Ellie. She's twenty-four and she says she thinks she's been abducted by aliens." He connected the call. "Hi, Ellie, this is Dale Greene."

"Hi, Dale." Ellie's voice was clear and mellifluous.

"You think you've been abducted by aliens, Ellie?"

From the ambivalent tone of Dale's voice, Ellie couldn't tell if he was mocking her or simply asking the question. "Yeah," she answered tentatively, guarding against possible ridicule. "Do you believe in UFOs?"

"Well, technically, a UFO is just an unidentified flying object. And I know that on occasion flying objects *do* go unidentified, even in official records. So I'd have to say 'yes,' I do believe in UFOs. But I suspect what you're *really* asking is: Do I believe that UFOs are extraterrestrial spacecraft?"

"Yeah!" she acknowledged, encouraged by Dale's analysis. "Do you?"

"I believe that some are. I've never seen one myself, so I can only say I hold the *belief* without experiential substantiation. But I've seen hundreds of photographs that have been documented as genuine by photographic experts, and read the testimonials of hundreds of people who have claimed to have seen craft that don't look like anything we fly and that exhibit maneuvering capabilities far beyond anything we can build. And that's only a drop in the bucket compared to the hundreds of thousands of reports and photographs that've been catalogued, some of which have been made by trained observers, including airline pilots, astronauts, and law enforcement personnel. If we aren't being visited by extraterrestrials, then *every single one* of those photos and *every single one* of the reports has to be either a hoax or a delusion. And I think the likelihood of *that* is vanishingly small. To put it another way, if just *one* of those photographs or *one* of those eyewitness reports is genuine—and I've gotta believe that, out of those hundreds of thousands, at least one *is*—then we are indeed being visited by extraterrestrials. So yes, I do believe that some UFOs are alien spacecraft."

Ellie's sigh of relief was audible.

"So what makes you think you've been abducted by aliens?" Dale queried.

"Well, for many years, since I was about five, I had a foreign object under my skin. I didn't remember injuring myself or being poked by anything that would've put it there; I just noticed it one day. And it didn't hurt or get infected, so I just left it there until about a five years ago when my curiosity got the best of me and I had my doctor remove it."

"What did it turn out to be?"

"Well, it was pretty unusual. I had it analyzed and it turned out to be a couple of short metallic rods, about a quarter of an inch long, put together in the shape of a 'T' with a covering of some hard organic substances. The weird thing about them was that the composition of the rods was like what they find in meteorites, and the organic substances covering the rods were not the kind of thing human bodies typically make. The analyst called the results 'mind-boggling.'"

"Really?! That's interesting. So on the basis of this object, you've concluded that you were abducted by aliens?"

"Oh, no. I have all the other classical signs: little scoop marks appearing out of nowhere on my body, vague fears all the time, missing time, nosebleeds at night, the sense that I'm being watched, nightmares of being experimented on that seem too real. It can be really terrifying."

"Yeah, those are the classic signs of the alien abduction phenomenon," Dale agreed. "How often do you believe this happens?"

"It's varied over the years. Sometimes it was every couple of months, especially when I was young. Other times it didn't happen for a couple of years. After I had the implant removed, I moved to another state and they didn't take me for about four years. Then I guess they found me again because suddenly they started taking me again, and there was another foreign object under my skin."

"Really?!" Dale found the probative nature of this sequence of events surprising. "Did you have it removed, too?"

"No. I figured they'd just find me again and do it all over again. So I decided to just go with it. I mean, it still scares me, but I don't think I can avoid it."

"I see! Well, that's very courageous of you, Ellie. So what can I do to help you with this?"

"Well, you seem to know so much about so many things, I thought you might be able to tell me something to make me less afraid."

"Well, of course, *I* can't make you less afraid. Only *you* can do that."

"Oh, I know," Ellie quickly assured. "But can't you tell me something that can help me do that?"

"Well, my channeled sources do acknowledge the existence of spacefaring civilizations on other planets, and some of them have answered questions of this nature. So maybe I can pass that information on to you. Of course, I can only tell you what my sources say. I've never spoken to any space aliens myself."

Ellie laughed. "I know. But I'd like to know what your sources say."

"Okay. Well, probably the most significant thing they talk about is that all these abductees have agreed to being abducted and having these experiments conducted on them."

"*Agreed* to them?!" This was something Ellie had not considered, and she gave it a moment of thought. Then, "Why would I make an agreement like that? And *how*?"

"Again, I can only tell you what my sources say, but they say that the civilization which is doing most of the abductions and experimentation is, for sake of brevity, dying out. And—"

"Dying out?! Why?"

"Well, the explanation I got said they had polluted the surface of their planet through imprudent use of their energy source and were forced to go underground. But in order to survive underground, they had to make some rather extreme alterations to their DNA, which they did through genetic engineering. But those alterations eventually led to genetic flaws and reproductive problems. So now they're trying to incorporate human DNA into their genome to strengthen their genetic structure. But they need to perform these experiments in order to learn exactly how to do it safely and reliably. So, to provide human subjects for their experiments, some of them have chosen to reincarnate in our reality with the agreement to allow themselves to be experimented on to save their race. Which means they aren't really imposing their will on you."

This concept struck Ellie as momentous. "Wow! So I may be helping them save their race?"

"That's my understanding," confirmed Dale.

"So they're not here to invade Earth or anything like that?"

"It wouldn't seem so."

"And I'm not helping them destroy mankind?"

Dale chuckled. "No."

Ellie sighed again. "Okay, but that doesn't completely make sense, 'cause they act like they don't know there's an agreement. They can be pretty cold—like, if they don't force me to come and submit to their experiments, I won't do it."

"*Would* you go along if they didn't force you?"

"Well, *no*. It's terrifying. O' course, part of the reason it's terrifying is because they're forcing me."

"Right. See, even though they know you agreed to submit to their experiments, they also know you have a human ego which doesn't remember the agreement and resists the process. So they think they have to force you."

"Oh! That makes sense. But if I've made this agreement, why do I feel so afraid when it happens?"

"Well, even if you have reincarnated into this reality from that one, you're still human, which means you had to forget your past lives and any agreements you may have made in them—at least consciously—in order to come into this reality, just like all other humans. And you've been educated with an earthly understanding of things, and your ego is human. So you have the usual human emotional responses to the unknown, and especially to things we've been taught by society to fear, like space aliens."

"I see. Well, is there anything I can do to not be so afraid?"

"Yeah, there are a few things you can try. Probably the first thing is to ask yourself if the fear serves you, or if it would be more useful to have a *different* response to these episodes."

"Well, I can tell you right now that the fear doesn't serve me; it only upsets me, and it doesn't seem to stop them."

"Yeah, the fear would suggest to them that you're going to resist their efforts. So what if you were to decide that, instead of simply being afraid, you could think of these episodes as *adventures* and find the *excitement* in them? Accept for the moment that you did make an agreement to participate in an effort to save their race, and see if you can't allow yourself to go along with whatever it is they're doing as a knowing and willing—and *excited*—participant."

Ellie thought about this for a few moments. "Yeah, I can do that."

"Good. If that doesn't get the job done, you can try to exhaust the fear."

Puzzled by his terminology, Ellie pondered for a second. "Exhaust the fear?"

"Yeah. You do this by totally feeling the fear until it no longer bothers you."

"How do I do *that*?"

"Well, when the fear comes up, place yourself in it, and willingly experience the full effect of it. Place all of your attention on that fearful feeling in your heart, or the pit of your stomach, and just *feel* it.

Don't try to escape it, don't try to avoid it—just immerse yourself in the feeling. Focus all of your attention exclusively on the sensations in your body and experience them without restraint. And keep that up. Pretty soon you'll realize you're not dead, and you're not even really being harmed. It's just that your heart is pounding really, really hard. But that's not much different than running around the block really fast. And after a while, that will subside. Then the next time the fear arises, it won't be as intense or last as long. If you do this every time the fear comes up, eventually these kinds of experiences will simply no longer scare you."

"Wow! That's kind of interesting. What else?"

"Well, you can try to let them know that you know about the agreement so they don't think they have to force you to go along with them."

"Really! How do I do *that*? I'm usually paralyzed and can't talk."

"Okay, well, one my sources described a mental exercise that you can do when you're having one of your abduction dreams. He suggested imagining a blue glow all around your body."

"A blue glow?"

"Yes. Just, with your imagination, envelope your body in a cocoon of glowing blue light. This is supposed to communicate to them on a level of consciousness that they pay attention to that *you* know you're there by agreement."

"Why blue light?"

"I don't know. Apparently it's a frequency that has meaning to them."

"Hmm." Ellie mulled the prospect briefly. Then, "Yeah, I can try that." Upon making this decision, she heaved a deep cleansing sigh. But she had more questions. "I've heard scientists say that it would be impossible for space aliens to reach Earth from so far away. What about that?"

"You mean because reaching even a *tenth* the speed of light would require so much energy as to be next to impossible, and even at *that* speed the closest civilizations would take decades to get here—the further ones centuries—so they wouldn't bother?"

"Yeah."

"Well, the way my sources explain it is that they don't actually *move through* space like we do. They have a much deeper understanding of space and time, and they're able to get from one place to another not by traveling *through* space—which they call 'sliding around on the skin of space'—but by jumping between spatial coordinates."

"What does *that* mean?"

"What they say they do is unlock the spatial and temporal signatures of the matter which comprises their spacecraft, then lock in new spatial and temporal signatures for the space and time of their destination. If you were outside their craft watching them do this, they would simply disappear from their starting location and reappear at their destination. Obviously, this is something our scientists haven't even thought of, much less figured out how to do."

"I guess! I don't even know what you said."

Dale chuckled. "It doesn't matter. Suffice it to say that they've developed technology that our scientists haven't even imagined yet. As a result, many of our scientists and government officials dismiss the claims of extraterrestrial visitation. It stems from their own fears and short-sightedness."

"You're telling me! It's like they forget what it means to be scientists or something."

"Yeah!"

"So do you think I've been abducted by aliens?"

Dale smiled to himself. "Well, there's no way I can know that. But by the same token, I have no cause to doubt you. There are so many things we don't know about the universe, the nature of physical reality, even ourselves, that to say something doesn't exist or isn't happening—that we aren't being visited by extraterrestrials—strikes me as the height of ignorance and arrogance. So I have to accept what you've told me as your experience."

Ellie sighed again.

"So did I answer all your questions, Ellie?"

"Yes, thank you. You've been really helpful. I'm gonna try that blue light thing next time it happens."

"Great! Be sure and let me know how it works, if you're ever abducted again."

Ellie giggled. "I will. Bye."

"Goodnight, dear." Dale disconnected the call.

Even after listening to Dale for all these months, the breadth of the man's knowledge continued to impress Elliot. *I guess that's what happens when you have a Harvard professor all to yourself,* he thought to himself as Dale announced a commercial break.

Chapter 21

"Elliot, it's Gene!" said the voice on the tape. "John Cochran's leaving 'Days of Our Lives' and they want to talk to you about joining the cast. This is your big break, partner. Get back to me the instant you get this message."

Elliot's jaw dropped. He signaled the machine to rewind and hung up in a catatonic state of shock. "Days of Our Lives" wanted to talk to him? The daytime drama had rejected him for a recurring role nearly nine months earlier because he looked too much like John Cochran. Now, Cochran was leaving and they wanted to talk to him again! What exactly did that mean? "...About joining the cast," his agent had said. To replace Cochran? That meant he would be an instant regular! Or in some other role? The intent of the message was unclear. But Gene had said this was his big break! So it must be to replace Cochran! No, that conclusion was premature; he had too little information to jump there.

These thoughts ricocheted around in his head as he dialed Gene's number as fast as his fingers would let him.

There was a screeching sound, then a mechanical female voice. "We're sorry, your call cannot be completed as dialed. Please hang up and—" He hung up and tried again, this time slower, making sure he got the numbers right. This time there was a ring.

"Agency," was the curt answer.

"Gene Weiss, please."

The phone receptionist didn't even acknowledge Elliot's request, she just put him on hold and executed the transfer.

"Mr. Weiss's office," came the voice of Weiss's secretary.

"Elliot Draupau returning his call," Elliot said flatly, purposely suppressing his excitement. He didn't want to sound *too* eager.

"One moment, Mr. Draupau."

Waiting for his agent to pick up, Elliot was as excited as he had ever remembered being. It had been a month since he had entered the tunnels beneath the Greene estate and he had made three "Dale Greene" appearances since then. They had gone well, and his new perspective and sense of service to Dale had made his malaise less punishing than before. But, as he soon discovered, they could not dispel it completely. The fact was that the role of Dale Greene had simply reached the end of its life for him and no amount of perspective could prolong it. He sighed as he admitted this to himself.

"Elliot!" Gene barked as he came on the line. "You ready to jump on your big break?!"

"Sorry, Gene . . . can't right now . . . got a hangnail," Elliot joked deadpan. Gene Weiss was a good agent, but Elliot didn't like being pressured by the man's unbridled enthusiasm, and this was his way of reining him in.

"Very funny," Gene smirked. "Do you want the job or not?"

"What exactly did you mean by 'joining the cast?' You didn't make that clear."

"Didn't I say John Cochran was leaving?"

"Yeah, but you didn't say whether they wanted me to replace him or what?"

"What do I have to do, paint you a picture?"

"It would certainly be clearer."

"Yes, they want you to replace him," Gene replied with mock condescension. It was *his* way of saving face after being reined in.

Yes! Elliot exclaimed to himself, finally getting satisfaction. Apparently, his resemblance to John Cochran was a blessing in disguise. This meant steady work, exposure, recognition, *acting* as it was meant to be! "What are they talking about for salary?"

"Well, they're kind of in a bind for someone who has the look and can do the job, so I told them not less than twelve a week to start, pending your approval." *Twelve* was short for *twelve thousand.* "They had to go for it . . . unless you want more."

"No, no. Twelve is fine. I don't want to start off upsetting them by quibbling over salary." At two thousand dollars a day, including weekends, Elliot was getting fourteen thousand dollars a week in the Greene employ. Twelve thousand was nearly as much, and being *free* again more than made up the difference.

But there was the matter of Dale.

"How soon do they need me?" Elliot asked. "I've got to wrap things up here."

"Well, they've still got Cochran for two weeks, and they can send his character out of town for a while. So three, maybe four weeks."

Elliot sighed. This meant he had a little time, but not a lot. "What started this? I mean, they're not gonna settle a contract dispute and change their minds or something after I end my gig here, are they?"

"No, no," Gene assured him. "They've been feuding for months—creative differences—and there's no settlement in sight."

"Creative differences can be resolved," Elliot averred warily.

"Not these. Cochran was recently 'born again' and wanted his character to get religion."

"Oh!" Knowing the role that John Cochran played, he knew such a transformation would be utterly inconsistent with his character's function in the show.

"The producers thought about killing him off, but he's central to the show. So they're replacing him. In any event, when his contract's up, he's outta there."

"Well . . . one man's loss is another man's gain!" Elliot observed.

"Two men's gain, in this case, partner. So I tell them 'yes?'"

"Tell them 'yes.'"

"That's my boy! I'll overnight the contract to you and talk to you later."

"Sound's good; I'll talk to you then."

Hanging up the phone, Elliot felt as if he had turned a corner and suddenly found himself on another planet. In the course of two minutes his life had changed. But he was aware that in the next two weeks, the life of another would also change. That he would be the cause of that change sobered him and alloyed his elation. He heaved a ponderous sigh and lay down to unwind from the excitement.

No sooner did his head hit the pillow than he was struck with a horrifying realization.

Chapter 22

"My next caller is Holly. She's forty-one and says she's worried about a decision she's made. Hi, Holly, this is Dale Greene and you're on The Brink of Tomorrow."

Fifty-three hours had passed since Elliot had talked to Gene Weiss; fifty-three hours of dread at the thought of tendering his resignation; fifty-three hours of procrastination he knew did no one any good. As of that moment, he was scheduled for only two appearances—one in two days, another two weeks later—and the prospect of telling Wil and Paul that they would be his last was at once suffocating him and eating him alive.

Had he not paid his uninvited visit to the catacombs—not seen what he saw, not known Dale for what he was—quitting would have been easier. But having seen and known, his sense of loyalty, compassion, and service, amplified by his horrifying realization fifty-three hours earlier, was playing havoc with his plans. Still, the thought of portraying Dale Greene for the rest of his life turned his stomach. And the lure of a real acting job was very powerful. But actually "giving notice" was proving to be harder than he could ever have imagined.

"What decision did you make that you're worried about?" Dale asked his caller.

"Well, a close friend of mine is in the hospital for a kidney transplant, and I've decided not to visit him or call him or even send him a card." Holly spoke in an effusion of words that Dale found enjoyable.

"Really?!" he queried curiously. "Why?"

"Well, it's kind of a long story."

"We've got another—" Dale checked his clock and did some quick math in his head "—eighty-seven minutes before midnight."

Holly chortled both at the DJ's generosity with his air time and the way he went about offering it. "Well, I've known him for about fifteen years, and I love him dearly. We went together for the first two years and we've been friends off and on ever since. In fact, now, we're kind of *best* friends; only I have *other* best friends and he only has *me*. But he's got this habit that just eats away at a relationship until you just can't take anymore."

"Mmmm. What habit is that?"

"Well, he won't work with you to resolve upsets with him. He's got this thing—some kind of ego or something—that resists any effort I make to enter into a healing dialog. If *I* make a mistake and somehow impose *my* will on *him*, he gets upset with me and won't accept my apologies—and I'm real good about apologizing when I cross someone's boundaries. But by not accepting my apology, he makes me apologize till I'm blue in the face, which is a form of control and manipulation. It's like he gets a whiff of an opportunity to control and milks it for all it's worth. Eventually, we sweep it under the rug and the thing blows over, but there's no forgiveness and I get stuck with this unresolved upset that I have to repress."

Mixed metaphors aside, Dale was impressed by his caller's grasp of the dynamics of her interactions with this man.

"And then," Holly continued, "if I get upset with *him* for some reason—'cause let's face it, he crosses *my* boundaries sometimes, too—he puts up this wall of resentment, like, 'How dare you be angry with me!' Like it's 'wrong' to be angry with him, and even worse to bring it up! And there's no way in hell of getting through *that* and having a healing dialog, much less getting any kind of apology out of him. And that gives him *another* opportunity to control and manipulate, which he milks like there's no tomorrow. So I'm completely stuck with any upsets I might have with him! And they've just built up to where I can't add another upset on top of all the others and still want to be around him." Holly released a healing sigh upon finally unloading this burden.

Hearing the release, Dale smiled softly to himself. "Have you tried explaining to him what you just explained to me?"

"Oh yeah, several times," Holly confirmed. "I'd wait till the upset blew over—way over!—and explain it to him as calmly and coolly as I could."

"Did it ever register with him?"

"I don't think so. He'd listen and all. But I don't think he really knew what I was talking about—what *behavior* in him I was talking about—'cause the next time we'd have an upset it would be like he'd forgotten everything I said to him. And nothing ever changed."

"I see. So what happened that precipitated your decision not to visit him in the hospital?"

"Well, he had a knee operation a couple of weeks ago and couldn't drive. And someone had broken his car window, so he asked me to take it over to get a new window put in before it rained. But it needed air in one tire and so I stopped at a gas station. But when I was putting the air in I accidentally cut my finger on the . . . you know, the thing that goes on the outside of the tire . . . ."

"The hubcap?" Dale suggested.

"*Yeah*, the—o' course!—the hubcap. And the only thing I could find to wipe the blood off with were these gas station paper towels. And I had this feeling of resentment toward him for asking me to take his car for repair when it needed air in the tire."

"But you did willingly agree to do this for him, didn't you?" Dale confirmed.

"Oh, yeah! And to put air in the tire, because he told me he thought it was low. And I knew the resentment I was feeling was just some weirdness of my own and that he really didn't do anything wrong. And I just wanted to tell him that I'd had this weird feeling of resentment and that I knew he hadn't done anything wrong—just to share my feelings like you always tell us to do."

"Well, I'm careful not to *tell* you to do anything," Dale reminded, "but I do *suggest* things for you to decide for yourself whether or not to do."

"Okay, right. Well, I just wanted to share my feelings with him, and because I knew it was my own weirdness, I wasn't going to express them angrily or anything. I just wanted to share them with him like it was a novelty. Well! When I got back to his place, I kept dropping things on the way from the car to his apartment and my finger was hurting and bleeding, and I started to get mad for real—but not at him, at myself. But when I got into his apartment, he picked up on the fact that I was upset and started putting up his wall. But it was all confused, because I wasn't mad at him at that time, and the resentment from before, that I wanted to share with him, like I said, was just kind of a novelty. But when I sat down to unravel it all with him, his wall was like solid brick, and he yelled at me for being mad, and I knew from past experience that there'd be no healing dialog, no understanding, no resolution, and it would just get swept under the rug and repressed. And I knew at that moment that I had repressed all that I could repress with him. There'd been upsets in recent months that he'd refused to resolve and I just felt like he was slowly but surely poisoning the relationship."

"That's not surprising. They call unresolved upsets like you're describing 'toxic emotion.'"

"Yeah! So when this last upset happened, I knew the relationship was dead, at least for me. I just didn't want to go through another attempt to enter into a healing dialog with him, only to have him refuse and add to the . . . the toxicity. So I left and decided to discontinue the relationship—which was weird, because I do love him. He's got a lot of real special qualities; he's smart and funny and creative, and it was fun to be with him—except when he got . . . *weird*, like I've been describing."

"I understand," Dale sympathized. "Is there any chance that, in the heat of the moment, your decision might have been just a little bit hasty?"

"Well, that's one of my questions. I've been checking my feelings on it ever since it happened, just to make sure I wasn't being hasty, and every time I thought about initiating a healing dialog with him—he would never initiate it himself—I got this real yucky feeling, because I knew he wouldn't go along. And again, I'd be stuck with an unresolved upset and just have to repress it. And I just wasn't willing to do that anymore—I wasn't willing to take any more poison. So it doesn't *feel* like I'm being hasty." Holly said this last with uncertainty in her voice—as though she weren't confident she could trust her feelings on the matter.

"All right. Is there any chance you're putting this distance between the two of you to get back at him or punish him or *force* him to initiate a healing dialog?" Dale probed further.

"I've been looking at that, too, because I *really* don't want to do that—that would make *me* just like *him*. But I don't think I am. 'Cause when I check how I feel about it, I'm willing to never see or speak to him again in my life in order not to take any more of his poison. I'm a pretty secure person—I have lots of other friends and make friends easily—and even though he and I have been very close, I just don't need any more of his poison."

Dale was impressed. "Well! That *is* secure. So now, did I understand you to say he's in the hospital again for a kidney transplant? Does this have anything to do with the knee operation? Last I heard, the knees and the kidneys were anatomically unrelated."

Holly laughed and Dale felt gratified that she had gotten his joke. "No, it's something else. He's been on dialysis for three years, waiting for a kidney, and one must've become available since our upset."

"Boy, he sure has his share of medical problems," Dale remarked. "Of course, that's not terribly surprising."

"Why?"

"Well, because all that toxic emotion has to express itself somehow, so it does it in the form of disease."

"Oh!" exclaimed Holly, as though this tidbit of information explained a great many things.

"So how did you find out about the kidney transplant if you're not talking to him?" Dale asked.

"His daughter called and left a message on my voicemail. She said he gave her a list of people to call and I was on it."

"I see."

"But I still didn't feel like having anything to do with him. But I felt bad about that, because I'd been through so much with him with his dialysis."

"You mean you'd been through *upsets* with him regarding his dialysis?" Dale clarified, interrupting.

"No, no. I mean I'd been there for him through all his pain and fears and self doubts. And after fifteen years of friendship—which was pretty intimate, as friendships go, outside of the upsets—I just felt bad about not wanting to visit him in the hospital or call him or even send him a card on this very important and triumphant moment in his life. 'Cause, see, I know he's thinking his good fortune of getting the kidney is way more important than some minor squabble."

"Uh-huh!" Dale acknowledged, beginning to understand Holly's inner conflict. "And when you look at it from *that* point of view, you're concerned that you're being petty and disloyal when you should be rising above all that."

"Yeah!"

"But what *he* considers a minor squabble is, for you, the last straw in a toxic pattern of defensiveness that's poisoned the relationship for good."

"Right! Exactly!" Her conflict finally articulated, Holly drew a relaxing breath.

"Hmmm. Do you feel as though you owe him something, or that he's been of greater service to you in the course of your friendship, and therefore you owe him for that?"

"No. Just the opposite. I've always been the giving one and him the needy one. I mean, he wasn't obsessively needy or anything—I didn't feel taken advantage of or victimized—but if anything, he owed *me*. But that's not a problem for me—I don't mind giving a little more than him; I'm perfectly comfortable with that."

"I see. Hmmm."

"So what do *you* think?" Holly pleaded. "*Am* I being petty and disloyal?"

"Well," Dale said, pausing briefly to consider the question, "of course, I'm not going to make that judgment for you. But I can give you a few principles—three to be exact—that apply here, that you can use to decide for yourself."

"Oh, okay. What are they?

"Well, first of all: Be true to your feelings—your *real* feelings. So what are your real feelings? When you strip away all the trappings, what feelings are you left with?"

Holly hesitated only briefly, then said, with utter conviction, "It feels really dishonest and yucky when I think about going to the hospital and repressing all that anger to make nice with him in order to help him through his surgery. 'Cause I know from experience that he'll just use his medical condition to try to manipulate me into not talking about the upset and it'll never get resolved. And that just feels too yucky."

"And are you *really* willing to give up the relationship forever and always?"

Holly heaved a decisive sigh. "Yeah. It had its beauty while it lasted, but I'm not willing to take anymore of the poison just to get the beauty. I can get the beauty with other friends without having to accept the poison at the same time."

"Uh-huh! Well, sounds to me as though you're being true to your real feelings. And the fact that you're being so conscientious about your motives suggests to me that you're not being petty."

Holly now sighed with relief. "What's the next principle?"

"The next principle is that of loyalty. Now, I believe that most people misplace their loyalty—they pledge loyalty to *people*, when pledging it to *principles* would serve them better. The problem is that if you pledge your loyalty to a *person* and that person starts violating principles you hold dear, then your loyalty to that person forces you to support a violation of your principles. If, on the other hand, you pledge your loyalty to *principles*, then, if one of your friends starts violating those principles, your loyalty to the principles will keep you straight, and set a positive example for your friend. And sometimes that example is the only rudder your friend has for getting back on course. But if you start wavering on your principles because of loyalty to your friend, then he's without a rudder and has a harder time getting back on course. So, in a way, loyalty to principles is indirectly loyalty to the person, because it offers him a reflection from which he can learn and grow most readily. *Your* loyalty is obviously to your principles, and if your friend uses your example as a rudder, he'll be able to learn and grow from this experience. And in my opinion, that ultimately represents loyalty to him."

Holly released a deep healing sigh upon hearing this. "What's the third principle?"

"The Platinum Principles. Are you violating the Platinum Principles with your decision? Are you imposing your will on him or somehow being of disservice to him?"

Holly sighed again, more contemplatively this time, and mulled the question briefly. Finally, she answered, "I don't think so. I'm not imposing anything on him by not going to visit him. I mean, I don't owe him anything and I'm not *obligated* to visit him. I mean, *jeez*, most of the population of the planet isn't going to visit him and they're not imposing *their* will on him."

"True."

"So neither am I. And I *am* preventing him from imposing his will on *me*. And I'm not being of disservice to him, either. I'm not doing *anything* to him, except not giving him something he wants, but hasn't earned. And the idea of going to see him, or even sending him a card, feels bad, so doing him this service *would* be a disservice to myself. So, no, I'm not violating the Platinum Principles." Having resolved it in her mind, she released a final healing sigh.

Dale gave it a moment to sink in before he spoke. "So, does that do it for you?"

After a moment's hesitation, Holly released a soft whimper. "No," she admitted forlornly. "I still feel bad."

"Hmmm," Dale murmured, a little puzzled. "Are you afraid he's blaming or judging you?"

"Uh . . . yeah, partly."

"Okay . . . . Are you concerned that, in this time of vulnerability, he especially needs your support?"

"Mmmm, maybe a little."

"All right. Hmmm . . . . Are you afraid he'll be *hurt*, knowing his best friend isn't there for him at this very important and triumphant moment in his life?"

Holly inhaled sharply as she heard the truth. "Yeah! That's it!"

Dale smiled to himself. "That's called compassion, my dear. Compassion is the pain you feel when you see others in pain, even when that pain comes at their own hand. You're simply mistaking the pain of compassion for the pain of *remorse*—which is the pain you feel when *you've* hurt someone. But as far as I can tell, you didn't hurt your friend in this case; he's done this to himself. You're simply very sure of your boundaries and not willing to let others trespass on them, but you feel badly when someone you love *does* trespass on them and you have to put a stop to it. But by trespassing on your boundaries, they're really hurting themselves. So the pain you're feeling for your friend is simply the pain of compassion."

Holly heaved another deep sigh.

"It's natural and it'll balance out in time," Dale continued. "It might help to think of yourself as a messenger bringing him a message that he's requested. The message is that he has this habit which poisons relationships. But since he won't let you deliver the message verbally, you're forced to deliver it in this way."

"You're right. I know you are. But it's so painful—for both of us."

"I know. And that's usually why people don't stay true to their feelings, much less loyal to their principles. But you can take comfort against the pain of your compassion by recognizing that some beings are in an extreme state of denial and resist learning what they're here to learn. So they attract very hard lessons as a way of breaking through the denial. He's giving himself the most effective lesson he can and it's entirely his choice. It's like they say: 'He's the instrument of his own destruction,' and, 'You can't save a man from himself.'"

Elliot suddenly quit listening and sat upright, abruptly focused on his own dilemma. He had been finding Dale's perspective on Holly's problem mystically applicable to his own, but this last instantly distilled the matter. Dale was the instrument of his own destruction—from his failure to face his fears, to his hiring of Elliot to impersonate him, to his broadcasting advice that Elliot needed to act against him—and in the grand scheme of things, there was really nothing Elliot could do to save Dale from himself.

Pondering this, Elliot missed the conclusion of Holly's call. His heart ached, thinking of the pain he was about to bring Dale, and he could no longer focus on the show. But in keeping with the DJ's advice, he knew he had to be true to his feelings and loyal to his principles. And the truth which spoke loudest to him was his excitement at the prospect of joining the cast of Days of Our Lives, despite his pain of compassion for Dale.

His course suddenly clear, he turned his radio down, placed a call to Wil, and requested a meeting for the following day.

Ken Gullekson

Chapter 23

Elliot had wanted a morning meeting, but Wil and Paul were not available until late afternoon, so the conference was set for 4:30. Too distracted to rehearse for his appearance the next day—or even to play casual sports—Elliot whiled the time aimlessly, which made the wait even longer and more difficult.

As for Wil and Paul, neither was looking forward to the meeting with Elliot. Having heard an unaccustomed gravity in Elliot's voice the previous night, and knowing that he and Paul had never spoken to Elliot about renewing his contract or adjusting his pay at the end of his second quarter, Wil immediately suspected trouble.

At 4:21, Elliot started across the estate to the manor house where the business offices were located. The sun was already low on the horizon, and its light shown through the leaves on the trees from behind, making them glow a bright, luminous green. There was a slight chill in the air. Having taken this first step toward tendering his resignation, Elliot found the sculpted beauty of the estate soothing, and he actually began to relax and breathe again, despite the onus of having to reveal his horrifying realization.

With marbled floors and padded velvet walls, the business offices were at once warm and majestic. This was only the third time Elliot had had occasion to visit them and he found them strangely compelling. Wil was pouring himself a cup of coffee when Elliot arrived and offered one to Elliot. The two men made idle chitchat until Paul joined them, not more than a minute later. Coffees in hand, the three of them sat in two plush black leather sofas, arranged facing one another just for meetings of this sort. Shel Boerman, Dale's financial advisor, had opted not to attend the meeting, having played almost no role in the daily interactions with Elliot.

"So, what's up?" Wil began, taking a sip of his coffee and trying to act calm.

Elliot drew a deep breath. "I've been offered a leading role on Days of Our Lives," he began, thinking it best to come straight to the point, "and I plan to take it. It's a great opportunity for me—for any unknown actor, actually—and I would be doing myself a great disservice if I passed it up."

Despite the bite of anxiety in his gut, Wil, upon hearing the word "disservice"—a term he knew Elliot had adopted from Dale—smiled to himself. It was an unexpected moment of pleasure in this solemn time of disaster. But the moment was very brief as the anxiety reasserted itself. For what Elliot had just said threatened to bring the Dale Greene public appearance train to a crashing halt. Wil consulted Paul with a silent glance, then decided it was time for an all-out *mea culpa*.

"I know we didn't call you in to renegotiate your contract at the end of your second quarter, and I'm profoundly sorry about that. It was a lapse of integrity on our part and there's simply no excuse for it. Thus, we're prepared to give you a substantial increase in salary, retroactive to the beginning of your third quarter. I hope you'll accept it with our deepest apologies."

Elliot had not expected an apology, and getting one made it even harder to assert his position, especially since he knew Wil's sentiment was absolutely genuine. But he was determined not to be swayed.

"I'm sorry, Wil," Elliot said, as gingerly as he could. "This isn't about money, or neglecting to renegotiate my contract. It's about my needs as an actor—as an evolving spirit, if you will—and I would be doing myself great damage if I didn't act on it."

"I can appreciate that," Wil replied, as dispassionately as he could, so as not to betray his mounting apprehension. In his mind, he was feverishly reviewing the insurmountable problems he and his colleagues had encountered before hiring Elliot—knowing that once Elliot left, the problems would be back—and racking his brain for ways to persuade Elliot to stay.

Paul was doing the same, although he was somewhat less demure about it. "All right," he chimed in with his Southern inflection. "What's it gonna take to get you to stay? Let's say we concede it's a buyer's market and leave it up to you to make the offer. What's it gonna take to make a deal?"

"Again, Paul, I'm sorry," Elliot replied sympathetically. "I'm not trying to position myself to get a better deal. I'm not interested in any deal at all. I'm only interested in moving on to my next challenge. I have two more appearances scheduled and I'll do those. But after that, I have to be moving on."

"How much are they offering you on the soap opera?" Wil tried again.

"Not as much as you can afford to pay me," Elliot allowed. "But like I said, this isn't about money. It's about my dreams, as corny as that sounds. It's about having the freedom to play different parts and grow. It's about being known and recognized as myself and signing my own name on autographs. And I just wouldn't be able to live with myself if I didn't take this opportunity." He paused a moment, then added, "I'm not here to negotiate anything, guys, and I won't be talked into anything. I'm just here to quit."

The earnestness and sincerity with which Elliot made his case utterly stumped the two Greene staffers, and they sat speechless for nearly a minute, frantically trying and failing to think of a solution that would make everyone happy.

"We've been talking to Lawndale Convalescent Hospital about an appearance next month," Wil finally said in a last-ditch effort to forestall the inevitable. "Would you be willing to stay for that?"

"Have you firmed up the date with them?" Elliot asked.

Wil could have lied and said he had, and possibly persuaded Elliot to stay a couple of weeks longer. But that would definitely have crossed the line, and it wasn't something he was willing to do, regardless of the enormity of the stakes. Even Dale would have agreed with that. "No," he finally admitted, his anxiety exploding into full-blown, rib-pounding panic.

"Thanks for being honest, Wil," Elliot acknowledged. "But, as you can understand, I have to draw the line somewhere. I'm sorry."

"You know what this is going to do to Dale, don't you?!" Wil snapped, letting his panic show through in a flash of impatience.

"I know. *Boy*, do I know!" As much as he had dreaded it, this appeared to be his moment of truth—time to drop the bomb, time to reveal his horrifying realization.

Even Wil picked up on the inordinate emphasis in Elliot's response. "What do you mean by that?" he queried evenly, reclaiming his composure.

Elliot drew a deep breath and glanced at each man before starting. "I know about Dale," he said simply, his voice hushed.

The two Greene staffers stiffened with alarm, though neither were yet convinced that alarm was warranted.

"What exactly are you referring to?" Wil inquired with steely self-possession.

"I know he's—" Aside from "thing" and "monster," Elliot had not characterized Dale's condition in his mind, so was at a momentary loss for a compassionate word. "Disfigured," he finally said.

"What gives you that impression?" Paul challenged.

It was time for Elliot to confess. "I went into the locked off section of the subway and saw Dale and Bobby doing the show in the broadcast booth."

"How did you get in?!" Wil probed testily, still unsure he was hearing the truth, but allowing impatience to rule his response.

"I had a key made. Don't forget, I used to be a locksmith."

The two men *had* forgotten, and now reminded, were all but convinced of Elliot's veracity.

"Do you have the key on you?" Wil asked.

Elliot had anticipated this question and slipped the key into his pocket before leaving his apartment. He now withdrew it and held it out to Wil, who was sitting closest. Wil took it and, extracting a ring of keys from his own pocket, compared them with Elliot's. It matched the elevator key in his set and he nodded an apprehensive confirmation to Paul.

"You realize this represents a breach of your contract," Paul asserted, hoping to scare Elliot into a weaker position.

"No, Paul, it doesn't. I had my lawyer check. There's nothing in the contract forbidding me to enter that area."

Knowing the truth of this—they had all figured that with locks on those doors, there would be no need to mention it in the contract—and recognizing how carefully Elliot had researched his case, Paul withdrew and shut up.

"So, uh, what do you intend to do with this knowledge?" Wil asked, suddenly sounding defensive and maybe a little threatening. "You know that if you reveal Dale's secret, you not only forfeit your trust fund, but also all your earnings for the past eight months."

"Oh, I know," Elliot countered, suddenly aware that his revelation appeared as a threat to the two men, and a little hurt that they would even think that that was his motive. "I have no intention of revealing the secret. I have a tremendous amount of respect and admiration for Dale—more than you might believe—and I would never do that. Only . . . ." His horrifying realization had been horrifying enough when he first realized it. Now he was finding it even more horrifying to say. He took a deep breath. "Anyone in Springfield who knows me as Dale Greene—which is half the city—and watches Days of Our Lives, will see me on TV with my name listed as Elliot Draupau, and know Dale and I are different people, or at least wonder what the heck is going on. Then Dale will get calls from his listeners demanding an explanation. But he won't be able to tell them anything that makes any sense, except . . . well . . . ."

As Elliot spoke, the picture of destruction grew more and more vivid for the two Greene staffers, striking even more horror in *their* hearts than it had in Elliot's three days earlier. Not only would this bring the public appearance train to a halt, it would also force Dale to reveal his disfigurement and the deception he had perpetrated to cover it up, and probably end his radio career for good. Wil and Paul were astonished and crushed that neither of them had foreseen this eventuality.

"In honor of my contract," Elliot continued, "I won't say a word. But the secret will be out anyhow." He paused to assess their emotional response and allow them to reply, but they were too stunned to comment. "I want you to know this hurts me very deeply. But I can't very well put my life on hold in order to shelter Dale from his own fears."

Looking quite pale—which, owing to his African-American heritage, made him appear very distressed indeed—Wil stood and silently left the room. His departure took Elliot by surprise, but did not seem to puzzle Paul, who just sat quietly, staring at the marble floor. As the seconds passed and stretched into minutes without a word from the man, Elliot, completely in the dark as to what was happening, became rather anxious. Was there more to come, or was the meeting over? Had Wil left simply to visit the bathroom—or to blow his brains out?

"Paul?" Elliot ventured tentatively. "What . . . ? Do you . . . do you know what's going on?"

Giving no sign that he had even heard, Paul continued just to stare at the floor, and Elliot gave up the effort even more concerned than before.

Finally, and much to Elliot's relief, Wil returned. But taking a position at Elliot's side and, like Paul, remaining strangely silent, he shed no more light on the puzzle than had Paul.

Presently, Elliot heard the faint whirring of a motor, and a moment later, the silhouette of a wheelchair and rider appeared in the shadows just outside the double-wide doorway. The details of the chair and its occupant remained indiscernible and the room was silent with anticipation for nearly a minute as the figure in the wheelchair surveyed the assemblage and assessed his willingness to join them. Finally, the motor whirred to life and Dale glided into the light, stopping just inside the doorway so that his guest could see him from a distance.

In the full light of the office, Elliot found the large lumps and droopy folds of mottled flesh which characterized Dale's disfigurement even more bizarre than he had expected—but not horrifying. He made a move to go to the DJ, but Wil discouraged him with a hand on his shoulder. Finally satisfied with Elliot's reaction— or lack thereof—Dale motored the rest of the way into the spacious office.

"Elliot Draupau," Wil said, gesturing toward his employer, "Dale Greene."

Fixing his eyes on Dale's, Elliot slowly got to his feet and approached the strange figure with his hand outstretched. "I'm honored to meet you, Dale," he said as their hands clasped.

Terrified of finally coming face to face with his doppelganger, Dale had been absently holding his breath. Now he released it, intoning softly, "The honor is mine, Elliot." In fact, the honor stretched well beyond meeting Elliot: Dale had not had face-to-face contact with a single person outside of the estate personnel in nearly two decades. So this personally momentous occasion was at once exhilarating and terrifying. He motioned for Elliot to retake his seat. "Wil tells me you have something to tell me," he concluded evenly, so as not to betray his nervousness.

Elliot looked to Wil for clarification. "You didn't tell him?"

"I only told him that you had entered the secured area and knew about his disfigurement, and that you had something to tell him," Wil explained. "I thought it only fair that, if you were intent upon this course of action, you tell him yourself—face to face."

Elliot looked back to Dale and saw a sharply focused, though apprehensive, look of expectancy in his eyes. The profound intelligence and wisdom that came through on the radio was plainly evident in those orbs. What a shame, he thought, that the rest of his body seemed to contradict that extraordinariness.

"I've been offered a major role on Days of Our Lives," Elliot complied, "and I want to accept it. It's a terrific opportunity for me and I'd be doing myself a great disservice if I didn't take advantage of it."

For several seconds, while the implications of Elliot's declaration slowly sank in, Dale just gazed at the Thespian, giving no indication that he had understood.

Seeing this, Elliot began explaining, "Days of Our Lives is a daytime—"

"I know what Days of Our Lives is," Dale interrupted, not unkindly. "I was just processing the shock of it." Now he looked away, gazed for several moments at the corner of the room, stared endlessly at his oversized, lumpy knees, felt his heart pounding against his ribcage, and trembled as unneeded adrenaline coursed through his veins. Commanding the room with a sort of magnetic presence as he did, none of the others even considered interrupting Dale's silence. "You realize that if you leave," he finally continued, doing his best to quell a fearful quaver in his voice, "there's no way that we can replace you. You *are* Dale Greene, as far as my public is concerned, and if you leave, Dale Greene will have to stop making public appearances. And that will disappoint a lot of people. You do realize that, don't you?"

Elliot cast an apprehensive glance at Wil. Even Dale did not foresee the deeper implications of the situation. "Yes, I do."

"Then, in the interests of public service, can't I get you to reconsider your decision?" On the surface, Dale seemed well composed and his entreaty was spoken with apparent dispassion. But underneath, he seethed with anxiety.

"It's like I told Wil and Paul here," Elliot replied sympathetically, "this opportunity is the kind of thing I've dreamed of. If I'm to act on my excitement, as you recommend to your listeners, I have to take this opportunity. If I don't, then I'd be being of disservice to myself. I know you understand that."

As much as he wished he didn't, Dale did understand—and agree with—Elliot's motives. And as much as he wanted to try to talk or cajole or bribe Elliot into staying, he found the manipulation that that would entail far too distasteful, so he did not press the issue. Instead, he nodded his misshapen head in acknowledgement, heaved a dispirited sigh, and swore vehemently to himself.

"It's not so much that I want to get away from here," Elliot elaborated, "although, recently, I've found all the restrictions pretty confining. It's that I need to move on. I need to play different parts and be recognized for myself and sign my own name on autographs . . . and find a girlfriend!"

Despite the pain of it, Dale had to smile at this. But not for long. "Well," he mused after a moment, sounding much more accommodating than he felt, "I guess Dale Greene will just have to stop making personal appearances. I suppose he could have an accident and be unable to get around easily. That would take some of the pressure off."

At this, both Wil and Paul turned a beseeching eye toward Elliot. Duly gathering their meaning, he shifted uncomfortably in his seat and took a breath. "I don't think it'll be quite that easy, Dale."

"Why not?"

"Because when the people who know me as Dale Greene see me on TV with my name listed as Elliot Draupau, they're going to know I'm not you and you're going to have a lot of explaining to do."

Like a wrecking ball from hell, the implications of Elliot's departure and new soap role hit Dale with devastating impact. The prospect of unmasking the counterfeit Dale Greene, the humiliation of being caught in a scandalous deception, the agony of revealing his disfigurement, the guilt of abandoning listeners who depended upon him for advice, the feelings of distrust and betrayal which that would stir in their hearts, the potential destruction of all the good he had done in the last eighteen months—it all crashed down on him with the force of a thermonuclear explosion. Every muscle in his body went weak; a fist seized his heart and squeezed out every ounce of will; an angry parasite writhed in his gut; and his life ground to a wrenching halt right before his eyes.

Suddenly driven by desperation and making no effort to conceal his rage, Dale now growled at Elliot. "You son of a bitch! This is going to ruin everything!! Goddamn you!!!" Slapping at his joystick, he angrily swung his wheelchair about. "Goddamn you!" he continued to mutter, "God*damn* you!!"

Elliot knew Dale was just responding to his fear and answered evenly but genuinely, "I'm sorry, Dale. If I could find a way to make us both happy, I would. But . . . I don't see how I can."

"I do!" Dale snapped, turning halfway back toward Elliot. "Turn the job down and I'll pay you whatever you want!"

"Money won't make me happy; I think you know that."

"Well, you can't go on TV and wreck everything for me!"

"I know that's what you'd prefer, but taking this job is what excites me and . . . that's what I intend to do."

"You seem to be forgetting that you're on my property and I don't have to let you leave." Being totally out of character for Dale, Elliot recognized this threat as no more than a desperate manifestation of his fear.

"I know this is terrifying for you, Dale," he empathized. "But what are you going to do, incarcerate me?"

"I could."

"Then you'd be committing a crime. And when the world got wind of it—'cause if my father and my lawyer and my agent quit hearing from me, they'd start asking some pretty probing questions—not only would your career be wrecked, but your reputation and all the good you've done would be, too." He paused to let Dale respond, but the DJ apparently had no response to make. "You might as well face the facts: You have no recourse but to let me go and deal with the problem head on. And given the kind of person I know you to be, I know that's exactly what you'll do."

Elliot's argument was powerful and Dale retreated, but only partly.

Turning to Paul, he asked, "Could his appearing on TV under his own name be construed as revealing the secret and violating the terms of the contract?"

Knowing the futility of this discussion, but not wanting to embarrass Dale in front of Elliot, Paul rubbed his forehead, then motioned for Wil to escort Elliot out of the room. "Would you excuse us for a moment, Elliot? I'd like to confer with my client alone."

"No, no," Dale chimed in, seriously in denial of the weakness of his position, "I want him to hear this. I want him to know what he's up against. Go on."

"Are you sure?" Paul queried. "This might not be—"

"I'm sure! Go on."

Ultimately, Paul knew, answering Dale's question with Elliot present would not reveal any meaningful legal strategy, so he made no further effort to talk his client out of it. With an air of reluctant resignation, he eyed Wil, heaved a sigh, and spread his hands toward Dale. "I wish I could tell you something reassurin', Dale, but I can't. Technically, the contract only enjoins him from revealin' the location and nature of his work here. Goin' on TV under his own name doesn't do that."

"But it does reveal the fact that *I* wasn't making those appearances," Dale pressed. "Surely that constitutes revealing the nature of the work."

"I s'pose," Paul allowed. "But even so, the most we could do at this point is hold back his pay. That wouldn't prevent him from takin' the job and lettin' the cat out o' the bag."

"Not to mention that without that money," Wil added, "he'd have no incentive to keep the secret."

Again, Dale swore under his breath. Slowly but surely he was realizing that the contract that was supposed to protect him from this very thing had been, from the beginning, no more than the proverbial paper tiger. Still, he did not yet see that his effort to hide from the world was the real problem. "Can't we get some kind of a court injunction to stop him or something?" he asked Paul, grasping at straws.

"Even if we could get a court to grant us such a thing, which is doubtful in itself, court proceedings are public record and your secret would be out of the bag right then."

"Goddamnit! We can't be *that* powerless!" Dale railed. "Isn't there something we can do?!"

Devoid of answers, the other three men eyed one another solemnly. Having been through these same discussions before hiring Elliot, the two Greene staffers in particular knew there was no satisfying solution. Despite their loyalty to Dale, they were ultimately more loyal to the principle of truth, and Paul decided it was time to acknowledge the validity of Elliot's position.

"We didn't exactly talk about it," he submitted gently, "but I think we all figured that whoever we brought in would eventually go on about his life after he was finished here. That's all Elliot's doin'."

"It's our mistake for failing to anticipate that any actor we hired might wind up on national TV and inadvertently reveal the deception," Wil added sheepishly. "I don't think we can honestly hold Elliot liable for that."

Feeling utterly defeated, Dale groaned and buried his head in his hands. He stayed that way for several minutes, his anger slowly giving way to exhaustion and resignation as he recognized the futility of his efforts.

Finally, he lifted his head and asked quietly, "What were you thinking when you went down there, Elliot? Didn't it occur to you that those locks meant we didn't want you in there?"

"Yes, but I was working without a contract, or any information at all. So I was in a state of mystery. Going into that section was the only way I had of solving it."

"You could have asked either Wil or Paul for information. They would have talked to you."

"Yeah, but would they have told me the truth?" He looked to the other two men for an answer, but they remained silent. "I didn't think so. The only way for me to get the truth was to go down there myself."

"But the result is the possible destruction of my life!"

"Not actually. Whether I went down there and found out your secret or not, I'd still be taking the Days of Our Lives job, and you'd still have the same problem. If anything, going through those locks gave you more time, 'cause I was climbing the walls by then and learning why I was doing the job gave me a reason to stay a little longer. It didn't totally take away the frustration, but it gave me some relief. And knowing your secret meant that I was able to warn you of what was to come so you didn't suddenly find yourself getting embarrassing calls you weren't prepared for. I could have just told you I was quitting and not told you why, and you wouldn't have had any warning at all that my face was about to show up on national TV. So I did you a favor by entering the secured area."

Although Dale understood Elliot's point, he couldn't derive any comfort from it, or really even acknowledge it, given his state of exhaustion.

"There's something I don't understand, Dale," Elliot went on. "Did you really expect to be able to keep me here forever doing appearances for you?"

Having no answer, Dale turned away and Wil replied in his stead. "We never expected the demand for appearances to last more than the three months we originally hired you for. We simply didn't anticipate the consequences when we conceived the idea. It just got out of hand."

"Well ... that's it for me," Dale conceded, finally recovering enough will to make a decision, premature though it might have been. "I'm quitting tonight. I'll give Stan the nine-to-midnight shift and bring in Harris to fill the hole."

Greg Harris was a standby DJ they used to fill in for sick or vacationing DJs.

"Are you going to tell your listeners what's happening?" Wil asked.

"Nah, I can't," Dale replied dismissively. "I can't—" he wanted to elaborate, but couldn't find the words for it, sighed, and finally just repeated, "Nah."

The haste with which Dale had made his decision gave Wil an extremely queasy feeling. This was a moment he had anticipated—and dreaded—for nearly two decades. Even when his disfigured student was little, Wil knew that someday, should Dale fail to face his fears on his own, life would step in and force him to face them. He had even helped Dale avoid facing those fears, along with everyone else. But that had to end. This was the moment in which Dale had to decide either to finally vanquish his fears, or let them vanquish him. Desperately wanting to help Dale rise to this challenge Wil decided, finally, to speak up and assert his opinion. "If I may suggest ..." he said, then waited for permission from Dale to opine.

For several moments, Dale did not move. Finally, he resigned himself to hearing the suggestion and signaled as much with a wave of his hand.

"Maybe quitting so suddenly isn't the best way to handle this, Dale," Wil said gently. "Elliot's got one appearance scheduled for tomorrow and another in a couple of weeks. If you quit now, we'll have to cancel appearances people have been counting on for weeks. You're going to disappoint people no matter what you do, but quitting tonight will disappoint more people than you need to and create more mystery than you need to deal with right now. I suggest you go on tonight, and for the next two weeks, and work on a way to handle it so as to minimize the damage."

"What's the point of that?!" Dale snapped, nearly taking Wil's head off. "What am I going to get out of it except a lot of pain and embarrassment?!"

"Well, maybe that's the point of it. No one ever suggested that doing what you're afraid to do is easy. But if you're to evolve, you have to face your fears. You know that as well as anyone. For most of your life you've been sheltered from your core fears here on the estate. And I think they've finally caught up with you. You can fire me if you want to, but from this point on, I'm going to encourage you to come clean and tell your listeners the truth."

Reminded of the prospect of coming clean and telling the truth, Dale felt another bolt of fear shoot like hot lightning through his body. He quickly suppressed the feeling and looked to Wil. "You're fired," he said blandly.

"All right," Wil replied, knowing Dale was not serious. "But do yourself a favor—go on tonight, and for the next few weeks, until you can work out a gracious way to handle this."

The thought of facing callers that night sent shivers down Dale's misshapen spine and made him want to get as far away from Springfield as possible. But he knew Wil had made a valid point and he could not, in all good conscience, mount a meaningful argument against it. "All right," he agreed, doing his best to push back the terror he was feeling. At least by going on tonight he would not immediately have to face the humiliation that lay ahead. And maybe, he thought, something would happen between now and then that would rescue him from it all. That thought brought a measure of relief and he finally relaxed.

Chapter 24

Elliot's appearance the next day went well, as did the following one two weeks later. Knowing these would be his last, he gave them his very best effort so as to make "Dale Greene" as memorable as possible in the hearts and minds of his audiences. That these audiences would possibly see *him* on TV in the not-too-distant future and form a very different opinion of Dale Greene was a bothersome detail he preferred not to think about, so pushed to the very back of his mind.

Two days after his final appearance, Elliot said goodbye and jetted back to Los Angeles. Though not a tearful one, the final farewell was a meaningful one for Elliot, for he felt honored to have worked in the service of a man he considered to be "great." And that Dale had invited him into the manor house a last time to say goodbye was a powerful validation of himself and his work.

Dale found Elliot's last days to be agonizingly painful. He continued to do the show, but now felt tentative about his answers, unsure of his philosophical footing, dishonest in his relationship with his listeners. That these were the final days of the one thing that gave his life meaning significantly disoriented him. A few times he was even short with callers. Although no one mentioned it, many noticed the difference in his mood. Naturally, their focus was on their own problems and it was outside the scope of the show's protocol to express concern about the well-being of the host, so they quickly dismissed any such observations.

As for bidding Elliot goodbye, when Dale first decided to hire someone to make personal appearances in his place, he had not expected ever to meet, much less say goodbye to, the man. But given his encounter with Elliot seventeen days earlier, he now felt differently about it. Since then, he had met and chatted several times with the actor. Unexpectedly, he found in Elliot a kindred spirit—a good-hearted soul and quality thinker—and came to appreciate more than ever the excellent job Elliot had done in representing him to his public.

Perhaps hiring someone to do his personal appearances had been a mistake, but he could have done worse—he could have hired an incompetent whose work would have embarrassed and discredited him. But he had had the good fortune to hire Elliot—mixed though the blessing might have been—and he had Wil and Paul to thank for it.

In the end, the two men exchanged best wishes, a promise to keep in touch, and a heartfelt handshake. The irony was not lost on Dale that, with Elliot gone, he was now free to roam the estate without restriction, but with the end of his radio career, his life would be more restricted than ever. And while he now had the opportunity to spend much more time with his friend, Bobby, he felt more like being alone, so took little advantage of the opportunity.

The "gracious way" to handle Dale's departure from radio, arrived at after numerous heated discussions between himself and his staff, was to make his resignation announcement a good week before Elliot's first air date. Then, instead of returning to a music format, a psychologist with talk-radio experience would take Dale's place on the nine-to-midnight shift so as to continue to offer WWKW listeners a forum for their personal problems. Phil Marovici, a popular Ph.D. out of Miami, had been hired, and all the elements were now in place. It was a Friday night, three days after Elliot's departure, ten days before his inaugural appearance on Days of Our Lives, and this was the night Dale would reveal the truth and say "goodnight" for the last time. All he had to concern himself with was his announcement.

As might be expected, he had grown increasingly anxious as the date approached. Dread of the consequences of what would surely be considered by his listeners a "shocking revelation" had occupied his thoughts without relief and the pit of his stomach had been host to a persistent knot. Much to his disappointment, nothing had happened to rescue him from his fate. He was going to have to come clean and tell he truth, and that's all there was to it.

Given that Elliot's appearance on Days of Our Lives would create an irksome mystery sandwich for his listeners, Wil and Paul had encouraged Dale to tell all, to openly bare his soul. Listing the various subjects he would talk about—his disease and the resulting disfigurement, the horror of rejection by strangers as a child, the shelter of the estate, the thrill of doing radio, the terror in the thought of picking up his Man of the Year award in person, the agony of deciding to hire a counterfeit, and the apologies to everyone from the Archers' Association to the patients at Lawndale Convalescent Hospital—forced him, again, to experience the fear that he had been hiding from all these years.

It was an excruciating exercise, one in which his heart alternately ached and beat so violently he thought it would burst from his chest. While the fear of rejection was agonizing enough, what really hurt was the knowledge that upon confessing betrayal to thousands of devoted listeners, he would change, in their hearts and minds, from being a trusted friend and confidant to a deceitful, treacherous stranger. That was the most punishing of all.

Unable to concentrate on anything else, he found the day unbearably long and, as show time approached, developed a case of the shakes that rattled him to the bowels.

At 8:50 p.m., he took the elevator down to the subway and motored out to the broadcast suite alone. He had asked Bobby to set the suite up for solo operation so he could make his announcement, hand the signal back to headquarters, and let them finish out the night with music. For some reason, even though Bobby knew the whole story, Dale was shy about making this announcement in front of anyone.

As always, Bobby had done his job well and was waiting in the broadcast booth as Dale arrived. "You okay?" he asked, showing a type of overt concern that was rare for him.

"As compared to what?!" Dale snapped, impatience bristling in his voice. Seeing a look of hurt come over Bobby's face, he quickly implemented damage control. "Sorry, Bobs, I just . . . you know me: life is okay, death is okay, feelings are okay. My life is about to end and I feel like shit, but that's okay."

Bobby smiled softly. Dale's answer had provided him with a lot more information than he had really wanted, but at least it had satisfied his question. "'Kay," he replied. "Everything's ready to go. All the lines are off hook so callers are getting a busy signal."

"Good. Thanks. Uh . . . ." Dale thought he should say more but found himself too distracted to think. "Thanks," he finally repeated.

"Sure. So, uh . . . I'll see you later," Bobby concluded.

"Right. See ya."

With that, Bobby left the booth and headed down the subway toward the manor house while Dale positioned himself at his microphone and checked his controls. He had not prepared a text verbatim—preferring to speak extemporaneously from an outline—so the last few minutes before show time were agony as different opening statements battled for dominance in his mind. He cursed himself for not having waited a few minutes longer before leaving the house.

Finally, 9:00 arrived and Dale accepted the signal handoff from headquarters. Now was his moment of truth.

"It's nine o'clock. You're tuned to WWKW, FM 102.4, and this is Dale Greene on The Brink of Tomorrow." Dale usually delivered this opening with a touch of flair and enthusiasm, but tonight he said it solemnly.

"Tonight's show is going to be a little bit different," he began. "Well, actually, it's going to be a lot different. I . . . basically, I have something to announce that . . . ." He was beating around the bush. *Get to it!* he thought. He gave a moment's pause. A sigh erupted as he drove to the heart of the matter.

"It seems I've made a terrible mistake . . . a mistake which is likely to hurt a lot of people . . . a mistake for which I am deeply, *deeply* sorry. I want you to know right up front that I feel very, very bad about this.

"Many of you know me as a handsome young guy who talks on the radio and speaks to various organizations around the city. But the fact of the matter is that the handsome young guy you see speaking at these engagements is not me. He's a man who sounds like me whom I hired to make personal appearances in my place. I won't give you his real name right now—you'll find that out soon enough—but the truth is that he isn't me. The truth is also that I've perpetrated a horrible deception upon you.

"'What's he talking about?' you're probably asking yourself right about now. 'Is this a joke? Has he gone nuts or something?' No, it's no joke and I haven't gone nuts. The fact of the matter is that I have a rare disease that makes me very difficult to look at. Its medical name is Proteus syndrome. But most of you will know it by its more common name, Elephant Man's Disease.

"Proteus syndrome is caused by a cellular mutation, which means the medical profession has no effective treatment for it. It's symptoms include rough, discolored skin, deformation and asymmetrical development of the skeleton, and both bony and fatty tumors. These symptoms can range from mild to severe; a mild case being characterized by a handful of small tumors that appear here and there; a severe case being characterized by large, lumpy tumors and severe overgrowth of parts of the skeleton. For people with mild cases, interactions with strangers can be uncomfortable, but not necessarily traumatic, and they can lead fairly normal lives. But severe cases are extremely disfiguring and for people with severe cases, interaction with strangers can be devastating. For them, a normal life is generally not possible. I happen to have one of the severest cases on record and most people find me very difficult to look at.

"My symptoms started showing up when I was about three years old and progressed to where, by the time I was five, I was very severely disfigured. By then, most people saw me as a little monster and wanted nothing to do with me, which really hurt my feelings. Strangers would usually gasp or yelp and jump back when they first saw me and a few of them actually ran away screaming. That *really* hurt my feelings. After all, I was only five years old, and even though I knew I had a disease that made me look weird, it still hurt my feelings when people did that.

"After a while, the people of the town we were living in became so nasty to us that, to protect me from all that, my parents bought land just outside of Springfield and built a large estate where I could grow up with as normal a life as possible under the circumstances. They provided me with all the activities I wanted, plus a Harvard Professor to educate me, and basically sheltered me from any need to interact with strangers.

"Now, I'm not telling you this to gain your sympathy or to make excuses for my behavior; I'm only telling you this so you can understand why I did what I did. When I first got the opportunity to work in radio, I was absolutely ecstatic; because here was a way that I could finally reach out to people without having to subject them to my appearance and getting my feelings hurt. Then, when I started the talk version of The Brink of Tomorrow, I was even more thrilled, because I knew it would enable me to really connect with people—to actually interact with them and even *help* them—without the barrier of my disfigurement. So when I was voted Man of the Year by the Archers Association and they wanted me to pick up my award in person—and I must say, they were very insistent about it—I was terrified that you all would get a look at me and freak out and never want to have anything to do with me again. And I thought we'd all lose out from that.

"Frankly, I didn't know whether that would happen or not, but I was too scared to take a chance on it and risk ruining everything. So I decided to hire someone—an actor—to accept my Man of the Year award for me. Believe me, I was aware of the deception it represented and I agonized over the decision. But it seemed that the benefits of this scheme—the fact that no one would be freaked out and I could just go on helping my callers—far outweighed the moral implications of the deception. And at the time, I honestly thought the Archers award would be all there'd be to it and that I could just go back to being just a voice on the radio.

"But then the various schools and charities and hospitals and community organizations started asking for appearances, and it was just so hard to turn them down that I hired the guy back to make those appearances for me too. I swear I didn't mean to hurt anyone, and if I could've seen a way to do it without the deception, I would have. But I felt pressured by all the demands and I was just too scared of the consequences of *my* making those appearances myself. So I succumbed to my fears.

"But my fears aside, the fact is that I deceived you. I didn't practice what I preached. And because of that, I know I've let you down. I take full responsibility for that and I am deeply—*deeply*—sorry for it. Please learn from my mistake so you don't have to make it yourself. I want you to understand that the man who made my appearances for me in no way shares responsibility for the deception. All he knew, at first, was that he was hired to play the part of a DJ making personal appearances. After a while, he came to realize that he was standing in for a real DJ, but by that time, the damage was already done and quitting would only have caused . . . well . . . what I'm doing now.

"In fact, the reason I'm doing this now is because he's accepted a major role on the daytime drama Days of Our Lives. Getting this role was a dream come true for him, but what it meant for me was that all you Brink of Tomorrow listeners out there who watch Days of Our Lives would see him on TV—and see his real name in the credits—and know he wasn't me. And I didn't want any of you to have to go through the wondering and questioning and doubting that that would cause. I wanted you to hear it from me first, so you wouldn't have to go through any of that.

"Now, because of the deception I perpetrated on you, I have no expectations of ever having your trust again, to be able to host a radio advice show. So, as of tonight, I'm resigning from radio. In order to continue to provide you with help with your problems, Doctor Phil Marovici, a brilliant psychologist from Miami, will be taking over the nine-to-midnight shift here on WWKW. Greg Harris will be filling in over the weekend with classic rock, and Doctor Marovici will be starting on Monday. I hope you give him the same warm reception you gave me when I first converted The Brink of Tomorrow to all-talk.

"Finally, I wish to apologize to the Archers Association for sending a pretender to accept my award. I'll be returning the plaque, along with a letter of apology, sometime in the next few days. And to all the schools and charities and hospitals and community service organizations, I apologize for deceiving you. I deeply, deeply regret what I've done, and don't expect your forgiveness. I only want you to know that this apology comes from the bottom of my heart. And it's my sincerest hope that this matter doesn't reflect negatively on the man who made my appearances for me. He's a very fine individual and doesn't deserve blame for any of this. And I wish him the very best in all his endeavors."

This said, Dale breathed a sigh of relief. He had the feeling there was more to say, but couldn't think of what it might be, so decided the feeling was just a residual phantom of the process.

"Again, I'm deeply sorry for what I've done. I don't know what more I can say or do. So I guess I'll just turn the show over to Greg Harris. This is WWKW, FM 102.4, and I'm Dale Greene on—" He was about to say "The Brink of Tomorrow," but thought better of it and simply concluded with, "Goodnight."

Ken Gullekson

Chapter 25

Slowly, solemnly, Dale threw the switch which handed the signal back to headquarters. Then he shut down the broadcast suite for the last time and motored back to the house.

His three advisors were waiting in the plushly appointed den with Bobby when he arrived. While they allowed their gaze to fall upon his form—as unthreateningly as possible—they all had the good sense to wait for him to speak, to let him set the tone for the interaction, if he wanted one. But he motored to the picture window and just stared out across the broad expanse of the estate, its grounds dappled picturesquely with soft patches of light cast by the lamps which lined its numerous walkways and edifices. *What good is all this beauty now?* he wondered. Only after several minutes did he speak.

"Well . . . that's it. It's over." He rotated his wheelchair toward his companions. "Did I say everything I needed to say?"

Wil was the first to reply. "That . . . and more, I think. I don't think you needed to be quite so abject in your apologies. But you always were harder on yourself than you needed to be."

Dale considered Wil's comment, then cocked his head. "Paul?"

"I'm with Wil."

Dale acknowledged with a nod, then looked to Shel, who shrugged in agreement. "Bobby?" Dale asked last.

"You get the broadcast suite shut down all right?"

Despite his dispirited state, Dale couldn't help but smile at Bobby's choice of focus. "Yeah, no problem. Thanks."

Then, unexpectedly, from Bobby, "You did a hard thing. I never thought having Elliot do appearances for you was so bad anyhow. He was a good guy and did you right. But I don't think I coulda done what you did tonight."

Dale especially appreciated this rare personal opinion from Bobby, a sign that significance and meaning were finding a place in his consciousness as he matured. "I think you could have, if you'd had to.

You've just never been foolish enough to put yourself in such a tough position to begin with. And I hope you never do. But thanks for the compliment, my friend."

Bobby acknowledged with a single nod and a soft smile.

The Saturday morning papers *all* led with the "shocking revelation by Springfield DJ, Dale Greene." To enhance the story, some of them ran pictures of the original "Elephant Man," Joseph C. Merrick—some of them identifying him by the moniker *John* Merrick, as he was erroneously denominated in the David Lynch film. The tabloids ran artists' renderings of the "real" Dale Greene—abominations ranging from a man with an elephant's head to an elephant with a man's head.

Leonard Greene had been careful to list the estate in county records under Dara's maiden name so as to maintain anonymity in the community. But that didn't stop a handful of zealous reporters from rattling the gates of every one of the four dozen or so manors that populated the outskirts of the city trying to find the disfigured DJ. None of the estates admitted to being the home of Dale Greene— including the Greene estate—but the eccentric master of one of them invited the reporters in to see the fifteen-foot-long tapeworm he had eliminated from his bowels the night before.

Of course, WWKW's headquarters were swamped with calls and visits from the media. But the folks who manned those offices during the weekend—for whom Dale's announcement was a jarring surprise—were just as much in the dark as everyone else. The only connection they had with the Greene estate was the private phone number—the mail was always picked up by someone from the estate, never forwarded—and it was promptly disconnected when the media got ahold of it and started making calls to it.

Ultimately, the Springfield media contacted the production office of Days of Our Lives, but the Los Angeles-based show knew nothing of the "Dale Greene affair" and wanted even less to talk to the likes of these small-town rags from halfway across the country. As might be expected, the daytime drama's "No comment" became big news in Springfield as the media milked the story for all it was worth.

Of course, true to his promise, Dale's Man of the Year award was promptly returned to the Archers Association, by private courier. No acknowledgment of this was made, beyond the signature of the Archers receptionist on the shipping receipt.

Over the weekend, Greg Harris played classic rock during the nine-to-midnight shift, confusing the few WWKW listeners who had neither heard Dale's announcement nor read the papers, and on Monday, Phil Marovici, Ph.D., started taking calls in that time slot. Dr. Phil called his show "The Night is Jung," a name whose wordplay was lost on any listener who didn't know "young" from "Jung"—which was most of them—and which tripped somewhat awkwardly off the tongue when used in program-I.D. patter. Ironically, Jung played almost no role in Dr. Phil's advice, which was a mishmash of traditional and pop psychological precepts.

As for The Brink of Tomorrow, it was dead and gone.

The reminders being all too painful, Dale found himself unable to listen to Phil's show. Even the music he used to have on in the background of his life was silent—music of any kind was just too cheerful to match his mood. What did match his mood was reading the ugly speculations printed in the papers about him and his counterfeit—who they were, where they were, how much money was involved, what were they really trying to cover up, what other illicit activities they might be involved in. All this ugliness served to feed Dale's own disgust with himself.

He got more of the same in the hundreds of letters he received from his listeners. The number of letters in the mailbag each day remained the same as before the announcement. But before the announcement, the mix had been about ninety-five percent positive, five percent negative. After the announcement, those figures traded places. Few of them said anything Dale hadn't already known and apologized for.

> We're very disappointed in you. Why does everybody who appears to be good and admirable always turn out to be some kind of crook or liar? We thought you were different. You have really let us down.
>
> Stan & Barb Farber

I'm sorry you're sick. But you had no right to lie to us. What kind of example do you think that sets for my kids?

Mary Donnelly

You son of a bitch! You gave me hope that I really could quit messing up my life. But if you can't keep from messing up your own life, what hope is there for me? I used to really admire you. Now I think you suck.

Evan Benowsky

Shame on you! That's all I have to say. Shame on you!!!

Laverne Shattock

We had come to govern our lives by the wisdom you shared with your listeners each night, believing it to be true and valid. Now we don't know what to believe and we feel lost.

Jerry & Terry Riggins

Fuck you and the horse you rode in on!

Frank Kellner

I have burn scars all over my face, so I know how hard it is to face strangers, and I'm sorry you chose to go off the air. Your philosophy is just as valid whether you're disfigured or not, or whether you deceived your listeners or not. If it were up to me, you'd go back on.

Alan Drake

With minor variations on the theme, the rest of the mail addressed to Dale was the same. Notwithstanding Alan Drake's loving and very welcome sentiment and the handful of others like his, Dale did not believe it wise to go back on the air. While he agreed that the philosophy was still valid, he did not believe that he could be trusted to dispense it accurately.

As if the letters weren't enough, there was the backwash of counterfeit autographs. While most "Dale Greene" autograph holders simply tossed the forgeries in the trash, others sent them back to the station, sometimes with nasty notes attached. Interestingly enough, a few shrewd souls hung on to the phony signatures, speculating that they might be worth something someday. In any event, Dale kept those that found their way back to him as punitive reminders of his duplicity.

That week following his resignation represented the bleakest period in Dale's life. Even the death of his parents did not compare. Although he had missed them terribly and felt extraordinary pain for himself, he genuinely believed they were in a place of greater light, beauty, and happiness. And their misfortune was not his doing—not the result of his choices.

This, by contrast, was a catastrophe of his own creation. His duplicity had wounded not only himself, but his listeners. No one came out of it better off . . . except maybe Elliot. And about this, he was conflicted. At one level—the level at which resided his despair and depression—he was angry with Elliot and begrudged him his success. But at another level—a more noble level that had somehow miraculously survived the debacle—he knew Elliot had done nothing wrong. Ultimately, he took relief in the knowledge that at least *some* good had come out of the disaster.

Other than that, his life held nothing for him. All the material wealth he had inherited from his parents, all the wisdom he had acquired, all the good he had done over the last eighteen months were of no value to him now. For all intents and purposes, his life was over. Withdrawing even further from the rest of society—if that were even possible for a man who hadn't been outside the walls of his estate in over two decades—he sequestered himself in his bedroom most of the time.

Each morning a breakfast was prepared and placed before him as he lay in bed. Each morning he stared at the repast without appetite. Afternoons were a little livelier. That's when the mail arrived and he could feed his self-disgust by reading it and absorbing its bile. Then, filled to the brim with his own ugliness, he spent the rest of each afternoon cursing his life, his staff, and his disfigurement while throwing things against the walls, ramming his wheelchair into the furniture, and knocking over whatever was left standing. He did this until he had exhausted himself, then slept through the late evening when the reminders of his foul deed were most painful.

Of course, everyone close to him tried to talk to him, cheer him up, reassure him that things would be all right. But he would have none of it. He didn't want to be cheered up. He wanted to wallow in the despair and self-hatred. He wanted to be angry. That's what was honest. He had been dishonest in having Elliot do his appearances and it had ruined his life. So he refused to be anything but completely and utterly honest. And given his mood, even the merest scintilla of cheer was false. Besides, right now, the despair and self-hatred and anger felt *better* than cheer. Go figure.

Watching him alternately mope and crash about, and having no success at cheering him up, Dale's advisors—and Wil in particular—felt terrible about having allowed their beloved employer to embark on a course that would lead to such ruin and despair. Of course, they knew they were ultimately not responsible for *his* choices; he had made the decision himself and was fully responsible for what happened in his life. But they *were* responsible for their own errors, for having neglected to state their misgivings, for having forsaken their own principles. They *were* responsible for bowing to Dale's "authority" and not encouraging him to face his fears. They *had* enabled him to hide from his fears. And for that they felt the terrible weight of their complicity and their own failures. Chastened by that weight, Wil tendered his resignation. Of course, Dale declined—with a terse "No"—to accept it.

The tenth day after Dale's announcement marked Elliot's debut on Days of Our Lives. As was the prevailing practice, some news had been made of the cast change from John Cochran to Elliot Draupau in the entertainment magazines and TV sections of the newspapers, but except for the residents of Springfield, it meant nothing more to soap opera fans than another player replacement, something they had seen numerous times before. And except for the fact that Elliot was obviously a different person—but with a satisfying resemblance to John Cochran, even if his voice was deeper—the transition was smooth. In fact, Elliot fell into the role with such ease that most viewers had fully accepted the change by the end of his second week.

By then, three and a half weeks after announcing his resignation, Dale's foray into despair and self-loathing had pretty much run its course. The processes of life having worked on his emotions, he had stopped reading the hate mail, stopped perusing the negative editorials, stopped throwing fits of anger, and started, once again, to listen to music—nothing cheery, mind you (he favored Wagner and Badalamenti), but he again had music on in the background.

This didn't mean, by any stretch of the imagination, that he had returned to his former chipper self. But he had quit punishing himself. And for that, those who loved and served him were grateful. Not unexpectedly, listener resentment and media interest in the Dale Greene affair waned with Dale's despair. The few stories which appeared in the newspapers now took residence on the back pages and the number of listener letters excoriating Dale had fallen significantly.

Perhaps things could never be normal again, but at least they had hit bottom and weren't sinking any further.

Ken Gullekson

Chapter 26

"Who's up first, Brian?" Dr. Phil Marovici queried, opening his fifth week on the air at WWKW. Dr. Phil had worked with an on-air producer in Miami and had insisted on a similar format for The Night is Jung. He had even imported his favorite Miami producer, Brian Conigliaro, and settled into a studio at station headquarters in downtown Springfield. During the first couple of days of his tenure at WWKW, some of Dr. Phil's callers had asked if Dale was as ugly as he said he was—Dr. Phil told them he had never seen Dale—and complained about Dale's failure to practice what he preached. As Dale was Dr. Phil's employer, the new host wisely chose not to comment. And after refusing to answer all such inquiries, all the questions about Dale had dried up and Phil had gotten down to the business at hand.

"We have Tisha on line two," Brian said, responding to Dr. Phil's opening question, "and she says she's having trouble in her marriage."

Dr. Phil connected the call and announced, "This is Doctor Phil and The Night is Jung." His style was very lively, very "up." It was no wonder he had been popular in Miami.

"Hi, Doctor Phil," Tisha said brightly.

"Hi, Tisha, how old are you?"

"Twenty-eight."

"And what kind of difficulty are you having?"

"Well, lately, I haven't been interested in sex. My husband and I have been arguing a lot; I feel angry with him about something, but I don't know what. And I was wondering what I could do about it."

"How long have you been married, Tisha?"

"Two years."

"And how long have you felt this way toward your husband?"

Tisha thought briefly, then, "Four or five months."

"No children?" Dr. Phil confirmed.

"No."

"What does your husband say about your lack of desire for sex?"

"He doesn't understand it."

"Does he pressure you for it?"

"Uh, no. He wants it and asks for it and wants to know why I don't want it. But I wouldn't call it pressure."

"Tisha-a-a-a," Phil said, drawing the name out and pausing briefly so as to appear thoughtful, "do you ever remember being sexually molested as a child?"

"No." Tisha's answer was prompt and unequivocal.

"Are you sure? The symptoms you described—feelings of hostility, lack of sexual desire, uncertainty about the relationship—are consistent with sexual molestation."

"Well, I'm pretty sure I wasn't molested. My parents divorced when I was ten and I lived with my mother after my father left. So I think I'd know if I was molested."

"Well, that is the common assumption. But you know, memories of childhood sexual molestation are typically very painful, and are usually repressed until trouble in later life starts bringing them to the surface."

"Well, like I said, my father left when I was ten, but he was a pretty tame guy and I'm sure he didn't molest me."

"Did you have uncles or brothers who showed you particular interest, who might have molested you?"

"I'm an only child and I never saw my uncle after my father left."

"So there's a period before you were ten during which both your father and your uncle were around."

"Uh-huh."

"And you have no recollection of being molested by them?"

"No."

"Well I hate to say this, but this is sounding more and more like repressed memory."

Tisha hesitated before responding. She didn't want to be so rude as to contradict the good doctor. Finally, "I—I really don't think so, Doctor Phil," she said delicately.

"I do," Phil asserted without regard for his caller's information.

Up till now, Tisha had been very patient, but she was tiring of Dr. Phil's persistence along this line of questioning and it came out in the tone of her voice. "I'm afraid you're wrong about this. I mean—"

Wil knocked on the door to Dale's bedroom.

"Come in," came the solemn voice from within.

The educator opened the door and stepped carefully into the partially darkened room. Dale was lying on his bed. Dour music played softly in the background.

"How ya doing?" Wil asked, just to break the ice.

"Never better," the younger man said sarcastically. Dale knew Wil was fully aware of how he was doing and it irritated him that the man would even ask.

"I guess you're not listening to Doctor Phil."

"No."

"Do you mind if I turn him on for a moment?"

"Why?!" Dale queried impatiently.

"I just think you might want to hear one of his calls."

"How could that possibly serve me?"

"Trust me . . . please," Wil entreated.

Dale let out a sigh of exasperation. "All right."

Wil switched on a light near Dale's stereo system and tuned in WWKW.

"Methinks the lady doth protest too much," Dale heard Marovici say. "The problem is, Tisha, you're in denial."

"But I *wasn't* molested. That's not the problem."

"Do you hear yourself, Tisha?" queried Dr. Phil. "Your protests are classic symptoms of denial. You're even denying your denial. And until you quit denying the problem, you're going to continue to have it. You have a dysfunctional relationship with your husband. You have a fear of intimacy. And you're in denial that it ever happened. These are the symptoms of childhood sexual molestation and memory repression. And the first step to getting better is admitting to yourself that it happened."

"But . . . it didn't!"

"All right, look, Tisha. There's nothing I can do for you tonight. I suggest you seek professional counseling—possibly hypnotherapy—to unlock those repressed memories. Then you can begin to get to the bottom of this problem."

"But isn't there something I can do to help myself?"

"Would a surgeon operate on himself?" was Dr. Phil's rejoinder.

Dale sat up, dangling his legs over the edge of the bed. "Are all his calls like this?"

"Well, they vary," Wil replied. "But he does tend to fix on a clinical diagnosis and stick to it rather than really listening to what his caller is saying. This woman is fairly assertive, but many of them just go along with what he says."

Hearing this, Dale rolled his eyes in disbelief.

Marovici went on. "The best thing you can do for yourself and your husband is to quit denying the problem and seek professional help." And with that pronouncement, he disconnected the call. "If more couples followed that advice," he added with a tone of authority, "the divorce rate would drop by half. Thanks for your call. Who's up next, Brian?"

Dale watched as Wil turned down the radio. The educator could feel his young student's attention at his back. This was the first spark of interest or concern about something other than himself that Dale had shown in weeks. "What did you have in mind?" Dale asked.

"Well, I don't think we can afford to keep him much longer," Wil replied. "He's not exactly breaking audience records. Have you been reading the mail lately?"

Dale hadn't been reading the mail. He had tired of it a couple of weeks earlier, but had assumed it was running about the same as before. "No."

"Our listeners aren't at all happy with him. The mix is still overwhelmingly negative, but now the complaints are about Doctor Phil. 'He's too abrupt.' 'He's too full of himself.' 'His advice really isn't very helpful.' 'When's Dale coming back?'"

"Right!" Dale challenged sarcastically. "Well, I guess we blew it with Marovici. What exactly impressed you about this guy, anyway? I mean, did you actually listen to him?"

"We listened to his sample tape. The station in Miami had already changed its format and he was off the air by the time he contacted us. His sample tape was all he had, and it was very impressive."

"Naturally. He would have put his best calls on it."

"His numbers and references were impressive, too. Apparently, his style played fine in Miami."

"Did you interview anyone else who can do the job?"

"No one we felt comfortable with."

"So we're stuck with Marovici?"

"For now, unless you want to go back to music in that slot."

Faced with another difficult decision in the wake of his debacle, Dale just heaved a ponderous sigh and buried his head in his hands for the umpteenth time as Wil turned up the radio again. Dr. Phil had just begun his next call.

"I think I was abducted by aliens," his caller was heard to say.

After a barely concealed snicker, Dr. Phil asked condescendingly, "And what makes you think you've been abducted by aliens, Sonny?"

"Well," replied Sonny thoughtfully, "I've got all the classic signs: missing time, odd scoop scars on my body, anxiety, nocturnal nosebleeds, the usual."

"Do you read UFO reports by other people?" Phil probed.

"Oh, yeah!" Sonny replied, unaware of the trickery in the question.

"If your signs are classical, don't you think it's possible that you've just imagined all those things as a result of reading all the other UFO reports?"

"But that wouldn't explain the scoop scars and the nosebleeds."

"Humans nick themselves all the time. Do you have an air conditioner at home?"

"Yeah."

"Well, nosebleeds can be triggered by dry air, caused by some air conditioning systems. Trust me, Sonny, you haven't been abducted by aliens."

Dale eyed Wil with concern. Even allowing that Dr. Phil had the right to doubt claims that space aliens were visiting Earth, Dale recognized Marovici's absolute pronouncement as arrogance born out of ego.

"What makes you so sure?" queried Sonny passionately, but not rudely.

"Well, first of all," Dr. Phil intoned, somewhat impatiently, "it would be all but impossible for aliens to get to earth. Even at tremendous speeds, the great distances between us and every other star system would make the trip last many decades or centuries. It's simply not likely that any civilization is going to make such a long trip just to abduct you. Even if they could travel at the speed of light, it would take people from the nearest star at least four years to get here. And Einstein proved that no one could travel faster than light. So it boils down to the fact that it would not be technologically feasible to make the trip."

"Well, see, this is what gets me," Sonny countered ardently. "Supposedly intelligent men—scientists even—seem to think that today's terrestrial technology represents the ultimate in technological potential. This is arrogant, if not just plain stupid! For one thing, what Einstein proved was that it would be impossible to *accelerate a mass* to the speed of light. That doesn't mean it's impossible to travel at superluminal speeds by means *other* than accelerating a mass, like using the quantum mechanics principle of non-locality, or some scientific principle we haven't even begun to become aware of. I mean, scientists didn't know the earth was bathed in electromagnetic fields until they learned how to detect them. But they've always been there just the same. For all we know, superluminal speeds *are* possible, but we just haven't discovered how to do it—and the aliens have. You dismiss UFO sightings as though the limits of *our* science represents the status of *alien* technology. Come on!"

Again, Dale eyed Wil, this time with a sort of pride that the caller had stood up to Marovici. After a nod of understanding from Wil, Dale refocused his attention on the radio to see how Dr. Phil would handle this argument.

Recognizing that Sonny had done his homework and that his reasoning, though speculative, was scientifically sound, Dr. Phil bristled at the threat of being bested by this young man. His defense mechanisms thus triggered, he emitted a derisive snicker. "Look, Sonny, I can assure you: You weren't abducted by aliens. You can believe what you want, but if you insist on believing you were abducted by aliens, I can't help you." He pressed the disconnect button and addressed himself to his engineer. "Who's up next, Brian."

With the end of the call, Dale looked at the floor. What he was hearing was troubling, but the prospect of dismissing Dr. Phil and subjecting his listeners to yet more instability was even more troubling. Still, he needed to know what was happening at his radio station, so continued to listen.

The next call, from Maureen, started out reasonably enough.

"My best friend's husband hit on me a few nights ago," Maureen explained, "and now I feel guilty when I'm around her."

"Did you accept the husband's overtures?" Phil asked.

"No! I told him I wouldn't do that to my best friend."

"Then what do you feel guilty about?" Marovici wasn't so much asking the question as challenging his caller's complaint.

"He pleaded with me not to tell her about it and I promised him I wouldn't. But now when I'm around her, I feel like I'm being dishonest with her."

"Why did you make a promise like that to a cad like him?"

"Well, since nothing happened—and I made him promise never to do that kind of thing to anyone else!—I figured telling her would only upset her for nothing."

"It sounds to me like you behaved yourself. So again, I have to ask, what do you feel guilty about?"

"I dunno. She doesn't know what kind of cad he is and I do. It just doesn't feel right keeping this secret from her."

"Okay, if you're not comfortable with the way things are, why don't you just tell her? Under the circumstances, I don't think you're obligated to keep the promise. Tell her what he did and let *them* sort it out."

"But wouldn't that be a violation of the Platinum Principles?"

"The what?" queried Dr. Phil.

"The Platinum Principles."

"What are the Platinum Principles?" Phil asked somewhat disdainfully.

"Oh!" Maureen had assumed that all therapists were familiar with the two essential principles that Dale had shared with his listeners. Having found them so useful in her own life, she was surprised that Dr. Phil didn't know about them. "Uh, they're two guidelines that Dale taught us for how to act with respect and responsibility."

"Never heard of 'em," Marovici said dismissively.

Dale turned to Wil. "How often does my name come up in his calls?"

"Every once in a while," Wil replied.

"But isn't the bottom line that you want to come clean with your friend?" Dale heard Phil ask as he redirected his attention to the broadcast.

"Yes," Maureen confirmed, "but I promised him I wouldn't tell her, and I think I should keep my promise. I don't want to impose my will on him by breaking my promise."

"Well, I've gotta ask you, Maureen: Which is more important to you, your friendship with your friend or your promise to this cad?"

"Well, they're both important. I take pride in keeping my word. I just didn't anticipate feeling bad about it."

"Seems to me you have to make a choice here," Phil asserted.

Maureen sighed. "I was hoping for a solution that wouldn't mean breaking my promise."

"Sometimes life just doesn't give you any options," Dr. Phil opined sagely.

Maureen hesitated before responding. She didn't want to argue with Marovici, but she didn't think the matter was so cut and dried. "See, I'm not convinced of that here. Seems to me I should be able to do *something*. I mean, I don't think I did anything disrespectful or irresponsible by making the promise. I just want to feel okay about it."

"But what if this guy tries the same thing with someone else? Do you want to be responsible for his cheating on your friend the next time?"

"No, of course not—" Maureen stopped as a realization suddenly burst upon her. After a few seconds of thought, she voiced it. "But *I* wouldn't be responsible for that. *He* would. And telling her about what he did with me—or tried to do—wouldn't necessarily stop him from doing it with someone else. *And* if he does keep his promise to me and never does it with someone else, telling her would just upset her for nothing."

"Okay, so you're back to where you started," Dr. Phil observed dryly.

Again, Maureen mulled her options. "Not really," she mused, more to herself than to Dr. Phil. "I can talk to him again, tell him how I'm feeling, and tell him that if he breaks his promise to me, that cancels my promise to him. And tell him I'm watching him like a hawk."

"There you go!" Dr. Phil acclaimed as though he had solved his caller's problem. Suddenly Maureen was off the air and Marovici was announcing a commercial break.

Dale eyed Wil again. He didn't expect Dr. Phil to be familiar with the Platinum Principles, but he certainly didn't think it was responsible of him to advise a caller to break a promise. At the same time, he was proud of Maureen for having understood the Platinum Principles and applied them on her own, despite the misdirection by Dr. Phil.

As much as he wanted to distance himself from the whole mess, after hearing Marovici's handling of these few calls, Dale started listening regularly to Dr. Phil and began again reading the daily mail. While admitting that Phil handled the majority of his caller's questions adequately, he found too much of his "advice" judgmental, or simply not helpful. Almost as disturbing as his advice, he found the man's on-air demeanor at times discourteous. One night, even one of Phil's own callers echoed Dale's observations.

"You cut me off last night," were Stan's first words to Marovici.

"What?" queried Dr. Phil, stunned by the unexpected assertion.

"You cut me off last night when I called you."

"Brian, did Stan get cut off last night?" Phil asked his engineer.

"No, I'm not saying I *got* cut off," the caller persisted. "I'm saying that when you ended the call, you didn't even say good-bye. You just hung up. You always do that. You make some pronouncement and cut the caller off. I didn't think anything about it till you did it to *me*, and then I realized how rude it is."

"Come on, Stan," Phil parried. "This is how talk radio works. It's different than real life."

"*Dale* never did it that way. He always said 'good-bye,' like he was talking to a friend."

"Well, I'm not Dale," Dr. Phil said in his own defense.

"You got *that* right," was Stan's retort, his respect for Dale layered in his tone of voice.

The support Dale heard in Stan's words and inflection took him somewhat aback. He had not conceived that his former listeners could ever respect him again. Likewise, he was surprised by the number of requests in the mail for his return to the air. He had been so focused on his emotional processes that he hadn't considered that his listeners were going through processes of their own and, despite his duplicity, were beginning to realize how valuable he had been in their lives, and to forgive him.

> I was angry that Dale had lied to us. But I realize now he didn't really hurt anyone but himself. I miss him.
>
> Kay Hastings

> I'm no psychologist, but even I can tell Dr. Phil is wrong half the time. When is Dale coming back?
>
> Phillip Sammartino

> This new guy sucks. Get him off and get Dale back.
>
> Rich Hempfling

Even some of those who had previously written letters critical of Dale were reevaluating their earlier position and writing again.

> I'm sorry I was so mean to Dale in my last letter. After listening to Dr. Phil for a month, I wish Dale was back on the air.
>
> Laverne Shattock

> We don't agree with Dale's choice to deceive his listeners, but at least he really listened to his callers and his wisdom was very insightful. Dr. Marovici seems to make snap diagnoses and stick with them, even when they are obviously in error.
>
> Jerry & Terry Riggins

> I'd rather listen to Dale anytime than Dr. Phuckhead!
>
> Frank Kellner

"I don't think we can wait any longer," Wil opined to Dale and his fellow advisors in their morning meeting, as he raised his cup for a sip of coffee. As usual, the four men were gathered in the den. "I think we have to let Doctor Phil go." By this time, Marovici had been taking calls on WWKW for eight weeks, and after the initial spike—always expected for a new personality—his audience numbers and write-in ratings were plummeting. Dale nodded his concurrence.

"I don't understand why he was so successful in Miami," puzzled Shel.

"Well," Paul drawled, "they didn't have Dale to compare him to in Miami."

Paul's argument was compelling, and Shel and Wil both nodded in recognition. Only Dale was not of a mind to agree. But he sat still and silent so as to avoid drawing the reassurances his well-intentioned advisors had taken to plying him with since he had emerged from the deepest recesses of his gloom.

Now turning directly to Dale, Wil said gently, "We're receiving so many letters asking if you're coming back on the air that I think we should consider this an option."

Pokerfaced, Dale surveyed the other members of his staff, looking for any dissent to Wil's proposal. They all seemed eager to support it. This annoyed him. "Absolutely not," he finally replied, rather indignant that they would consider this to be an option after the embarrassment he had sustained in retiring from radio and the humiliation he would surely suffer in returning to it.

Disappointed that their employer was still so adamant in his refusal to face his fears, but not terribly surprised, Paul and Shel sighed and settled back in unison.

Wil opened his mouth to mount an argument, but realized the futility of it and retreated. "Then it's back to a music format," he concluded.

Dale nodded curtly and the decision was finalized. Dr. Phil was given two weeks notice and Greg Harris, always eager to get the work, was lined up to take his place with the same classic rock format he had overseen after Dale left the air.

Having undertaken the major move from Miami just two months before, Marovici was not happy. But his contract had a mutual escape clause and he had no legal recourse to stay the termination. When he was unable to charm the Greene staffers into reversing their decision, he angrily refused to finish out the two weeks, and Greg Harris was called to take over that night, forcing him to cancel a hot date.

The callers who had begun dialing the station even before 9:00, hoping to talk to Dr. Phil, were puzzled to reach only a busy signal.

And the few listeners who tuned in to The Night is Jung were mystified when they heard only music, though none were all that disappointed. As for Dale and his staff, they were certain the era of talk radio at WWKW had finally come to an end.

Chapter 27

As had been the case several times since Dale launched his talk format, the fans of The Brink of Tomorrow had their own plans for the show. They had begun a process of personal growth—applying to their lives the wisdom Dale had shared with them—and were not content to merely abandon that evolvement. Having had a couple of months to process the events that took their once-beloved radio advisor from them, they were now able to see Dale and his acts, as already expressed in some of their calls and letters, in a more compassionate light.

Bottom line, they wanted Dale back. If he thought he could hide from his deepest, darkest fears while encouraging his listeners to face theirs, he had another think coming. Now deluging the station with letters and email, Dale's former listeners urged—sometimes demanded—the reclusive host return to the air. Someone even circulated a calligraphed petition entreating him to reconsider his resignation, using a website on the Internet to promote it.

Fundamentally in agreement with Dale's fans, the Greene staff made sure every letter addressed to Dale or about Dale arrived on his desk, along with the petition, which had ultimately been signed by six thousand, seven hundred and twenty-two people—a mighty turnout for talk-radio listeners in the relatively small city.

The intent behind the massive pile of letters heaped on his desk each day was not lost on Dale. He knew what his staff were up to. But the thought of returning to the air—of actually facing people he had lied to, people he had betrayed—was still too awful to even imagine, despite their pleas for his return. Yet the daily pile of correspondence held a strange and compelling attraction for him. He read each letter, and kept returning to the somewhat formal text of the petition.

Petition

We, the Undersigned Listeners of WWKW, being of one mind and intent upon one course of action, hereby make this formal declaration and petition:

Whereas Dale C. Greene formerly hosted a call-in discussion program known as The Brink of Tomorrow, hereinafter "The Show," on radio station WWKW; and,

Whereas Dale C. Greene shared his Wisdom with the Undersigned Listeners of The Show; and,

Whereas We drew strength and benefit from said Wisdom; and,

Whereas We miss the Wisdom of Dale C. Greene on The Show;

Wherefore: We, the Undersigned Listeners of WWKW, hereby request the return of Dale C. Greene to The Brink of Tomorrow.

It all raised so many questions for Dale. Sitting in the gloom of his bedroom, he mulled them over and over. Could he *actually* return to talk radio? Could he *actually* talk to people who knew his secret? Could he *actually* counsel people he had betrayed? Would he *actually* be embraced by people he had deceived? The letters and the petition seemed to suggest it was possible.

But how many listeners held an opposing view? Dale was aware that the letters represented only that small portion of WWKW listeners who were unhappy with the status quo, who were eager enough for Dale to return to go to the effort to write. Those who were satisfied with music from nine to midnight would have no reason or incentive to write. Thus, the letters gave a skewed profile in support of a return to the air. In truth, what proportion of WWKW's listeners still held Dale in contempt? This was not known, and maybe not precisely knowable.

And if he did return, how many challenging questions would he have to answer? How much ridicule would he have to endure? He would no longer be able to evade such questions. He would have to be completely honest in his answers. How deeply into his pain would he be forced to reach? *Could* he endure the questions? *Could* he endure the ridicule? Just the thought of sitting again at that microphone—of taking calls from victims of his treachery, of answering questions that penetrated to the darkest quadrants of his soul—stiffened his muscles and made his heart pound in his chest, its turbulent thrashing seemingly too intense to endure.

Flogged by this fear, he could not even guess at the answers to these questions, and trying only raised more of the same. But the pleas of his listeners couldn't be ignored. By their sheer volume and persistence, they cracked open a door that had been sealed shut for months—the urge to explore his options, and to seek help with them.

"How are Greg's numbers?" Dale asked, raising a forkful of capellini primavera to his mouth. He had requested a private lunch with his closest advisor. They were sitting on the veranda under warm sunshine. A gentle breeze ruffled their napkins.

"They're all right, for a music format," Wil replied. "He's holding his own." Greg Harris had been on the job from nine to midnight for six weeks. Bobby made the trip to WWKW headquarters each night to engineer for Harris. Wil took and thoroughly chewed another bite, allowing the silence between himself and Dale to gestate before probing gently, "You didn't ask to meet me privately to discuss Greg Harris. What's on your mind?"

Dale was no quicker with his answer, unsure he even wanted to explore the subject. He released a breath. "I . . . never thought I'd ever hear myself ask this, but . . . all these letters, and this petition, have me wondering: If I went back on the air, could I possibly be accepted . . . *trusted* . . . after what I've done?"

"I'll answer that with three words," Wil replied, "William Jefferson Clinton."

Understanding the reference, Dale raised his shaggy eyebrows in recognition.

"But that's not what you're really worried about, is it?" Wil had always been quick to detect the inner structure of Dale's concerns.

"No," Dale admitted.

"You're afraid the embarrassment their questions might stir up will be unbearably painful," Wil continued.

Dale nodded his large, knotty head.

"No doubt there will be pain. But let me put it in perspective. At base you have only two choices: You can hide from it, or you can face it head on. If you hide from it, you'll either have to face it later, or remain hidden and off the air for the rest of your life, wondering what might have been if you'd faced it."

Dale grimaced at this prospect.

"If you face it head on," Wil went on, "you'll either get through it and put it behind you once and for all, or you'll wind up right back were you are now, in which case you'll have lost nothing in the attempt. And you'll have gained some experience, if nothing else."

"But how embarrassing will it be to be talking to people I deceived so ignominiously?"

"I know you know that's something only *you* can determine. But let me paint the broad picture: It will be as embarrassing as you want it— or don't want it—to be."

Dale furrowed his bulbous brow at this unrevealing pearl of wisdom.

Seeing Dale's expression, Wil elaborated. "It's not as though you gave them bad advice and are no having to eat your words. Your error—our error—had nothing to do with the advice. So you have nothing to be embarrassed about with regard to what you'll be talking with callers about. Plus, I believe you're overlooking the compassion and forgiveness of which people are capable in response to humility and remorse of the kind you showed in your apology."

Dale had not considered the matter from that perspective. Maybe he wouldn't be called upon to face his deepest fears after all. Maybe it wouldn't be so painful after all.

"So it boils down to how you wish to respond to the matter," Wil continued. "You can approach it from a perspective of poise and self-possession, or you can approach it from imbalance." He started to say more, but stopped. He knew there was a deeper issue—a core issue of which Dale seemed unaware. But something told him Dale was not ready to address it, and the current situation wasn't forcing Dale to deal with the core issue . . . yet. "The choice is really yours," Wil concluded.

Though not really satisfying, Dale knew Wil's counsel on personal matters would always steer Dale back to his own choices, and never impose a direct opinion without a direct request. "All right, I know the choice is mine. But I'd like your opinion about my choice."

Wil fixed his young charge in his gaze. "I'd like to see you back on the air."

Dale drew a deep breath. Though he knew his beloved advisor was only expressing his personal wish, Dale took comfort in the fact that by it he was expressing a belief that Dale's return to talk radio would not be as rigorous as Dale had feared.

"I don't mean to suggest there will be no pain in returning," Wil continued, dabbing his mouth with his napkin, "but whatever pain there is can only promote further growth."

Dale tipped his head slightly as if to concede the point. Gratified to see his young charge arrive at this understanding, Wil sat silently by, allowing Dale to mull the proposition without interruption. Though Dale wasn't sure he was ready to face his listeners again—or his fears—he was now beginning to think it would be endurable. After some moments, he arrived at a decision. "All right. What do we have to do to get ready?"

After some discussion with all three Greene advisors, it was decided that announcements would be made—on the air, in the local papers, and on the station's website—that Dale was considering returning to talk radio. Listeners were invited to call or write with their vote for or against the proposition. Though less than scientific, at least this approach held the promise of collecting a reasonably representative sample of listener sentiment.

As much as Dale wanted to get back to doing what he loved, he half-hoped the response would be negative so he would have an excuse not to face his fears. But such was not his luck. Although a statistically significant percentage of WWKW listeners voted *against* Dale's return to talk radio, the figure nevertheless represented a minority. The majority cast their votes *in favor* of the proposal.

With the WWKW listener vote in, Dale's return to the air was scheduled for the first Saturday of the following month—a fortnight away—starting as a weekend show and phasing in to a daily show if Dale was well received. After the date was first announced, the local papers kept repeating it, happy to have a reason to recycle the story of the "disgraced DJ," and now making hay with the news of his "comeback." Committed to two shows on the designated weekend, but still unsure of himself, Dale was in a constant state of anxiety— and commensurately cranky—for two whole weeks. Both he and his staff couldn't wait for the waiting to be over.

Chapter 28

"This is Jay Leavenworth closing the curtain on The Saturday Evening Concert," announced the DJ who emceed the six-to-nine shift on weekends. "Stay tuned for Dale Greene, coming up just six minutes from now, at the top of the hour. In case you haven't been keeping track, Dale's been on leave for a few months and he's returning tonight. Welcome back, buddy. I, for one, missed ya." Of course, Jay had never met Dale, but he had always listened to The Brink of Tomorrow during his drive home from the station after his shift and, liking Dale's way of looking at things, felt a kinship with him. "Be sure to tune in tomorrow night at six for The Sunday Evening Concert with Jay Leavenworth, here on WWKW, FM 102.4."

Dale had arrived in the estate broadcast booth a couple of minutes earlier. It was the first time he had used the access tunnel between the house and the broadcast booth since the night of the "big apology." The ride triggered painful memories—of his lapse in integrity, his betrayal of his listeners. The remembrance stiffened his muscles and sent a shudder down his spine. Bobby had been there for some time, setting up the booth for the show. Calls were already coming in and the call queue was full.

In comparison with the anxiety of the last two weeks, these last six minutes were agony. At least the seclusion that followed his big apology had been known—painful, but known. What was to follow here was completely unknown. That made it all the more terrifying. To remain focused, Dale muted the news-and-weather brief and commercial messages that filled these final six minutes.

Thirty seconds before the hour, Dale received the "get ready" signal from Bobby. At nine, station headquarters handed signal control off to the estate booth. With his eye on his instruments, Bobby faded the opening music and gave Dale the "go" sign.

For a few seconds, nothing happened. Those tuned to WWKW—of which there were an inordinate number, given all the hoopla made by the media over the event—heard only silence. Dale's advisors, listening to the broadcast in the den of the manor house, held their breath at what seemed to them a loss of nerve. Registering only dead air in his headset, Bobby jerked his head up, anxious to find out what was happening, and studied Dale through the glass panel that separated them. The DJ sat motionless, a glaze in his normally keen eyes.

Over the intervening two weeks, Dale had rehearsed his opening words many times, trying out numerous different approaches. Now that it was time to say them, he was stuck. His practiced plan didn't feel right. He had nearly resorted to habit and begun with the upbeat opening of the previous incarnation of the show, but that definitely wouldn't have fit. He was returning to radio at the request of his listeners, so this had to be on their terms. It had to be respectful and extemporaneous.

"Thank you, Jay, for that warm welcome back," he finally said in utter earnest. In the den, his advisors simultaneously released their breath. Likewise, listeners across the city relaxed. "And thank you to all of you who asked and encouraged me to return to the air. I want you all to know that I read every letter addressed to me—and, of course, the charming petition so many of you signed—and the only reason I'm here is because of the warm and loving invitation you extended to me in them. I feel truly humbled, and I'm not quite sure I deserve your support. I'm painfully aware that I deceived and betrayed you, and for that, again, I am deeply sorry. I will never lose sight of my error.

"But at the same time, I'm also aware that my error is a lesson, an opportunity to grow, to strengthen my honesty and integrity. As a way of showing you I've learned my lesson, I promise to answer all your questions honestly—at least all questions suitable for family radio. And just to be fair tonight, I'm going to take your calls in the order they arrived."

He turned his gaze to the computer monitor which displayed the call queue. "My first caller is Quentin. He's called before and he just wants to—" He stopped mid-sentence. The remainder of Quentin's reason for calling read "—welcome you back." While Dale was warmed by Quentin's sentiment, relating it to the audience himself felt self-serving, and he just felt too humble to be doing anything self-serving at this moment. "Well, I'm going to just let Quentin say it." He connected the call. "Hi, Quentin. You're on the air."

"Hi, Dale. Wow! First in line! That's a first . . . uh, no pun intended. I don't know if you remember me; I called last year when I was losing my job, and you helped me a lot."

"I *do* remember you, Quentin. Did you start your skydiving school?"

"I sure did!"

"How's that going?"

"Great! Business has been great! It's the best thing I ever did, next to marrying my wife . . . and calling you."

Dale chucked at the compliment. "Well, that *is* great. Congratulations!"

"Thanks! Look, I don't want to take up much of your time—I know you have other callers—I just wanted to call and say 'welcome back.'"

"Well, thank you, Quentin. It's good to be back. Like I said before, I'm not sure I deserve to be here, but I'm truly grateful to everyone for being invited back. Is there anything else you wanted to talk about tonight?"

"No, I'm good. I just wanted to say I'm glad you're back."

Both touched and relieved, Dale relaxed. "Well, thank you again, Quentin. You've made getting started real easy. Have great evening."

"Thanks. See ya."

Dale disconnected the call and consulted his monitor for the next caller in the queue. Her name was "Cindy." But more than her name, Dale was interested in her reason for calling. What he read sent a chill down his spine: It was to find out what Dale really looked like. He had hoped not to have to tackle this subject quite so soon, but having promised to answer all questions honestly, and to take the calls in order of arrival, he didn't feel he could make an exception just because he was afraid it would be painful.

"Next up is Cindy, and she's calling to ask . . . what I really look like." He engaged the call and tried to sound cheerful. "Hi, Cindy. You're on the air."

"Hi, Dale."

"How are you this evening?" he stalled.

"I'm fine, thanks. How are you?"

"As well as can be expected," he equivocated. He didn't really want to start the ball rolling on Cindy's subject, but felt even more uncomfortable with the silence. "And how can I help you?" he asked cautiously.

"Well, some of the papers published these stupid drawings that I didn't think could really look like you, so I was just wondering what you really do look like."

Inhaling deeply to calm his nerves, Dale pondered his answer for a moment. He had already revealed that he was disfigured. Now that the cat was out of the bag, what could it hurt to give the details? Still, the potential of being ridiculed had not vanished and the prospect terrified him.

"Well," he drawled carefully, "I'm just over five feet tall, with a bit of a hunch. If I could straighten up, I'd probably be three or four inches taller. My head is about twice the size of a normal man's and pretty lumpy. The disease has caused my skull to grow all out of shape and proportion, with knobby protuberances that appear externally as large nodes, or bumps."

"Do you look anything like that movie the Elephant Man?" Cindy queried ingenuously.

"A little." Then, "Maybe a tad more handsome—"

Even Dale was stunned by what had just come out of his mouth. He had never indulged in morbid humor before and, especially after his ignominious departure from radio, was startled at his capacity for it. But this had been an instantaneous impulse he hadn't been able to resist. He wondered as to its import. Cindy too saw the humor in it, but didn't know whether or not it was intended, so sat silent for several seconds. In the den, his advisors were caught short by the unexpected quip. Secretly, though, Wil found it an encouraging sign.

"What else?" Cindy finally asked.

"Well ... my spine is curved and my ribcage is enlarged," Dale replied, returning to form, "which accounts for the resonant quality of my voice."

"Does the disease cause you any disabilities?"

"I have limited use of my left arm and my legs, due to asymmetric hyperostosis—uneven and kind of gnarled overgrowth of my bones. And my feet are misshapen by osteomas—bone tumors—and plantar hyperplasia—deep lines and overgrowth of the soft tissue on the soles of my feet.

"Can you walk?"

"Yes, but with difficulty. Most of the time I use a wheelchair."

Cindy was silent for a moment. Then, "It's really hard to imagine you that way. You sound so good-looking on the radio."

Dale didn't know whether to thank Cindy or point out her foolishness. But his indecision was short-lived as Cindy picked up where she had left off.

"I guess that doesn't make much sense," she said. "But I guess I'm trying to say that what really matters to me is how you sound and what you say, not what you look like."

This came as a pleasant surprise. "Well, thank you, Cindy. I appreciate that. Of course, because you can't actually see me, that's easier for you to say than if you were looking right at me." Dale gave Cindy a second to say anything else she might want to say, then asked, "Is there anything else you'd like to know or talk about?"

"No. That's all."

"All right, then. Thanks for calling and have a pleasant evening."

"Thanks. Bye."

"Bye."

Dale disconnected the call. He'd gotten through it alive. But he hadn't heard the last of the difficult questions. On the very next call, Simon asked, "You always seemed to stand for honesty and stuff. So why did you hire that other guy to make those personal appearances for you when you knew it was dishonest?"

Though this was a perfectly legitimate question, it shot through Dale like a shiv. He gasped for breath and reminded himself that he had no right to overreact to their questions. He had brought them on himself by his own actions, and they deserved to have their questions answered calmly and rationally.

"Well," he began, after collecting himself, "when we decided to hire Elliot to accept my Man of the Year award, someone suggested I was given both the disfigurement and the award to deal with in the least objectionable way possible. To my fear-addled mind, that rationale seemed perfectly correct. But in retrospect, I realize it *wasn't* correct." As painful as it was to admit to this error, Dale found the confession liberating. He took a breath and went on. "What was correct was that I was meant to deal with it in the most *courageous* way possible. But that's one thing I've been lacking for most of my life: courage. The world is a judgmental place, and it scared the daylights out of me to even think about having to face that world in person. I've gotta tell you, I have tremendous respect and admiration for anyone who lives his life with a disfigurement, even a slight one. It takes tremendous courage to face a judgmental world, and any soul who's chosen to incarnate into that kind of life is exceedingly strong."

After a short silence to allow his mind to incorporate this concept, Simon mused simply, "I agree."

Dale's next caller, Palmer, observed, "I notice you're not calling the show 'The Brink of Tomorrow.' Why is that?"

"I don't feel I've earned it yet."

"What do you have to do to earn it?" Palmer persisted.

"Well, practice what I preach, to invoke the old saw."

"Okay, I can dig that. So what went wrong? Why didn't you practice what you preached before? I mean, what was so hard about doing it before?"

"Well, like I told Simon," Dale explained, "I was extremely fearful. The same thing that causes all of our problems. I'm no more immune to it than anyone else."

"But you help *other* people with their problems. How can *you* have problems? I mean, how can you help other people with *their* problems when you have problems of your own?"

"Well, I'm able to help other people partly because I know the philosophy and I have an agile mind. But more importantly, I have an objective point of view on *their* problems. One of the reasons people have trouble solving their own problems is because their fears cloud their perspective and get in the way of the resolution process. But I'm not wrapped up in *their* fears. *My* perspective on *their* problems isn't distorted by *their* fears. However, when I was being asked to make personal appearances, the fear I was feeling distorted my perspective— kept me from having an objective point of view on my own problems—so I was unable to apply my own philosophy. This isn't an excuse, it's an explanation. It was a mistake and a learning experience that I intend to use in the future in the application of my philosophy to my *own* life, and, I dare say, to help people through the haze of fear that prevents them from resolving their problems on their own."

"Okay, I can dig that," Palmer acknowledged.

Then there was Irene.

"What right do you have to pull the dishonest stunt you pulled and then come back on the air and think we're all gonna make nice and forgive you?!" she demanded angrily.

After his opening statement and the previous calls, Dale was perplexed by Irene's question. It was as though she hadn't heard a word of what had gone before. Well, at least she wasn't attacking him for his disfigurement. He steadied himself. "I'm not here because I feel I have any right to be here," he said patiently, "I'm here because I was invited back by so many people. And—"

"*I* didn't invite you back!" Irene interrupted invectively.

Dale took a deep breath and reminded himself to be calm. "All right, I respect that, as well as your right not to forgive me. Did my mistakes directly harm you in some way?"

"No. But you shouldn't have done what you did!"

"I know that. I realize that now and my apologies were sincere." Although Irene's anger seemed excessive and inappropriately aimed, Dale thought he might still be able to temper her upset by soliciting a solution from her. "What would you like me to do?" he said earnestly.

"Go back to whatever hole you crawled out of and get off the radio."

Recognizing that Irene's complaint was not coming from any real injury, but from some generalized judgment, Dale found maintaining his patience progressively easier. "May I ask you a question, Irene?"

"I guess," she drawled suspiciously.

"Can you receive other stations on your radio?"

"Of course!"

"Then I invite you to tune to a different station and forget about me. No one is forcing you to listen to WWKW, or this program."

After a few seconds of silence by the apparently stunned Irene, a sharp rap on the line told Dale and his listeners that she had hung up on him.

"Goodnight, Irene," he concluded.

Partway through the night, something seemingly miraculous happened: The calls ceased to be about Dale and became about the callers. Some were rather light. Political correctness was the current watchword at Bret Harte High, and seventeen-year-old Justin wanted to know if affectionately touching a girl on the arm or shoulder was really politically incorrect.

"The concept of political correctness," Dale explained, "is just someone's idea of what's 'right' and what's 'wrong.' So political correctness is basically a judgment, which, as you know, I don't endorse. And political correctness is made all the more ticklish by the fact that those who set the standards of political correctness often have socialist agendas and are imposing their ideas of 'right' and 'wrong' on the rest of the populace in order to further those agendas. So I would encourage you not to try to conform to political correctness."

"But I don't want to make anyone mad or uncomfortable!" Justin interjected.

"And I salute and support that desire. But I don't believe political correctness is the answer. I believe the answer lies in the Platinum Principles. If you're a regular listener to this show, you know the first Platinum Principle is the principle of respect. The second Platinum Principle is the principle of responsibility. If you simply treat everyone with respect and responsibility, you won't make anyone mad or uncomfortable."

"Okaaaaaay," Justin drawled, not sure how to apply this advice. "So how do I do that?"

"Well, instead if applying a single rigid standard to everyone, which has the potential of missing the mark for everyone, you find out what the other person is comfortable with. Some people don't mind a friendly pat on the arm or shoulder, others do. But *they* set those boundaries for themselves; *you* don't set those boundaries for them, nor does anyone else, including the proponents of political correctness. So it's for you to find out what each person's boundaries are and be respectful of them. That way you don't have to worry about conforming to anyone else's ideas of what's correct and what's not, or concern yourself with applying a rigid single standard to people who are different."

"But what if I don't know what they're comfortable with?"

"You ask them. And until you find out, simply treat them with respect."

"I'm kinda surprised," Justin said. "I thought you'd agree with political correctness."

"Why did you think that?" To Dale, the difference between political correctness and the Platinum Principles was crystal clear.

"Because *they* don't like judging and *you* don't like judging."

"Ah! I see. Well, the similarity goes only so far as not endorsing judging. When it comes to what to do *instead* of judging, I completely disagree with political correctness."

"Oh. What do you do differently?"

"Well, let me start by giving you a little background. The proponents of political correctness understand only half of the equation. And, as it turns out, the *opponents* of political correctness understand only the *other* half of the equation. Neither side understands the whole equation. As I've said before, judging— thinking or asserting that something is good or bad or right or wrong— reflects only someone's personal opinion, deceptively couched as an absolute or a fact. As such, as I've said many times on this program, if you wish to evolve spiritually, you have to cease judging. But for most people, that leaves a sort of void, a need to replace judgment with something else.

"The proponents of political correctness want you to replace *your* opinion of what is right or wrong or good or bad with *their* opinion of what is right or wrong or good or bad. The *opponents* of political correctness want you to continue to judge. I propose a third solution which dispenses with the judging, but doesn't substitute someone *else's* opinions. I propose replacing judgment with *preference*, which is an expression of personal choice that reflects personal responsibility for one's thoughts, choices, and actions.

"I once read a treatise which argued that Shakespeare was a 'better' poet than T.S. Eliot." Dale mimicked the judgmental tone he imagined the author of the treatise using. "The author of this treatise claimed that this point of view was 'factual and objectively correct,' and he used that to justify his judgment. But the truth is, the appreciation of poetry is purely an aesthetic consideration. And aesthetics—beauty— is only in the eye of the beholder. So if you want to make a distinction between Shakespeare and T.S. Eliot, you don't have to think Shakespeare is a 'better' poet than T.S. Eliot, all you need to do is *like* him more. Or, as in my case, like T.S. Eliot more. Call me uncultured if you must, but I've always preferred T.S. Eliot. In any event, preference provides an utterly simple way of making those distinctions without judgment. It celebrates the differences between people and things, but without resorting to judgment or adopting someone else's rigid single standard."

"Hmm," Justin mused. "I used to think that ceasing judgment would make everything seem the same to you. Like everything would be the same dull gray. But it's not."

"No, it's not," confirmed Dale. "If you substitute preference for judgment, you make all the same distinctions you did before, but now you're taking responsibility for them.

"That's really cool! So I just need to find out each person's preference, and treat them that way."

"That's it," Dale acknowledged.

"Wow, that's really simple."

Other calls were quite serious.

"My next caller is Jackie. She's fourteen and . . . contemplating suicide." He punched the button to engage the call. "Hi, Jackie, you're on the air."

"Hi, Dale." Her voice was sweet, but melancholy.

"You're contemplating suicide, dear?" Dale asked with great concern. "What's happening?"

"I just feel so awful. I just don't want to live anymore."

"Why?"

"Well, to start off, my mom was murdered eighteen months ago and that was bad enough. But now my dad's been convicted of the murder." As the case had been big-time news in Springfield, this was usually all Jackie had to say, so she stopped there.

Dale had followed the media reports on the incident, which included accusations of sloppy police work, prosecutorial misconduct, and a rush to judgment. A heartfelt groan of sympathy escaped Dale's throat. "I'm familiar with the case."

"He didn't do it, I know he didn't. They didn't have any evidence, only circumstantial, but they convicted him anyway, and now I'm in foster care, which I hate. I love my dad and I know he wouldn't kill my mom."

"I understand that his conviction is being appealed."

"Yeah. But it may take a long time. And in the meantime, everyone at school calls me the killer's kid and won't talk to me, except to taunt me. It's awful, and it makes me not want to live anymore."

"Pretty challenging, huh?" Dale sympathized.

"Yeah." She was nearly in tears.

"Okay," he said softly. "I understand the impulse to take your own life. I've had some pretty dark moments of my own and contemplated suicide myself. And in the sense that you have a right to do with your life what you will, I have no argument against suicide. However, from a metaphysical point of view, it may not be an effective way to get out of the situation you're trying to escape."

"Why not?"

"Well, the impulse to commit suicide is always an impulse of the ego, not of the soul. As I've told my listeners before, we come to this reality to learn specific lessons, and ending your life before you've finished that process prevents you from learning those lessons. As a result, according to my sources, when you end your own life, you reincarnate right back into the same situation in the next lifetime. In other words, your soul is going to learn the lessons it came here to learn, one way or the other. So if you stop it from doing that *this* time, it'll just come right back and put itself through the same pain again."

Jackie groaned at this prospect.

"Some people even get caught up in a *cycle* of suicide," Dale elaborated, "repeatedly ending their life before completing their lessons, reincarnating into the same sort of circumstances, finding it unbearable and committing suicide again, then repeating the process. The only way to stop that is to realize that you're here to go through these challenging experiences and grow from them, to learn how to be courageous—or at least to embrace your fear without acting on it. So I urge you to trust that whatever challenging situation you get into, you've chosen it for a reason, and find the growth in that reason. And if you stick to your principles and act with integrity during these challenging times—don't let yourself start imposing your will on others or being of disservice to others, or yourself—you'll learn the lessons most quickly and the situation will soon resolve itself. I say that from personal experience. I had *many* dark days and I *never* thought I'd be able to return to radio again. But here I am. I've benefited more from the pain of this ordeal than you could possibly imagine."

"Why do you think I chose to create this for myself?"

"That's always an excellent question. Of course, *I* can only speculate on it. It's for *you* to determine yourself so you can derive from the lesson everything that's in it. In fact, I encourage everyone to ask themselves what message they're trying to send themselves when they create really challenging circumstances for themselves. Ask yourself 'How does this serve me?' and see what answer you get back. The answer might come as a strong voice in your head, or it may be just a subtle feeling. Or it may not come right away, but be revealed to you at some other time in some other way. It doesn't matter how it comes, all ways are equally valid, and just right for you for that experience.

"But to get back to your question, two things strike me right off. One, we often allow ourselves to share a challenging experience with someone in order to be of service to them—to set a positive example for them—so they can get the most out of the experience. Seeing you maintaining faith that things will resolve according to truth could help your dad keep faith while he's going through his ordeal. And, if you ended your life, it would probably hurt him very deeply, and he may even give up trying to bring the truth to light. So it might be very important to *him* for you to stay really strong."

"Hmm ... I hadn't thought of that," Jackie confessed, seeing her ordeal in a fresh new light, "I don't want to make it any harder on him than it already is."

"Right. The second thing that comes to mind is that you may have wanted to experience the same *feelings* your dad is experiencing without having to go through the same *experience* your dad is going through. In other words, you may have put yourself close to someone undergoing this experience so you could learn from it vicariously without limiting yourself in the same way. Or it might be something completely different that I couldn't possibly imagine. So just trust that what you're going through is exactly what you came here to do, and that by sticking with it and facing it with integrity—the Platinum Principles will help you there—you'll experience the growth you came here for."

This made great sense to Jackie, who silently allowed the insight to settle in. "So I need to stay here for both of us," she concluded.

"I'd say so. And when he gets out, he's going to need you more than ever. Besides, we need more sweetness in this world, and you can help provide some of it."

Jackie giggled, then heaved a big sigh. "Thank you. This has really helped."

"You're very welcome, dear. And promise me you'll call anytime you're feeling down. Just tell Bobby who you are and he'll make sure I talk to you."

"I will. I really love you and I'm really glad you're back."

Now it was Dale's turn to heave a cleansing sigh. "Thank *you*, Jackie, for giving me the opportunity to be of service."

"You're welcome." She giggled again. "Bye."

"Goodnight, sweetheart." He disconnected the call. "This is Dale Greene on WWKW, FM 102.4. Back after these commercial messages."

Ken Gullekson

Chapter 29

As the evening closed in on midnight, Bobby signaled Dale that he had time for just one more call. "I've got time for just one more caller," Dale announced as he glanced at the next name on his call queue, not bothering to read his reason for calling. "This is Kurt, and he's calling—" He stopped short as he looked for the first time at Kurt's reason for calling. A shiver shot up his spine as he read it. He contemplated skipping to the next caller. But he had already committed himself to Kurt, never mind the promise he had made to take all calls in order. "—To urge me to make a personal appearance," he finished. With great trepidation, he pressed the button to connect the call. "Hi, Kurt, you're on the air," he said, as cheerfully as he could manage.

"Hey, Dale! Welcome back, dude. I think I speak for everyone when I say we missed ya."

Well, at least Kurt seemed friendly enough. "Thank you, Kurt. How can I help you?" He hoped to sidestep the reason for Kurt's call.

"Well, man, you can start by making a personal appearance so we can all see the real you." The tone of Kurt's voice was not demanding or threatening, but it was ardent.

So much for the sidestep. Having to respond to this direct entreaty left Dale speechless. He had exhausted all his excuses the first time this request was made so many months ago. And the events that had taken place between then and now had illuminated the shadowed crevices into which he had ducked in order to avoid this issue then. He had to address it. But how? He was at an utter loss for words and the silence that ensued over the airwaves only highlighted his difficulty. In the den of the manor house, his advisors hung breathless on the edge of their seats. Watching for signs of Dale's next move, Bobby was poised to spin a disc to fill the dead air.

In a flash of recognition, Dale realized that he was frozen with fear. This was what his life had finally come to. This demand to show his face to the world was appearing to be inescapable. This was what would finally define him. There were five more minutes of show time to fill. Would he seize this moment to vindicate his philosophy of life and his advice to his listeners? Or would he shrink from it and back into the shadows of obscurity as a coward and a hypocrite? Both options terrified him.

At the same time, he realized he had nothing left to lose. He opted for honesty, finally ending nearly twenty seconds of dead air.

"To be honest with you, Kurt," he said calmly, "the thought of doing a personal appearance—even now that everyone knows I'm disfigured—terrifies me to the core. Just sitting here hearing you ask the question and thinking about it does that. I can't imagine what I'd feel if I were faced with actually stepping out in front of an audience. I mean, it's been over twenty years since any stranger has laid eyes on me and I just can't imagine it."

"Okay, but you're always encouraging your listeners to face their fears, to do what they're excited to do and do what they're afraid to do. If you believe in your own philosophy, shouldn't you do the same thing?"

Dale was tempted to call Kurt on his use of "shouldn't," but knew that would just be a stalling tactic. He drew a breath. "Yes, if I were to follow my own advice, I would face my fears and make the personal appearance. I have no excuse for not doing that. But as they say, it's easier said than done."

"What are you afraid of exactly?" Kurt queried. "We already know what you look like, sort of."

"What, indeed?" Dale mused. "When I was young, before we moved here, my parents would warn their new friends about my disfigurement before they met me, and even then, the extreme reactions they had to first laying eyes on me deeply hurt my feelings. So I don't even trust people who have been warned about my appearance to react any more respectfully."

"Okay, but you told a caller last year that people with defective bodies chose those bodies because they had some very extreme feelings they wanted to experience. So you must have chosen your body for that reason. Right?"

Kurt had a point, and Dale was unable to deny it. "Yeah," he began. "But it's so painful to think that I've chosen this body that it's difficult to take responsibility for doing so. But essentially, yes, that's what I believe."

"And you said earlier tonight that you're supposed to deal with your disfigurement in the most courageous way possible. What could be more courageous than making a personal appearance?"

"I can't argue with you on that, Kurt," Dale conceded. "There's no logic to it. It just scares me to death."

"But like I said, what are you afraid of exactly?"

"Rejection. Judgment."

"By whom?" Kurt countered. "The people who want to see you already accept you."

"I'm not so confident of that," Dale argued. "No one's actually seen me. Actually coming face-to-face with me is a lot different than imagining what I look like."

"So even though the people who want to see you have already quit judging, you're afraid their going to judge you anyway?" Kurt queried most logically.

"Yes, essentially, that what I'm afraid of."

"Well I'm tellin' you, man, we won't."

"I really appreciate the reassurances, Kurt, but you're just one guy with one opinion, and you can't very well speak for everyone else. I've experienced the opposite enough to have a legitimate concern that that *will* happen."

"But you *don't* know that'll happen with *us*," Kurt said sagely. "You're only speculating it'll happen. And I'm saying your speculation is wrong. There're thousands of us out here who've taken your words to heart and seen the wisdom in them and quit judging. And we love you and would never judge you, especially on your appearance."

"Even if what you say is true, there are plenty of people who *will* judge me."

"Okay, say that's true. Why would any of 'em would even want to be there?"

"To gawk. To ridicule."

"But even if some of those people did show up and gawk and ridicule, so what? They'd be in the minority, and probably be shouted down. They'd be the ones looking foolish. I don't mean to be critical, but I just think you're underestimating us. And it hurts to think you'd do that."

Dale drew a spontaneous sigh. He finally understood that he was, indeed, being selfish. "I'm sorry, Kurt. That's not my intention."

"So give us the personal appearance. I kinda feel like you owe us one after dodging us for so long." There was an edge of insistence in Kurt's voice.

"Don't forget," Dale countered with equal insistence, "insisting on my making a personal appearance is what started the problem in the first place!"

"No it's not!" Kurt shot back, assertively, but not unkindly. "What started the problem in the first place was your *fear* of making the personal appearance and ducking it by hiding behind an impostor."

Of course, Kurt was right—absolutely right. But knowing that didn't banish the fear from Dale's heart. He had hoped that returning to the air would do the trick. But now, again faced with the prospect of *actually* appearing before his listeners, the core of his fear was right back in his face. At the level of his ego, he wanted to fight Kurt and deny the truth of it. But at the level of his soul, he knew Kurt spoke the truth. Still, he could not bring himself to accept his caller's invitation to appear in person. Fortunately, by this time, the end of the show was only thirty seconds away.

"I appreciate your call, Kurt, and your desire to see me in person. But I can't commit to anything like that right now. It's just too scary for me. I'm sorry." And with that, Dale disconnected the call, dispensing with his usual parting courtesies. It was not his intention to deny Kurt this courtesy, but he was just too rattled to observe it. "This is Dale Greene on FM 102.4," he announced hurriedly. "Stay tuned for the Midnight Express with Stan Furness, coming up at the top of the hour. Good night."

As Dale had signed off a few seconds early, Bobby let the closing theme music play a little longer before he rolled the top-of-the-hour commercials and prepared to hand off signal control to station headquarters.

Agitated by the subject of conversation and his hasty exit from it, Dale mostly sat silently, feeling afraid, trying to suppress the awful gnawing feelings. Then, as he pushed the fear down, he moved into the shell emotion of anger. He wasn't angry at anyone in particular, just at the situation, at the fact that he was still receiving requests to make personal appearances—and having to turn them down. He angrily spun his chair around, yanked open the suite door, and crashed through it, marring the paint on the molding as he went.

In the den, his advisors were prepared for some apprehension in their employer, but not for the level of anger Dale brought into the room. "That's it!" he declared without waiting for comment from them. "I'm not doing it anymore! See if you can line up Greg Harris for tomorrow night. I'm through." He waved his hand dismissively.

Paul and Shel looked to Wil, making an offer with their eyes to vacate the room. Wil acknowledged with a subtle nod and the two other men quietly stood and left Wil and Dale alone. Dale watched them go, knowing what Wil had in mind, but wasn't eager to enter into discussion.

"Forget it," he said, anticipating Wil's encouragement. "It's just too scary. I can't do it. And I'm not interested in being talked into it."

"I would never presume to talk you into anything," Wil countered gently. "Haven't I always only urged upon you your own choices?"

Dale answered with a mere raise of an eyebrow.

"But I hasten to remind you that you made a commitment to your listeners to do shows on both Saturday and Sunday. Are you going to renege on that commitment?"

Dale groaned. After deceiving his audience with Elliot, he didn't now want to compound the error by breaking promises. Even in his disheartened state he knew that *that* would be a slippery slope to complete disintegration of his principles. "No," he conceded reluctantly.

On Sunday, fearing more of the same kind of questioning, Dale just moped through the day, not even bothering to bathe and dress until dinnertime. He used to look forward to doing his show. Now he dreaded it. *So this is what I've come to*, he thought, sitting in front of a rerun of "Gilligan's Island." *What an awful feeling to have what you love most turned into what you fear most. Worse to know it was your own treachery that did it.*

A few minutes before nine, he motored to the broadcast suite, mechanically retracing the path alone, isolated in a mental fog. Without even bothering to look at the call queue, he waited numbly for the top of the hour, wondering how he was going to fake being "up" for the show, resigned to accepting any beating his listeners might wish to administer. The fiction and cynicism of it all sickened him. This was not what he was about. But how could he avoid it? The alternatives—making the personal appearance or fading forever into the background—were worse. Presently, Bobby gave him the "go" cue.

"Good evening," he said without conviction. "You're tuned to WWKW, FM 102.4, and this is Dale Greene." He looked for the first time at the call list. The thought of screening the calls for safe ones occurred to him, but in his despondency, he didn't care enough even to do that. He took the one topping the list. "Our first caller is Bonnie. She's twenty-three, and she says she's having trouble accepting the news that she's adopted. Hi Bonnie, this is Dale Greene."

"Dale?" Bonnie queried, surprised to be first up.

"Yes. You're on the air, Bonnie. How may I help you?"

"Uh, well, when I was seventeen, my parents told me I was adopted. It was a complete shock to me and I've never gotten over it."

"What about being adopted shocks you?"

"Well, I always thought I was their real child. I didn't have any reason to believe otherwise. And then they tell me different after seventeen years. I felt lied to. I felt . . . ." She searched for a word that described her feeling perfectly.

Sensing what she was doing in the silence, Dale offered, "Betrayed?"

"Yes!" Bonnie confirmed.

"And you've felt like this for six years?"

"Yeah. I thought it would just go away. But it hasn't. And it's really started to bug me."

"Okay," Dale mulled. "First of all, do you feel loved by your parents?"

"Oh yeah. I'm sure they love me. I just feel suddenly like I'm not really theirs, like I'm some kind of alien or something that they've come to love, like a puppy dog or something."

"I see." Dale had some experience with feeling like an alien. "Have you talked to your parents about this?"

"No."

"Why not?"

"I don't want to hurt their feelings."

"Why do you think their feelings would be hurt?"

"Because I'm questioning their motives and stuff. I just think they would feel hurt by that."

"And you don't want to hurt their feelings because you love them," Dale confirmed.

"Yeah!"

"All right, Bonnie, what would you like to accomplish with this call?"

"I just don't want to feel this way. I just want to feel like I did before, like I'm their daughter."

"Okay. You do know that I can't change the way you feel. You have to do that yourself. Sometimes the way we feel about things depends only on how we're looking at them, and we can change the way we feel about them simply by changing our mind about them. What *I* can do is suggest different ways of looking at things. Then *you* have to apply those different ways to your life, change your mind about some things, and see if that changes how you feel about them. Do you understand?"

"Yeah."

"Good. So let's start off with the feelings of betrayal. Do you think your parents should have told you that you were adopted when you were younger?"

"Yeah."

"What would that have accomplished?"

This stumped Bonnie for a second. "Well, I guess I wouldn't have felt they had kept the secret from me for so long," she finally speculated.

"Uh-huh. And at what age do you think they should have told you?"

Bonnie hadn't really thought it through to this extent. "I don't know."

"Okay," Dale acknowledged. "Why do you think they told you when you were seventeen?"

"Oh, I needed my birth certificate for something and it came out that I was adopted."

"So they were forced by circumstances to tell you that you were adopted."

"Yeah."

"All right. So let's assume your parents had told you at a younger age that you were adopted. Do you think you would have felt less like an alien *then* than you do *now*?"

This *really* stumped his caller. Dale could hear her take a deep breath and release it. "I don't know. Probably not," she ventured.

"Okay. Could it be that your parents were concerned that you *would* feel like an alien if you learned you were adopted, and didn't tell you at an earlier age in order to spare you from that feeling?"

This had not occurred to Dale's caller. But realizing it now made an impact. "I suppose."

"Could it be that *they* felt that you were really their daughter and never felt the need to tell you that you were adopted?"

"I suppose," she said thoughtfully. Then, after a brief moment of mulling, she said a little brighter, "Yeah, that could be."

"Good," Dale acknowledged. "Now, can I give you the metaphysical perspective on this?"

"Okay."

"All right. As I understand it, we have all chosen to be exactly where we are, for purposes that our soul knows, even if we don't know them consciously. So we are all exactly where we belong. If we took an unusual route getting there, it's only because we wanted to take that route, not because we started in the wrong place, or ended up in the wrong place. In other words, I believe that you were adopted specifically because you belong with your adoptive parents. It wasn't a mistake being born to your birth parents, because both you and they— at the level of your souls—wanted to have the experience of your being born to them and then of being adopted by your adoptive parents. In other words, it has all happened exactly according to plan and you are exactly where your soul wants you to be. The feeling of being an alien is only something fed to you by your ego—your thinking mind—not your heart. And you're free to change your mind about it."

For the first time since learning she was adopted, Bonnie began to feel some relief, as though the weight on her shoulders was lifting. "We all end up exactly where we belong?" she queried.

"Yes," Dale confirmed. "You chose to be exactly where you are."

Bonnie gave this concept a moment to sink in. Then, "Wow! I never thought of it that way. That's really wild." With this, she heaved a huge sigh, the signal to Dale that she had released the trauma.

"Feel better?" he asked.

"Yeah. *Lots* better." Bonnie drew another deep breath and released it. "Oh, thank you so much! I just love you so much!"

"You're quite welcome, my dear. I love you, too." Softly, through the phone line, Dale could hear his caller's trauma continuing to release in waves of sighs and sensed the timing was right to end the call. "Feel free to call any time, dear," he concluded.

"I will. Wow! Thanks! Bye!"

"Good night." Dale disconnected the call.

Despite his personal despondency, the philosophy was still there, still working its magic, and it buoyed his spirits somewhat. He took the next call with more enthusiasm.

"My next caller is Patrick. Patrick is forty and says he's having trouble with his career. He pressed the button to connect the call. "Hi, Patrick, this is Dale Greene and you're on The Brink of Tomorrow."

"How's it going?" The tone of Patrick's voice was a dirge of discouragement.

Dale recognized the somber sign immediately. "What's happening with your career, Patrick?" he asked sympathetically.

"Well, it's ... ugh." Patrick heaved a big sigh. "It's going nowhere. It's ... I ... no matter what I try, I can't seem to catch a break."

"Hmm, that doesn't sound very good. What kind of work do you do?"

"Well, what I *do* and what I *want* to do are two different things. The career I'm talking about that's not going anywhere is what I *want* to do—although, what I'm doing isn't in such great shape either."

"All right," Dale said. "Let's start with what you do."

"I write industrial video scripts, and sometimes direct them, when I get the opportunity."

"Oh, that sounds kind of fun. What do you *want* to do?"

"I wanna write—and hopefully direct—major motion pictures . . . and television. Well, I write them; I just can't seem to sell them."

"I see. Well, that certainly is an ambitious goal. Do you have an agent?"

"Yeah, I have an agent." There was a hint of dejection in Patrick's voice.

Prompted by the tone of his caller's voice, Dale asked, "What about that do you find dissatisfying?"

"Well, he's not as vigorous in shopping my work as I'd like him to be. I mean, he does send it out, but not as aggressively as I would. I can't really blame him, though, I haven't made a dime for him."

"Well, he must have *some* confidence in your work, to continue sending it out for you."

"Yeah, I guess he does. I mean, there are a few things I've written that he's chosen not to represent, so he's certainly discriminating. And the fact that he's chosen to represent some of them must mean he thinks they have potential."

"What do *you* think?" Dale inquired.

"About what?" Patrick was unsure exactly what Dale was referring to.

"Whether your stuff has potential."

"Oh, *I* think it has potential, if I say so myself. I've had a lot of producers compliment my screenplays, and in my video work, I always get compliments on my scripts. One producer said I was the best writer he'd ever worked with, and the last video I wrote and directed won two media awards. So I'm pretty sure my work is good—at least the video work."

"What about your film scripts?"

"I think they're good too. I mean, I think my ability to write industrials translates over into the film scripts, although they are completely different animals. When it comes to writing, it's something that I've always had a talent for, no matter what I was writing. But in the end, my screenplays always seemed to get turned down. Or some freak thing happens to get in the way."

"Freak thing?" Dale puzzled. "Like what?"

"Okay, well, I wrote a couple of scripts on spec for 'The X-Files' when it was still on. I got going on these kinda late in the game, so they were already in season eight when my scripts were up for consideration. This was the season where David Duchovny wasn't sure he wanted to continue with the series, and he kept them guessing about that for nearly a year. They held on to my scripts for eight months—which indicated they were seriously considering them—but the moment Duchovny decided he wasn't going to be in the show full time, they sent my scripts back. These scripts featured Duchovny as he'd been featured in all the episodes before that, so they weren't of any use after he decided not to be on the show full time.

"I also wrote an episode for Star Trek: Voyager. They kept it for nearly a year—right up to the last eight episodes of the series—indicating, again, that they were seriously considering it. But ultimately, no go. I also wrote a screenplay for a sequel to 'Blade Runner,' that film starring Harrison Ford back in 1982?" Knowing Dale was a young man, Patrick wasn't sure if he had seen the science fiction classic and ended his statement on an intonational upswing.

"I know the film," Dale assured, "I have it in my DVD collection."

"Oh, good," Patrick acknowledged, "so you know what I'm talking about. Well, before I wrote the script, I had my agent query the producer of the original film and ask two questions: Is he working on a sequel to the film and is he interested in seeing a screenplay for a sequel? He said he *wasn't* working on a sequel and he *would* be interested in seeing a screenplay. So I wrote it up. Of course, it took me several months to get a polished draft, and by the time my agent submitted it, the guy had hired two other writers to work on a sequel. So now my script's sitting on the guy's desk in an sealed package that he can't open because he'd have to pay me if there's anything in my script that's similar to what his writers wrote. In other words, I got him thinking about doing a sequel, but I'm screwed out of it. It's one of those freaky things that always seems to happen to me. And that's what makes it so frustrating. Like I said, no matter how hard I try, I can't seem to catch a break."

"Hmm. You said the same thing just a minute ago."

"Well, it's true. The same kind of thing happens in my video work. I work freelance and when I'm not working, I'm constantly calling around, sending out resumes, trying to drum up work. Once I called one of these places to see if they had any work for me—a place I'd done work for before—and they said 'Oh, you should've called last week, we just hired someone.' Great! Now you tell me! In fact, that's happened twice in the last two months, with two different places. The breaks always seem to go to someone else. I mean, this kind of thing happens to me all the time! I thought sure I'd get more work from the place I did the award-winning video for, but *nooooooo*, they closed their video department right after I did that show and now all their shows are made by their sister division on the West Coast. Another place went out of business after I did a show for them. It's always some freak thing, totally beyond my control, that screws me up and it's been like this for years. I'm just barely getting by—and not because there's anything wrong with my work—but because ... well, like I said, I don't know why. It's just really frustrating."

"I can see that," Dale acknowledged. "Did you study writing in school?" he asked now, curious to know about Patrick's educational background.

"No, no, I studied electrical engineering. I have a B.S. and worked as an electrical design engineer for ten years before I got into video. This is my second career."

"Wow! That seems like a one-hundred-and-eighty degree turn! Why did you get out of engineering?"

"I didn't like it. I mean, it didn't fulfill me."

"Did you not feel successful as an engineer?"

"Well, no. I mean, I was a *good* engineer—I was successful in that my work was good and I was paid well enough and getting promotions and so on—but I didn't *feel* successful. I felt like I was wasting my time. It's ironic that I could be successful at something I didn't like and fail at something I really want to do."

"So, engineering didn't excite you," Dale averred for clarification.

"Right! I wanted to be making movies," Patrick affirmed.

"Ah! And that's what you're doing now."

"Well, yeah, to a degree. But like I said, I want to be doing so much more, and I just can't seem to catch a break."

"That's the third time you've said that," Dale asserted.

"Well, that's how it is."

Dale took a deep breath and released it in preparation for what he was about to do. "Patrick, as I'm sure you're aware, this is not an easy problem to solve. I mean, it seems like you know how to market yourself, so it's not as though I can just give you a few job-hunting pointers and send you on your way. But if I'm going to help you with this, I'm going to have to get into some very deeply metaphysical concepts. Do you have any objection to that?"

"Uh, I guess not," replied Patrick, "although I don't exactly know what you mean."

"Okay, well, let me just get into it and see how it works for you."

"Okay," Patrick agreed.

"Good. What really stands out to me is the fact that, three times tonight, you said you can't seem to catch a break. Now, according to metaphysics, we create our own reality, and we do that according to our *beliefs*." Dale spaced out the latter half of this statement to emphasize its message. "And your statement that you can't seem to catch a break sounds like an underlying belief that may be dictating your reality and undermining your success."

Patrick was silent for several seconds as he tried to fathom Dale's assertion. Then, "Our *beliefs*? You say we create our reality according to our *beliefs*?"

"Yeah."

Again, there were a few seconds of silence from Patrick. "What do beliefs have to do with it?"

"Well, it's our beliefs which shape our reality. And the fact that you've said you can't seem to catch a break three times in five minutes suggests to me that this is a belief that you hold which, unbeknownst to you, is creating the very reality you're complaining of." Dale waited for some indication of his caller's understanding. When nothing came, he asked, "Do you follow?"

"Not really," Patrick answered.

"Okay. Well, like I said, this is the metaphysical perspective on reality, and it's different from what we're typically taught and what we feel in our daily lives. So you have to think outside the box of conventional wisdom to understand it. You okay with that?"

"Uh, yeah, I guess. But I don't really know where you're going with this."

"Okay, well, just bear with me for a minute." Dale took a breath. "We tend to think that our reality exists and we just live in it, buffeted by the vagaries of chance. Isaac Newton started us thinking like that in—" he had to think briefly to retrieve the date, "1680, I think it was, when he hatched the notion that the world functions according to relatively simple equations involving forces and velocities and so forth, independent of the life that inhabits it. And we thought like that until the early 20th Century when guys like Einstein and Bohr and Heisenberg and Schrödinger discovered that Newton's so-called 'classical,' or mechanistic, description of reality failed to describe the behavior of subatomic particles, and they formulated quantum physics. Of course, Newton was limited because he could only see the world on a macroscopic scale; he had no concept of atoms or subatomic particles, much less that they follow completely different rules than the stuff he could see. But this all changed with the advent of quantum physics. And after a century of quantum physics, which has been astonishingly successful in describing the behavior of subatomic particles, quantum physicists have arrived at the conclusion that consciousness plays a role in the very existence of physical reality. To be honest, most of them found the implication that reality doesn't exist without the involvement of consciousness very disturbing, and many of them refused for many years to believe what their equations and experiments were telling them. But when they kept getting the same results over and over again, they finally had to admit to themselves that this is how it is. Anyhow, metaphysics goes a step further and tells us that it's our *beliefs* which shape that reality, and those vagaries of chance are actually a product of those beliefs. You with me so far?"

"Well, I understood the words, but what you're saying sounds like voodoo or something. But I don't think you'd be trying to lay that kind of thing on me. So I'm not really following you."

"All right. Well, you're right" Dale confirmed, "I'm not trying to lay some kind of voodoo on you. I know that, to the mainstream, what I'm saying may sound like voodoo, but I believe it's an accurate description of the creation of our reality, as viewed from the metaphysical perspective."

"Okay, so tell me again what you're saying."

Pausing for a few seconds, Dale contemplated how he might put this to Patrick in a way that would make sense to him. Finally, "Okay, well, let's see . . . . All right, let me ask you this: You were a science and engineering student. In your science curriculum, did you ever study quantum mechanics?"

Patrick thought briefly back to his college days, then replied, "I got a little of it in my physics classes, but I didn't take a whole course in it, if that's what you mean."

"All right. Well, in what you did get of it, do you remember learning about wave functions?"

"Uh, I remember something about that. But I don't remember what they are."

"Okay, well, according to quantum physics, the state of a particle of matter is governed by an equation called a wave function, and the wave function predicts the *probabilities* of where a particle can be. Another way of saying that is that the particle exists everywhere in the universe all at once, and doesn't have a precise location—doesn't have physical existence—until *observed*. Does this ring a bell for you at all?"

"Um . . . I dunno."

"Okay, well, let me go a little further with it. When the particle is observed, the wave function is said to 'collapse' and the particle settles out at a particular location. In other words, the act of observation is what causes the particle to come into existence. This fact has been born out repeatedly in countless experiments and has been accepted as an accurate description of material reality. Now, the important thing to recognize in this is that the act of observation is a function of *consciousness*. It's *consciousness* that performs that observation, so it's consciousness that causes reality to take form." Dale paused to give Patrick an opportunity to respond, if he had a response.

"I guess I'm missing your point," Patrick confessed after a moment, a hint of irritation in his voice. "What are you getting at?"

"I'm trying to cite the scientific underpinnings of what metaphysics says about how our reality comes into being. And that is, as I said, that *we*, as beings of consciousness, create our reality, by the operation of our consciousness." Again Dale waited for some confirmation of understanding.

"I'm sorry," Patrick said, "but when you say *we* create our reality,

I'm just not sure I understand what the big fuss is all about. I know we have to take the bull by the horns, so to speak, and assert ourselves in the world, and take affirmative action in our lives to make it happen. That's obvious. So I don't understand why you're making a big deal about it, like it's anything new."

"Well, I agree that we have to assert ourselves in the world to achieve success, but that's not what I'm talking about."

Patrick seemed stumped. "Okay. Then what *are* you talking about?"

"I'm saying we *literally* create our reality, we *literally* create the matter of the world around us. This all happens below our level of awareness, of course, but in the final analysis, it's we—our spiritual selves—who create our reality."

Somewhat taken aback, Patrick was silent for another moment. "Okay, now this is why I didn't understand what you were saying. You're talking about ... like, acts of *God*, creating the universe? You're saying that *we* create the universe, like God?"

"Yes, that's what I'm saying."

"That doesn't make any sense to me!" Patrick was becoming more irritated.

"I understand," Dale assured evenly. "It *doesn't* make sense, at least to our physical senses. To our physical senses, it seems like our physical world exists and we just live in it. And it's practically inconceivable that *we* 'puny humans' would have anything to do with the creation of it. But that's not what modern science—what quantum physics—is telling us. As I said, countless experiments conducted over the last two or three decades have confirmed that physical existence is very tenuous at best—in fact, it's completely virtual—until consciousness steps in and coalesces the subtle energy fields of creation into discrete particles. It *is* Godlike. And I believe that that's what the Bible means when it says we are created in the image of God. We have powers of creation, and the world around us is the result of that."

Patrick inhaled deeply as he considered Dale's words. "Well, I'm not sure I believe you, but if what you're saying is true, then ... well, it's mind-blowing!"

"You're right! It *is* mind-blowing! The great Danish physicist

Niels Bohr once said that anybody who isn't shocked by quantum mechanics hasn't understood it. It's *totally* shocking. But it does explain a great many things that otherwise defy explanation. But I'm not asking you to believe me. You can read the research findings yourself and draw your own conclusions. The works of contemporary physicists like, uh, Fred Wolf, Nick Herbert, Amit Goswami—guys in that crowd—would be particularly helpful. Many of the other quantum physicists are still too timid to embrace the mind-blowing implications of this interpretation."

"Okay, so let's say, for sake of argument, I accept what you're saying. How does that help me?"

"All right, that's a good way to proceed." Feeling he had finally broken through a wall with Patrick, Dale took a breath before continuing. "As I said, our reality—the context of our lives—is shaped by our *beliefs*, beliefs we often hold at a subconscious level of awareness. You've expressed what sounds like a belief: 'I just can't seem to catch a break.' If you have a subconscious belief that you can't catch a break, then no matter what you do, you *won't* be able to catch a break, because that *belief* will create a reality in which you *can't* catch breaks. And it will defeat any action you may take in pursuit of a break. Fortunately, you've arrived at a point where you're able to see this pattern and formulate a description of it: your statement that you can't catch a break. Is this beginning to make sense?"

"Mmm, sorta. Okay, if our beliefs shape our reality and that *is* a belief of mine, I can see how it could undermine everything I do. But before I accept that as an axiom, I'd like to know *how* we create reality."

"Ah! That's your engineering mind at work. To be honest, Patrick, I don't know how it works. No one does. That's like asking 'How did God kick off the Big Bang?' We're just beginning to understand that He *did* kick off the Big Bang. For that matter, we're just beginning to realize that quantum mechanics provides a sort of confirmation that there *is* a God. But we're still a long ways from knowing *how* He did it—or how *we* do it. For now, we have to be satisfied just knowing that He did do it, and that *we* do it."

"Okay, I suppose I can live with that." Finally engaged in the effort to sort out his problem, Patrick devoted several seconds of thought to his next question. "So, what do I have to do to get rid of this belief?"

"Well, let's not think so much in terms of getting rid of the belief, but changing the belief, or at least recognizing that you don't have to use that belief as the blueprint for your reality."

"Oh, okay, that makes sense. How do I do that?"

"Well, sometimes it helps to identify the event in which the belief was formed. Do you remember anybody ever saying or doing anything to make you think you couldn't catch a break?"

Asked to remember his past, Patrick heaved a spontaneous sigh and thought about the question. After several seconds he said, "I'm drawing a blank here. If something like that happened, I don't remember it."

"Okay," Dale acknowledged. "That's not unusual. These things are often deeply buried, and they take a little while to surface."

"Well, maybe you can just tell me how to change the belief," Patrick suggested.

"Okay, well, the simplest way to do that is probably just to change your mind. Or, you can change your past, although those two things are really the same thing."

"Wait a minute, wait a minute! Change your past? How can you change the past?!"

"Well, pretty much by changing your mind."

"Whoa, whoa, whoa, you're losing me!" Patrick exclaimed, suddenly put off by the direction of the discussion. "This is beginning to sound like voodoo again. How does changing your mind change the past?!"

"First, let me say, I understand your resistance to this idea. It's almost harder to believe than the idea that our beliefs shape our reality. But if you think about it critically, you'll see how it happens. Let me ask you this: Where is the past?"

Sensing trickery in the question, Patrick thought about it for a moment. But failing to see any deception, he replied plainly, "It's what happened before now."

"Well, see, that doesn't really answer the question. But we can use it to ask another question: How do you know what happened before?"

Again feeling deceived, Patrick gave the question due thought, but still failed to find the trickery. "I remember it."

"Right. In fact, that's the *only* indication you have of what the past was, or even that there *was* a past. So the answer to my original question is: The past is in your memory. Right?"

"Riiiiight," Patrick drawled dubiously.

"In fact, the past is *only* in your memory. It doesn't exist anywhere else."

"But what about photographs? They're records of the past."

"Photographs exist only in the present. And if your memory of a photograph were changed by, say, brainwashing or something, then that new memory would completely change the history of that photograph for you. But forget about photographs for the moment. You don't have photos of every event in your life. For most events, the only thing you have is your memory of them. If you were to change your mind about what happened—and I mean completely replace an old memory with a new one, so you had no recollection of the old memory—then, for all intents and purposes, your past would change, at least so far as it affects you today. It's really quite simple."

"It doesn't *sound* simple."

"Granted, it may not be *easy*, but it *is* simple, if you catch my meaning."

"All right," Patrick conceded. "So how do I change my mind?"

"You just change it. Okay, I know that's sometimes easier said than done, but that's really what it boils down to. Sometimes the belief is relatively close to the surface and you can change it simply by making a conscious decision to do so. Other times the belief is deeply buried and it only surfaces when you're troubled or faced with hardships. Then the process of changing your mind may take more work."

"What kind of work? How do you do it?"

"That's the key question in this whole discussion," Dale observed. "First of all, you have to recognize that, vis-à-vis our beliefs, the universe is a reflective system. It shapes itself exactly according to your beliefs, so it exactly reflects your beliefs back to you. If you can't catch a break, you can be sure that, at some level of awareness, that's what you believe. The trick is to become aware of the pattern. If you can do that, as *you* have, then you can recognize the belief and change it. If the belief is deeply buried, you may have to look very attentively at your life—at what the universe is reflecting back to you—to learn what your belief is. Once you've done that, it helps if you can articulate what it is—put it into words that accurately describe the pattern. That way, when the pattern recurs, you have a way of identifying it. With me so far?"

"I think so."

"Good. Now when you become aware of a belief in this way, the first thing to do is acknowledge it. And you do the same thing each time it recurs."

"Acknowledge it?"

"Yeah. Basically, you just say, 'I see you there,' or 'I acknowledge you,' if you prefer to be more formal about it. Or 'There's that belief that I've been using to keep myself from creating the reality I prefer.' You might also add an affirmation like, 'Perhaps I can allow it to change, now that I'm aware that I've been using it to keep myself from realizing my dreams.' It doesn't matter how you do it. The point is to consciously spot the belief when it expresses itself in your mind or in your speech, and make a point of acknowledging its existence and the fact that you can allow it to change."

"Hmm." Patrick was somewhat surprised by the practicability of Dale's methodology.

"Now, here's an important point to remember," Dale continued. "The belief may never actually go away. It—and all the negative beliefs which shape your reality in ways you don't prefer—are part of your shadow self. The shadow self is the negative side of your energy structure. It's part of you and will always be part of you; you can't get rid of it. But you can dispel its power by acknowledging it whenever it pops up and tries to dictate your reality. At the same time, you supercede the old belief with one you like better. Of course, since the old belief may not go away, it may continue to surface, even after you've decided on a belief you prefer, and maybe even after your new belief has begun to shape your reality. And if it does that, you just continue acknowledging it anytime it pops up. You remind yourself that it's part of your shadow self and that the shadow will always be part of you, but that you don't need to allow it to dictate your reality." Dale paused momentarily for a breath. "Is this making sense to you?"

"Yeah, it is. And you know what?"

"What?"

"I just remembered something that might be the cause of all this."

"Oh! What?" Dale found this new development intriguing.

"Well, when I was in college, I saw a Japanese movie called "Woman in the Dunes" at the local oldies theater. I don't know why, but that movie really knocked me out and after that, all I wanted to do was make movies. But I was in the engineering program. So my choice was either get my engineering degree and try to get into the film industry with it, or switch over to the film program. Anyway, when I told my mother that I wanted to make movies and was thinking about switching to film school, she said, 'How are you going to find a job in the film industry?'" In quoting his mother, Patrick applied an intonation of disdain. "She wasn't asking to get the information; she was challenging my ability to get a job in the film industry. But I didn't have an answer. I'd heard it was a hard industry to get into and really didn't know how people got jobs in it. So that discouraged me from studying film and I went ahead and got my engineering degree. I don't think about that all the time, but every once in a while, when I'm really down about my career, that scene comes flying back to me. She was a very unsupportive influence in my life. I can see now how she really did a number on my head."

"This is excellent!" Dale said. "This is very good. You can acknowledge that as a major source of your old belief. Now, it's *possible* that that's the only incident that's been feeding that negative belief, but there could be others. So be open to the possibility that you'll remember other incidents that could have contributed to it."

"Oh, okay, that makes sense."

"Then," Dale added, "simply acknowledge whatever negative beliefs come up and replace them with affirmations of what you prefer to believe."

"Yeahhhh." Dale heard Patrick draw a healing breath and release it. "Wow!" Patrick continued. "When I called this evening, I really didn't have any hope that you'd be able to help me. I didn't think there could be anything anyone could say that would be different than what I'd already thought of myself. But you came at it from a *completely* different angle and given me something specific, something concrete, I can work on. So . . . *thanks!*"

Dale chuckled at his caller's surprised enthusiasm. "You're quite welcome, Patrick. Keep in touch and let me know how it goes for you."

"I will; count on it. Thanks again, man."

"My pleasure, my friend. Goodnight."

"Goodnight."

Dale pressed the button which disconnected the call. With the success of his conversation with Patrick, Dale's concerns about being asked for a personal appearance had completely evaporated and he took the next call without concern.

"My next caller is Dane, and Dane says he has a personal issue he'd like to discuss with me." He connected the call. "Hi Dane, you're on the air with Dale Greene."

"Hi, Dale." Dane's voice was strong and confident.

"Your reason for calling is a little bit cryptic here," Dale began. "Is this because you're embarrassed by what you want to talk to me about?"

"Not really," replied Dane. "In fact, I'm not really calling about myself."

"Oh." Already this sounded suspicious to Dale. "Who are you calling about?"

"You."

This answer caused Dale's buoyed spirits to sink again. He had hoped all the questions about himself had been answered and exhausted the previous night. "All right," he said guardedly, "what would you like to know *now*?"

"I'm the director of the Springfield Civic Auditorium, and I've been authorized by mayor Braunmuller to extend to you an official invitation to appear in person at the Springfield Civic on the day of your choice."

Ambushed! Dale thought, the cheap tactic piquing his anger. In the den, his trio of advisors eyed each other, simultaneously cursing the caller for the anguish this invitation would cause their employer and cheering him for pushing Dale to do what they secretly knew he needed to do.

In the broadcast suite, Dale felt like lashing out, but his internal compass urged him to keep cool. Not only would an outburst be unprofessional, but it would betoken just how desperate he was about this subject. "I appreciate the invitation," he lied, "but if you heard last night's show, you know how much that sort of thing scares me."

"Yes, and that's why I called. I've listened to you from the beginning of your talk format, and I know what you advocate: 'Do what you're excited to do and do what you're afraid to do.' As you acknowledged last night, you weren't taking your own advice, so I thought I'd give you an opportunity to do that."

"But that's a decision for *me* to make."

"I'm acutely aware of that. And I'm not trying to make any decision for you. I'm only offering you the opportunity, which you can seize or not."

"But it puts me in an awful spot!" Dale replied, now somewhat heatedly.

"Well, yes, I'm aware of that, too. But it's only a 'spot' as long as you hold onto your fear. Isn't that right? Isn't that what you'd tell your listeners?"

Using my own advice against me! Dale thought. *Damn him!* Of course, what really irked Dale about Dane's argument was that it was absolutely correct.

"I happen to agree with that advice," Dane continued. "So I decided to put the opportunity in front of you. You can accept it or turn it down. It's entirely up to you. However, the invitation is sincere. I've admired your work from the beginning, and I'm truly only interested in offering you a safe place to make an appearance."

"Well, I have to be honest with you, Dane, I'm a little offended that you surprised me with this, not being forthright about the nature of your call."

"I understand, and I'm sorry about that. But would you have taken the call had you known the true nature of it?"

Dale didn't want to answer this question and delayed responding for several seconds. "Probably not," he finally allowed. "But it was still dishonest."

"Do you think it was more dishonest than sending an imposter to make personal appearances for you?"

Stumped! Mulling what response he could possibly make and coming up with none that would effectively rescue him from having to face either a personal appearance or the outrage of his listeners, Dale said nothing for several more seconds. Finally, aware that he couldn't turn down the invitation on the air, but not feeling comfortable accepting it, he said, "All right. I won't accept the invitation right now, but I won't decline it either. I'll think about it. You've gotta at least give me that."

"Of course!" was Dane's reply. "But to help you decide, your listeners could write in, telling you what they want."

Dale buried his massive head in his hands. He knew in advance the outcome of *this* and was already dreading it. "All right," he surrendered. "Whatever."

"Great!" exclaimed Dane. "I'll draft a formal invitation and get it in the mail tomorrow. I promise you, you won't regret it."

"That's not something you can promise," Dale warned.

"All right," conceded Dane. "I promise to treat you with the highest degree of respect."

This was something that Dale couldn't argue with. "I know I'm supposed to thank you for the invitation," he confessed, "but I feel more like cursing you. I'm sorry, I'm just being honest."

"I know. Under the same circumstances, I would probably feel the same. So I won't take it personally."

Dane was certainly being understanding and gracious about this, so Dale found himself genuinely unable to dislike the man. "Okay, Dane. Why don't we compromise, and I'll just thank you for calling."

"Sounds like a deal," Dane said, laughing. "Goodnight."

"Goodnight," Dale concluded. "This is Dale Greene, and you're tuned to WWKW, FM 102.4. I'll be back with more calls after this commercial break."

Not again, Dale lamented to himself. Again his fate was in the hands of his listeners. He knew what the result of the write-in vote would be—even before the first listener laid pen to paper—and he knew he wasn't going to like it.

Chapter 30

Despite the troublesome invitation from Dane and prodding by subsequent callers to make the personal appearance, once Dale had pledged to give it consideration, the Sunday night show went well. Two days later, a letter arrived from Dane Huttman officially confirming the invitation. This was followed over the course of the next two weeks by another mountain of mail from listeners asking for the personal appearance.

But still, Dale couldn't bring himself to commit to it. He knew he needed to face his fears, but just couldn't find the courage to take that step. Again he met privately with Wil. Taking advantage of some unseasonably pleasant whether, they strolled along the winding walkway between the manor house and the recreation pavilion—Dale motoring at minimum speed, Wil sauntering beside him. Again Dale listed all the reasons his fears were justified.

"No matter what Mom and Dad did to prepare people for my appearance, they always freaked. Yeah, because everyone has promised to accept me and not to judge me, this personal appearance *sounds* like a good idea in theory. But practice has told me differently. They talk a good game, but when they see me, they won't accept me. I just believe that in my heart."

Wil regarded his young friend for a moment before responding. If this were not the time to address Dale's core problem, there would be no other. "I've got to be honest with you about something, Dale. Your problem isn't one of acceptance by your listeners," he observed carefully.

"Oh?" queried Dale, a tad skeptical. "What's my real problem?"

"Acceptance of yourself."

"I accept myself!" Dale asserted, somewhat defensively. "I've always accepted myself!"

"Only conditionally," Wil returned evenly. "Only when others accept you. And of course, here," he spread his arms to embrace the estate, "everyone accepts you. It's easy to accept yourself here. But outside, you still allow your feelings to be hurt by a fearful look. You depend upon *their* acceptance for self-acceptance. As you well know, we attract to ourselves people and situations to reflect back to us our own beliefs. Thus, the judgment you've attracted from others must necessarily reflect your own self-judgment and lack of self-acceptance. Only when you can accept yourself—only when you can love yourself as they cringe in fear—will you have conquered your fear."

"I disagree," Dale countered, still challenging Wil's observation.

Seeing his young charge's resistance, Wil was forced to acknowledge something he had denied for more than two decades.

"Dale, there's something I have to share with you," Wil said, taking a seat on one of the park benches that lined the walkway. Bringing his wheelchair to a stop opposite the bench, Dale eyed Wil tentatively. Wil took a steadying breath. "For twenty-two years," he continued, "I've been party to a metaphysical crime, if you will. And, in many respects, I've been in denial of that fact." Now intrigue crept into Dale's gaze. "In their efforts to shield you from the judgmental stares of society, your parents failed to recognize your core life lesson: that your reality—your physical body—reflects your own self-judgement and lack of self-acceptance. The state of your body screams that at you every instant of your life. But achieving that self-acceptance—by putting you out in society, in public—was so painful for you that your parents couldn't bear to watch it, couldn't bear to see the pain in your eyes. So they hid you away. Unfortunately, all that did was help you deny your core lesson of this lifetime. And I went right along with it. I enabled them to deny it, and I enabled to you deny it.

"But as you well know, life lessons will not be denied. Despite our efforts to shield you, I believe you've created this whole personal appearance dilemma as a means of forcing yourself to face the lesson, of forcing yourself to achieve true self-acceptance, painful as that might be. I'm ashamed to say that, by enabling you to hide from that lesson, I've enabled the lesson to be much more dramatic than it had to be, to be so much more painful than it would have been had I helped you face it when you were a child. Your parents and I only wanted to make life easy for you, comfortable for you. Had we known it would come to this—that, in the final analysis, we *couldn't* protect you from the truth of living in a judgmental society—I'm sure we would not have been so ready to sequester you. *I* wouldn't have anyway. And I'm deeply sorry for my role in it."

Uncharacteristically, Wil looked at his lap. More than his miscalculations in the Elliot Draupau scandal, having failed Dale in his most important lesson shamed him the most.

Dale slowly drew a breath and released it. "So what're you saying?" he said softly, fearful of the answer.

"You have to make the appearance," Wil said, lifting his head. "There's no other way out of this."

Dale's stomach leapt into his throat. Wil's assertion had shot directly to the core of the problem. In his chest, his heart pounded with violent fury and he suffocated with the awful, choking feeling he had endured so many times since becoming aware, as an innocent five-year-old, that his mere appearance frightened people away. Too panic-stricken to speak naturally, Dale forced air through his larynx and out his mouth. "Just . . . hearing you say that . . . really makes my heart . . . ugh. . . *pound*!"

"I know," said Wil softly. He could see the panic in Dale's eyes. He had seen his young employer in all manner of emotional states—angry, dejected, depressed, anxious, insecure, grief-stricken—but never paralyzed with fear. "But that's what you have to do to get through this," he added. "I'll help you any way I can."

Despite the offer of assistance, which he knew was always available from Wil, Dale felt no better than before. But he also felt he had no choice.

Still unsure he could ever vanquish his fears, Dale had two weeks to prepare. While he did use his mirrors to check his dress and grooming, he rarely used them to look at himself as others saw him. Faced with the prospect of showing his face to the outside world, he now parked himself before his full length mirror and took a long, lingering look at himself. He did not like what he saw. In fact, he hated the monster that stared back at him. He didn't feel monstrous on the inside, but there was no denying the monstrosity on the outside, and the pain of seeing the shocked reactions on strangers' faces when they looked at him flooded back to him. All his fears of presenting himself to the world, all his reasons for hiding from it, reasserted themselves in this moment. It made him angry—angry at himself for choosing to incarnate into such ugliness, angry at his parents for conceiving such ugliness, angry at God for creating a world that contained such ugliness. At the limits of his frustration and knowing there was no changing it, he grabbed a nearby vase and flung it with abandon into the mirror. The glass shattered, instantly dispelling his image.

Hearing the tintinnabulous crash all the way down the hall where he was working, Wil rushed to Dale's aid, fearing the worst. He found Dale slumped over in his wheelchair, his hands covering his face. He touched Dale on the shoulder. "Dale?" The younger man did not respond. He tried again, more urgently. "Dale, you're scaring me."

Finally, Dale lifted his face. Tears filled his eyes. He did not look at his advisor. "I can't do it, Wil. I can't face them."

"Your listeners, or your fears?"

Dale knew they were one and the same. "Both."

Wil inhaled deeply. He couldn't force Dale to accept himself, to find within his heart love for himself. That was something only Dale could do. Nearly at a loss for something to suggest, Wil took a seat in a nearby chair and sat quietly, unthinking. In an instant, an impulse moved him to speak and he said, "Dale, do you doubt that you are an expression of God/Spirit/All That Is?"

"No, I don't doubt that," Dale replied, a little surprised by the question.

"And as one of His expressions," Wil added, "do you doubt that God/Spirit/All That Is loves and accepts you?"

Dale furrowed his brow, not detecting where his advisor was going with this. "No."

"Then what flight of arrogance possesses you to reject yourself?" Wil asked, a tad sternly.

This kernel of logic was so compelling as to straighten Dale's back.

"I know you're having difficulty arriving at a frame of mind of self-love and self-acceptance," Wil continued. "But sometimes you just have to go through the process in physical reality to make the change at the spiritual level."

Hearing this started Dale's heart again thrashing in his chest. Unfortunately, as painful, or embarrassing, as it was for him, Dale knew his trusted advisor was right. But knowing that didn't quell the seemingly lethal pulsing of his heart. "It makes me feel like I'm going to die."

"How many times have you felt like that?" Wil asked.

"Too many to count."

"And how many times have you died?"

Dale was startled by the obviousness of this question and its answer, something that had never occurred to him before, despite having used the same line of questioning with his callers. He marveled at how this fierce emotion could so handily mask truth that would otherwise have been so evident. His silence told Wil he knew the answer.

"You must realize," Wil added, "that their reaction to your appearance is *their* problem, not yours."

"It *feels* like mine!" Dale argued.

"Of course! That's the nature of fear. But I seem to recall your telling your listeners on more than one occasion that they're responsible for their own emotional responses."

Dale couldn't argue with that. But in the two decades he had been disfigured, he had not been able to see *this* particular problem from that perspective. "It's *so* overwhelming," he confessed.

"But you *know* the futility of trying to suppress or avoid it," Wil countered gently.

Dale did know the futility of it, but the thought of facing this monster seemed impossible. "What can I do?"

While Dale had meant the question as an rhetorical emblem of hopelessness, Wil took it as an invitation for counsel. "Embrace the fear. Feel it completely. Immerse yourself in the feeling and allow yourself to totally experience it. You know the process."

Indeed he did. Many times Dale had urged his listeners to totally experience their fears and by so doing exhaust them of their power. His own words flooded back into his awareness: *Place yourself in the fear, then willingly experience the full effect of it. Place all of your attention on that fearful feeling in your heart or pit of your stomach and just* feel *it. Don't try to escape it, don't try to avoid it—just immerse yourself in the feeling. Focus all of your attention exclusively on the sensations in your body and experience them without restraint.*

You'll soon realize that you're not dead, you're not even being harmed. And after a while, the fear will subside. Then the next time it arises, it won't be as intense or last as long. And eventually, it'll simply no longer bother you. Yes, he knew the process. But he had never applied this wisdom to himself. Isolated on the estate, he had never had to. And feeling it now—in all its chest-thumping ferocity— he had doubts that it would work for *him.* "That's so easy to say; so much harder to do," Dale lamented.

"Yes it is. But are you going to allow 'easier said than done' to stop you from doing it? Don't forget: Avoiding the fear doesn't get rid of it—it merely defers it till later. It rears its ugly head again the next time you face—or even think of—the dreaded situation. And by fearing the fear, you stop yourself from taking action." Wil cocked his head as if to ask, *Eh?*

Aware that none of his other options—options he had already tried—produced satisfying results, Dale hesitated to commit to what he knew would be the most painful, though effective, solution. Finally, "I guess I don't have any choice."

"On the contrary: You still have choices. You can continue to hide for the rest of your life . . . if you think you can be happy doing that. Or you can face your fear and get back to doing what you love."

"I'm not convinced I'll ever be able to do that."

"I know. But *not* facing your fears *guarantees* that you won't be able to do that."

Despite the terrifying implications, Dale knew Wil was right. Confronted with this truth, Dale released a troubled sigh.

"I'll be nearby, in case you need me," Wil said, standing and moving toward the door.

Dale nodded an acknowledgement, and Wil left.

For the next thirteen days, Dale struggled to face his fear, attempting—and often failing—to immerse himself in the crushing emotion. Each time he did the drill, he felt as if he were dying. But each morning he woke up alive and well.

As he prepared for bed the night before his personal appearance, the fear gripped him again. He knew there was no backing out at this point, that he would finally have to come face-to-face with his public, that they would finally see him for what he really was. Although not convinced that the result would be satisfying, he had set himself on this course of action and knew there would be no going back now. He fully expected to be humiliated, to be completely destroyed, but was resigned to it, like a kamikaze pilot making the final run of his life. The fear knotted his stomach and squeezed his heart.

Laying in bed staring at the ceiling unable to sleep, he again did the drill, immersed himself in the fear and willingly experienced the full effect of it. The next day would show what he was really made of.

Ken Gullekson

Chapter 31

It was the day Dale feared. Rain poured from a lowering sky as if from gargantuan buckets. Suddenly at the loading dock of the auditorium in the Plymouth Voyager, Dale found himself completely without recollection of the trip there. *I must be really out of it,* he thought to himself, blaming his lack of focus on the impending event. Just as suddenly, he found himself wheeling through the dusky backstage vaults of the auditorium.

The gloomy darkness of the hall was at once forbidding and welcome. While creepily eerie, it provided a comforting veil of obscurity for Dale's hideous form. Occupied with the facility director, his advisors were not around and he was on his own in this strange place. Navigating cautiously through the dark backstage catacombs, macabre sets looming around each corner, Dale made his way uncertainly to the dim wings of the stage. The echo of his wheelchair motor in the cavernous expanse of the theater and the haunting acoustics of the gothic vaulted ceilings sent jagged shivers up his crooked spine. There, in the wings, Dale waited for what seemed like forever as an announcer droned in incomprehensible tones, further jeopardizing his fragile courage to go through with the plan.

Presently, he heard his name announced. He expected applause, but none came. Instead, the murmurs of the crowd as it waited for Dale to emerge more resembled a low rumble.

Finally throwing caution to the wind, Dale nudged his joystick forward and guided his wheelchair beyond the wing curtains. The stage was enormous and too brightly lit. Beyond the lighted edge of the stage, the audience sat in complete darkness. A lone microphone sat center proscenium. From the invisible audience came a collective gasp, then a chorus of disgusted groans. Dale tried to stop, but the control stick on his motorized chair jammed and the machine carried him the rest of the way to the microphone. Deposited directly behind it and driven by his promise to speak to the group, Dale slowly rose to his feet.

But before he could utter a word, he heard the voice of a girl in the crowd warn, "I'm gonna be sick!" followed by a gagging, retching sound. Out of the corner of his eye he saw an amorphous object hurtling his way. Unable to move out of its path in time to avoid it, he could only turn his head in time to be hit square in the face. It was a rotten tomato. He froze as its slime and stench enveloped his lumpy features. The crowd laughed viciously. Immediately, numerous other pieces of rotten fruits and vegetables flew toward him, hitting and splattering all over his hideous face and gnarled body.

Dale was at once terrified and utterly humiliated. And while the physical experience was degrading enough, the injury to his pride was worse. *They came prepared with rotten produce?!* he thought to himself, stunned by the treachery of what was now obviously a deliberately plotted ambush. Then, within instants, the people in the front seats began to rush him. Unable to dash off stage, and perhaps too stunned to move, he found himself powerless to stop the attack and was forced to simply to wait for its impact.

Suddenly, he was in bed, drenched in sweat, looking up at the ceiling of his darkened bedroom, his muscles stiff with terror. Another nightmare! The reality of the vivid experience now in question, he breathed a sigh of relief, but was unable to relax completely. His previous nightmares about encounters with the world outside his walls had been accurate enough to scare him off. Was this also an accurate portent of things to come?

While the nightmare was obviously just a fiction of his imagination, it haunted him all through breakfast. By lunchtime, its vivid simulacra seemed to be fading, but then as the hour of the appearance neared, it again imposed itself on his consciousness. In fact, as they drove to the auditorium, that was all he could think about. He tried to concentrate on his speech, but the uniqueness of this venture—being outside the walls of the estate and facing strangers for the first time in over twenty years—defeated his best efforts.

To ensure that some unforeseen incident didn't disrupt the event, the backstage entrance had been locked and made off limits to the public. Paul and Shel had gone ahead to meet Dane Huttman and the program emcee and coordinate Dale's arrival at the facility. Although Dale was familiar with the sights and sounds of the city through television, he hadn't seen and heard them directly in over twenty-two years. He wished he could appreciate them, but preoccupied with the prospect of meeting strangers face to face, he didn't.

After a fifteen-minute trip that seemed to take forever, the unmarked Plymouth Voyager containing Dale and Wil pulled up at the backstage entrance. Wil dialed a number on his cell phone. On the other side of the backstage door, Paul answered his. "We're here," was all Wil had to say, and the backstage door opened, revealing Paul's lanky frame and smiling face.

Dale had not wanted anyone to lay eyes on him prior to his address, so his advisors had made arrangements for the facility director and emcee to see him for the first time only at the same moment as his audience. Before his horrific nightmare, he had felt the numbers of the crowd would afford him some measure of safety. Now he was not so sure. However, the plan had already been laid, and was now being executed. Slowly, Dale and his advisors made their way from the backstage door through the corridors of the historic structure to the wings of the stage. For Dale, this journey brought a procession of unfamiliar senses: the musty smell of moldering carpet and stale floor wax, the grating buzz of a faulty fluorescent light, the reciprocal eyesores of marred walls and peeling paint—conditions carefully groomed out of the estate.

Waiting in the darkened wings for the show to begin, the fear of rejection grew to bone-rattling proportions and Dale grew steadily more sick to his stomach. The temptation to turn his chair around and run away was powerful. But the awareness that that would be "chickening out"—and only confirm his reputation as a coward—was more powerful. So he stayed, guided by the maxim Do what you're excited to do and do what you're afraid to do.

The din from the audience suggested a full house. In the wings on the far side of the stage, the handsome, white-tuxedoed emcee checked his look in a mirror, straightened, and put on his show face. Ten seconds later, at exactly the top of the hour, he strode onstage to appreciative applause.

"Ladies and gentlemen, boys and girls, good afternoon and

welcome to Springfield Civic Auditorium for this special event. Because of the special nature of this program, I know that you all know why you're here, so a lengthy introduction of our special guest would seem unnecessary. I haven't met him myself, but I'm told he's waiting in the wings. So without further ado I give you WWKW talk radio guru, Dale Greene."

Thunderous applause erupted from the crowd, and Dale thought, Maybe this won't be so excruciating after all. The same thought occurred to Wil and Paul and they both gave him an affectionate pat on his shoulders. Wishing to take advantage of the acceptance expressed in the ovation, Dale cautiously pressed the joystick of his wheelchair forward and eased up to the edge of the wings. But he remained in the darkness of the perimeter for another couple of seconds. Building his nerve to actually take the leap out of obscurity, he looked back one last time to Wil, who gave him a gentle nod of encouragement. Finally, he could delay no longer, and motored tentatively out into the light of the stage.

The instant the light hit his face, the applause fell off and a collective gasp was heard, peppered with breathy exclamations of "Oh, my God!" and "Jesus Christ!" Dale couldn't tell if these were expressions of judgment or sympathy and his heart pounded wildly in his chest. This was what he had feared. Had he been walking to the microphone, he would have frozen in his tracks, his muscles too rigid to move. He briefly considered swiveling his chair and returning to the refuge of the wings, but he knew that would only prove his cowardice and he proceeded to center stage in complete silence.

Stopping near the microphone, he struggled to his feet and, with the help of a cane, hobbled the next few feet to the public address device. During the several seconds that this took, an insistent murmur grew within the audience. Finally reaching the microphone, Dale looked out into the dimly lighted auditorium, and the murmuring gave way to deadly silence. Though the light was subdued, he could see their eyes, and every one was on him.

Much to his chagrin and very much against his will, he found himself uncontrollably choked up, a fact keenly observed by the audience. It was a very long time before he was able to make a sound. Finally . . .

"Seeing all of you . . . in the flesh," he began haltingly in his familiar basso profundo, his eyes so wet that he could barely discern those he proclaimed to be seeing, "after speaking to you only on the phone . . . is proving to be a bit overwhelming. I'm discovering that talking about fears and facing them are two different things. I'm Dale Greene and . . . um . . . I feel like I really am on the brink of tomorrow."

There was a soft, appreciative chuckle as the more comfortable members of the group responded to the young man's humor.

"Although I fought this tooth and nail with some of you," Dale continued, finding it increasingly easier to talk, increasingly easier to open up, "I suppose I have to thank you for not letting me get away with hiding. I've been talking with many of you this last year about breaking the habit of judging—and, as so many of you have discovered, judgment can be a very hard habit to break. But I failed to take my own advice: I've been judging you, my dear, devoted listeners, because I didn't trust your ability to accept me. After watching you work so diligently to apply to your lives the principles we've talked about—and succeeding—I still didn't trust you when it came to not judging me by my appearance. For that I am deeply sorry. You deserve more credit than I gave you and I've learned about my own fears—and pettiness—from it. And, hopefully, I've learned to trust. Sometimes respect and responsibility come only after a painful lesson, and that's surely true for me. Thank you for sticking with me and allowing me to learn my lesson. I love you all."

This was what the audience had come to hear and, much to Dale's surprise, they broke into spontaneous applause. Then, prompted by some in the front row, they all rose to their feet in a standing ovation.

As Dale stood before his admiring public, finally feeling free of the onerous weight of hiding who he really was, Archers Association president Roger Hampton strode onstage carrying the Man of the Year plaque that Dale had returned after his ignominious retirement from radio. His appearance on the stage took Dale completely by surprise.

"I believe this belongs to you, Dale," Mr. Hampton said with a warm smile as he approached the stunned DJ.

Genuinely astonished, Dale accepted the plaque with humility. Never believing he could accept such an honor in person, tears of gratitude streamed from his eyes.

"Thank you," he said, shaking Mr. Hampton's outstretched hand with his good right hand. Again, the assemblage erupted in thunderous applause, accompanied by cries of "We love you, Dale!" It took several minutes for the assemblage to quiet down, but when it did, Dale delivered an address which again brought the group to its feet.

As might be expected, the local papers all ran stories about the special event at the Springfield Civic Auditorium. This time, the truth being far more sensational than any fiction they might have concocted, the courage that Dale had shown in making the appearance was the focus of the reports.

In North Hollywood, California, Elliot Draupau happened upon the story in a national newspaper and, between scenes of Days or Our Lives, called Dale to congratulate him. In their matching voices, the two men chatted amicably for several minutes before the actor was called back to the set.

Although the prospect of making personal appearances still sent twinges of apprehension through him, Dale continued to accept invitations to worthy events, where he signed autographs and actually touched his listeners.

And after finally facing his most terrifying fear, the DJ felt—with the full support and encouragement of his listeners—that he had earned the right to again call his show The Brink of Tomorrow.

www.ingramcontent.com/pod-product-compliance
Lightning Source LLC
Chambersburg PA
CBHW070539260626
47161CB00002B/449